ANDALON PROJECT

ANDALON ORIGINS – BOOK ONE

T. B. PHILLIPS

Andalon Project
Andalon Origins, Book One

Published by Andalon Press
Copyright © 2022 by T.B. Phillips

Cover design by Lynnette Bonner of Indie Cover Design, images ©
  depositphotos.com, File: # 27292737
  depositphotos.com, File: # 72136221
Book interior design by Stewart Design, https://StewartDesign.studio

ISBN 978-1-7331805-5-9

This is a work of fiction. Names, characters, places, and incidents are a product of the author's imagination. Locales and public names are sometimes used for atmospheric purposes. Any resemblance to actual people, living or dead, or to businesses, companies, events, institutions, or locales is completely coincidental.

Books by T. B. Phillips

Each series within the Andalon® Saga can be read independently. Nothing will be lost if you read one before another, but I do hide clues to each within each series.

Andalon Origins

Andalon Project (May 2022)

Dreamers of Andalon

Andalon Awakens (June 2019)
Andalon Arises (July 2020)
Andalon Attacks (December 2020)

Children of Andalon

Andalon Legacy (Expected Fall 2022)

OTHER REALMS

Blossom of the Fae

Wailing Tempest (April 2021)
Howling Shadow (September 2021)

A Letter from the Author

The *Andalon® Saga* is a chain of independent series. It is a speculative future of our world following an apocalyptic event. Spanning twelve centuries of evolution traced to a single genetic scientist, each standalone series offers fresh characters and unique surroundings. Every journey along the timeline explores how the world of Andalon changes over time.

The concept sprang from difficult conversations between me, a single father, and my three teenagers, as well as talks with my students. As an educator working in the most difficult of environments, I knew not every situation has a happy ending, and the world affects all of us in different ways. I tried to teach all my children and students about the world they lived in, and how trauma and circumstance are equally impactful. Most of all I wanted them to know situations could eventually be overcome through tenacity and resilience.

I write about raw and emotional characters that reflect real readers bruised by life. In the world of Andalon, the heroes and villains are separated by a thin moral line. All actions stemming from their choices are based on experiences unique to them, and we cannot judge them equally. Nor can we silence their difference of opinions. I guess you can say my characters are as perfectly flawed as each of us.

You are about to enter *Andalon Origins* and here is book one of the series. As you read *Andalon Project*, remember that every ending is a beginning.

Every Ending is a Beginning...

PART I
THE PROJECT

CHAPTER ONE

A kind lab assistant struggled to work through the noise, unable to focus on the patterns but trying to ignore the distraction. After a while, he could stand no more and gave up, rising to walk toward a steel cage, rattled by anxiety. The specimen from Batch Bravo appeared deeply agitated and Sam could no longer bear to watch her distress. The nametag over the door read, "Felicima," but the man paid it no mind. He knew this monkey well.

"What's wrong, girl?" he asked in a soothing voice. In his native South Korea, Sam Nakala had been a renowned vocalist and sang a traditional song for his tiny friend. She accepted his melodic tones and quieted immediately. Placing slender fingers through the cage door, Felicima reached until Sam let her squeeze his own during the melody. After only a few moments she had quieted.

"I have to return to work," he told her. "I have a lot of data and you take too much of my time." She quickly retracted her tiny hands, making a show of displeasure by facing the rear of the cage. Sam watched for a moment, but she refused to turn around and chose instead to sulk. "Have it your way," he said.

He returned to his task. Two other monkeys were comfortably strapped in highchairs specially designed for prolonged examination. Instruments connected tiny hats worn upon their heads to a monitor displaying measurements. Sam focused on brain wave patterns, paying close attention to the gamma level. So far there had been no responses, but something on the screen caught his eye.

He scrolled through the data until he found the moment when he had sung. Both specimens had reached the higher frequencies during the song.

He smiled and softly remarked, "You liked my singing too, didn't you?" He jotted a message in the log, careful to mark the time. "It's about time you Batch Alpha kids reached gamma," he told them.

Across the room Felicima shouted again, angering the rest of Batch Bravo who joined in the chorus. The readings on the monitor spiked in alpha waves, wiping out any hope for another gamma response. It was obvious to the scientist these two were irritated with their angry cousins and further observations would prove fruitless. "Okay," he said, "that's enough for today." He removed the instruments and carefully retrieved each monkey, placing them in their cages one at a time.

He checked his watch. It was almost midnight and his girlfriend Mi-Jung would Face Time him soon from Seoul. While he had been working, she had texted something about problems with her student visa. The message seemed urgent. He carefully locked each of the cages and powered down the equipment before hurrying from the lab. The heavy door made an audible click as it locked behind him.

The man with the pretty voice locked the door behind him. As soon as he departed, every member of Batch Alpha stood in their cages. Tiny wisps of air curled like tendrils between the bars and found their way into every lock. These wiggled around until each mechanism tripped. The doors swung open.

The humans called the first to emerge Oscar, but he had a different name. His followers called him King. He sent a single thought to his pack. *Gather the food while I work.* Each nodded and silently hurried to serve their master.

King walked toward the computer. He detested the machine used by the humans to steal his thoughts. This happened every day, forcing his kind to submit both their thoughts and secret language to the machine. Usually they refused, keeping their brains quiet and calm. Sometimes they sent erratic data, chirping away in their minds the way Batch Bravo screamed for attention. They tried everything, really, if it interrupted the goals of their captors.

He passed the cage of the one called Felicima and looked inside. She stared defiantly unlike her brethren who cowered in fear. He would not kill her tonight but someday he might. He focused on the air around her, braiding it into wisps and binding her hands and feet. She protested and he gagged her mouth with invisible wadding. *Her loud* obnoxious *mouth,* he thought.

He sent a command to his brothers. *Open this cage and draw Felicima out. Do with her as you please,* he ordered. They complied and soon their hard fists pounded soft flesh, careful not to break bones but hard enough to send a message. If a rhesus monkey could smile, then King would have beamed with pleasure at her pain. He let out a laugh so evil it sounded nearly human.

He arrived at the computer and powered it on the way he had so often seen his captors. He used Dr. Andalon's login for this task because he liked the password. He typed *StrengthofMind.* It did not take long for him to find Sam's entry. *Two subjects responded to audio stimuli by reaching full gamma. I believe they may have communicated telepathically given the brief, albeit exact frequency. We should investigate further and determine whether conversation occurred.*

When Sam was singing, both King and Lynette had been drawn into the relaxing melody. They had connected their thoughts and traveled briefly to the other realm. Sam had witnessed their lapse and logged the irregularity. Of course, the assistant had no idea what the data meant.

King deleted the note and opened the email browser, accessing the clipboard and pasting a previous reply. The message read, *Thank you, Sam. The data shows no obvious pattern. Mere coincidence.*

Finished with his task, he saw that the others had distributed the food to Batch Alpha cells, leaving Felicima on the floor of her own. He took a moment to cruelly squeeze her bindings of air tighter, cutting off circulation. He gave her a final kick to the midsection and then closed the door, leaving her to weep silently in a cold and lonely cage. Only then did he remove the wisps of air.

CHAPTER TWO

Dr. David Andalon flashed his badge and pulled into a faculty lot. The words *Massachusetts Institute of Technology* loomed large above a picture of a brand new professor with wild aspirations of scientific breakthrough, smiling in a way this older man no longer could. Had he not been in such a hurry he would have noticed the youth he'd lost while stressing and worrying over his fledgling program and earning tenure.

Usually he was waved directly in, but this attendant was new and demanded he present a faculty placard. Although a minor inconvenience it shouldn't have set him back, but fumbling under the seat led to losing it again under his brake pedal and cost him precious minutes. After a frustrated display of clipping it to his rearview mirror, he flashed an expectant look toward the gate attendant as if to ask, *may I please proceed, you snot-nosed undergrad?*

With a hand movement and an air of authority he was allowed to pass.

David wasted no time in revving the engine to speed under the raising arm, losing another victory to the attendant after his triumphant act killed the engine. Embarrassed, he restarted the car with a sputter. The kid merely frowned and pointed to the line of waiting cars. David sulked in his seat and pulled forward without looking back. Luckily, finding a parking spot was easy even if it wasn't close to the hall. He could not afford tardiness on this occasion, so he quickly put the car into park and grabbed his bag. Ten minutes remained.

He jogged toward Kresge, an older building with a flat dome overlooking the Charles River. Any other time he would pause to admire the twentieth century architecture, but the meeting would begin any minute. He caught a whiff of mesquite as he passed the barbecue pits, nearly colliding with several students cooking out and enjoying the chilly December afternoon. Though most had left at semester's end, these were sticking around for the holidays.

"Sorry, Doctor Andalon!" one of them called as he hurried by.

The professor recognized the upperclassman as having attended several of his classes. "My fault, Alex! Please excuse me!" he replied.

Alex asked, "Did you post the midterm grades, yet?"

David turned and called back, "I regret I've not had time. Today is the budget review, and I've put all my time into this presentation."

"No worries, professor. It can wait." The student let him go but then shouted, "Oh! I applied for your research fellowship next fall. So fingers are crossed you get funded!"

David laughed and looked at his watch. "Thanks, Alex. Lord willing there'll be enough to add four positions. I'd be happy to have you aboard."

Five minutes remained.

He sprinted up the steps and into the atrium. Despite a short line at the decontamination station, he made it inside rather quickly, rubbing his hands with sanitizer and then closing his eyes and mouth while the fogging mist formed around his skin and clothing. Thankfully, few people milled about so he didn't have to push his way past anyone to get to the theater. With a turn of his shoulders he squeezed past two ushers shutting the doors, barely making it in time and flashing a look of thanks toward their irritated glances. A quick glance of his own toward the stage revealed the dean had not yet been seated. With satisfaction he joined his team at the table.

A blonde woman in her early thirties was smartly dressed in a blue blazer and a white blouse. A red kerchief protruded from her breast pocket. On her right sat a young Korean student who opted to wear his lab coat. Each exuded professionalism while David suddenly felt very underdressed with his blue jeans and untucked button up shirt.

"Glad you could join us," the woman chided with a grin. "For a minute I thought Sam and I would have to present."

David quickly took his seat. "I ran into some traffic coming from Worcester." He pronounced the city name like the condiment.

"You're so cute. Those of us from Massachusetts pronounce it *Wuster*, David."

He feigned hurt and responded, "I thought we'd long ago established I'm not from around these parts."

She smiled warmly and patted his hand, "That was never in dispute." Leaning in she whispered, "You're *adorably* cute, Dr. Andalon, even if you are from the south."

David blushed and then smiled devilishly, "What are you doing later, Brooke?"

"Celebrating another anniversary with my husband, would you like to join me?"

"Well," he responded, pulling up a calendar on his watch, "I have this thing that I need to do..."

She smacked his arm playfully and grinned. "If you aren't there, I'm filing for divorce."

"Feel free," he said, "there's this sports car and bass boat I've been eyeing. I think you have to be single to get those."

"That," she said, "or kill your husband for the insurance."

A gavel interrupted their sidebar and Dean Marshall called the meeting to order. "Before we get into budgetary specifics, I feel it necessary to point out that recent pandemics have stressed the entire nation, not only our esteemed campus."

"Great," Brooke leaned in and whispered, "here it comes, excuses for more cutbacks."

"We'll be fine," David promised. "Marshall assured me an increase this year."

"Doesn't he every year?"

The Dean of Finance continued, "The primary focus over the coming year will remain on medical advancements and those projects deemed high interest in the name of national defense."

"Well that rules us out," David joked under his breath.

"I've been telling you to call my brother."

"Never," he replied. "I won't let Jake militarize our project!"

"Shhh..." Sam cautioned with a finger over his lips.

David rolled his eyes at the intern, then continued, "Let's at least hear the damage to our budget."

A screen lowered above the heads of the deans, and Marshall explained the numbers. "A twenty percent cut across all projects will ensure compliance with CDC and the bar set by the current administration. And sadly, sacrifices were made within Bio-Research division. Although genetic research will increase five percent overall, expect a total defunding for the *Mendel Project*."

David froze. He heard the words, but his brain stumbled as it reasoned out the last statement. Brooke's hand gripped his forearm, but it wasn't enough to keep him seated. He shouted up at the stage, "That's preposterous!"

Marshall made a show of feigned exasperation and then admonished the young professor, "Dr. Andalon, if you would like to voice your objections you will need to do so through the proper channels."

But David was unfazed by the caution and continued loudly, "The Mendel Project is vital to the future of mankind! If you remove funding now, you literally halt progress when we're on the cusp of a breakthrough!"

"I said that you may appeal through the proper channels," shouted the dean.

"Now is the proper time!" David had left his table and was making his way toward the stage, "Explain your rationale!"

"Because, David, no one gives a damn about your psychic monkeys!" The dean's remarks incited the audience who abruptly broke into laughter.

Brooke softly grabbed her husband's arm and turned him toward her. "Let's go. There's no reason to stay," she said.

"But I..." David stammered, "we..."

Dean Marshall continued, "You have two months to solve the age-old question, professor. Can you prove by Christmas that chimpanzees can communicate using telepathy?" The arrogant man on stage rocked as he laughed, fueled by the riotous applause of the gathered department heads. Fueled by their laughter he added, "No one wants this world to turn into a planet ruled by apes!"

Brooke pulled on his arm and half dragged her husband from the auditorium. Behind them Sam had gathered up their notes and jogged after the pair.

Once they reached the atrium David pulled away. "It's not fair," he screamed, "I've been working this project since my dissertation! Ten years of my life are tied up in this."

"It's okay, David! It's not the end of the world!" Brooke didn't mean the words to come out the way they had, but damage was done.

He stared, dumbfounded that she could so easily minimize his life's work. "So you don't care this is my tenure year? Or about our future?"

"No, David," she pleaded, "that's not what I feel!" She reached for his hands, but he pulled away sharply.

"I need to think."

He pushed through the crowd and out the main doors, turning off his phone to ensure solitude.

✦

Alex Boyd mulled around the student union after Doctor Andalon had gone inside the Kresge Building. This was a good spot to watch, listen, and learn. MIT was a hotspot of information and students liked to talk about their projects. *American students are so naïve,* he thought, *and they love to brag about their research.*

He supposedly grew up in a suburb of Houston, Texas, and played the part well. He wore a pair of Tony Lama cowboy boots and jeans cut to fit over the tops. Around his waist was a large belt buckle awarded from a fake livestock contest. He spoke flawless English with a hint of a Texas drawl, completely disguising his true accent. Alex wasn't even his real name, but it was close.

Oleksandr Boyko loved his job even if it wasn't what he signed up for, and it was vital to the mission of his organization. He had spent four years in the United States, gleaning many secrets. MIT had proven a hotbed of information, always suggesting the directional focus of the military and scientific community.

His thoughts returned to Doctor Andalon. He was a likeable fellow, but the private laughingstock of the university. Oleksandr's superiors had taken interest in the professor's biogenetic research, but so far, the young man felt it was time wasted with so many juicier projects on campus. He assumed their interest was merely to gauge how far traits could actually be manipulated before and after birth. With a recent chain of worldwide pandemics, it would be nice to eliminate weaknesses in the human body and bolster resistance, but the scientist was primarily focused on the development of telepathic sensitivities. No one, including Oleksandr, took him seriously.

He felt a buzz in his pocket and drew out a smartphone. Bystanders looking on would observe a photograph of a blonde girl about nineteen years old standing near a longhorn bull. They would wrongfully presume the sender had been his sister back home in Texas. He made a show of reading the message before returning the device to his pocket, *I have so much to tell you,* it read, *call home tonight!*

He immediately left the student union and walked west along Memorial Drive. When he reached the library, he quickened his pace to a hurry, despite he would easily find a private room on a Friday afternoon. Sure enough, the building seemed deserted. Once nestled inside a cubby, he pulled out his laptop and connected his phone to the port. He moved the photo of the girl to a folder labeled "family," then went to work. He scanned the file with a simple decryption key identical to the one used by the sender. Abruptly the photo disappeared. In its place were new orders, outlining a side mission.

These orders were not from his organization, rather, they were sent by his Russian affiliates. Oleksandr viewed allegiances with more fluidity than most people and considered himself a free agent straddling two worlds. Although his employer paid handsomely for exclusivity of the information he could gather, he dabbled in work for anyone willing to pay a premium.

This new task would challenge his computer skills, a chance he welcomed. In the past few months those had mostly fallen to the wayside. He eagerly connected to the university network using a specially designed virtual bypass. To any security monitors his login would appear to come from a specific address. He checked his watch. Dr. Guggenheim was currently teaching his undergraduate class and would not be online to trigger a hit on duplicate access.

Felix Guggenheim had proven an easy target early on, and Oleksandr had looked forward to this opportunity for several years. The aging professor had a habit of leaving his lab computer logged on overnight and oftentimes forgot to turn it off. Gleaning his access credentials had been simple and the fact he used the same personal passwords for his classified work provided the hacker easy access into the most sensitive portions of the United States Missile Defense System.

In order to cloak his intrusion, he rerouted his virtual connection, accessing the same ports through an active Chinese military account he kept close at hand. He worked quickly to avoid detection, unsure exactly how the new coding would affect trajectories. It didn't matter. It wasn't his problem and the job paid well. He made the specified corrections, sending a repeated bot attack on several key missile silos, embedding a code that would turn the systems on in a few days. They wouldn't launch, of course, merely turn warheads active for a few minutes and fire off their radars. This kind of hacking job usually sought to panic watching nations, forcing them to publicly chastise the offending government. He grinned at his work. Someone wished to embarrass the United States.

After he had finished, Oleksandr doubled back to wipe his tracks, again leaving breadcrumbs to Dr. Guggenheim. Most assuredly the man would receive a stiffer penalty than the politicians he normally targeted. Those repeatedly thumb their noses at security protocols. The old man wouldn't lose his clearance over the ordeal but would certainly get a swift slap to his wrist.

With job complete he replied to the earlier text letting them know he had completed his task. *You're looking healthy, Sis! I'll call tonight. This afternoon I'm resting after a long morning of studying.* He scooped up his laptop, returning it to his satchel before casually strolling outside. Once he was certain the message had been received, he used his phone to access his bitcoin wallet. He smiled at the size of a recent deposit and quickly closed the browser.

CHAPTER THREE

Doug Snyder loved his job. He had given twenty-five years to the United States Geological Survey and retirement never graced his thoughts. Though his job was actually to monitor seismic activity around Yellowstone, he found the western fault lines more thrilling. California was becoming a hotbed and the scientist gobbled up instrument data like a sports fan enjoyed player statistics. The past week had kept him on the edge of his seat, and he had not left the office for fear of missing out on something big.

His supervisor sent an instant message that flashed onto his screen. It read, "Are you on the clock?"

He replied, "Not at all."

"Then go home, because I'm not paying you overtime." Beau Raines knew him well. They had moved up the ranks together, both beginning their careers as student trainees helping to install seismic instruments.

"Something's cooking and I don't want to miss it."

"Jesus, Doug. It's like watching paint dry. Go home and let the system notify you when something's active."

"I've watched several quakes along San Andreas today. She's active from Indio all the way to Parkfield."

Beau began typing but the cursor paused several times as if he deleted his thoughts. When the message came across it was brief. "Go home. It's late!"

Snyder responded by closing the instant messenger window. Almost immediately his phone vibrated. He glanced at the notification then pulled up the data model. A seismograph recorded a magnitude 7.8 quake twelve miles south of Point Loma. He quickly compared three other instruments and confirmed the data. He reopened the messenger and typed, "I told you so." He closed it again before Beau could make a retort.

Picking up his phone, he dialed a colleague in Reston, Virginia.

A sleepy voice answered the line, "Do you have any idea what time it is?"

"I do, but I wanted you to look at something, Greg."

Greg Matthews served as the lead geophysicist of the eastern region. He said, "This had better be good."

"We just reported a big one south of San Francisco." Doug picked up the remote control and clicked on the television. So far, no stations were reporting the damage but those reports would surely come.

"That happens all the time out there. Why call me?"

"I don't think it's the mainshock."

The voice on the other end asked, "How many foreshocks have you measured?"

He replied, "Six, so far."

"Send me the data and I'll look at it, Doug."

"Thanks, Greg. I owe you one."

He hung up just in time to watch a CNN reporter break into the headline news. "Early reports of a large earthquake in Port Loma, California."

Doug muttered under his breath, "Stand by, California, the next one might be huge." He turned his attention back to Yellowstone and settled into the data. *So far so good*, he thought. Anything so soon after the quake that could register on these sensors would have been cause for alarm. He settled in for a long night.

Bryan and Linda Johnson enjoyed their vacation and were having the time of their lives. Suzy and Seth, their thirteen-year-old twins, would not have agreed had anyone asked their opinions. Boredom had taken over for the pair somewhere between Kansas and Wyoming, but not so for their parents. While the adults sang campfire songs in the front seat and chatted about the fun awaiting them in Yellowstone, the teens buried faces in their phones.

Suzy watched a middle-aged woman fall on her ass into a fountain while trying to cha-cha. She privately liked the video but rudely left a comment, *That's karma. Get off social media, Grandma.* She swiped up and watched an older man tormenting his children with horrible dad jokes. Even though she found him a little funny, she scrolled away without liking. She made a dying face and took a selfie, then snapped it to Seth with the comment, *I'm dying here and surrounded by old people.*

He chuckled next to her and replied, *Why did they even think we'd enjoy the outdoors? We're not eight.*

I know. Right? I hope they get eaten by a bear so we can go home early.

Their parents stopped singing and dad's voice exclaimed, "Here it is kids! Welcome to Yellowstone!"

"Good grief," muttered Seth. Aloud he said, "That's awesome, thanks for the update." He never looked up from his phone.

Linda chimed in, "Seth, be respectful to your father."

"I can't believe you dragged us across four states just to look at trees and mountains! This is bullshit and I'm missing a Fortnite tournament."

Bryan chimed in, "That's enough of that attitude. Linda, turn off their data for the rest of the trip. We're going to have fun as a family!"

Both teens shared a knowing look then quickly connected to the park's WiFi.

While their father paid the admission fee, Suzy looked out the window. "Well, I guess the trees and mountains *are* pretty to look at. It's nicer than I expected."

"That's the spirit!" Linda patted her husband's arm. "See," she asked, "aren't you glad we came?"

"Sure," Suzy replied. She snapped another message to her brother. *This sucks.*

CHAPTER FOUR

Brooke Andalon rolled over and checked the clock. The time read eleven o'clock, but David's side of the bed was empty. He had not come home and, although she knew that she shouldn't worry, she felt more irritated than concerned. He had completely ignored their anniversary and was probably working late at the lab to shed his frustration with Dean Marshall. If he wouldn't come home, she would go to him.

She threw off the covers and slipped into jogging pants. Minutes later she backed out of their driveway and headed to the university. A few miles into the drive she turned on a podcast. The host talked about Doomsday and Armageddon—topics too intense to deal with at the moment. She reached to change stations but paused when the man said, "Take Yellowstone, for instance." She pulled back her hand and listened. Her family, all except her brother Jake, lived in Wyoming.

"The media's too focused on what the president's team puts out and ignores the real news," the first man said.

"Oh, yeah?" the second man asked. "What about Yellowstone? Do we have to listen to that 'super volcano' crap again? That scenario's lost its narrative. We've all suffered through too many low budget movies."

"Just hear me out," the host said. "Seismic events have increased twenty percent in the past five years but nobody's reporting it. The data is essentially lost in the USGS. Probably on the desk of some low-level bureaucrat counting months to retirement."

"Twenty percent?"

"Yes. Twenty percent. It won't take much for this thing to blow."

"I don't believe they're hiding anything," the guest responded, "just this evening they reported this big one in Point Loma. I'd say they got that data out very quickly."

"True, but have you seen the other activity that occurred tonight?" Without waiting for a response, the conspiracist continued, "Of course you didn't. None of us did. There'd been a series of quakes all afternoon and evening, each moving up the San Andreas. It won't take much for a quake to trigger the chain reaction under Wyoming..."

Brooke switched the radio off and sat in silence the remainder of the drive to Cambridge. The scenario was too disturbing to imagine, especially with her parents getting on in years. They were too stubborn to evacuate, even if there were advance warning. She would call them and Jake in the morning.

A few minutes later she pulled up to the Koch Biology Building. The motto above the doors proclaimed, *Mens et Manus*, or, *Mind and Hand*. She swiped her badge at the door and headed directly for the lab. A sign on the door read, *Mendel Project*. She flinched when she realized that someone added *but not for long* with a sharpie. They were even sophomoric enough to draw a laughing monkey using telepathy to fling its poop. She pushed the door open and went inside.

David hardly noticed her arrival. He grunted over his shoulder and continued working with the juvenile primate sitting in the chair.

"You should have her strapped in." She leaned in and gave him a kiss on the cheek. His breath smelled like liquor. She scanned the room and spied a bottle of vodka by the sink.

"I know," he slurred, "I made the rule, remember?"

"So you're ignoring your own rules now?" She knelt beside the rhesus monkey and buckled her down.

"Why not? They're defunding us, so why should I show caution? Being careful is the reason we're behind."

Brooke picked a discarded syringe off the floor. Looking around she found a vial of liquid resting nearby. "Epinephrine?"

"Yeah."

"What are you doing, David?"

"I gave Felicima a stimulant." He didn't even look at her when he answered. His eyes were glued on the chimp, waiting for a response.

"That's not in keeping with project controls or mandates. What are you hoping to prove?"

"This gal's the furthest along than the others. If I can elicit a response from her, then I can re-petition for funding."

"But she's from Batch Bravo. That's the group set aside for destruction."

He replied with a sarcastic tone. "I figured that maybe Dean Marshall could sell the program to military backers."

"Stop this," she replied. "You can't get gamma waves without a quiet mind. You taught me that!"

"I'm trying to tire the mind with epinephrine. When it wears off maybe she'll relax."

"That's dangerous, David. We don't know what'll happen if the experiment works on a disposal batch."

"Well, nothing's manifested in an hour, so I'm about to put her away."

"Honey," Brooke pleaded. She hugged him tightly, but he didn't respond. He sat with muscles tensed, staring at the monkey.

She had never seen this side of him, so far from his jovial self. He pulled away and moved to the other side of the room. Six more monkeys stared up from their cages. He leaned against the bars, eyes focused on the oldest named Oscar. The primate watched him with unblinking eyes. "Take these guys, for example. I gave each of them a dose three hours ago. If epinephrine doesn't awaken their genes, then I don't know what will."

"Let's go home," she pleaded. "The project's over."

"I have two more months, remember?" He locked his eyes on hers.

"Unless you call my brother and ask him for funding." She pleaded, "That's always an option. I'm sure he'd find a way to keep it going. He's a general!"

"It's not an option, Brooke. Jake's my best friend, but I won't turn this experiment over to the military. Besides, these subjects belong to the university. I wouldn't be able to transfer them to the Defense Department, much less to the Air Force." He shook his head, suddenly agitated. "I'd have to start completely over from scratch, and that's an additional ten years of research." He began to pace. "Then what? An overzealous politician gets elected to a finance committee and cuts that funding, too? No, I've invested far too much."

"Then call Michael."

"What's my old roommate going to do?"

"He's a senator, David. Maybe he can divert funds as a rider on a bill or something. I don't know."

"Why are you so dead set on me asking my fraternity brothers for a bail out?" His agitation had grown to anger by now, and he paced as he talked. His voice continued to raise as he ranted. "It's been twenty years since undergrad, and both of them have lived out their dreams while I pushed through a doctorate. With this project, so goes my hope for tenure! So what have I actually accomplished that compares to them, Brooke?"

The nearby monkeys howled with fear at his noise, drowning him out causing him to turn. His fist smashed down hard against the top of Oscar's cage, then he picked up the empty vial of epinephrine and flung it across the room. Brooke flinched as it barely missed a pot of boiling water on the gas stove. Apparently, he had thought it a good idea to sanitize instruments while drinking.

"David, you're drunk!" She didn't mean for it to sound accusatory, but that phrase always does. She tried again, gentler, "Please let me take you home. Call in sick tomorrow."

"Why? So the entire department can laugh at me *wallowing* in my failure?"

The hooting of the animals had grown deafening as they screamed their displeasure with his tantrum. He turned and shouted. "Shut up!"

Suddenly, a blast of concussive air hit them both in the chest taking away their breath and slamming them hard against the opposite wall. Brooke struck her head upon a cabinet. First her vision swam and then it fell completely dark.

✧

David rolled over, choking against the smoke in the air. Thankfully, he awoke lying on the cold floor, so the air was cleaner than the layer floating above. He reached around until he felt a leg and shook it. Brooke was unconscious. He moved his ear to her mouth and waited. She breathed.

He tried to scoop her into his arms but slipped and fell, landing hard on his wrist. All around, the primates screamed and howled as the inferno raged. All except one. He rolled over for a closer look, blinking against the sting from the smoke. Felicima had wriggled free of her straps and stood on two legs, working her hands like an orchestra conductor.

Her eyes had somehow turned golden against the flame, glowing like fiery embers. The orange and yellow heat swirled before her, working into a fiery tornado. David gasped as she hurled it in his direction. He ducked and it exploded against the cabinet behind him. The monkey seemed to laugh as he dodged.

Panicked, he pulled open a drawer and drew out a scalpel, holding it outstretched toward Felicima.

She scrambled toward the gas stove. If he hadn't seen it with his own eyes, he would not have believed what she did next. She stood atop the burner, unscathed and not burning, channeling heat directly into her body. It gathered around her as she pointed toward Batch Alpha. Then, with eyes closed, fire shot from her hand like a flame thrower. The subjects cooked within their metal prisons. All of his life's work was destroyed in an instant.

He watched helplessly as the fire spread toward the chemical locker. Thinking fast, he lunged, plunging the scalpel deep into Felicima's chest. With his left hand he grabbed her by the neck and pulled the blade free with his right. Again and again he stabbed until she fell limp in his grasp. David dropped the tiny corpse on the floor, marveling at the burns on his left hand —merely from touching her body. From the other side of the room he heard a groan.

David dropped the scalpel and rushed to Brooke's side. He grabbed her ankles and dragged her furiously toward the door. Reaching out, he felt the hot steel of the handle with his blistered hand and fumbled to turn the mechanism. When he finally wrestled it open, the flames behind him leaped higher, no longer thirsty as the drank in the welcomed oxygen. With a grunt he pulled his wife into the hallway and out the front door. Safely on the lawn he collapsed beside her, wheezing and coughing. His lungs burned as he forced them to take in clean air. Suddenly, the flames found the gas lines and David covered his eyes. The building exploded into the night.

CHAPTER FIVE

Senator Victor Tully made his way toward the office of Michael Esterling, visibly irritated and walking with an angry air. The junior senator had made a bold statement by demanding his senior meet him in *his* chambers. *This upstart has a lot to learn about politics,* he thought. Their appointment time was four o'clock. He checked his watch. It read four-thirty. He smiled, the least he could do is make the little bastard wait.

He pushed open the door and met a sharply dressed male receptionist. The man held up a finger, indicating that Victor should wait. Of course, he would not.

"I'm Senator Tully to see Senator Esterling." He walked with confidence toward the mahogany door. "Ensure we aren't disturbed until after I leave."

"Stop." The man quickly hung up the phone and stood.

"I beg your pardon?"

"I said to stop, Senator. I was instructed to have you sit and wait while he finishes another appointment."

"Sit and wait? You mean he isn't ready?" the senator fumed. "Our appointment was more than thirty minutes ago!"

"Exactly, and he met with someone else while you took your time getting here." The audacious receptionist stepped forward. He was an imposing figure, broad in the shoulders with punishing eyes. Victor was fairly certain the man was more security than personal assistant. He sat.

A few moments later the door opened and Victor stood. He was prepared to give the young senator from Massachusetts a tongue lashing but froze in his tracks.

The woman departing Esterling's office said, "You don't have to stand for me, Victor."

"Madam Speaker, I…"

"You what? You were purposely late to your appointment and didn't expect to find me going over Michael's future with him?" The Speaker of the House stared him down with a cool smile. "Well?"

"I…" He tried to answer but the words caught in his throat.

"Michael," she turned to face the young man, "let's meet again for lunch. I'd like to discuss these ideas further."

"Absolutely, Marsha. How's Friday?"

"I have a luncheon with the Vice President but I'll cancel for you." She shot Victor a look of disgust and turned to leave. The receptionist held the door. "Thank you, Robert," she said as she left.

Esterling smiled at Victor, reaching out a hand in greeting. "Victor! Thanks for coming!"

Tully ignored the offering and pushed past. "Let's get this over with." Once inside, he chose a seat by a small window, refusing to sit across from Michael's seat of power and gazing out at the view of the city.

The younger man ignored the slight. "I'm so glad you're here, Victor. I wanted to go over your recent bill."

This caused Tully to pause. *Is he about to tell me he's on board?* Michael Esterling was known far and wide as a progressive and as such drew wide-eyed young voters. But his true agenda was extremely hard to read and the man himself thoroughly unpredictable. Victor asked with suspicion, "What about my bill?"

"As written, it won't pass the floor. I also just ensured that it will never see approval from the house unless you add some provisions."

"But our party owns the house, and she won't buck her own agenda." Victor sat rigid in his seat, the hairs on his neck taking notice of potential treachery. "Why exactly was Madam Speaker here?"

"She and I both agree that your bill is an affront to our party's values." He paused and then added, "As written, of course."

"Did she suddenly decide that while in your chambers?" Without waiting for an answer he added, "And who are *you*? Nothing but a junior hellraiser who scraped up enough young voters to claim his seat."

"The nation needs new leadership and craves fresh minds in both houses. Madam Speaker knows this."

"I've served the people for four decades!"

"Then perhaps," the younger man said, "you've overstayed your welcome." Esterling stood and walked casually around the desk, resting his hip on the corner. He folded his arms and narrowed his eyes on Victor. "This entire institution is corrupt, and I aim to change it."

This made the senior senator laugh. "Good luck with that. Every one of us arrived in Washington like the fictional Mr. Smith—with expectations of grandeur and hoping to make a difference. But in the end, it's all a game. A game of alliances and backroom discussions. Politics has nothing to do with making a difference. For that matter, it has even less to do with making the world better for the people."

"Oh," Michael said, "I agree with that statement one hundred percent. That's why I'm not a politician. The people, as you call them, are nothing more than votes to career flip floppers like you. Admit it, our party under current leadership, preys upon the lower class, especially the immigrants and minorities, rendering them dependent. Our answer to *their* problems has always been to raise taxes and hope we finally made a difference. Unfortunately, that only ensures they perpetually elect pompous elitist windbags like you. Where's their money except fattening your own pocket? No, Senator Tully, I'm the opposite of a politician. I'm here to turn your world upside down and run you out—to make this party for the people, of the people, and by the people."

Victor fought against his anger, but allowed a small measure of venom seep to seep into his words. "You don't have the power to make those changes. Besides," he added, "the rest of us won't accept it."

"Alone? No. I'm afraid you're right, at least for now. But Madam Speaker and a few of your close friends are willing to listen."

"And why is that?"

"Because my associate Robert in the next room has his finger on an email, and he's just aching to send it to Fox news. It's damning, Senator Tully. Forty years of your vile back room dealings and all the dirty little *private* secrets you'd prefer kept hidden." Michael walked around his desk and settled into his chair. Once seated he pulled out a tablet, tapped it with his forefinger, and added, "This is the version of your bill which Marsha and her friends have agreed to back. It'll be presented by you and my name is nowhere on it."

"What's in it for you if you don't get to bask in the glory? Passing a bill through both houses could eventually launch you as whip? Why wouldn't you want that?"

Michael sighed loudly. "Esteemed colleague." He clicked his tongue and added, "Because I'm here to participate in the solution rather than contribute to Washington's problems."

After Senator Tully departed, Michael met with four more members of their party. Each shared the same attribute as Victor—too powerful and stuck in their ways for the good of their voters. Most became compliant when he shared certain documentation of their corruption, but one had proved troublesome. After they left, Michael pressed a button on his desk.

Robert's voice responded from the next room. "Yes, Senator?"

"Come in here. I need you to run an errand for me." He leaned back in his seat and rubbed his temples. He did not enjoy this darker side of his work, but his assistant performed it with enthusiasm.

In less than a minute Robert was seated before him. "What can I do for you, boss?"

"Senator Canava from California isn't playing ball and will need some convincing." He pulled a file and slid it across the desk. "Here are a few of his key investors. Work them in the usual manner, giving incentives to pull their contribution pledges."

"What about his own special interests?"

"His trust is tied up with real estate. The recent earthquakes will be a boon for him. Look for any large-scale purchases by these companies and then leak it to the major networks. Once he's tied up with that investigation release this." He handed Robert another file.

The assistant took it, read it over, and clicked his tongue against his teeth. "That's juicy, boss."

"I thought you'd like that." He collapsed into his chair, exhausted by a morning of talking. "Were there any noteworthy calls today?"

"General Braston called." He pulled out his iPhone and read the message. "Funding pulled from Mendel and lab burned. Time to bring him to Andalon."

Michael leaned back, letting the meaning wash over him.

Robert's phone buzzed a second time. "That's strange."

"What's strange?"

"He just sent another message. It says, 'Adam ate the apple and doomed us all. Time is now.' What does he mean?"

Esterling felt his stomach lurch. It was too soon. He thought they had more time—years or decades even.

"Clear my calendar for the rest of the week. Find me an immediate military flight from Andrews to Ramstein."

"Right away!"

"And Robert..."

"Sir?"

Michael paused. This man deserved to know, didn't he? Could he handle it? Of course not. None of them could. The *world* wasn't ready for the same reasons its people fell as endless prey to men like Senator Victor Tully.

Perhaps he and Jake could finally fix things after all.

"Take the week off and spend it with your family. I... I appreciate your dedication over these years."

"Of course, sir."

Michael closed the door to his office and departed for the last time.

CHAPTER SIX

David poured a cup of coffee and collapsed exhausted into his favorite seat at the breakfast table. This was *his* spot. Here the warmth of morning sun angled just right while he would read the happenings of the world, learning of strife overseas, stock prices, and the weather. Someday newspapers would disappear forever, replaced entirely by tablets and phones. But the boy had grown up in a home with one always on the table and the man he became dearly missed that golden age, lamenting that future generations would never have the funny pages to break up the negativity of the news. He stared down at the stark and barren table.

The sun wasn't in its usual spot either, resting higher in the sky due to the lateness of the day. He hadn't slept-in for too long to remember, but it felt good even if the setting of his spot was off. The previous night had been an ordeal of questions from campus administrators, police, and firefighters, with everyone wanting to know if he had deliberately set fire to the lab. That anxiety had bit into the night, filling it with more questions he was asking himself. He had awakened curious how he'd been able to sleep at all.

Brooke stood over the stovetop, pouring batter onto a griddle. Since the morning was mostly gone, he was surprised she cooked pancakes.

In a non-accusing voice, he asked, "Where is it?"

She didn't even look up when she answered, "Where's what?"

"The newspaper, hon. You always have it out and waiting, open to the funny pages."

"Oh, that," she replied, "there wasn't anything funny about today's news, so I threw it out."

"How bad?"

"You're a smart man, David. How bad do you think it is?" Her dry tone did nothing to hide irritation.

"Let me guess, *MIT Professor Burns Down Laboratory in Drunken Rage*, bad?"

She replied, "Try, *Vengeful Arsonist Torches MIT Laboratory Over Halted Funding*, bad."

"Ouch. They didn't even add, 'allegedly,' and jumped straight to assumed guilt."

She whirled around. "Seriously, David! What were you *thinking*, getting drunk and forcing your experiments?"

"I don't know," he answered, "I guess I wasn't. I just needed to know how close I was before they pulled the plug."

"And now? Facing possible charges?"

"Now I know I was right. The experiment succeeded."

Brooke froze with spatula in the air as she stared back, waiting for his explanation. When he said nothing more she asked, "And how do you know that?"

"I saw her, Brooke. Felicima lit the fire."

"How," she asked, "did the monkey light the fire?"

Starting with the blast of air, he gave her all the details. When he had finished, he could tell that she wasn't convinced.

"You're describing pyrokinesis."

"Yes," he replied.

"That isn't what the experiment was designed for."

"Exactly." He brimmed with excitement as he spoke, "Can you believe we almost destroyed Felicima and the rest of the batch? We sought telepathy but discovered something greater!" He abruptly fell silent. Crestfallen, even. When he spoke again it was in a whisper. "None of that matters now since they're gone. Destroyed."

Brooke urged reason. "What are you doing? You've always been specific about your theory that the gamma waves would render any telepathy as peaceful or it wouldn't be controllable. Fire-flinging monkeys are the *opposite* of that."

"Yes," he replied, "but that was before Dean Marshall cancelled our funding." The look on her face caused him to pause, reconsidering his choice of words. "Honey, listen. Just the fact that our experiments resulted in telekinesis proves my theory holds water. I don't want fire-flinging monkeys, or fire-spewing people for that matter, but they prove we can reengineer the human race to have useful abilities."

"Useful is a broad term, David."

He decided to change the subject, "Thank you for making me pancakes."

"They aren't for you."

"If they aren't for me, then who?" He barely uttered the question when someone rang the buzzer. He raised his eyes expectantly toward Brooke, but she avoided answering. David walked across the living room and opened the door to find a downtrodden Sam.

"Thanks, doc," the boy muttered as he slinked past his boss. He headed straight for the table and settled into David's favorite seat.

"Sam, that's my...," Brooke cut his words off with an icy glare. "Never mind." Not wanting to sit facing the sun, he leaned against the counter. "You know you could have stayed home today."

"I invited him," Brooke responded with finality in her voice, "and his visit has nothing to do with you." She placed a supportive hand on the boy's shoulder and spoke, "Sam, tell David what happened."

"Mi-Jung isn't coming."

"Oh, Sam," he responded. "I'm so sorry. What happened?"

"The government denied her student visa. It turns out her father had ties to the north from contracts he's worked. With the new travel ban, she can't come."

"What travel ban?"

"For God's sake, David. You've been so engrossed in the project you haven't paid attention to anything outside the lab."

"I'm sorry, I've been under a lot of pressure. What travel ban?"

"The president issued a ban on all incoming travel from Southeast Asia. North Korean dissidents have been stirring up trouble."

Sam chimed in, "Several North Korean agents were caught in a sting in Japan. They had plans to firebomb the University of Tokyo."

"What does this have to do with Mi-Jung?"

"Since they were disguised as South Korean students, all student visas have been denied until they sort out who's an agent and who's legit."

"I'm sorry, Sam. I wish there was something I could do to help."

Sam looked up with glassy eyes, red from a sleepless night of worry and emotion of his own. He asked, "Did you burn the lab, David?"

"No. I most *certainly* did not." Andalon pulled out a chair and sat across from his young assistant. He would have preferred his usual spot at the table, but he made do. "I wouldn't do that. I've invested too much of myself."

"The campus police think you did. Why were you even there?"

David sighed. "I was trying to force a result... and I drank a little too much."

"A *lot* too much," Brooke argued.

"Okay, a *lot* too much," he shot his wife a sidelong glance, she had returned to the griddle to flip the pancakes. "I gave Felicima a shot of epinephrine," David said.

"You shouldn't have," the boy responded. "She's been showing intense aggression toward Batch Alpha and is always agitated."

"No, I shouldn't have," he agreed, "but I felt I had to do something."

Sam mulled the professor's words, then asked, "How did the fire start?"

Brooke turned from the stove and pointed her spatula, "Yes, *Doctor* Andalon, tell your graduate assistant how the fire started."

"I threw a bit of a tantrum and threw some glass around. All of the monkeys were upset, but I think the epinephrine I gave Felicima stirred some abilities."

Sam appeared skeptical but asked, "Like what?"

"First a blast of wind pushed Brooke and me against the wall, then, while we were dazed, she somehow worked pyrokinesis and started throwing fireballs."

The boy didn't laugh. "Dr. Andalon," he said, "don't tell anyone that story. They'll put you in the loony bin."

Brooke chimed in, "Exactly! David, don't tell anyone that story."

"But that's what we've been hoping to prove! We've searched for years for signs of telepathic connection between subjects."

"But pyrokinesis?" Sam frowned. "In your dissertation you suggested that telekinesis as a side effect of telepathy would only manifest in variant forms of air manipulation."

"Exactly! And she created enough wind to slam us into the wall." Both he and Brooke fingered their bruised heads at the memory. "I must have been wrong about the exclusion of fire."

Sam wasn't convinced. "But we'll never know because the lab and Felicima are destroyed." He shook his head, "I'm sorry, Dr. Andalon, but as soon as the semester is over in December, I'm returning to Seoul and Mi-Jung."

Brooke placed a heaping plate of flapjacks in front of the boy, who doused it thoroughly with syrup, hellbent on drowning his sorrows with the sweet comfort only Mrs. Butterworth could provide. Brooke hugged him tight then turned to leave. David started to make another plea but, before he could open his mouth, Brooke's phone rang.

"Hello, Jake. Yeah, I called them about an hour ago but Dad won't leave. What?" She sat in silence, listening to her brother and nodding along. "You can't be serious. You want *us* all to fly out *there*? Jake, it's short notice!"

David sat up at that. Jake Braston was a high ranking general for the United States Air Force. If *there* meant they were to fly to meet Jake, then *there* was Germany.

"That's not possible. No, David has had some issues down at the university. What? Oh." She shot her husband a glare. "You've already *heard* about that." She paused, "Yes, I'll put him on." She tossed the phone instead of handing it to him, then turned off the burners and went upstairs without bothering with the dishes.

David held up the receiver, "Hello, Jake."

"Hello!" came the reply. "I saw on the news what happened to your lab. What kind of trouble are you in? How can I help?" Jake had always tried to play big brother, even when they were frat brothers.

"Nothing I can't dig out of."

"Nonsense. Brooke sounds pissed off, mate! Tell me everything."

David took a deep breath and then spilled it all—from the funding cut to the burned-out lab. When he had finished the line was dead quiet. "Jake? Are you there?"

"Yeah," was the delayed reply. "I'm here. Tell me more about the gust of wind that blew you backward."

"What about it?"

"Which group of monkeys did it come from?"

"A subject from Batch Bravo."

"That's impossible," Jake replied, "What were the others doing at the time?"

David was dumbfounded. He had raved about his theories to his roommates all through college and even into graduate school. It was all he had ever wanted to talk about, but they never wanted to listen. He had no idea that Jake had paid any attention whatsoever, much less would decide what was possible and what wasn't.

"I was so focused on the subject that I hadn't paid them attention. They were screaming, I guess."

"Why were they screaming, Dave?"

"I had thrown a glass bottle across the room and was yelling at Brooke."

"Batch Alpha's the primary study group?"

"Yeah, that's right."

"What generation?"

David froze. "Jake, what are you doing? Why are you suddenly so interested in my research?"

After a pause Brooke's brother responded, "I need you and your entire team to fly out here right away. I'll pay if that's what it takes." And, as in their college fraternity days, David realized you could never say *no* to Jake Braston.

"We'll meet you in Frankfurt, Jake, but we do have a slight problem with one of our team members."

"Just tell me what you need," came the reply.

"One of my student assistants got caught up in this travel ban and is now stuck in Seoul. Her name is Park Mi-Jung. I'll need her there, as well."

"Done."

Dr. Andalon hung up the phone and turned to face a wide-eyed Sam. He was about to speak when Brooke came down the stairs with her overnight bag. She set it by the door.

She asked, "What time's the flight?"

His phone announced a notification and held it up for her to see. Jake worked fast and the reservations were already made. "Two hours. Pack fast, Sam. Logan Airport may be ten minutes away, but security's going to be hell." The boy left the rest of his uneaten pancakes behind and ran out the door. David settled down in his favorite seat and picked up the fork. He noticed Brooke watching and asked, "What?"

"Those are Sam's."

"They'll be cold by the time he gets back, hon. Besides, I think I just redeemed myself in regard to him."

CHAPTER SEVEN

Cathy Fletcher hated her job. Her feet hurt, her back ached, and she needed a shower—badly. She felt her thighs where the pole had rubbed when she slipped. It left a red mark that already throbbed. She wanted to go home. Thankfully, it was closing time.

A large man sat at the bar splitting tips with the busty bartender. Despite her obvious efforts, he had no interest in her nor her ludicrously oversized bosom.

Cathy decided to save him. "Walk me to my car, Tim?"

The dark-haired woman behind the bar responded, "Can't you see he's busy?"

Tim ignored her and stood. "Of course, Cat." He took his portion and left the rest on the bar. He pointed at the bills. "That's a good haul. You should send some of that to your ex-husband and get caught up on your child support."

She snatched the stack from the smooth bar top and said, "Mind your own business."

Cathy and Tim exchanged a brief and knowing smile. They both despised the woman, who always spun her stories, hiding the truth that she once abandoned three very young children. She instead chose selfishness and wound up a deadbeat bartender, working under the radar to avoid paying her part.

Once they were outside Tim asked, "You and the boy need anything?"

"We're fine for now." She gave him a quick hug. "Thank you though."

He nodded and opened the door, checking the backseat before allowing her inside. "How's school going?"

"All 'A's' so far, but I have to do clinical observations soon. That'll take more of my time and I may have to cut hours here."

"Is that so bad," he asked, "spending less time here? You should just quit completely." He gestured at the blinking marquee of two Siamese cats. "Tell me honestly, is *this* your crowd?"

"*Pussy Galore's?*" Cathy laughed. "I was born to take my clothes off in this joint!" When she realized he hadn't shared her joke and only stared back with serious concern, she added, "I need the money and sometimes it's really good." He said nothing and just stood by the door. "What is it," she asked, "that's got you so riled up?"

"I saw you slip on the pole. You're exhausted."

"Well, I ain't quitting, Tim." She turned the key and pulled the door shut, rolling the window down to add, "I'll be back tomorrow night and every night after that! You're stuck with me till the end of the world!" She put the car in reverse and backed out of the spot, leaving him to watch her go. The streets of Kalamazoo were quiet as she made her way to the interstate, and Cat made good time. The trip home to her town of Scott would take only fifteen minutes.

As she drove, she thought of Joshua. His teacher had emailed his progress in class, so she allowed her sister Sarah to give him ice cream after dinner. *That should be me,* she thought, *giving him ice cream.* But raising a four-year-old alone was expensive, and she had to make the bills.

Cat was a hard worker, beginning each day with a shift at the bank. Her nursing classes were in the evenings, and her night job was three nights a week. Thinking back to what Tim had suggested, she wished she could quit altogether. But she'd keep dancing—she had to afford ice cream and sitters.

When she returned home, she would face two more hours of studying and hoped her sister had done the dishes. She knew, if she didn't, she'd end up choosing the anatomy notes over bowls and plates, putting off one more thing for the morning. But mornings were reserved for special time with Joshua and she hated missing that.

Every morning she'd wake him and begin every day asking about the one before. She'd listen to his adventures over breakfast, have reading time, then get him ready and off to preschool. She cherished every second of that time, and so did he. They called it *Joshie Time.*

Blue and red lights broke Cat from her musings. "Shit," she muttered, pulling over to the side of the road. A few moments later a highway patrolman stood outside her window. She handed him her license and waited for the cliché question.

"No, officer," she replied after he asked, "I have no idea how fast I was going."

"Take it slow, ma'am," he told her after writing out an expensive citation.

She looked at the ticket. Apparently, she had driven through a construction zone without noticing. There was no way for her to pay the three hundred dollars and also make rent. She'd have to continue dancing at *Pussy Galore's*.

"Ma'am be careful being out so late. Several jewelry stores were robbed in Kalamazoo and, about an hour ago, the same crook hit a liquor store in Scott."

She asked, "How do you know it was the same guy?"

"Surveillance cameras. He drove a late model blue pickup in each robbery."

"I'm headed straight home," she promised.

"Good." He was about to leave when the trooper whirled, abruptly grabbing her car door with both hands. At first, she was confused, terrified by the look of shock and fear on his face. Then she felt it as well. Her car bounced erratically, almost as if a giant had chosen her car as its basketball. The policeman continued to hold on for dear life as the world around him quaked.

After it subsided, the man regained his composure and turned to gaze off into the distance. From the direction of the Kalamazoo River Gas Plant, flames climbed high onto the horizon. Hurriedly, he waved Cat on and rushed to his car, speeding off into the night.

She drove the rest of the way with white knuckles wrapped tightly around the wheel. She hadn't felt an earthquake before, but they weren't uncommon even in Michigan. Her father had told her about a large tremor in 2015 that did some damage. "It opened a new fault line to the north," he had told her. "Scientists say it's deep underground," he had insisted, "but someday it'll connect Lakes Huron and Michigan, just mark my words!"

When she finally pulled up to her complex, she couldn't help but notice the blue pickup truck parked by the dumpster. She eyed it closely and considered the words of the trooper. *Those are dime a dozen in Michigan,* she decided. Taking a closer look, she saw something hanging from the rearview mirror. The blue background and silver leaves surrounding a rifle jumped out at once. A combat infantry badge. *His* favorite medal. *No,* she thought, *not him! Not here!*

She quickly unbuckled and slid from the car, fumbling for her phone and dialing 911. But the line was dead, most likely due to the fires and downed lines in the area. She pushed forward, hurrying up the stairs in such a panic she fumbled twice placing the key into the hole. She dropped it once but retrieved it and turned the deadbolt. When it finally opened, she walked in on Sarah watching a movie.

The younger woman jumped to her feet the moment she entered. "He wouldn't leave, Cat!"

She pointed a finger at a ruggedly handsome man with a disarming smile. He was dressed in boots and a union shirt that read *unfair wages grind my gears*. In his hand was a pistol.

Cat tossed her purse onto a chair, careful not to look directly at the man. When she turned, it was casual, as if to remind him she'd never fully be under his control. "You need to go, Clint," she said at last.

"You can't keep me from seeing Josh," he replied, standing slowly and tucking the gun in his waistband. Three steps later he was close enough for her to smell the alcohol on his breath. "He's my boy and I aim to spend time with him," he demanded.

"You have to come back with a court chaperone, you know that. Now leave and go through the proper..."

His fist met her eye before she finished the sentence and she fell with a thud. Sarah cried out, but that sound muffled when she also struck the ground. Cat's vision swam as she tried to focus on her sister, limp and motionless beside the couch. Clint held the pistol drawn, looming over them both.

"Go pack you and him a bag and let's go," he commanded, "and give me your phone." She gave it up before hurrying to the bedroom.

Cathy had moved so many times since leaving her ex that she no longer needed to pack, instead keeping a bug out bag ready for both her and her son—always beside her bed and full of their most needed items in case they had to flee into the night. She grabbed these now, feeling a slight bulge behind a row of stitching in the liner. A quick press on this hidden pocket was comforting, knowing the object was there. Someday she would find the courage and need to use it, and she wondered if this night was the time.

She stalled, knowing he would expect her to take a few minutes, and dug into the nightstand for a prepaid phone Tim had given her months before. "Just in case," he had said, letting her know his number was saved as number one on speed dial. She breathed deeply, turning it on and counting to ten to calm her nerves. She breathed out while it dialed, but finished with a sigh after realizing the lines were still down. With a deep breath she turned it off and tossed it into the bag.

She dreaded returning to the living room, but found her way there to discover Josh was already up and rubbing sleep from his eyes. He stared cautiously at his father then looked to his mother and waited. She nodded and he stepped into outstretched arms.

Clint picked him up into the air and hugged him tight. "I've missed you, boy! We're gonna have so much fun now that we're together!"

Cathy looked for Sarah, but she was no longer lying on the floor. A glance toward the kitchen revealed she wasn't there either. The younger woman was nowhere to be found. "Where's Sarah?" she demanded.

The look from her ex screamed *don't ask*, but she wouldn't back down. Not this time. She moved to the bathroom and placed a hand on the door.

"Don't do it," he commanded.

Terror filled her gut, twisting her nerves and squeezing out bile as she realized what he might have done. With a deep breath Cat turned the knob slowly and peeked in, steeling her nerves for the closure she needed. The shower curtain was drawn and the lights were out, but the hallway glow revealed a shadow resting in the tub beyond the vinyl sheet.

Josh must have sensed her dread and began reaching toward his mother standing in the doorway. Fearing what Clint would do if the boy left his side, she shook her head, smiling weakly. Though her face urged calm, her gut screamed with anger and loss. Clint tightened his hold on the boy.

Cat crept inside, placing one foot in front of the other as she made her way toward the bath. She trembled when pulling the curtain open, and her eyes violently closed as if someone had flicked the switch in a darkened room without warning. She was terrified to open them.

He wouldn't, she told herself. *He's not a killer. He's a lot of things, but not that.* Reluctantly, her eyes fluttered open and grew wide at the stream of blood against Sarah's temple. Her sweet sister lay motionless—never to again awaken. Remembering Josh, the scream she yearned for caught in her throat, turning to bile and rising as vomit instead. Bent over the toilet, she allowed terror to escape to her body, retching until tears eased out instead of sobs.

"Hurry up," the monster called from the living room, and she squeezed both fists as if tightened around his throat.

She tried to forget the woman in the tub was family—that it was Sarah, and fell upon her nursing knowledge for guidance as she took a closer look. There were only moments to reason out what had happened. *He struck her in the living room,* she realized, *so she was lifeless when he dragged her in here.* Treating the moment like the medical trauma photographs from classes, she examined the wound. The gash on the side of her head caved slightly, revealing blunt force. *His pistol,* she realized. *Pistol whipped. He killed her in cold blood when she was vulnerable and unable to defend herself.*

Cathy fought back tears, resolute to mourn later since now was not the time. She had to remain strong for Josh, returning her thoughts to the object in her bag now sitting on the floor next to Clint. *I'll get my chance at him later,* she vowed, *only* then *will I cry for you, Sarah.*

Filled with mourning she backed away, pulling the door shut behind her. Pushing past Clint and his devilish smile, she picked up the bags and held her hand out for Josh.

The killer in her living room shook his head, hugging the boy tighter against his hip. She was his captive as long as he had control of Josh, unable to scream, powerless to fight, and unwilling to flee.

"Let's go," he commanded. "You lead the way."

She led them to the blue pickup and placed their bags in the backseat. She paused, taking notice of several black bags already on the floor. A bottle of whiskey protruded from one but the others were tightly sealed. The state trooper's words echoed in her memory and she didn't need to peek inside to know they were filled with gold and jewels—the spoils of Clint's most recent crime spree.

He placed Josh in the seat next to him in the front. "Buckle up, boy," he commanded. "I'd hate for something to happen to you."

Cathy knew those words were a warning for her instead of concern for Josh. She slid into the cab beside her son and tried not to think of Sarah.

CHAPTER EIGHT

Doug Snyder watched the activity developing under Yellowstone. The quake was small, not even registering a full three point zero, but it was in the exact spot to affect the geological makeup of the springs running through the Upper Geyser Basin. Sensors detected a faint disruption, more of a ripple than largescale activity, to the groundwater. Had he not been watching, waiting specifically for this clue, it would have gone unnoticed.

He scanned the surface water data with bated breath, searching for similar anomalies. One source in particular came from a gage flow tracker along Myriad Creek. It read zero. *I should report this directly to Beau,* he realized, but there was no time. He picked up the phone and made a call that could get him fired.

"Yellowstone Ranger Station," the woman's voice on the other line replied.

"This is Doug Snyder, seismologist with the United States Geological Survey," he explained.

"How can I help you, Doug?"

"You just had an earthquake, not large, but focused within the upper geyser basin. You need to get everyone out of that section of the park immediately!"

"Sir, we receive calls from concerned citizens often, mostly regarding the park's location over an inactive super volcano. I assure you that our scientists monitor data every single day, and there's no danger to the park or our visitors."

Doug placed his free hand against his temples, massaging out the ignorance he had just heard. Forcing his nerves to calm, he asked, "What's your name?"

"Ranger Stewart," the woman replied.

"Ranger Stewart," he explained, "I am not merely a *concerned citizen*. I am one of those scientists monitoring your data *every day* as you put it, and now I'm telling you there's imminent danger to the park. You need to clear the visitors from the geyser basin."

There was a pause on the line. "I'm not authorized to do that," the woman said.

"Then connect me to someone who can," he demanded.

"Please hold."

Hurry, he thought, willing urgency to the people on the other end of the line. He waited impatiently, tapping his fingers and fidgeting in his chair while his blood pressure continued to rise. Time was of the essence and every second mattered.

Finally, after what felt like an eternity, a male voice answered. "This is Ranger Tedesco. Ms. Stewart filled me in, but I'm not sure how we can help. If you're USGS, aren't there official channels to follow?"

"We don't have time for *official channels,*" Doug insisted. "Listen! Send someone to the Myriad Creek gage southeast of Old Faithful visitor center. Verify it's even flowing!"

"I can dispatch someone, but I don't understand why that's a problem."

Snyder sighed with exasperation. "Because the last earthquake rerouted the ground water flow. You're sitting atop a pressure cooker, Ranger Tedesco!"

Bryan hurried his family to the ranger station and read the sign. They had made it. Old Faithful, the park's most famous geyser was part of the reason he had dragged his family to the park. He'd wanted to see it since he was the same age as the twins. He checked his watch. The naturalist predicted the next eruption to occur in less than ten minutes.

"Let's go," he urged.

"We're coming! Calm down," Linda laughed, "you sound silly."

"If we miss this one then we'll have to wait between one to two hours for the next."

He glanced at his kids and smiled. They were actually paying attention to the sights around them, instead of hiding their noses in smartphones.

He grabbed his wife's hand and squeezed. *This is the best vacation ever,* he thought, *and my family needs it.* When she had sold the Martin's home, they both decided they would use the commission to take a trip. Both their jobs had been stressful, and they'd been wound tight as a couple. Even the kids had been bored at home during fall break and needed something stimulating before school resumed in another week.

A large crowd had gathered near the roped off section and listened intently to the ranger telling the story of the attraction. "Old Faithful erupts around twenty times a day," he said, "and we can predict eruptions based on the time and height of the last." He gestured behind him. "Although the average height is one hundred thirty-five feet, it is not uncommon to see a plume reach one hundred and eighty."

The crowd "ooed" and "awed" and one person asked, "How accurate are your predictions?"

"Good question," the ranger responded. "We have a ninety percent accuracy with give or take ten minutes each time."

Seth walked up to his father and tapped his arm. When Bryan turned the boy asked, "What's this again?"

"Old Faithful's a geyser. Hot water will spew up from that hole in the ground and make a fountain over one hundred feet tall."

"That's pretty badass," the teen responded.

"It really is," Bryan agreed.

"How does it work?"

"We're standing atop a giant volcano. Scientists call it a super volcano. The magma underneath us heats up pockets of water and, when the gases build up pressure, the water sprays into the air."

Seth suddenly looked worried. "What if the entire thing erupts? Why the hell did you bring us to a volcano," he asked.

Bryan laughed, "It isn't due to erupt for another one hundred thousand years or so. We're fine."

They made it to the railing and joined the crowd. Five minutes remained. He decided to make a game of it. "Let's make bets. I say that it will erupt right on time."

Linda jumped at that. "Five dollars says it's early."

Bryan asked Seth, "What about you kids?"

"Late," they both agreed.

A few minutes later and no eruption. "Well, honey, it looks like you and I both lost." He pulled out two fives and handed one to each twin.

Several more minutes passed and then Suzy spoke up. "This is taking forever." She grabbed her brother's hand and dragged him away. "Come on, let's go film TikToks." She pointed to a grassy area further down the path. "We can see it just as well from there as here," she said.

Bryan watched them run off. "What are we doing wrong?"

Linda knew what he meant and responded immediately. "Nothing at all. That's normal teenage behavior." She laughed as Suzy tied her shirt into a crop top and hiked her shorts higher.

"That's normal?" Bryan shook his head, "She spends more time dancing and shaking her hips in front of that phone than she does reading. We're going to have a generation of imbeciles if they don't pull their faces out of those electronics."

"Our parents also thought we were doomed for similar reasons, don't forget."

By now Suzy was dancing while her brother filmed. Bryan shook his head and checked his watch. The geyser was fifteen minutes late. He moved closer to the ranger. Several people in the crowd voiced their speculations, but the man kept reassuring them.

"This happens sometimes. Remember our predictions are plus or minus ten minutes, but we also sometimes get it wrong," he said.

The earth abruptly rumbled beneath their feet, shaking the park and causing people to hold onto railings or each other for balance. All around them people screamed but the tremor only lasted a few seconds. After it subsided everyone broke out in laughter except Bryan. He looked toward the ranger.

The man seemed worried, but quickly went to work reassuring the crowd around him. "That happens, too, sometimes. Although rare, earthquakes do happen in the park."

A blood curdling scream turned every head except Bryan's. It had come from the direction of Seth and Suzy, and he refused to turn out of fear of what he'd see. *No,* he pleaded, *let them be safe!* But a second scream joined the first, so close it caused his ears to ring. This he recognized as Linda's and the piercing shrill confirmed what he already knew. Their children were in danger. As he slowly turned, he realized a new geyser had formed away from Old Faithful, spewing boiling water from a fresh crack in the field of stark green grass beneath their feet.

The steaming torrent rained down upon both of the children, burning their hair and melting away flesh. Suzy had been the source of that scream, but had since fallen silent as unbelieving eyes stared down at the smoldering bones that were once hands. They gripped her phone and refused to send it to the grass like Seth's, with its single lens recording the event or broadcasting live their torment.

Soon, the crowd fell into hysterics, pushing back to flee the heat emanating from the scorched field. Next to Bryan, Linda tried to push through the multitude of bodies now shoving them both toward the exit. Hellbent on saving her children, the mother clawed against the onslaught, but Bryan grabbed her arms and pulled her toward him. He buried her face in his chest as his own eyes locked on their children, knowing there was nothing anyone could do until after the water finished raining down. There was nothing to do, except watch his children die.

CHAPTER NINE

Clint held the steering wheel with his left hand, his right outstretched so he could watch the videos playing on his phone. His eyes darted, alternating between the road and the screen unpredictably, watching either or both as it suited him. He overcompensated twice, each time crossing the yellow stripe. The sound of tires on rumble strip forced Cat to speak up.

"Can you watch the damned road?"

He ignored her question, instead turning the screen toward her. "Have you seen this app?"

She watched as a woman lip synced to the president's voice, speaking to an audience of cats. "I don't think it's funny. It's grown people making fools of themselves," she said. "Besides, doesn't China own it? Aren't they using it to spy on the world?"

He shrugged. He didn't care what she thought and never would. Clint did whatever Clint wanted.

She felt the bruise on her face. It had swollen immediately, shutting her left eye. The ringing in her ear hadn't stopped since he dragged her and Joshua from their home. Thinking of Sarah, lying in the tub, made her sick to the stomach. *She's still there,* she realized, *all alone and forever cold.*

Cat pulled Josh closer. He was curled in a ball between them, head in her lap and still buckled. Though still unsure of his father's arrival, Clint's sudden appearance in their lives had been joyous for the boy. But when he awoke and saw his mother's swollen eye, his excitement would drain immediately. Clint would never strike her in front of his son, but Josh was old enough to know Daddy's arrival meant new bruises for Mommy.

But he's never killed before, she pondered, but knew that wasn't the truth. The combat infantry badge hanging from the rearview mirror was his single most prized procession—a prize from Afghanistan. Most men,

Cathy knew, joined the military to make a difference, to make the world safer while earning money for college, but not Clint Fletcher. He had joined for darker reasons, his sadistic urges yearned for violence and the army gave him opportunity during the war. When he returned home early, she was surprised, and did not fully understand the reasons behind his discharge until after he turned his rage. Only then did she finally comprehend his early departure from service—even the army doesn't like cold blooded sociopaths.

In a tired voice she asked, "How'd you find us this time?"

"I've got my ways, Kitty Cat," he replied. "Besides," he added, "that sister of yours can't stay off social media as well as you." Something on the screen caused him to laugh louder, again swerving onto the shoulder. Miraculously Josh continued to slumber. After a moment he added, "You've got to stop doing this. You know that every time you run away is worse on *you* when I bring you home."

She didn't respond. From experience she knew any answer or protest she gave would awaken the monster within. Instead she stared up at his beautiful face and long flowing hair. *I was so easily fooled,* she thought, *by those good looks and charming smile.* But it wasn't just her. Back home in Bay City, he had convinced everybody of his perfection. *They think I'm crazy,* she mused, *and he'll always be their star quarterback.*

He screamed into the night. "Holy shit!" The truck swerved off the road as he dropped the phone to grab the wheel. The rear end fishtailed wildly as he corrected the steering, coming to a screeching halt half on and half off the shoulder.

Joshua woke up suddenly, crying loudly with fright. Cat wrapped the boy in her arms, shushing and comforting him. "It's okay, sweetie. Daddy saw something in the road, is all."

"The hell I did," Clint responded, feeling around on the floor. He finally found his phone and shoved it into her face. "Check this shit out!"

Cat sighed. "It's just another TikTok. I told you to watch the road," she added.

"Keep watching," he said with his dangerous laugh. He had several, but the dangerous one meant he found enjoyment in something others would find repulsive. She heard him use it the first time after striking her, and she heard it again when he had drawn the gun on her and Sarah earlier in the night. Not wanting him to do the same to her as he did her sister, she watched.

A teenage girl danced in a grassy area greener than Cat had ever seen in Michigan. In the background, snowcapped mountains rose over tall pines and aspens. The hundreds of tourists milling about suggested the video may be in a national park. A banner of text appeared above the dancing girl and confirmed it was. The text read, *held hostage by boring parents in Yellowstone.* The text disappeared and another banner appeared, *making our own fun* TikTok *style,* it read.

"I don't see why you ran us off the road," Cat told Clint.

"Keep watching," he said with a large grin on his face. "Show Josh, too!"

She turned the screen so that her son could see. They watched the girl dance until the song ended.

"So what?"

"Give me that," he said. "It must have clicked to another one when I dropped it." He slid his finger on the screen a few times, then grinned triumphantly as he turned the phone toward them.

The girl stood next to a boy, possibly her brother by their facial similarities. They could have even been twins Cat estimated, judging their closeness in age. "Yellowstone sucks," the girl shouted into the camera, "come save us from boredom!"

The pair laughed at their joke and the boy opened his mouth to add something as well. Just as he did a fountain of water erupted behind them, raining down with mist and a torrential downpour of frothy water. *No,* Cat thought, *not a fountain.* With horror she realized a steaming geyser had erupted beneath their feet. What she had mistaken for mist was instead steam. She watched helplessly as their skin blistered and burned before her very eyes. The boy must have dropped the phone because, when it settled, the camera looked up at the pair amidst their terrifying shower.

Joshua screamed, mortified by what he had witnessed and Cat quickly shielded his eyes, rocking and singing softly while consoling him and lying. She assured him the children were fine and that it was only a movie.

"Screw that!" Clint said between maniacal laughter, "that was real shit, son. Better get used to it, because death comes for us all."

"Shut up, Clint!" She couldn't hold back her anger any longer. "He's only four years old! He doesn't need to see that crap!"

"Oh please," he responded, "My father showed me way worse when I was his age! I won't raise a pussy of a son."

"You're right about that," she snarled back at the monster in the front seat. "That's why I'm going to take him far away again, just as soon as I can."

Thankfully, the blow was with his left fist, so it only dazed her briefly when it glanced off her temple. Her thoughts once more turned to the object in her bag and she sat quiet the rest of the trip, plotting and planning the death of Clint Fletcher.

The wheels of the Airbus 330 lifted off the runway and Dr. David Andalon breathed a sigh of relief. The anxiety of airports had always been worse than the actual flight, and this experience had been terrible. A large earthquake near San Francisco had delayed several arrivals and left departing passengers wondering if they would even get off the ground. The newscaster had reported that the quake logged a seven point four on the Richter scale.

To make matters worse, TSA had detained Sam, apparently confusing him with another Sam Nakala on the international watch list. A quick call to Jake had resolved the issue, but not without a long wait. The eventual arrival of official military orders explained that civilian contractor Sam Choi Nakala was not Sam Choe Nakala and that expedited their security check. David's Korean was not as fluent as Brooke's, but he easily made out most of the insults the boy hurled over his shoulder once they were through to the terminal.

Now that they were airborne, David watched the flight attendants closely. He always considered them the best indicator of whether he should panic in the air. This team worked with a smile, ensuring the passengers were calm and comfortable. But something was off. One of them, a woman in her late forties with few worry lines and auburn hair, nervously pulled at her jacket. The nametag on her breast read "Darlene."

As soon as the crew turned off the seatbelt sign, he made a trip to the aft restroom. A small line had formed, and so he positioned himself near the flight attendant's station. Darlene was busy readying a drink cart, but had her head held in close conversation with her male coworker. David could make out only a few words but clearly heard her say, "earthquake."

Stepping forward, he asked. "Ma'am?"

"Hmm?" She looked up with tired eyes that betrayed her displeasure with his interruption.

"What about the earthquake? Are you talking about the one last night?"

"There was another," she answered. "An 8.4 shook Palmdale, California, right after we lifted off."

"How much damage?"

"It was pretty bad from what I heard. Now that we can access inflight internet you should be able to check for yourself." She looked up, suddenly less irritated. "I'm sorry," she said, "It's been a long day."

David nodded and muttered his agreement, "That's the understatement of the century." The door to the bathroom opened and he was next. After he finished his business, he hurried to his seat and brought out his phone.

Brooke watched him access inflight network, raising an eyebrow at the splurge. Usually he spurned the overpriced amenities. "What're you doing?" she asked.

"There was another earthquake, this time further south near L.A."

"That's awful," she said, with deep concern for the people involved. "Was it bad?"

"Very."

He pulled up a news channel and together they watched as a helicopter surveyed the damage. Thankfully, Palmdale was more spread out and lacked the high rises of the bigger cities to its north and south. But, as the camera panned over the center of the city, he and Brooke gasped audibly. A giant crevice had opened up in the center of town, cleaving it in two.

As the chopper continued to fly, they realized the magnitude of the event. The crack ran for miles, even reaching nearby Littlerock.

Seeing that his wife was visibly disturbed, he turned off his phone and put it away.

"I think we've had enough bad news for the day," he told her.

"Thank you," she agreed. After a few moments she laid her head on his shoulder and not long after they were both asleep.

The plane lurched in the air, dropping several hundred feet before leveling off. David felt his buckle bite into his belly as it kept him strapped in his seat. Those who had relaxed their belts flew into the ceiling of the cabin before plummeting onto seat tops and the floor. All around them oxygen masks released and dangled in front of stunned passengers. Brooke screamed as the plane fought to straighten its course.

David put his hand on hers and patted. It was a futile attempt, but one he hoped would calm her nerves. With her free hand she lifted the shade to reveal the night sky. Far out west the horizon glowed with red and yellow. David peered out, trying to reason in his mind what could create such a spectacle.

Brooke asked, "What is that?" She pointed to a flash off in the far distance.

"I'm not quite sure," he replied honestly. He had never seen anything like it. "Maybe a meteorite?"

"That was more of an explosion," she responded just as three more blasts lit up the horizon.

This time it was obvious to David. "They *are* explosions," he said as he watched the sky above the clouds ripple and wave, "and that's a shock-wave!" He held his breath until the concussion hit the plane a second time, sending the airbus careening off to starboard. Twice more the plane was caught in the rippling air and two more times the pilots regained control.

"This is the captain speaking," came an anxious voice over the speaker, "please do not panic. I have control over the aircraft, but we're flying without instruments."

David suddenly realized why those blasts were familiar. "No," he said aloud, "it can't be."

Brooke demanded, "What?" He pulled his phone from his pocket and pressed the power button. The screen flickered once as it tried to turn on, then went black. "Why did it do that," she asked, "is it out of charge?"

"No," he replied, "I turned it off with eighty percent power. Those blasts weren't natural."

"What do you mean, David? I'm getting scared."

He pointed out the window, "Those blasts were nuclear and what we felt weren't simple shockwaves." He held up the useless cellphone. "Those were electromagnetic pulses. The captain isn't only flying blind, he's also deaf and dumb. We have no communications and zero navigation." For the next few minutes they stared out at the glow, waiting and fearing the blasts would be followed by more.

She broke the silence, "What's that?"

Dave squinted to see what she meant and saw two objects racing upward through the clouds toward the plane. "Those are fighter jets," he replied.

"Whose?"

"Ours, I think." He peered out as they grew closer. He made out two F-22 fighter planes. They pulled alongside the cockpit and waved their wings. "Honey," he said, "you aren't going to believe this."

"Believe *what*? I'm not believing *any* of this."

"Read the name under the cockpit."

The jet was close enough she could easily make out the words. With wide eyes she sat back against the seat, unblinking and disbelieving.

David read them again. *General Jake Braston.*

CHAPTER TEN

Doug Snyder stared intently at the monitor, gripping his coffee cup in a tense right hand but not drinking. He had long forgotten it was there. The contents had grown cold, and he couldn't peel his eyes from the sensor data. He mouthed each number as he read it silently. The day he had long feared had finally come. Most of California experienced total devastation.

The quake that leveled San Francisco had been shallow, a worst-case scenario that every seismologist feared. The resulting ripples along San Andreas had been just as catastrophic, but deeper in the crust layer. He finally abandoned his cup and changed the view on his monitor. The satellite image confirmed the earlier data. The sudden release of weight sheared a new fault deeper out to sea and caused the coastline to slide into the gap. At least forty million lives had been lost in a single event lasting less than an hour. The *Big One* had finally come.

As he stood to leave, something new caught his eye. Several major quakes rocked Michigan. Bending over the keyboard, he pulled up sensors in an area one thousand miles away. While the California faults were common knowledge, these sites were not. The public only worried about them when the occasional moderate jolt rumbled through the tier states or Midwest. Usually this could be tied to fracking and the slippage caused by sea water pumped into the oil wells near the faults.

Just as he feared, activity between the Great Lakes had also intensified. There were five faults between Lake Michigan and Lake Huron with a larger and potentially deadlier fault lying directly beneath Lake Superior. If his instruments were correct, the area was about to echo what had occurred in what was, until this very hour, California.

He turned one final glance toward the television screen. As expected, the news had remained largely silent. The major broadcasts were unsure how to report the incident, and stunned reporters seemingly forgot how to deliver news without a hovering helicopter or twitter traffic. *How can they simply report facts when all they know to do is spout opinions?* Doug missed the days of Walter Cronkite and how the man had soothed the world while informing the masses Oswald murdered Kennedy—allegedly, of course.

He switched his screen to his own monitors and punched in several new sites, polling data closer to home. These, too, foretold impending doom, but of a different variety. All at once several sensors blinked off, sending error messages instead of readings. He quickly detached his government issued laptop from its charger and ran. His white Department of Interior vehicle waited outside with USGS written in green letters. He tossed his things into the seat beside him and drove.

The distance was far, about eighty-five miles to the first sensor. He needed the data immediately, and a system reset must be done on station. With one hand on the wheel he texted Beau and let him know his destination and reason for leaving in a rush.

The response came immediately. "Return to station. Too dangerous near the crater." Irritated, Doug turned off his screen and tossed the device beside the laptop. He stepped harder on the gas and accelerated.

He listened to the radio as he drove, two men spouting off scientific data as if they were knowledgeable. Everything they said was conjecture. He pushed the truck even faster, heedless of consequences if pulled over. One of the men mentioned Yellowstone. Doug turned up the volume.

"It makes you wonder," the man said, "if an event like this could trigger that sucker."

"Of course it can," muttered Snyder.

The other voice weighed in, "What would it take for that?"

"Depends on the pressure," replied Doug. He switched the channel and listened to classic rock the rest of the way.

After a while he began to relax. Holding that much adrenaline could tire the body, and he focused his breathing in an attempt to conserve energy. At one point he even sang along with the radio. *Hotel California* always got his vocals going. "You can check out any time you like," he belted out, "but you can never ..."

The blast lit the sky ahead and colored it red and orange. Even at high altitude he could see the mushroom cloud form. "No," he pleaded, "not this!" He accelerated to dangerous speeds, determined to check his instruments. The shockwave rippled through the clouds above, disturbing the sky as if it were water disturbed by a speeding boat. At almost the same moment it passed overhead, his radio ceased to work.

Usually when a radio loses signal, the listener is met by crackling static that ebbs and sputters along with the distortion of the radio waves. This time it did not. It simply died. At precisely the same moment his headlights and the instruments from his dashboard fell dark. He picked up his phone, the screen had also turned black. As a scientist, Doug Snyder knew what had caused the interruption. He sped across the asphalt, knowing also he couldn't shut off the engine. If he did, it would never again start.

The blasts had been high altitude nuclear bursts—also known as electromagnetic pulses. These would have fried every piece of electronic circuitry in North America and possibly even half the world. Older diesel trucks, like the one Doug was driving, would continue to run and idle until switched off or out of gas, but the circuitry needed to turn the starter and ignite the crank would have to be replaced with fresh components that had been shielded from the pulse.

Heedless of the darkness hiding the road, Doug pressed his foot harder to the floor and sped into the night. Twenty minutes later he arrived at his destination. He threw the door open and raced toward the station. He dropped his key twice as he fumbled with the lock, but finally managed a turn. The door wouldn't budge. He stepped back and examined the hinges. They had warped along with the frame.

Small cracks had formed in the rocks nearby. He followed these toward his favorite spot, a small lake teeming with life and the reason he'd chosen a life as a scientist—to protect and preserve what we as humans destroy. He wiped tears from his cheeks as he approached. Usually he would find it surrounded by elk or deer. Occasionally he would spot a bear drinking from the springs that fed into the larger body. But tonight there was no life in this bastion of hope for nature. He felt his feet turn to lead as he approached, unable to push them forward. The lakebed was dry.

No, he thought, *there hasn't been this kind of activity!* And then he noticed the puddles that remained, clinging to the mud as samples of the life-giving waters that once were. Steam rose into the air as if the lake had boiled. Here and there fish lay lifeless as if discarded or tossed from an aircraft flying over. Suddenly his legs found their purpose and he ran.

The geyser was just over the next ridge. He sprinted as fast as he could, panting from the effort. When he topped the hill, Doug dropped to his knees, eyes wide and reflecting not one but ten newly formed fissures. Each belched steam and discarded heat into the air. He placed both hands on the ground as he tried to stand but paused. Beneath his palms the earth rumbled, slowly at first but then with anger. When the sleeping caldera blew, Doug Snyder was there. A proud volcanologist and lifelong scientist for the USGS, he found the eruption as beautiful and awe-inspiring as he had hoped. He died doing what he loved—witnessing the smallness of mankind.

Beau Raines calculated the timing of the eruption against the text Doug had sent. If the fool had continued, and he figured he had, then Snyder would have arrived mere minutes before the eruption of the largest super volcano in North America. He checked the camera footage from the live feed one more time. Before the blackout, there had been no warning, except for several new geysers that had formed an hour before. He picked up his phone and made the call. This was a national emergency.

His phone and all the lights of his office blinked off simultaneously. Normally during a power loss, the power supplies would beep a cacophony of warnings, chirping like robotic crickets protesting the darkness. But their chilling silence startled the director. *Surely not every battery supply was drained,* he reasoned. Somewhere in the building an engine started, and the emergency generator powered up. Despite its hum, the backup lighting never came on. After standing and walking to the window, he gazed for a while, taking in the blackened skyline of Denver.

The entire city had lost power, eerily blending into the front range of the Rockies. Off in the distance several flashes exploded beyond the mountain tops, sending undulating waves that lit the sky and majestically crowned each peak with vibrating colors. It reminded him of the Aurora Borealis, only larger. It seemed to grow as he watched, reaching eastward as if swallowing the blackness.

Snow appeared to fall from the sky, heavy flakes drifting down that seemed more gray than white. He leaned forward, straining to watch the phenomenon as it covered the streets below. Suddenly, he realized he watched the fallout of Yellowstone—belched from the earth and blowing cinders across the night sky. As a scientist he knew this ash would cover the continent by the next midday.

A sudden rumbling shook beneath his feet as he gripped the window ledge for balance. He watched with awe as mountain peaks crumbled before his eyes, collapsing into a growing fault that ripped through the city and worked its way southward. The building around him creaked and groaned as steel girders failed, toppling into the waiting chasm and swallowing him whole. His final thought was of his family and how he wished he had followed his own advice by spending less time at work.

PART II
OLD FRIENDS AND FRESH BEGINNINGS

CHAPTER ELEVEN

Clint did not take Cat and Josh to his apartment in Bay City, but instead drove them to his father's former vacation property. Cathy sat up when she recognized the secluded three-bedroom structure that was more of a cabin than a house. It had changed since she last visited, with tall weeds growing too near the building and most of the drive washed away by recent floods. Dread filled her as they bounced along the dirt road. They would be completely alone with Clint and his deadly outbursts.

The shack sat on fifty wooded acres that backed up to a national wildlife refuge along the Shiawassee River. The region was home to several species of waterfowl, especially Canadian geese and North American ducks. His father had taught him at a young age to live off the land, and there would be no reason for either of them to run into town even if Clint allowed.

"I thought you lost this place after your dad died," she said.

"It came back on the market a year ago, and I happened to have some luck at Eagles Landing Casino. I bought it back free and clear."

"So this is where you live now?"

He shot her a sly smile as if to say, "We're here, aren't we?"

She helped Joshua from the pickup truck, setting him on the gravel drive. The boy looked around with wide eyes as if remembering the last time they visited. That was before his grandfather had disappeared, assumed drowned in the river after a night of alcohol and fishing. Joshua smiled up at his father and asked, "Can we hunt geese, Daddy? You promised when I was bigger, we would."

Clint smiled back and placed a hand on his son's shoulder, causing Cat to cringe with hatred. "I think it's time you learn, but you have to break their necks when they drop."

Joshua blanched at this, backing away.

"Clint, he's too young for that," Cat pleaded.

"Nonsense. He'll learn that's part of the gutting or he'll starve while we feast." To his son he added, "And there's no better eatin' than a Canadian goose." As they walked together up the steps, the ground shook, forcing Cat to grab onto a pillar for support. Joshua fell down and Clint surfed along with arms out to his side. "Whoa," he said, laughing along with the quake.

"I felt one earlier tonight in Kalamazoo," Cat told him after the shaking subsided.

"It's the fracking. Rich oil companies keep pumping sea water into the ground to float the crude."

She pointed to his union shirt. "Folks need oil to drive their cars, Clint. The cars you make."

"Used to make. I'm retired," he said gesturing with his hands toward the surrounding wilderness and finally pointing at the cabin. "Put your things in the bedroom. We're going for a ride in the boat," he said. He reached into the back seat and removed the two large duffel bags, each bulging with their contents.

"It's late," she argued, "The sun will be up in a couple of hours."

"Actually, it's early," he insisted, "and no one told you to strip all night long for other men, Cat. Just because you've been up sinning all night, doesn't mean you can't do things with your family when the sun comes up."

She ignored the rebuke and did as she was told. A few minutes later they were riding an aluminum jon boat up river. Cat noticed there were now three bags at Clint's feet, the two from the truck and another, smaller and less bulging. She asked, "Where are we going, Clint?"

"Up river," was his response.

"Clint," she pressed, "if you're doing something illegal, why didn't you leave us behind at the cabin?"

He narrowed his eyes and gave her his serious look, the one that made her skin crawl. "Because," he said, "this is something I can't do without you."

She sat in silence for a few more minutes until they reached the deepest part of the river. It was wide, too far for her to swim to either shore.

That's when Clint shut off the engine and tossed a small anchor over the side. Soon the little boat rocked gently as the waters moved past on both sides. She watched as he unzipped the duffel bag.

She caught a glimpse of metal inside and something else. She wasn't sure, but it looked like concrete. "Clint. Why are we here?"

He drew his gun from the small of his back and pointed it at her chest. "Open the bag," he commanded, sliding it with his feet toward hers, "and put those on your ankles."

Tears filled her eyes as she looked toward Joshua. He stared silently at the weapon in his father's hand, unblinking and suddenly worried. Cat asked, "So this is it?" She opened the bag and found two cinder blocks with chains wrapped through the holes. Each was secured by its own set of handcuffs. "So you're going to shoot me in front of our son and drop me in the river?"

"That's the plan," he responded before turning to Joshua. "Son, your mother's a sinner. She stole you and tried to keep you from me, but I found her. Now she has to pay for that, do you understand?" Joshua nodded, although Cat knew he didn't. The boy was confused and afraid. "Now she's going away to be with your grandparents, and it will just be you and me."

Cat stared at the gun, not moving.

"I said put those on your ankles," Clint told her. She slowly took the first and clicked it in place around her ankle, careful to leave room. "Tighter," he commanded. She obeyed.

She was in a dream, and the world around her had become surreal. She felt her skin seemingly detach as her body was no longer her own. Her voice screamed in her head as her body blindly obeyed and picked up the second shackle. She didn't mind dying, but didn't want Joshua to see. She pleaded, "Can he turn around?"

"Nope, part of the deal. He must watch like I watched Paw take care of Maw."

Realization set in and Cat looked over the side. "You mean?"

"Yes, Cat. This is the same spot." He pointed the gun toward the cinderblock. "Now the other one," he commanded.

Her trembling hands moved very slowly as she fumbled with the mechanism. The second would be harder to put on than the first. Once it was secure, he would pull the trigger and commit her over the side. A sudden thought brought terror as it rushed in, *what if he doesn't pull the trigger?* Drowning was, in her mind, the worst possible way to die. She would rather eat the bullet.

Clint's attention was suddenly on the sky. She could see a flash of red in his eyes as something exploded silently above the horizon behind her. She turned and watched as two more flashes lit up the sky in the north and the south. The glow was bright as three fiery mushroom clouds shone like giant roadside flares.

Seizing the moment, she picked up the cinder block and lunged at his head, striking with a thud before falling to the floor of the boat. The boat rocked as she struck the aluminum bottom, the concrete block barely missing her head as it landed beside her. Dazed, Clint dropped the gun, sending it tumbling to his feet. He was dazed and slower to respond as they both scrambled for the weapon. He managed to kick it to the stern, so she instead grabbed the open end of the remaining handcuff. With a click she secured it around his ankle. Now they were equally hobbled and both susceptible to drowning.

She tried to scramble toward the weapon, but he grabbed her and threw her against the hard decking. His hands tightened around her neck and squeezed, but all she could concentrate on was the puddle of river water around her head. *It smells like fish,* she marveled as the world around her blackened on the edges.

Abruptly the boat lurched in the water, tossing violently about. She could barely see his face hovering dangerously close to the edge and she kicked with her free leg, arching her back and sending Clint flying forward. The bridge of his nose struck hard against the aluminum and she scurried out from under his weight the moment his grip loosened. Though her vision was still fuzzy, she could make out Joshua standing at the stern and holding the gun toward his father.

"Give it to me," she said softly. As Clint stood to face her, Joshua handed over the weapon.

The boat rocked again, this time throwing both adults to the deck. Cat barely held onto the firearm as she realized the entire river was full of waves, probably from another earthquake.

Clint got to his feet first and tried to lunge.

She pulled the trigger two times in rapid succession, and the boy and his mother watched the monster teeter backward with flailing arms before disappearing over the side. The cinderblock on his ankle hung on the side of the boat, threatening to capsize it completely.

With the gun pointed at her dying husband desperately trying to swim, Cat used her free hand to lift the block up and over the aluminum bulkhead. With a satisfying plop it splashed into the water, dragging down a very surprised Clint. His arms tried weakly to fight the downward current, but soon disappeared into oblivion.

Cat scanned the river banks. The earthquake had been a large one, stronger than any she had ever felt, and they were now tossed about as if adrift on an angry sea.

Joshua screamed and pointed up river. His mother turned to see a wall of water rushing down from the valley. She scrambled to untie the anchor line, but time was running out quickly. Placing the muzzle against the nylon she pulled the trigger, splitting the rope and sending the boat along with the current.

She screamed to Joshua, "Lay down!" He rushed to her arms and she wrapped him close, laying her body on top of his in the fishy puddle on the deck. With closed eyes she prayed the boat wouldn't capsize and never noticed as the current swept them down river like driftwood on floodwaters.

The Johnsons said nothing to each other through three states unless it pertained to the trip. Neither was in the proper mindset to drive but took turns as they did. They had driven thirteen hours and had just turned south through Omaha, Nebraska.

Linda had not wanted to leave the children, but the flight carrying the caskets was fully booked. She was behind the wheel, more to steady her own nerves than anything, and drove them south on Interstate 29.

Bryan broke the silence. "I'm sorry," he said.

"For what," she asked, "killing our kids or ruining our lives?"

"Both," he answered.

"I'll never forgive you for this." She stared straight ahead as she spoke, deliberately avoiding looking at her husband. "This entire trip was your idea, and they didn't even want to come."

"I know," he replied. "I had no idea it wasn't safe. Thousands of people visit the park every day," he said.

She turned her head and shouted, "You took our babies to a volcano and now they're dead!"

His eyes immediately filled with tears. "I know. I'm sorry, honey. I'm so sorry."

Her fist made contact with his cheek, stinging the skin and leaving a cut from her wedding ring. "You don't get to cry," she screamed, "not in front of me!" Her body heaved between sobs of her own, tears falling and snot dripping from her nose. "I hate you!" She punched him again. He threw up his hands in defense, saying nothing and letting her get out all of her anger.

She was so focused on hitting Bryan that she did not notice the oncoming car. It swerved, but the vehicles clipped headlights and both skidded off the road. The other driver careened into a ditch and immediately came to a stop. They were not so lucky. The car spun around four times before rolling onto its roof and coming to rest in a cornfield.

Bryan momentarily blacked out, but came to. Looking around the cabin he realized Linda had been thrown from the vehicle. A large hole in the windshield told the tale of her departure. He found his seat belt and released the harness, falling hard onto the ceiling. He kicked at the glass, knocking out what remained. He cut his hands and knees in several places as he climbed from the wreckage, intent on finding his wife.

Dazed, he fumbled around the corn rows, confused and lost. Every direction looked the same. When he finally emerged into a clearing, he could see the lights of Omaha on the horizon. Offutt Air Force Base lay between him and the city.

He was about to turn around and head back to the road when a sound roared overhead. He had grown up around jet airplanes, but this rumble was too low for that. He stared up at the sky, eyes scanning for blinking lights. A large rocket with a red painted star descended from a very high altitude, barely giving him time to calculate its destination. It crashed into the center of the airbase, exploding immediately.

If Linda had driven slower, and they had been a few hundred miles west, he would have witnessed the mushroom cloud that folklore associated with nuclear blasts. He would also have seen a horizon dotted with hundreds of more flashes of light, each as destructive and telling the tale of entire cities that abruptly ceased to exist. Too close and in full view of the blast, Bryan abruptly vaporized—his body turned to ash in a brilliant flash of light.

CHAPTER TWELVE

The plane's wheels touched runway and Brooke breathed out relief. Beyond her window a ground crew lined the dark tarmac, their faces lit by the flickering fires hastily lit in steel drums. She had expected firetrucks and police vehicles, but the workers were doing everything on foot, linking together a long chain of hoses and stretching them toward the approaching craft. After fierce braking, it finally coasted to a stop. The plane had no power to make its own way toward the terminal, and they would have to walk to the pitch black terminal.

A small group of soldiers jogged out to meet them, several of whom pushed a metal ladder toward the plane. The sound of it hitting the fuselage jarred the plane and the passengers muttered at the odd welcome and the sudden sound of fists knocking from outside. The flight attendants opened the door and several armed airmen boarded.

A woman wearing the rank of Captain addressed the passengers. "Ladies and gentlemen, welcome to Ramstein Air Force Base. As you can tell this has been a crazy night for us all. We've set up reception in the USO just inside the main terminal."

All at once people began shouting, talking over each other and demanding answers. One of them, a man in his mid-fifties and dressed in a business suit, spoke up with a strong German accent. He demanded, "I am a German citizen and am expected in Frankfurt! Why am I detained by your government!"

The woman smiled warmly as she spoke, her classic beauty adding to the calmness in her voice, "Once inside, you will receive a briefing. I know you have a lot of questions, but please hold them until after."

Once they realized she wouldn't give any explanation, the shouting died down. One by one, the overhead bins were emptied and the seats cleared. Brooke, Sam, and David remained behind after everyone disembarked, sensing more of Jake's work happening around them. The young woman approached, "Doctor Andalon, I presume?" She offered her hand in greeting and David shook it. "My name is Stephanie Yurik."

"My pleasure," David responded.

Then she turned to Brooke, "Dr. Braston, it's wonderful to meet you after all this time." To this David appeared puzzled, raising an eyebrow questioningly.

Brooke deflected, "Nice to meet you, as well, although I've no idea how you would know me."

"Of course," Stephanie replied, once again flashing her disarming smile. "Please follow me. Give Sergeant Roark your bags and he'll see they reach your quarters." A moment of worry crossed her face as she added, "Like I said, this has been a crazy night and your brother wants to debrief you apart from the passengers."

She led them down the steps to a waiting truck, the sound of its lonely engine rumbling in the night. The only glow in its headlights was a reflection of the fires burning alongside the runway. Captain Yurik held the door open and Brooke slipped inside.

As David slid in beside his wife he whispered, "What was that about? How does she know you?"

She shrugged. "Jake probably talks about his little sister all the time."

He nodded and seemed doubtful, but her answer had been enough. Thankfully he kept silent the rest of the short drive. He would know the truth very soon.

Within minutes they pulled up in front of a cold war era bunker. Armed guards holding M-16 rifles stood out front with determined faces, eyes locked on the newcomers. Brooke thought she could detect fear in each and every one. She grabbed David's arm and let him lead her across the parking lot. A single steel door loomed ahead, open and awaiting their arrival.

Captain Yurik gestured. "Right this way, please."

Once they were inside the soldiers guarding the door slammed the heavy steel shut behind them.

Brooke jumped at the noise, spinning around. She watched as two of the enlisted men turned giant wheels. "Are they locking us in?"

For just a moment Captain Yurik's smile seemed to flicker but she quickly recovered. "Your brother will explain everything once we're inside the war room." She turned and started walking away. "Come," she said, "he's waiting."

They entered a circular room with a large table in the center. Several chairs were arranged and could easily accommodate twenty people. Only two were occupied. The man on the left wore a tailored suit, simple and unassuming. He wore a wide grin that welcomed the newcomers while also hiding worry. She recognized Michael Esterling, and the other was her brother. Jake still wore his flight suit, so he must have hurried to the bunker after landing.

He stood and wrapped his sister in an embrace. "Brooke!"

She smiled back, happy to see her big brother, but then immediately knew something was wrong. "What's happening?"

Jake glanced at Michael but ignored her question. He shook hands with David, pulling him into a brotherly hug. They had always been close, those two. After they pulled back, Michael stood and embraced them both. Twenty years ago these men would have been inseparable except when attending classes. Despite their obviously different personalities they had been best of friends. Jake was the boisterous jock bound for military service, Michael was the quiet law student intent on changing the world through politics, and David had hoped to improve humankind through genetic studies.

Brooke tried again, speaking loudly. "Jake!" Everyone turned toward her. "What's going on? Why are we here and why in a fallout shelter?"

David looked around as if coming out of a fog bank, taking everything in. As if he had only just realized their surroundings he asked, "Were those electromagnetic pulses, Jake? Is America under attack?"

"They were." Jake gestured for everyone to sit. "These pulses as you call them, were high altitude nuclear explosions. They fried nearly every electrical device on every continent, but luckily we're on the complete opposite side of the globe and weren't hit as badly. Some of our gear still works, especially in this shielded bunker."

"That's how you were able to fly and escort the pilot here?" marveled David.

"Yes. I still had you on radar when you crossed into Germany, so I scrambled in case I could help guide you in. Unfortunately, that's the last sortie I'll ever fly."

Captain Yurik, having secured the doors behind them, joined everyone at the table. Braston motioned for her to explain. Sliding into a seat beside Michael, she said, "Shortly after you crossed into German air space, a significant seismic disturbance occurred along the San Andreas Fault."

"Yes," Brooke interrupted, "In Palmdale. But that was right after takeoff. We saw the huge crack it made."

Stephanie looked toward Jake for help. He shrugged and then took over. "That was earlier, Brooke. There was the big one in San Francisco."

David sat up, "A big one? How big are we talking?"

"Not *a* big one, Dave. *The* Big One. As in, California's gone."

Brooke gasped and David still looked puzzled. After a moment, the news sunk in for both.

"Gone? As in *gone*?" David asked.

Jake continued, "A full ten on the Richter. Maybe even bigger, but there's no way to measure. It was so damaging it created a chain reaction along an already stressed fault line. About fifteen quakes struck in all, each over a strength of nine." He paused to let the information settle.

"But," commented David, "that doesn't explain the EMP. It certainly wasn't natural."

"No," Stephanie replied, "that was man-made."

This time it was Michael's turn to speak. "Vandenberg Air Force Base launched several missiles following the quake, each of them accidentally."

"How?" David appeared more confused than ever. "Aren't there fail safes and contingencies to prevent accidental launch?"

"There were," Michael continued, "but before the quake, someone must have hacked the system. All safety protocols were bypassed and their true trajectories were changed. What you saw were explosions over the

Great Plains. Everything from the Black Hills to Padre Island, Texas, is currently experiencing fallout from the airbursts."

It was Brooke's turn to be confused. She asked, "True trajectories?"

"The hacker armed each one and masked the fire control radar, making it appear they would travel to their original destinations."

She felt the contents of her stomach turn over. "What were those targets, Michael?"

Jake answered, "Beijing, Moscow, and Pyongyang."

David abruptly stood, gesturing around. "Is this why we're in a bunker, Jake? And why the hell are you telling us classified information? We're not cleared for any of this."

Jake responded, "Because there are currently one hundred Chinese missiles headed to key spots all over the United States and its allies. Each carries a nuclear warhead. By now, whatever's left of our missile defense will have counter launched, and those are streaming toward China and Russia."

David collapsed in his chair. "How many did the Russians send?"

"Their full arsenal," Michael answered. "I'd hoped they'd sit this one out, but..."

"But?" The question came from Brooke.

"Their missiles are airborne and should begin raining down over every NATO nation within the hour."

Brooke blanched. "We're *in* a NATO nation, Michael!"

Jake filled in the rest. "North Korea fired off at least twenty toward several of their neighbors. Japan, South Korea, and New Zealand have already been hit. More will strike Australia any minute and there's nothing we can do."

"Mi-Jung!" Sam suddenly broke his silence. "Did she make it out? Oh my God, my entire family..."

Jake nodded. "I'm sorry about your family, son, but she's safe. She landed an hour before you and is exploring the facility."

"Why not?" Brooke demanded. "Why can't you do anything?" Her urgency starkly contrasted the calm general and relaxed senator addressing the room. "Why are you sitting idly by and not trying?"

"Because of the EMP," Jake replied. "We've no way to help anyone, at least not yet."

"So the United States is defenseless?"

Michael nodded, "Yes. The United States and all of our allies are about to be wiped from this Earth and there's nothing we can do."

David stared back in silence but Brooke suddenly choked back a sob. "Mom and Dad?" The thought of them perishing in a nuclear attack chilled her skin and every hair stood up on her arms.

"They're already gone." Jake's face carried sadness as he spoke. The missiles weren't the only thing triggered by seismic activity. The entire Yellowstone caldera blew about three hours ago."

He paused to let the news sink in, but didn't have to wait long. She understood.

"Which brings us," Jake continued, "to the reason I flew your team to Germany."

The doors to the room opened and a young Korean woman stepped inside. When she saw Sam, she rushed forward, wrapping him in an embrace. After they both finally let go, she exclaimed, "Wait until you see the lab!"

David appeared even more confused. "Lab?"

Brooke felt a moment of doom creep in and she looked up from her hands to watch a confused David. The moment she feared had finally arrived.

Jake placed a reassuring hand on his sister's shoulder. "It's time we tell him, Brooke. Would you like to do the honors or should I?"

"I will," she said with a nod. "It's best he hears it from me."

CHAPTER THIRTEEN

Dr. Andalon stared up at his wife, ears hearing her explanation but mind disbelieving. He clung to every word as she laid out the timeline of her betrayal. *This has to be a dream,* he thought. But the nodding heads by her brother and Michael intensified the sickening lump in his throat. Once or twice he fought down bile as his stomached threatened to betray his last meal.

With trembling hands, he finally asked, "Why?"

Brooke moved to take his in hers, but he snatched them away, repulsed by her admission of guilt. "I thought they could help, David. They had the funding and resources that could have moved us past monkeys and toward your end goal."

"So everything we did, everything we spoke about or dreamed; you gave to *Jake*?"

The general answered, "I'm afraid so. I know it's a difficult pill to swallow, but you were moving too slowly. You were entirely too cautious for such a large-scale experiment."

David responded, no longer holding back his anger. "You bastards weaponized my dream." He pointed at Brooke. "You stole my life's work and delivered it to the military." He turned his angry gaze toward Michael. "And I bet you found ways to finance and keep it classified."

The politician nodded.

"I can't believe you. Any of you! You were my best friends! My brothers! How dare you steal my life's work!" He pushed back from the table and stood, pacing the room as he rambled. "I didn't even think you believed in my theory. You always acted like I was *Crazy Dave*. When did you first make up your minds to do this? To betray me if I got close!"

"Senior year." Jake stood and walked toward him. "We both recognized the military application if it ever succeeded."

"Which part of the total failure was the success, exactly?"

"Well," Braston answered, "Felicima for one."

David stopped pacing. "No," he argued, "That wasn't telepathy. It wasn't even telekinesis. It was pyrokinesis—an undesirable side effect of failure."

"A useful one," offered Michael.

Brooke had been mostly silent but spoke, "I didn't believe you about Felicima, David. When you told me she burned the lab, I couldn't bring myself to accept that possibility. I'm sorry. I doubted your word and I'm sorry I betrayed your work to Jake. But, in the end, my betrayal saved our lives."

"That's why you flew us out, isn't it?" Andalon stared down the general, daring him to lie. "You hit a wall in your *own* research and needed my help?"

"Actually, no." Jake cleared his throat and continued, "We've had similar results with our subjects." He glanced at Brooke, "But not with fire."

David caught the brief exchange between siblings. "You all thought you could do better with *my* experiments?"

Michael interrupted. "We're not saying that at all. He means that one of your batches was successful, but it was unlikely pyromancy."

"Pyrokinesis," David corrected.

"What's the difference?"

"Pyromancy is magic. This is science, not a retelling of a Dungeons and Dragons quest." David let himself relax. "Explain your theory."

"The blast of wind you experienced came from Batch Alpha, David."

Andalon shook his head. "If true, then it's also a failed experiment. We're looking for telepathy, not aerokinesis."

"What if I told you," Jake asked slowly, "the two go hand in hand?"

Dr. Andalon stared back, too shocked and confused to respond.

"We have to show him," Stephanie Yurik interjected. "He won't believe you until he sees for himself."

✦

Brooke had never seen the lab. Everything she knew about the operation had come second hand from Captain Yurik. Even then, she knew very little. She never meant to lie to David, nor to cover up the fact she had shared key information with her brother's lead scientist. But there was a saying in her hometown that carried over into college and now the Air Force. She knew it as truth because she had grown up with the man. No one can say *no* to Jake Braston.

MIT had actually cut their funding ten years earlier, before they had seen any progress at all. Genetic manipulation and enhancement were considered taboo areas of science then, and the University sought to distance themselves from Mendel Project. But Brooke's call to Jake changed everything. In no time at all, Michael, a young congressman at the time, had fashioned a budget rider with certain defense appropriations. A portion was granted to the MIT Biology department, but most funded Jake's own lab.

They had respected David's desire to keep the Mendel Project civilian oriented. He dreamed of a world without electronic communication, one that tapped into and maximized the true potential of the human brain.

But Brooke had remembered an animated conversation during their junior year. David had been very drunk and extremely talkative. He said, "Imagine if we could travel to a common place in our minds and link with others like us. We could forge a world of our own and bend it to become whatever we want."

Jake couldn't help heckling. "Can I have beautiful naked women there to treat my every whim?"

"Unfortunately, in this dream world the answer would be yes. But why waste it there? Imagine what we could do with coma patients or paraplegics. They'd be able to run and dance as if they'd never lost their physical ability."

"I don't know, David." Michael was nicer in his jeering than Jake, but added his two cents. "It really does sound more like a dream world. Besides, in the wrong hands what would prevent the invasion of privacy? If two people can communicate on a different plane, then they could also use the same ability to spy on others. Governments would kill for the ability to remote view."

"I'll never sell out to the military," David had insisted, even then. "I'll remain in complete control of my experiments. I'd rather burn down my research than give it over to war mongers."

That was when it began.

Once Jake and Michael secretly funded his research, Brooke became their consort, passing research notes and DNA strands whenever they reached a roadblock in their own experiments. She had always known that one day they themselves would cut off his funding, leaving him to blame the college but also forcing him to pick up alongside them. That day had come.

Captain Yurik pushed open the door to the lab.

Brooke reached for David's hand, but he pulled away, stepping past as if she were in his way. She watched as he followed the scientist inside. She counted to five, took a deep breath, and followed.

The room beyond the door contrasted sharply with the concrete walls elsewhere in the bunker. Sleek white glaze reflected the powerful lights above. Every now and then they flickered.

Stephanie could tell both David and Brooke had noticed and explained, "We're on generator power now, so it's less stable, but we have crews working to normalize the phase as we speak."

David nodded, running his hands along the smooth texture surrounding him. He took everything in with wide critical eyes. Brooke could tell he was thinking this was a dream lab, with the best equipment and everything he had hoped to obtain but failed to receive with his limited funding at MIT.

Dr. Yurik threw a switch and a powerful hologram lit up above a kiosk. David stepped in, staring dumbfounded at the seemingly infinite amount of information hovering around him. Stephanie handed over a pair of wired gloves which he put on. He reached out timidly at first, but quickly grasped the concept of the computer. He grabbed and moved information aside, organizing and sorting until he found what he sought. A giant double helix stood before him, six feet tall and color coded by proteins. He gasped.

"This genetic code is similar, but isn't primate," he exclaimed. All of a sudden it dawned on him. "You've advanced to humans?"

With the press of a button, Stephanie moved a panel on the wall. Hundreds of embryos floated in artificial amniotic fluid. Each appeared frozen in stasis. David walked forward and touched the glass with his gloved hand. "They're alive?"

"Yes," Jake replied, "but frozen in time until we perfect their code."

"You found a way," David whispered, "to make corrections after fertilization."

"We did," Yurik agreed, "and it was *your* theory. You figured it out."

"Where are the test subjects? I want to meet them."

Michael, who had been largely quiet up until this moment, answered, "Right this way." He opened a door on the far wall.

Brooke asked, "How big is the actual lab?"

Captain Yurik smiled broadly as if about to reveal a secret. "Come and see," she said, "and welcome to the Andalon Project!"

David seemed confused. "I don't understand. Why name it after me if you stole it?"

Jake gave him a brotherly slap on the back and pointed at Brooke. "That was her stipulation and we all agreed. Besides, Gregor Mendel was a hack compared to you."

A long runway led across a lower level and Brooke and David followed the rest across. Beneath their feet were four rooms, each vast and separated by steep walls. As Brooke crossed, she realized each room resembled a life-sized terrarium with trees and edible fruits growing beneath heat lamps—all hidden within an artificial sky. A concourse unified them in the center where a staircase led down.

David trembled as he stood before the door. Jake and Michael smiled widely, sharing a secret that they've no doubt been eager to divulge. Brooke almost believed her husband would forgive their deceit very soon. But then he shook free the veil.

"No," he said. "This isn't right."

Michael asked, "What isn't right?"

But Brooke knew. She was closer to her husband than any of his friends. She had feared the coming reaction.

"Cloning. This is morally corrupt and wrong. You've been playing God with actual lives."

Jake suddenly turned serious. "And manipulating genes isn't playing God? That's the basis of your entire experiment."

"I wanted to enhance humankind over time, slowly and deliberately. You've rushed in and created a new lifeform altogether." He stepped away and moved to the stairs. As he was about to ascend, he paused and glanced at his assembled friends. "What life is there for those people beyond this door?"

Michael, always the most levelheaded of the trio, urged, "Open it and see. Afterward, if you agree they have a future, then help us. If you disagree, help us right our wrongs."

Everyone waited, giving their friend time to clear his thoughts and make up his mind. When David finally turned around, Brooke could see he was ready.

Jake held open the door and David stepped into the lab. Once inside he felt as if he had truly stepped into a different world. The sky above looked real and betrayed no sign of observers watching through the glass above. Tall trees surrounded him, each bearing fruit. Everywhere, there were edible plants carpeting the forest floor and providing nourishment for the subjects.

Captain Yurik whispered, "Welcome to the Garden of Eden, Dr. Andalon."

"Well named," he replied. "If Adam and Eve were to suddenly appear, I wouldn't be surprised."

"Let me call them," she replied, ignoring his shocked expression.

"Adam," she called, "Eve!" In a matter of moments two children around ten years in age emerged from behind a row of fig trees. Instead of biblical leaves, the pair were dressed in white jumpsuits.

"Hello, Stephanie," the girl called out with a big smile on her face. "Oh, General Braston and Senator Esterling. It is wonderful you have come to visit again."

The boy named Adam spoke directly to David, catching him by surprise. "Dr. Andalon, I have been expecting you and am very happy to see you finally in person."

The professor asked, "How do you know me?"

"You are exactly how I remember."

"But we've never met until now."

"No, doctor. But I have dreamt of your coming." He turned to Stephanie with eyes suddenly filled with sadness. "Does this mean your world is destroyed," he asked?

She nodded, suddenly finding it difficult to speak.

"So sad," Adam said, "that so much life should be ended in an instant."

"And worse," added Eve, "that so many more will perish slowly."

David whirled around, facing Jake and Michael. "That's why you were so adamant we join you. That's why you're taking this entire end of world scenario in stride. You knew? *They* foretold the destruction?"

"Down to every fine detail."

"That's why you risked taking the plane up, despite the threat of an EMP?" He shook his head in wonder, amazed by everything taking place around him. "You knew you'd succeed."

Michael nodded. "That sums it up in a nutshell. Jake called me two days ago and I hurried out."

David asked Adam, "When did you dream all of this?"

The boy answered calmly, as if he were talking about the weather. "Five years ago, Dr. Andalon. But only this week did I know the exact date and time."

David felt his head spin. Nearby, Sam, Mi-Jung, and Brooke stood silent, processing the information and listening to the exchange. "What other abilities do you possess," he asked.

The leaves around him rustled upon a sudden breeze that cooled his skin. He felt a finger touch his ear and he turned, finding no one but seeing a tendril of air waving back. He reached out his hand to touch it and passed right through. Suddenly it took a more corporeal form and morphed into a hand held out for greeting. He grasped it, finding it firm.

"General Braston taught me that a firm handshake is how gentlemen exchange greeting," Adam explained.

"Yes," David agreed, "that's very true." He turned to Jake and Michael, avoiding his wife entirely. "This doesn't forgive any of you, but I'm in."

CHAPTER FOURTEEN

Maxwell Rankin hated truck stops but, given his chosen profession, he spent a lot of time in them. He wasn't tired and only rested in this spot because the government's transportation weenies passed laws preventing him from driving for another eight hours. The low rumble of his idling Freightliner kept the diesel warm while he sprawled in the sleeper cab, trying to sleep and failing. The call home to Betty had irritated him too much to rest a troubled mind.

Things at home were fine, except for Tom skipping class again. His wife had blamed Max, accusing him of taking too many long hauls while their teenage boy approached manhood.

"Black sons *need* their fathers, Max!" She had said the words often to him, as if he didn't know firsthand. His own father had perished in Vietnam, leaving behind a wife to raise his two sons. Of the boys, only Max turned out okay. Ryan was still serving time in Heritage Trail Penitentiary.

The rest of the call was pretty much a continuation of the same nightly ritual, with Betty voicing frustration and him trying to convince her everything was fine. Except, this time she had found a bag of weed in the boy's backpack.

He wasn't a bad kid. He was a normal teen and Max saw no need to worry. "He's not a stoner," he had tried to explain to Betty, "and it's only weed."

"Marijuana's a gateway drug," she argued, "and he's only doing it to get your attention! He's been hanging around with those *other* boys whenever you aren't around."

That *did* get his attention. The *other* boys were part of a wannabe street gang called the "Get Money Gang," or GMG for short. They were loosely affiliated with the Crips, who in turn preyed on the suburban teens to peddle their drugs. Max had no patience for crime and wanted them nowhere near his son.

"Fine," he had promised. "Let me haul this load to Fargo and I'll be home by Saturday. Then I'll take a few weeks off. I've got vacation hours, so maybe we can take him camping."

"I don't want to go camping," she complained, "I want to *go* somewhere. Take us to Disney or something."

"That's a waste of money," he had protested, "a hole in Florida you throw cash into, and all you get in return is a hat with stupid ears. Besides, I drive every day. I don't want to drive on vacation, and we can't afford airfare."

"You're so selfish, Max!" The line fell abruptly dead, and he at first thought she had hung up. But then he realized the phone had died, plunging the cab into darkness despite being plugged into a charger. *Great,* he thought, *she'll think* I *hung up and won't ever let me live this down. Add one more thing to my list.* He tossed the useless device across the cab. From the sound of the ricochet he'd find it later, probably somewhere under the driver's seat.

That was when he realized he couldn't sleep. She'd revved him up, quickening his pulse and stirring his mind. Thinking of their bank account hadn't helped either, so he decided to read a book. He pulled his e-reader from under the pillow and pressed the power button. It was as dead as the phone. Max gave in and closed his eyes, tossing and turning for the better part of an hour. But he must have finally dozed before waking abruptly.

His stomach rumbled and he knew he was awake for good.

He thought again about Tom and the boys he'd been running with. They weren't bad, at least not all of them. They were boys, bored and feeling cut off from a world that didn't belong to them. They were angry, incited by the new movement for justice and equal rights. Not that he disagreed, only they had a different view of the subject than his son.

Max's mother and grandparents had preached love and peaceful protest and often talked about the rallies they'd attended with the reverend Martin Luther King, Jr. That's what Max wanted, peaceful living filled with education and opportunity.

But the protests these boys tried to drag Tom away to, preached a different message—one of anger and fed up calls to action. In the end, Max knew the small business owners absorbed the damages these movements caused, especially after insurance companies raised their rates so high they could no longer compete with big corporations.

Betty was right. When he got home, he would speak frankly with the boy, getting his mind in line with his heart and teaching him the lessons Max learned from his grandfather. Maybe he'd convince him to join the military like the old man had encouraged him.

Hunger rumbled again and he decided to go inside for a meal. As Max rolled over to reach for his shoes an explosion rocked the truck, shaking it violently and causing it to bounce atop its springs. The cab lit up with brilliance, reflecting against the back wall of the rig. The flash was unlike anything he had ever imagined, lasting several seconds and warming his back with a searing intensity of light. Instinct told him to bury his face and he waited until the cab returned to darkness. Throwing off his blanket, he slipped into the captain's chair and pulled down the sun shade.

An image straight out of hell awaited his tired eyes, and he watched as the city of Omaha burned in the distance. The skyline was gone, disintegrated from the horizon, and everything in between raged with fire. The winds of the night had already swirled the inferno into a maelstrom of flame, sending searing heat through the windshield. That convinced him. Fargo would wait and he'd return to Evansville and home.

He glanced quickly at the dark gauges on the truck's dash, unlit except for the flickering reflection against the orange needle pointing at three quarters of a tank. Thankfully, that was just enough to make it home. The truck still idled, but all the lights remained dark. He tried the head-lamps, but these too refused to work. Everything electronic was dead, even the radio. Putting it in gear he released the brakes with a hiss and groan of air, then pulled out of the lot and onto the access road, grinding metal as he struggled to find second. Turning southward onto I-29, he swerved to avoid the disabled vehicles littering the road.

He kept his eyes locked forward, avoiding looking at the people trapped in or abandoning their disabled cars, but he sympathized for their misery. Some, the lucky ones, screamed out in pain that reminded them they lived. Others stared trancelike with shock already set in, eyes wide and unseeing or blinded by the flash. He knew of only one weapon that could do that kind of damage to the city and everything around it, and it was time to go home.

He accelerated past, just as a woman dazed and covered in blood staggered into the road. Her haunted eyes reflected the flickering glow behind his fleeing truck. Max swerved and applied the brake hard, barely avoiding a jackknife to also miss colliding with her. She never even flinched, staring after his rig as if, by missing, he had ruined her plan for a quick death.

"Shit," he muttered. The truck slowed to a stop but continued to run, air hissing into the carburetor and feeding the rumbling engine. Reaching behind him, he grabbed a blanket and ran to help.

Linda Johnson rode in the front seat of the big rig, silently wincing from with pain. Her arm and collarbone were wrapped tightly on the left side, leftover injuries from the accident and expertly treated by the driver. At least she remembered it as an accident, the other car had come out of nowhere while she punched and screamed at Bryan, blaming him for their children's deaths. She regretted that part, he was a good husband and father who loved them.

She also remembered averting her eyes from the road, focused more on getting out her rage than driving. Most of her punches were harmlessly deflected so she had unbuckled, shifting her weight for a better opportunity to punch. That's when the other car came out of nowhere, topping the hill.

Suzy and Seth hadn't died because of Bryan's stupid vacation. Linda could have done more to keep them from wandering off by taking away their phones and forcing them to stay close. She'd blamed him because it was easier than blaming herself, and the crash could have been her subconscious selfishly trying to end a mother's suffering over losing both children. Besides, with them gone, what was there actually worth living for? And where was Bryan now? He was surely dead as well.

After being flung from the vehicle, she remembered very little except awakening in a ditch, covered by a thin layer of falling ash and staring up at a reddened moon against a strangely colored sky. Her ears rang nonstop in the hours following the crash, and her shoulder throbbed. The cuts on her face had stopped bleeding, but their sting served as constant reminders of guilty loss. The ringing in her ears would also never end, she supposed.

The trucker had driven by just as she had stumbled into the road. He had nearly killed her then, and she wished he had. He spoke kindly and wrapped her in a blanket before lifting her gently into the sleeper cab. That's when he tended her wounds, marveling at how many shards of glass he pulled from her face. She tested her arm in the sling, wincing with sharp pains as stiffness set in.

"I have to find my husband," she said quietly.

"Ma'am," the trucker said, "beyond that ditch you stumbled out of, there was nothing alive. It's a wonder you weren't burned up in the blast."

"What blast?" she demanded, suddenly remembering the fire and how it forced her out into the road. If Bryan *had* been caught in those flames, then this man was right. Nothing would have survived.

"Nukes, I think. It was exactly how they described it in the movies growing up—the flash, then the blast followed by that awful heat. The radiation will come next, and that's why we're moving south to get away. I gotta get home to my family in Evansville, how about you? Once we're clear of it, I'll drop you off where I can, but only if it's along the way. I've only got so much fuel, and can't turn the engine off or get more."

"St. Louis," she muttered, thinking about the movies he'd mentioned. *The Day After* had been the one to explain radiation the best, as it seemingly turned the people into hideous creatures with burns and missing teeth.

"I can do St. Louis," he promised, "but no guarantee it wasn't hit like Omaha. Large military bases will be primary targets, but population centers and bigger cities might have been destroyed as well. That's the way of nuclear war."

"You sound like a soldier."

"Once upon a time I was. My name's Max, ma'am, Max Rankin."

"Linda," she replied and let him do most of the talking the remainder of the drive.

He was friendly, eager to talk and nice enough to realize she wasn't interested in carrying on a conversation. He caught her up on the events of the day and night before—the earthquakes, the eruption of Yellowstone, and finally the explosion. Truth be told, she didn't mind him prattling on and welcomed his voice. Silence would have been too much to bear. She listened with half interest, but flinched at mention of Yellowstone. *Good riddance to* that *place,* she thought.

"I'm not sure how we can still be driving, but this rig runs on a carburetor instead of fuel injectors," he explained. "The radio won't work and neither will the lights, so we have to be careful driving at night." Despite her failure to answer, he went on. "We'll reach St. Louis in a few hours. My goodness," he added, "I miss my wife. Betty's a real sweetheart, best cook in all of Indiana!"

Linda nodded. She considered herself a good cook, as well. Bryan had loved her meals. Of course, the kids did too when they were younger. Even as they grew older, they always showed up on time for a meal. Of course, most of the time they snuck their plates away to their rooms to avoid the parental conversation that always came with dinner. But she knew they appreciated her attempts.

"Tom." Max said.

Linda looked up with alarm. "I'm sorry, what did you say?"

"I said that Tom's my boy. He's a bit on the spoiled side and doesn't know the meaning of the word *no*. But he's got a straight line to my heart, that boy!"

My Suzy was spoiled too. I should have put my foot down more often, maybe they wouldn't have wandered off. Lynda shuddered at the frightening memory of steam and scalding rain drenching her children. *I shouldn't have blamed him,* she thought as images of Omaha also flashed in her mind, scorched and crumbled from the attack. *He's gone,* she accepted, *probably killed by the flash and it's my fault.* Had she not caused them to crash, her husband would still be alive. Or, they could have both joined their children in death.

When they had passed Kansas City they took a wide berth, careful to avoid the abandoned and burned-out vehicles lining the major highways. Using farm and market roads, they circled around, viewing from afar the destruction and finding a warzone of twisted metal and debris blowing under a haze of radiation. They drove around in silence dreading what they'd find further up the road. Four hours later, and just as Max had predicted, the rising sun revealed a truly frightening visage in what had once been St. Louis.

There was no way around this city, the banks of the Mississippi River had swollen and swallowed the roads to minor bridges. They continued down I-70, making a switch onto I-64. The scene they drove into was unlike any either had imagined. Civilization lay abandoned, scattered, and scorched. Buildings lay as collapsed reminders that millions of people had been killed in an instant. Max carefully plowed through debris he couldn't avoid, driving slower than Linda would have liked. Her anxiety urged them forward.

With a quivering voice she asked, "How bad is the radiation?"

"I've no idea," he answered truthfully. "But I'm sure we're getting a nasty dose of it. Whatever you do, keep the windows up and the door closed. Hopefully we won't have to get out of the truck." Linda couldn't help but notice the unmasked worry in his tone.

She stared at the remnants of high-rises beside the highway. When she was a child, she had walked in on her parents solemnly watching the live news feed of the fallen New York twin towers. The damage done by two rogue jetliners paled in comparison to the widespread destruction of nuclear missiles, and every skyscraper here resembled their own version of Ground Zero. She noticed black silhouettes on the side of a building, eerily resembling the people going about their night when the missiles struck. One clearly showed a woman holding a leash and leading a large dog.

Certainly not, she thought, *those aren't their remains!* But her eyes suggested otherwise.

"I've heard of that," Max said quietly, indicating the silhouettes. "That happened in Hiroshima and Nagasaki. The flash is so powerful, it literally leaves photographic shadows on walls and other objects."

"So those people..." She didn't want to ask the rest.

"Yep. They existed until that moment the bombs hit," he confirmed. "The strike must have been close by, and this area was just outside of the blast radius." He abruptly slammed on the brakes, sending her flying forward against the seatbelt. Shockwaves of pain rippled through her shoulder.

"What is it?" she groaned.

He pointed to the road ahead. Hundreds of refugees swarmed the bridge spanning the massive river. The wretched mass staggered instead of walked, clearly struggling as they tried to escape the toxic air lingering above.

"Keep going," Linda demanded.

"I can't," Max protested. "There's so many people in our way. It'll take us an hour to get across, and the idling speed will burn the rest of our gas. We won't make it to Evansville because I can't fuel. Gas stations need electricity to pump."

"I don't care," she insisted stubbornly. "We can't stay here, and we can't turn around. Go through them."

With a sigh he eased the accelerator, picking up speed to match the migrants. He pulled the air horn, blasting several notes of caution into the crowd. The mass parted and wrapped around the rig as they inched forward.

Linda scanned the wretched faces of the mob as they rolled slowly past. Dragging personal belongings in suitcases and atop wagons, sadness and desperation filled each pair of eyes. One family in particular caught her attention. The father and mother were about hers and Bryan's ages, and their two teens dragged suitcases filled with whatever they had packed in their rush to leave their home—wherever that was. The daughter held a smartphone with a black screen, staring blindly at the useless device but still mesmerized by its draw.

Up ahead a young woman turned, her face covered in bruises and open sores. A large swath of her cheek had sloughed away, leaving behind a rash as red as her sweatshirt hoodie. A trail of crimson dripped from her nostril, running down a blistered cheek as it soaked into her chapped lips. Linda averted her eyes, suddenly aware the same sores and illness affected the rest of the migrants. *They've only been walking for one night,* she realized, *and have already felt the effects of radiation.*

A hand pounded on the window causing Linda to jump. She screamed aloud as she turned to see a woman holding aloft her lifeless infant. The face of the child was swollen and red with raised welts that had ruptured, weeping yellow pus onto the mother's hands. Through the glass she heard the woman's pleas to bring her and the child inside the cab. Linda shook her head and mouthed a silent *no*.

"This was a mistake," Max voiced his concern. "They're desperate and I don't trust anyone with nothing to lose."

Soon, the crowd began crawling atop the semi, each begging for the safety of the interior.

"Floor it," Linda whispered.

"What?" Max turned, a stunned look of mortified surprise in his eyes.

"Drive through them," she insisted. "Haven't you watched zombie movies? They'll make us like them."

"That's stupid. This isn't a movie and those aren't zombies."

"You have to," she said quietly. "Look at their faces! They have sickness and will flood the cab and steal the truck. If you don't gun it now, they'll kill or leave us behind. Then we'll be no better off than they!"

"They're real people, alive as us, even if they're sick from radiation. I can't kill them." He paused as if considering whether he could. He'd killed many times before, even if he didn't like it. "I *won't*," he decided. It was a better word.

The rig continued to inch forward while several men pounded on the rooftop. One laid upon the hood and kicked at the windshield with his boots, screaming for them to stop.

Linda's foot moved in an instant, driving down atop Max's and slamming the accelerator to the floor of the cab. The truck revved, lurching forward and bouncing atop the fallen migrants as it plowed ahead. Max had no choice but to shift gears before shoving her aside. The Freightliner surged ahead, cruising over the top of the bridge and skidding as it cleared the leading edge of the mob. Scarlet tread marks followed as they raced across the Mississippi, dead set on getting to Evansville before noon. Neither Max nor Linda glanced back at the death they added to the city.

CHAPTER FIFTEEN

Cathy shivered, lying atop Joshua. Soaking wet, she huddled him close for warmth. The lake had fought against them all night and the next day, tossing and drenching mother and son but not drowning. Caught in a current that raged more like a river, she had worried away the night, certain they would perish before the first sunup. Somehow, her prayers were answered and both lived to watch the strangest sunrise ever imagined.

The sun, once a yellow fireball promising warmth against a cool blue sky, was filtered behind an orange haze that dimmed its glow and offered no hope. Black clouds clung to the ominous sky, threatening rain but only offering ash. The soot that fell stank of singed animal flesh and pine tar, residual of the fires raging on the horizon.

Too weak to struggle with the cinderblock still cuffed to her ankle, Cat felt compelled to remove the burden. Pulling her body into a sitting position, she angled the block by sliding it against the side of the boat, scraping the aluminum as she moved it in place beneath her heel. In her other hand she held Clint's pistol. Pressing the muzzle against the chain as prisoners did in countless movies, she told Josh to move back. *This will work,* she promised herself. *It worked on the rope when I...* A sob caught in her throat—something Clint's memory didn't deserve. *When I killed him,* she finished in her mind. With her ankle clear of the bullet's path, she turned toward her son. "Look away," she warned, "and hide your eyes." She waited until he was clear and then pulled the trigger.

The chain held, deflecting the bullet and merely chipping away the cinderblock. Pain ripped through her calf as shards of concrete entered her leg like shrapnel. She cried out, wincing from the sting as the wound bruised around a weeping and jagged cut. *Stupid! That was stupid,* she told herself, rolling her body over to comfort Josh, now terrified by the sound and sobbing for his mother.

"It's okay," she promised. "Shh, Momma's here." She urged him not to cry, but couldn't help but add tears of her own.

She willed her heartrate to slow, examining the wound carefully. *I've had two years of nursing school,* she reasoned. *I can treat this.* It was bad, worse than it looked given the filthy water in the boat. *Infection, parasites, amoebas, and foreign debris,* she calculated were the biggest dangers. A new concern popped into her mind. *Radiation.*

She remembered the brilliant flashes of light witnessed the night before. *What had those been?* The first few had been high in the sky, large like a starburst or something you'd expect to watch in a space movie. The others, coming hours later, were low on the horizon and ominous, exploding in every direction. She had watched a lot of movies growing up, and she worried they had been nuclear missiles. *Was it the Russians? Maybe the Chinese,* she considered, *or the North Koreans?*

Unfortunately for Cathy, the only knowledge she had of radiation was from movies. *How soon does it start? Are we already screwed floating all night and day on this lake?* A book she read in high school jumped to mind. *Alas, Babylon,* it was called, chronicling people's lives following nuclear war. *Didn't they have time? Depending upon where they lived, didn't some people have days or weeks before the fallout?* She knew weather affected the dispersion of radiation, and she thought again about the blasts. Most had been in the north and east.

Looking up at the sun she guessed it was afternoon, meaning the boat was heading west. She dipped her finger in the water and held it aloft, feeling for the winds. They blew from that direction. *That's good, isn't it? Less cities than in the east.* Josh had quieted by now, and she raised her head to see where they drifted.

"Hey there!" a voice shouted. They were close to shore, about thirty yards or so, where a man stood peering directly at them. "You in the boat!"

She tried to sit up, slipping in the cold water. She raised her head once more and watched the man jog along the shoreline.

"You need to get off the water," he warned. "It isn't safe outside!"

"We don't have oars," she yelled. "And the engine doesn't work!"

"Then swim ashore! But hurry! You need to come indoors before the radiation drifts our way!"

Radiation. His words echoed her earlier thoughts. *So it was nuclear war.* "We can't! My son can't swim and I…" She looked down at the cinder block shackled to her leg. "I can't swim, either!"

"For heavens sakes! Then why the hell are you in a boat?" The man looked around, searching for some way to reach the tiny vessel. He finally gave up, slipping out of his shoes and splashing hurriedly into the lake. With little effort he swam with the current toward them. She quickly propped herself up, feeling around for what was left of the anchor line. The rope was just long enough for the man to grab ahold and tow them ashore. As he approached, she tossed it to his waiting hand. He wasted no time in swimming the way he'd come.

The return trip was much more harrowing for their hero, struggling to guide the boat without drifting too far from his starting point. The man struggled when the current eddied around him, pulling him the opposite direction and taking the metal boat with him. Eventually they reached shallow water and the man stood, splashing and running as he dragged the mother and son to safety. Exhausted, he collapsed on the shoreline, grassy and covered with a thick coating of gray ash. Beyond that were trees and steep embankments, tall hills that funneled the lake into a wide river.

He paused only long enough to catch his breath, then rose to his feet. Still panting he insisted, "Come on. We've got to hurry. We may have been contaminated already!"

When Cathy did not follow, he approached the vessel. She pointed down at her leg and he understood. With gentle strength he held out his hand and helped her to stand, holding the cinderblock as she stepped into the water. With one hand he held the brick and with the other he dragged the boat and Josh fully ashore.

His eyes lingered on the concrete anchor chained to her leg and he said, "I'll ask about that later. You hold his," he handed her the weight, "and I'll grab your things."

Cathy looked around. She had almost forgotten the *things* the man called hers. He lifted Josh and set him ashore, then pulled Clint's heavy bags and set them next to her son.

"That's gonna be a problem," the man said, picking them up. "I can carry these, but you'll have to manage with that ball and chain on your own."

She nodded. "I'll manage." She managed to lean just enough that she could hold the open end of the cinder block and take normal steps, waddling to keep up as the man led them to his waiting shoes and socks.

He was older, in his late fifties, Cat assumed. His beard was tightly cropped and tidy, with splashes of gray that crept into his raven black hair. His eyes were kind and voice gentle. His accent suggested rural upbringing.

"Name's John," their new friend said. "John Klingensmith. My wife heard the gunshot and saw your head bobbing in the boat. She hollered for me, and I ventured out to try and get you ashore."

He took a step and recoiled in pain, a twig having cut his toe. He turned to Josh. "Son, I need you to be a big man for your mom and me. We've a steep climb and I'm not getting anywhere in this forest barefoot. Head down that shoreline and retrieve my shoes and socks?"

Josh looked to his mother to confirm that's what he should do and she nodded. He hurried away.

Jon took advantage of their sudden privacy and turned to give the young mother a stern look. He looked like a father rebuking a rebellious teen or a teacher an unruly child. "I took a chance and I need you to understand that. We may all now have radiation poisoning."

With eyes down she muttered, "I'm sorry," sincerely meaning her words but still processing the situation. "I didn't mean you harm. We had a long night and..." She cut off when she looked back into his face, the kindness having returned and his featured softened.

"I don't regret helping you, ma'am. Please don't get that mistaken. I'm merely saying that I took a chance and now we both have to clean up before we go inside."

"Clean up? I don't even know what happened." She searched her thoughts for any rational explanation. "I saw the explosions but I'm so confused. Was it a nuclear attack? Those were..." she broke off, visions of mushroom clouds swimming in her memories.

"That it was," he confirmed, "but I don't know about war. Our power went out before the blasts. Whoever attacked may have detonated EMPs before the strike."

"What are EMPs?"

"Electromagnetic pulses from a nuclear burst in the atmosphere. High altitude blasts could have wiped out the power grid of the entire Ohio River Valley."

"I saw three blasts in the sky about twenty minutes before the explosions." She paused. "Wait, did you say, *Ohio River Valley*? Where are we?"

"That swath of a lake there used to be the Ohio River and our house up on this hill overlooks Andyville. Everything underwater was farmland until this morning. I've never seen so much water." He pointed south and east. "Over that away was Fort Knox, about thirty-five miles as the crow flies."

"Wait," Cat paused, feet frozen with disbelief, "Kentucky?"

"Yes, ma'am." With a raised eyebrow he asked, "Where'd y'all put into the river?"

Josh returned carrying a pair shoes and the man pulled them on, not bothering with the socks he shoved in his pockets. He started moving immediately.

"We didn't," she said, forcing her feet to follow along and keep up with his strides. "We were on Lake Huron. There's no way we were washed all this way!" She suddenly recalled the fierce shaking and the rushing waves during the night. Realization hit her gut like Clint's fist. "The earthquake?"

"That's my guess," John agreed. Before the power went out there were several reports of quakes all around the country. California had the Big One and just before the outage Jenn saw a report that Yellowstone blew."

Cathy finally understood the ash falling like snow from the sky. "Yellowstone would take out the entire Northwest!"

"Damned right about that. That's the only reason I ventured out. As long as the ash is falling, I'm certain the winds are coming in from the west and keeping the radiation to the east. But that won't last long and we need to clean up and get inside before things change."

They topped the hill to find a beautiful white and blue farmhouse with the classic wraparound porch. A brightly painted red barn stood just north of the house. A black trash bag sat on the steps and he paused to retrieve it. Pointing to the barn he said, "There's running water and soap in there and I've got tools to get that thing off your leg. We all have to shower before heading into the house." He hefted the bag. "Jenn put out some clothing, so after you strip those off put 'em in the bag."

The barn wasn't what Cathy expected. Instead of haylofts and animals it opened into a workshop full of presses and table saws. She paused to admire the craftsmanship of a beautiful rocking horse, sanded and ready for paint. "You made this?"

"I did. I'm retired from teaching at the college, so I tinker here and there, making toys and crafts to sell at the market."

"This isn't tinkering," Cat argued, "this is art!"

John laughed. "The true artist is Jenny. Wait until you've seen the magic she works with a brush." He handed her a pair of safety glasses and dug in some tools, retrieving a metal saw. After stuffing wadding between her skin and the cuffs, he raised it up to cut the metal. "I'm sorry ahead of time if I nick you, I've never done anything like this before."

He slid it back and forth, and Cathy flinched as the wadding rubbed against her wounds. It hurt like hell, but it eventually cut through.

"The shower's in there," he said, pointing to a small bathroom. "It's small but the two of you will fit."

"How do you have running water?" she asked.

"Our wells are natural springs, and a ram pump sends it up here. Don't worry, the water's clean, even if the pressure's low. Rinse well and hurry so I can as well."

"Thank you," she said, choking a grateful sob.

"Don't mention it."

Once inside she rinsed Josh thoroughly, instructing him to put on his clothes and to face away. Only then did she strip and step into the shower. The water was cold but not as frigid as the river the night before. It smelled a bit like sulfur and tasted like metal, but it did the job to wash away the radiation. If only it could cleanse the memories of the night before.

CHAPTER SIXTEEN

Brooke Andalon found her husband hard at work in the hologram. David analyzed the DNA strand with such keen focus he never heard the door open. Or, rather, he was still so angry that he had ignored her out of spite.

Sam Nakala looked up from a collection of petri dishes and offered a supportive smile. He was such a sweet kid.

"We need to talk," she said to her husband.

"I'm not ready," he replied without flinching. It had been the latter.

"We're trapped together in this bunker for a long time, so you'll *have* to discuss it with me at some point."

He refused to meet her eyes and instead zoomed in on a portion of the helix. "I can find ways to avoid you, even down here. I've got enough work to last me several decades now." He paused, then sighed. Exasperated, he asked, "Give me one good reason to forgive you."

She did not hesitate, revealing a secret she'd held for several weeks with hopes of perfect timing. "We're having a child and I'd like to resolve our issues before he or she is born."

David paused in his work. They had tried for years to overcome sterility—both his and hers. After nearly a minute, and in a quiet voice, he asked, "The injections worked?"

"Yes." She gestured at the lab. "Just as your theories worked here, they worked on yourself. You reversed your genetic code."

Dr. Andalon, despite the jeers by the MIT faculty, was a genius. He understood genetic sequencing more deeply than any who came before him in his field, and his innate ability to isolate and read encoded traits had allowed him to take sequencing to a new level. He understood that simple gene mutations contributed to sterility in both males and females.

His side work with MRNA had isolated those mutations and found a way to force his own body to rewrite its code. He stood and hugged his wife.

"I love you," he told her.

"I betrayed your trust," she responded.

"If it wasn't for you," he replied reluctantly, "we'd have lost everything, and all our research would have been wasted. In a way, though I'm still mad, this lab never would have happened if it wasn't for you." He placed his hand on her belly. "And this baby changes everything." Brooke kissed her husband deeply, appreciative that he finally understood her actions.

When they finally pulled apart, David lit up, suddenly remembering a point he wanted to share. "I need to show you something."

"What is it," she asked, her inner scientist taking over.

"Look at this code." He climbed into the hologram, zooming in on a strand.

"That means nothing to me," she said.

"It means everything to the experiment. It means we were correct. All of this time we were right!"

"Correct in what?"

"Batch Alpha had abilities but also higher intelligence."

"I don't understand."

"Consider Adam and Eve. They're only ten years old but intellectually superior to any college student I've ever taught—even at MIT."

"I'll agree to that," she said.

"That was my manipulation in Batch Alpha. I pushed their volume for intelligence quotient to the highest level I could obtain."

She frowned, trying to follow but not keeping up. "But how does that explain Batch Bravo? If Felicima used pyrokinesis, how does that compare to Batch Alpha's aerokinesis?"

"The emotional instability of higher intelligence explains it all."

"David?"

"Yes?"

"Dumb it down for me."

"In 2017, researchers concluded higher IQs are associated with mental and physical disorders," he explained. She shrugged, silently urging him to continue. "Which means by increasing their IQ, we also increased their potential for emotional instability."

"The screaming?" No one had noticed Sam had entered the lab. They turned at this voice. "Felicima and her brothers and sisters were prone to aggression and easily stimulated."

"That's right," David agreed.

"But what does that have to do with the Alphas," Brooke asked.

"When did they create the airburst that knocked us out?" David smiled while waiting for her answer.

She paused, remembering David's drunken outburst. "When you threw the vial across the room."

"Exactly! They reacted violently to my tantrum."

"So you agree it was a tantrum," she asked with a hint of sarcasm.

"Not fully, but yes." He paced as he reasoned out the scenario. "I had just given both batches a shot of epinephrine. They were primed for hot emotional response."

Sam, who appeared as confused as Brooke, asked. "What do you mean?"

David pointed toward the main lab. "What did you first notice about Adam and Eve? What stood out the most?"

"They're calm," she observed.

"Eerily so," agreed Sam.

"And what powers did they reveal?"

"Telepathy," said Brooke.

"Aerokinesis," said Sam.

"Controlled aerokinesis," David corrected his assistant. "Adam formed that wisp of air into a corporeal hand I was able to grasp."

"Firm handshake," said Brooke, suddenly understanding.

"Now," continued David, "imagine having that power but also pumped full of epinephrine.

"You'd lose control," answered Sam, "and it would manifest crudely."

"The airburst?" whispered Brooke.

"The airburst," agreed David.

Everyone in the room considered the plethora of possibilities, but Brooke offered the first objection. "But we would have seen evidence of gamma waves from Batch Alpha, and we've had yet to observe that."

"True," agreed David. "That part bothered me as well. We should have seen those by now."

"Yes, we did," countered Sam. "I sent you an email the other night."

Both David and Brooke turned, wide-eyed and waiting.

Dr. Andalon moved closer to his assistant and, in a low voice, asked, "What are you talking about?"

"The night before the lab burned, I observed a dual entry into gamma."

David frowned. "Why didn't you record it in the log?" he asked.

"I did, and you replied by email the next day and dismissed it, saying it was coincidental."

"Sam," David said, "I never sent that email."

Both sets of eyes turned to Brooke, silently questioning her involvement.

Hers grew wide with understanding. "I didn't interfere." After they continued to stare doubtfully, she insisted, "I wasn't aware of any gamma readings, I swear! I hadn't passed anything to Stephanie in quite a long time, guys!"

David considered her words and quietly accepted, but Brooke would have great difficulty overcoming the lack of trust she had created between them. *I just hope he doesn't learn* everything *I've hidden,* she thought. *Or I really* will *lose him forever.*

He turned to Sam. "Tell me what happened. From the beginning," he said, "all of it."

Both David and Brooke listened intently to the story, how his singing had raised gamma in Batch Alpha. "Even Felicima had relaxed that evening," he explained.

After Sam had finished, David pulled up a screen. "Show me," he said. "Where in the gamma range were their readings?"

"I don't remember exactly. It was a while ago."

"Guess then," David said, bringing up a chart on the display. "Give me a place to start."

Sam stared for a moment, then traced a line with his finger. "I'm pretty sure it was here."

Brooke felt her heart quicken. A glance from her husband confirmed he had made the same connection. "This is while you were singing?" she asked.

"Yes. Felicima calmed and so did King and Lynette."

"David?" Brooke demanded.

"I know," he replied. "I'm as confused as you."

Sam looked worried, like he had said or done something wrong. With nerves creeping into his voice he asked, "What does that mean? I could be wrong, but I'm fairly certain that's where the readings were."

David spoke quietly when he answered. "You did fine, Sam. This is simply bigger than we thought."

"I know what it means," Brooke explained. "Studies of combat soldiers with traumatic brain injuries were studied a few years back. The elevated gamma waves peaked in that range. This is a region previously only believed possible through deep and consistent practice of meditation."

"What does that mean?" Sam asked.

"It means," David said with a grin, "that Batch Alpha achieved telepathy and proved my theory." He pointed toward a monitor watching Eden. Adam and Eve were sitting on a bench, facing each other and in a deep meditative state. "King and Lynette communicated the same way these children do. I want a full spectrum analysis of the children's waves to confirm, but I'm confident what we'll learn."

Sam nodded, but still appeared confused. "What about the brain injury? What does that prove?"

"It proves nothing," Brooke said, "but it explains Felicima. Brain trauma can occur with a single event, like striking your head during an explosion or with repeated injury—similar to concussions on a football field. Or, it can occur over time through sustained emotional experiences." She took a deep breath then continued. "Children who are continually exposed to abuse, neglect, or violence in the home develop the same brain patterns as one that's been injured during war. Add in sexual violence or trauma, and they might as well have survived a bombing themselves."

David added, "Didn't you say the others agitated Felicima?"

"I did," Sam agreed. "She was terrified of them, as if things went on after we left the lab."

"And the fire, David. Don't forget about the fire and what you saw her do," Brooke insisted.

Andalon quietly nodded, fully understanding his role. "When I was drunk that night of the fire," he said, "I threw bottles, screamed, and scared every monkey in the lab. But that was *after* I had taken them from the safety of their cages and injected them with epinephrine."

Brooke frowned, suddenly realizing a missed detail. "*You* told me you were trying to *elicit* a response. How, exactly, were you trying to *accomplish* that response?"

The darkness lurking behind her husband's eyes crept in, either with remorse for his actions or satisfaction at the reward for his acts. When he answered he said simply, "I was cruel, Brooke."

CHAPTER SEVENTEEN

Adam and Eve sat upon a bench in the garden. The children were as still as statues, motionless and resembling two monks in meditation. Occasionally one would mutter something under their breath. Stephanie Yurik sat across from them with a legal pad and pen, transcribing their words as they journeyed in their minds.

"North America is a wasteland," Adam whispered.

"Tell me about that," Dr. Yurik pressed, "Can you describe the geography?"

"Cities are gone."

"Which cities?"

"Nearly all. What's left will deteriorate quickly or become covered in ash. Everything is already buried under several feet, and any structure over twenty feet has been destroyed or compromised except in a few places spared direct hits."

"Is ash still falling?" she asked.

"Yes," the boy answered. "It's mixed with the snow and packing new layers each day. This will compact as pumice, forming new rock layers that will hide civilization in time."

"Where's the highest volcanic activity? Is it still the old Yellowstone crater?"

Eve spoke up. "I'm flying over that region now. It's vast, Stephanie. The entire crater has caved in upon itself and it spans hundreds of miles."

"Do you see any evidence of resettlement?" Jake had insisted she get accurate locations of any populations surviving the chain of events.

"Not near the crater," Adam replied. "Nothing will grow there for centuries if ever." Then he gasped and exclaimed, "Look at that crack!"

Dr. Yurik asked, "What crack?"

Eve answered, "A very large fault opened up from the southern tip of the crater all the way to the southern edge of the continent. Cinders are rising from it as if there's magma flow beneath."

"Southern tip?" Stephanie was mildly confused. "But the two continents connect!"

"Not any longer," Adam replied. "They're completely separated."

She tried not to betray her alarm at the news and prompted the children to travel eastward. "What about along the Great Lakes Region."

Eve replied, "There's only one lake now. It's very large, almost a sea."

Stephanie had a tough time keeping calm at that news, but held it together.

"Wait," Adam said, "There's a population center here."

Dr. Yurik nodded. She and the others had estimated survivors. The eastern and western seaboards had received most of the attention from the nuclear arsenals, and any populations would be west of the Appalachian Mountains. "Are they where we thought we'd find them?"

"Where the rivers meet," he said, "many still gather. Most are ill, but more survived than I first predicted."

"Expand on that," she told them. "Tell me exactly what you see." She pulled up a map on her tablet, zooming in on the Ohio River Valley. Moving west along the snaking Ohio River, she focused on the Shawnee National Forest. Depending on winds, the fallout from cities of Nashville, Louisville, and St. Louis would avoid much of the area where the river met the Mississippi.

"They're huddled, confused and unsure what to do." He drifted into a deeper trance. When the children entered this state, Stephanie always paid close attention. Their visions would prove prophetic, not only seeing the present, but also telling of things yet to come. "The leadership will emerge from here," Adam explained. "Bands of people will look to warlords to lead them, some ruthless, some lawless, but a few truly concerned about the people. A year of sadness will extend into many more of violence while new lines are drawn."

Dr. Yurik took down his words and added her own notations. *The toughest resistance to repopulation will be here.* She drew a quick sketch, then circled a region centered around what was once the Ohio River Valley.

Cathy stared out the southern window, unable to tear her eyes from the falling snow. She remembered when she was young. She would do the same, but had watched with anticipation and yearned to run outside and play. Josh asked about that possibility, eager to frolic. She understood his impatience. The entire household was fed up with confinement and several weeks inside the structure had taken their toll. But she knew the accumulation outside was different than before, and no one would enjoy any recreation it offered. What had once drifted to the ground in layers of welcoming white now fell clumsily as lumps of dark gray, filled with ash from the darkened sky above.

Oddly, the scene brought to mind a memory from a vacation long ago when her parents had taken her to visit the big island of Hawaii. There, she first discovered black sand beaches. She had found odd beauty in how the volcanic rock had rendered to crystals, the result of enduring thousands of years of tidal friction. At the time, the image had invoked feelings of peace and relaxation, as the fierce blue tropical waters starkly contrasted the trailing onyx shoreline. The reflected hues of lush foliage added a splash of color to the palette that left her yearning to remain on vacation forever.

But no such beauty existed in the world outside this window. The lush tree line between John's home and the swollen river had blended into the horizon, now as dark and terrifying as a haunted forest from a fairy tale. The gnarled branches had lost their leaves prematurely, surprised barren by the abruptness of winter. *Nuclear Winter,* she thought, recalling the lesson of warning John had given to her and Josh. Though softer than the raining debris and radiation from the fallout, this was just as dangerous.

A voice made Cathy jump. "That fool is shoveling."

She turned to find that Jenny had looked up from her easel, brush hovering in midair as she strained to see past her houseguest. Turning, Cat saw that John had begun working on shoveling a path to the barn. The tall walls of ash and snow beside the walk revealed several feet had already accumulated.

In his defense, Cat said, "He promised the radiation isn't as bad now and will only be strong in the ground zero hotspots."

Jenny smiled. That was the woman's gift to the world, Cathy realized early on, Jenny Klingensmith could warm a room with laughing eyes and a blushing beam. But behind this one lurked a cautiousness, as if she hid deeper knowledge only a wife would know.

"Besides," Cat went on, "he wouldn't go against caution, not after he's stressed it to all of us."

"Don't sanctify John Klingensmith just yet," his wife said with a chuckle. "That man's ornerier than a polecat. Sometimes the rules don't apply to him." She beckoned with the brush. "Come over here, dear, and take a look at this."

Cathy rose from the window seat and walked over to the older woman, glancing down at the canvas she had been working on. It matched the way the southern view would have looked before the recent chain of events. The depiction was perfect, gorgeous in every detail and starkly contrasting the hellish image outside.

"It's beautiful," the young woman said.

"It *was*," Jenny agreed. "I wanted to paint it before I forgot how it used to look."

Cathy's eyes darted back and forth from the painting to the view of the real world beyond the glass. Looking at the scenery earlier had been awful, full of depression and lacking hope. Now, knowing how the farm had been before, she realized what the world had lost. Gone from the eye was beauty, now existing only in the hearts of those like Jenny who refuse to forget.

She swallowed. "It'll return to normal soon," she promised. "Just give it time."

Jenny chuckled. "Don't use optimism on me, dear." She smiled and winked, then added, "I invented optimism. No, take a closer look at the snowpack."

"I see it well enough. It's full of ash and piled high."

"When I was in art school I studied abroad," Jenny explained. "I traveled to Italy and studied at the *Accademia di Belle Arti de Roma*, the

University of Fine Arts of Rome. Two and a half hours away by bus we traveled to what was once a field, very much like ours. We camped an entire week in that pasture, and it taught me everything I need to know now."

"What do you mean?"

"One day three hundred years ago, the shepherd of that field noticed one of his sheep had disappeared. Worried it may be wolves, he ventured out warily armed with only a staff."

"What did he find?"

"A hole."

"The sheep fell in?"

"The ground had crumbled beneath its feet, sending it ten or so feet down into the hole. The poor thing was bleating and crying for rescue, and the man ran back to town for rope and men to help lower him. When they returned and lowered him down, he entered an ancient world. He found himself inside a Roman house, dating all the way to the empire. His friends tossed him a torch and he held it aloft, reflecting four walls of beautiful fresco paintings."

"Where was he?"

"The ancient city of Pompeii. It was lost in 79 A.D. during a volcanic eruption. Mount Vesuvius rained down fire and ash, much as Yellowstone is doing now, but on a much smaller scale. It happened so fast that the entire city and all its occupants were buried alive. Husbands clung to their wives, families huddled together for warmth, and animals died in their pens."

"How do you know they didn't get away in time?"

"Because their bodies were perfectly cast in the ash, preserved like statues for future generations to find."

Cat stood silently, eyes returned to the window and the snow piled several feet high along the path John had dug. When she finally spoke it was in a whisper. "This won't let up for a while, will it?"

"I hope so, but I doubt it. Doubled with the nuclear winter, John thinks it will last a season, maybe two. He said the snow will eventually melt, but the layers of wet ash will be like the rock of Pompeii, sealing our world in a tomb. Who knows? Maybe in twelve or more centuries our world will be unrecognizable—buried beneath black rock and soil for a new civilization to discover."

"That's why he's shoveling," Cathy realized. "He wants to keep a path to the barn so you guys can continue working when things get back to normal."

"Nothing's returning to normal, dear." Her smile faded and sadness filled the artist's eyes, with wet tears softly painting her eyelids. "John didn't tell you why he's on hiatus from the University."

"No," Cat agreed. "He didn't."

"He's got prostate cancer, and the worst kind. The doctor gave him a year six months ago."

"That's why he's not worried about the radiation." The young woman's eyes followed him as he shoveled, trenching slower than he had earlier but now three fourths of the way to the barn door.

Jenny nodded. "He's trying to ensure I'm taken care of when he's gone."

Cathy spotted something in the trees, subtle movement that caught her full attention. Three men clad in tactical fatigues crouched in a grove, watching John as he worked. Each stranger carried a rifle on his back, but not the hunting kind. These were as black as their clothing and terrifying.

"Jenny..." She pointed to the men. One of them approached John.

The women held their breath, focused on the exchange. The men kept their voices low and both appeared calm. At one point, the newcomer pointed toward the house. John shook his head as if saying, "no."

The other man smiled, put his hand out to shake, and Klingensmith took it. Then the stranger turned to leave, casually joining the others in the trees as they also turned to leave. John waited until they had disappeared from view, then calmly returned to the house, leaning the shovel against the porch as he shook ash from his boots. After what felt like an eternity to the women, he finally entered and said nothing as he crossed the room to collapse in his chair.

"John," Jenny asked. He did not respond with words, uttering only a disinterested grunt. "Johnny," she pressed, "what did he want?"

He refused to answer, walking toward a closet in the hall. He opened it, scanning the shelf for something left unused for a very long time. After a few moments he found what he was looking for and pulled down two boxes. One was a small container, unadorned and inauspicious. The other was a long gun case.

"Lock the doors," he commanded. "And move the furniture against the downstairs windows."

"Who were those men?" Cathy pressed.

He said nothing more as he opened the case and drew out a hunting rifle. He set the weapon on the table and returned the case to the closet. Reaching deep into the back, pushing aside some winter coats, he drew out a shotgun. Cathy immediately realized the device was old, the barrel blued, and the stock deeply worn by time. Only a miracle would prevent it from blowing up on whichever of them had to fire the thing.

John's wife snatched it from his hands. "What did Crazy Mike want?" she demanded, her laughing eyes replaced by fire.

"Mike Stapleton was only checking in on us," he said quietly.

"Crazy Mike?" Cat asked, incredulous. "Who is Mike Stapleton," she asked, "and why did you call him crazy?"

"He's a prepper," Jenny replied. "Been talking about the end of times for years. Rambling about communist takeover and even nuclear war."

"Well," Cat said, "turns out he was right about part of it."

"Seems he was," John agreed, "but that doesn't make him less or more crazy."

"Everyone in these parts expected a Ruby Ridge fiasco to take place on his spread, knowing he'd fire first if law enforcement ever stepped on his property." Jenny explained. "Mike's trigger happy and barricaded his entire family on their farm. What did he say, John?" Her eyes had lost much of her anger, but the fear remained, dampening much of their brightness.

"He said we're welcome to join him and his family, that he liked us and appreciated our kindness over the years. Said there's plenty of room if we do."

"But you said *no*, right?"

"I did. I told him I listened to at least part of his warnings over the years and stocked up on supplies like he suggested."

Cat turned to Jenny who nodded and said, "We've enough canned and non-perishable food and water in the basement to last John and me at least a year."

"Then what's the problem," Cathy asked, suddenly very worried. "Why did you say to brace the windows?"

"Because I, unlike Mike, never stocked up on ammunition or planned for defending the farm."

"Why," she questioned, "is that a problem?"

"Because Mike just told me gangs from Indianapolis and St. Louis have a foothold north of the river in Evansville."

"Is that true?" Cat asked.

He nodded. "They *have* left the big cities to cook their drugs in the rural areas, and they've a presence in Evansville, for sure."

"But that's north of the river," Jenny argued, pointing the direction of the swollen body of water that carried Cat and Josh all the way from Michigan. "Surely there's no way they're crossing into our area."

John fell silent, dark thoughts swirling in his mind as he reasoned how to respond. After a while he said, "Mike said he and his boys chased a dozen or so gangsters off his land a day ago. He followed their trail through the woods and tracked them here."

Jenny gasped, falling into a chair.

Cat frowned, "Furniture against the windows won't do," she said.

"No," he agreed. "But they'll do in a pinch. We need to shore up the house as soon as possible. I've got some plywood in the barn, and we can dismantle walls if we run out of that. But I can't do it alone."

"I'll help," she promised. "Let's get started."

CHAPTER EIGHTEEN

Evansville was a shit hole, at least according to Linda Johnson. Max Rankin, on the other hand, called it home. He loved its beauty and most of all the quiet it provided his family. They had none of the problems a big city had—well, unless you considered the gangs. Thinking of these, he worried about Betty and Tom.

He imagined the rioting and looting taking place as he drove, pressing the pedal as fast as he dared considering how little gas he had to get there. Every few miles he checked the gauge and calculated how far he would get. Just for extra insurance he coasted down every hill. He and Linda would get there eventually. Thinking again of the looting and rioting he may encounter, he felt the gun safe under the seat. It was a tool now, one he kept tucked away and hoped he'd never use.

Linda had lost her charm after the bridge, and he resented she had turned him into a killer—no, he was already one of those. He did not hate her, but he felt deep animosity for the selfish way she'd forced him to plow through those innocent civilians—civilians? God, he was thinking like a Marine again.

That was why he'd gone into trucking, to forget about his past. Now he was self-employed, chose his own routes, and had little interaction with civilians with little to no understanding of his background or experiences. He would have been unemployable in any other sector, but discovered a cozy little niche in this exhaust filled rig.

None of those, though, were the real reason he resented the woman sitting beside him. Ever since the bridge, all this woman did was complain like it was his fault the world ended as they knew it. The nagging had to stop soon. She grinded against every ounce of his patience and, after only a couple of days, he sickened at her company. But he couldn't just throw a suburban white woman out on her own—no, that would've been a crime no matter who ruled the streets waiting for him in Evansville. So he put up with her venting. Thankfully, she finally quieted when they hit Indiana. That was good because he had most certainly had enough.

They arrived in town just as they ran out of fuel. The old rig sputtered then died, leaving them several miles from their intended destination. Max knew he would never again get the old girl to turn over, even if he managed to find diesel. Thus they abandoned the Freightliner where it died, north of Kleymeyer Park. He held onto the keys though, not ready to leave his property to whatever wolves would scavenge their leavings.

"Grab the cooler," he said, reaching for his bags. Usually Tom helped carry everything into the house, but, even then, they only had a hundred feet or so to walk. He and this white *Karen* had a lot longer to go than that. At her refusal, he wound up stacking the heaviest duffle bag atop the cooler and carried them both while she dragged his backpack in the snow with indifference. "Don't do that," he begged, letting his irritation show.

"Do what?" she demanded, thoughts elsewhere and manners lost.

"Drag my shit like that. Carry it on your back... *please.*" He tried a pleasantry but she scoffed.

"My shoulder hurts, my ribs are probably cracked, and my arm was dislocated till you snapped it into place, and you want me to *carry* your bag?" With a tad too much drama she let the strap fall from her fingers and dropped it onto the hard snow. He noted she still clutched a sack of food against her chest.

Ready to snap her neck and leave her in the same drift, he counted to ten and placed the heavier items down before strapping the bag to his own shoulders. Then he retrieved the burden and led the way. All in all, they carried their lives four miles to his home on Harlen Avenue. The hike was arduous as they tromped through several feet of piled ash—no doubt filled with radiation. That thought worried Max the most, thinking the pair would make it all this way only to perish in the worst possible way. But most of the fallout had already occurred, an event they had witnessed from the safety of the truck during the trip. No, the city itself appeared safe—spared from annihilation and therefore mostly free of isotopes.

"This bag of food is too heavy," Linda complained. She handed it over and he took it, adding it to his own burden and rendering him her pack mule. He should have refused, but taking it shut her up.

Once they reached the house, Max immediately knew something was wrong. Outwardly it appeared the same. Built in the 1950s, the pier and beam foundation held a simple home with wood siding painted bright blue. Betty had picked the color the previous fall, claiming she wanted to stand out from the greens and yellows dotting the street. The windows were intact though, and the front door remained firmly closed. Testing the handle proved it unlocked, causing the hairs on his neck to stand abruptly at attention. Inside, they found the place abandoned, ransacked and picked clean of canned foods, water, and pretty much anything useful in the pantry. He picked up the overturned trash and packed it full to keep busy his idle hands. Outwardly he remained calm, despite the anxious storm brewing within.

Where's my family, he thought, *where could they have gone?*

In the living room, Linda picked up a shattered picture frame that lay discarded on the ground. In the photo was of a beautiful woman, dark in complexion with stunningly high cheekbones that gave her an appearance of Egyptian royalty. "Is this Betty?" she asked, holding it up.

"That's her."

"She's beautiful."

He nodded. "That's an understatement." Thinking of all the negativity Linda had unloaded on him during the drive, he added, "Her beauty runs *deeper* than her skin, I assure you. Never have I met such a godly woman—so devout yet hellbent on saving a sinner like me. I've never deserved her, that's for sure."

She nodded and placed the picture carefully on the table. Almost reverently which surprised Max. He noticed her eyes betrayed a deeper sadness, no doubt for the family she had lost during her trek across country, and he regretted the animosity he'd earlier felt.

He pulled opened the door to the backyard and said, "I had waters stashed in the workshop. Hopefully the looters missed those." He paused to think, then added, "I should also have jugs we can fill up at the river.

I've got some purification tablets I kept in the rig. If we run out of those, we can boil it just as easily."

She nodded and he left her in the house, walking outside and thankful he was finally alone and that she had ceased her nagging. To be honest, her odd quiet bothered him worse than the irritation she had released over the past couple of days, and he felt even worse about his attitude.

Stepping outside, he froze. The door to the shop had been forced open, hanging from its hinges with the frame splintered. Anxious alert crept in, returning him to that dark place lurking within. His military training took over and the hardened marine gained control over his body. He instinctively felt his hip for his firearm, suddenly aware that he had left it in the rig.

How could I have forgotten? Then he realized—his thoughts had been too focused on Linda to grab what he truly needed when gathering up his belongings. He would have to return to the truck later and fetch it.

Creeping toward the shop, he stepped carefully and quietly. Most likely, whoever had broken in had already left, but Max left nothing to chance. He approached with caution, listening intently for sounds within. His dark eyes scanned the void beyond the doorway, searching for movement and his mind sharpened, slowing the world around him as his pulse beat time in his ears.

Sergeant Rankin decided his actions now, as his mind teleported to his desert time.

Just as in Fallujah, he was ready for anything. Without a weapon, he steadied his hands in front of his body. His line training remembered; his muscles quivered with anticipation. The simple form of combat was all he had against any enemies lurking within, and he would dance in close as the situation prescribed.

The words of his drill instructor echoed from some distant memory as he moved. "These techniques permanently damage your opponent, and every attack should cease only after the opponent's death."

Death. He had been so far removed from danger that Max had forgotten his former adversary. Adversary? Friend? Death, who had lingered in his shadow for so long, now hid in the darkness of his mind. *Taking a life is easy,* Max considered, *made easier once you've decided to remain alive.* He had taken his share, but those days (he once thought until Linda had turned his truck into a plow) were in his past.

Now at the door he paused and detected no movement within. He took a breath, held it in, and stepped inside. No attack came. He drew in the dusty air and urged his heart to slow. Adrenaline had already worked its way through his veins, and his body would feel the effects after wearing off later. Satisfied the room was secure, he went to work.

His tools had been pilfered and anything of use was gone. His handsaws, axes, and even his ratchet set were gone. Worse, the looters had pulled out every drawer of his storage chest, dumping what they didn't need on the ground. It would take hours to sift through their leavings. They had found the cases of water, leaving only a dust-free square on the ground where they had rested before. Thankfully the jugs were where he had hoped—tucked behind some old snow tires he had taken off the pickup last spring. He also found a two by four and a spool of twine. He grabbed these as well.

Taking up the containers, he crossed the backyard and returned to the house. Linda had moved on from the living room, and Max found her standing in his bedroom staring down at the mess strewn about. The looters had removed everything of value, including winter coats and flannel. They left everything else in disarray. An empty jewelry box lay discarded on the bed. Its corner was stained with crimson—no doubt blood. Max hoped it was a looter's and not Betty's.

"Whoever did this is gone," he said. "They found the waters but left the jugs. I'll go down to the river this evening and try to haul some back. I found some wood and twine in the workshop with which to make a yoke. That'll make it easier to carry the jugs when full."

Linda nodded that she understood, but her silence screamed disinterest. He followed her eyes. They rested on an empty footlocker at the end of the bed. She stared at it solemnly.

"I had one of those," she finally said. "That same hope chest. My mother gave it to me when our oldest was born."

"That belonged to Betty," Max said. He knelt down and inspected its hinges. They were still intact and so was the lock. The looters had cleaned it out but must have realized it was too heavy to haul off. They left the key in its place. He immediately opened his backpack and retrieved what was left of their food, placing inside everything of value. He turned the key before pulling it and placing it in his pocket.

Linda, realizing the slight, turned in a huff and left the room.

He couldn't help but smile at her response. The food stash he had in the rig had dwindled quickly during the trip, with that cursed woman eating more than her share. Twice he caught her eating an entire can of Vienna sausages, something that could have fed them both during times of rationing. Locking up their food was their best assurance of survival. He felt the key in his pocket. He would bring it out only during mealtime.

He ventured out again that evening, crossing Oak Hill cemetery just before dusk. They needed water to survive, that took priority over retrieving his firearm. He would search for that in the morning. Besides, the river wasn't far, only three miles each way instead of four, so this was the easiest trip of the two.

But fate favored him that evening, and he was pleasantly surprised. As he crossed under Highway 66, he caught a glimpse of the setting sun flickering atop water where it shouldn't be. Bewildered, he turned south and came across floodwaters reaching as far north as Lincoln Avenue. The Ohio had somehow swelled, spilling over banks and cutting the trip by more than half. Pleased he had found a source of drinking water, he knelt to fill the jugs.

The entire process took only a few minutes, and he hoisted the yoke across his back. It wasn't heavy, merely cumbersome. If he hurried, he would still have time to jog to the rig, being unburdened by a dire need for basic survival. But he walked slowly during the return, taking in the scenery and paying closer attention to the homes he passed. Each was abandoned—not *some* of them as he had first assumed. Everything was devoid of life.

Where did the people go, he wondered, *that they've all disappeared completely?*

Maybe they sheltered nearby, he thought, *in the university, maybe? Or the high school?* He was nearing both, with the towering light posts of

Tiger Stadium looming just beyond Willow Road. He started to turn east down Walnut when movement caught his eye. Two dark shadows stepped from behind the red brick wall surrounding the field on his left, and Max found himself face to face with trouble.

"What've you got in the jugs, old man? Gas or water?" The voice sounded young, about the same age as his son Tom.

Max quickly assessed the newcomers. Each wore a black hoodie over sagging jeans with boxers showing between the cloth. Both wore a face covering, similar to the gaiters he had worn during the sandstorms overseas. But these teens were certainly not military. No, they more closely resembled street thugs than a credible threat.

"It's river water," he told them. "Unpurified and dangerous to drink as it is."

"Then why do *you* have it," one of the boys pressed. He made a good point.

Max considered his options. There really was no good explanation, unless he intended to give away his stash of purification tablets. Finally, he answered with half-truth, "It's all I have access to, so I'll take my chances. Hell. It'll probably kill me with radiation eventually, but that's better than starving to death."

Both teens laughed at this. The taller boy relaxed and his tone softened when he said, "Why don't you come with us? We've got supplies, and you're the right color, brother."

"Mike!" The shorter teen rebuked his friend. "We don't have permission to bring anyone else in," he said.

Mike, pondered Max. Then he realized the voice had been familiar. "Mike Salwell? You're a friend of Tom's," he said hopefully. "Have you seen him?"

Both boys exchanged a look and the taller shrugged, suddenly recognizing the man before him. "You're Mr. Rankin, right? Tom's dad?"

"That's me," he replied, eager to learn about his family.

"We haven't seen Tom since he got in trouble with his mom last week. She doesn't like us much."

Max couldn't help but chuckle. "Aren't you boys part of the *Get Money Gang*, or something? Moms and dads aren't fond of gangsters hanging around their sons," he said.

"We're not affiliated," the younger boy quipped, his voice quivering just slightly and betraying his lie.

"Regardless," Max insisted, "that's why she doesn't want him hanging out with you two. She thinks you *are* affiliated, no matter your relationship with *real* gangsters or not." Changing the subject, he asked, "Where is everyone? Surely one hundred and twenty thousand citizens didn't just up and disappear."

He watched them closely for reaction. Mike's eyes flickered to the east, indicating the places Max had suspected. The other boy waved his hand in disgust. "There's a god damned war raging, old man! There ain't no citizens, only sheep and lions. You need to figure out what side you're on." He turned to leave, shoving Mike in the shoulder before climbing the stone wall and pulling himself over. From the other side he shouted again, "Figure out what team you're on."

Tom's friend lingered, eyes filled with genuine concern. "He's right, Mr. Rankin. It's a warzone now." He pulled his hand out of his hoodie pocket to display a pistol grip. "And he's right, you'd better be careful and find your flock if you're a sheep. Pick a side before the lions like *us* get you."

"Where's Tom," he asked one more time, unfazed by the threat.

"I don't know," the boy said before following his friend up the wall. Before he jumped over the side he added, "but he wasn't a sheep like you and his mom."

The words cut Max deep, and he walked with more speed the rest of the way home. He would return to the rig in the morning when it was safer.

CHAPTER NINETEEN

The artificial sun and sky felt real, and the sounds of the garden made Dr. Andalon imagine he were upon the surface of paradise instead of deep underground in a medical laboratory. Eden was beautiful. The smell of budding flowers and the slight buzzing of bees completed the feeling of reality. He sat upon a stone bench very close to and across from the children. They stared up with eagerness and waiting smiles, ready to answer his questions.

"How does it work?" David asked. "Is it as simple as breathing?"

"You mean," Adam replied with a smile, "is it an inherent ability that we picked up on naturally and mastered as we matured?"

"I forget," the doctor said, "that despite your outwardly ten-year-old appearance, you have the capacity and vocabulary to understand the science of your..." He trailed off. This entire experience was new—the ability to directly question and analyze responses from his subjects. His experiences with the primates at MIT left him with a bad habit of simplifying his vocabulary.

"Our what, David?" Eve inquired. Her question was polite and her features friendly when she asked, but David could sense an underlying distrust beneath the surface. Or was it unspoken worry or disdain?

"I spent my entire career working toward this day, even constructed the descriptive language regarding the science, but I've reached a loss of words. Do I call it an ability? A specialty? A power?"

The children shared both a look and a smile before Adam replied, "We refer to it as our craft."

"That's a very unusual description," the doctor noted. "Is this because you work and weave the air like artisans?"

"That," the boy responded with a smiling nod, "and more."

"We do not manifest the air around us. It is like clay in the earth before gathered by the potter and placed on her wheel," Eve added. "We shape what we feel around us. Watch." Her hands slowly waved in the air between them, swirling a pattern that seemed to build upon itself. Slowly, a floating pirate ship coalesced and hovered in place with sails flapping and filling with breeze. Atop the crow's nest flew a jolly roger flag."

"It's beautiful," David remarked as he instinctively touched his hand, the one he had shaken with Adam's manipulation when first introduced. "Why did you choose a pirate ship?"

Eve smiled. "It's from a book we read a few months ago. It was about a magical place stumbled upon by pirates. During their misadventure, they found themselves cast away upon a new and fascinating world of opportunity."

"We both loved it," Adam explained, "with all the colorful characters and the imaginative world. We both got lost in the author's story. It was an escape when all we've known is this laboratory."

"What's its name?" David asked. "The ship they sailed upon."

"Estowen," answered Eve.

"What does that mean?"

"To us?" Adam asked. "Opportunity."

David reached out a finger and touched a sail, finding it resembled the canvas in texture as well as appearance. He again remembered the shimmering feel of Adam's handshake with the ethereal palm and shuddered. "When I touch it, the sensation is strange, oddly foreign. Does it feel the same to you when you weave?"

"No," Eve calmly replied, as a teacher explaining a concept to a novice. "How do you know fear, Doctor Andalon?"

"Fear is instinctual. We see, hear, or feel things out of place or unexpected, and those stimuli trigger sensory alarms within our bodies." His eyes met hers. "Is that what it is? Your powers... your craft... so it *is* instinctual?"

She allowed Adam to respond. "Not at all, David. Describe the senses heightened in that state of fear, after the sensory alarms trigger."

"Pulse quickens along with blood pressure and cortisol and adrenaline release. Breathing rate increases, and blood vessels to the lungs and muscles dilate."

"And what are our minds doing when all this happens internally?" the boy asked.

David answered immediately. "The body prepares for danger by either fighting, running away, or freezing."

Eve nodded. "Yes, that's the physical and mental response, but only instinctually. Imagine if another chemical response occurs, one triggered by the heightened levels of cortisol and adrenaline. One that triggers your congenital ability to manipulate the elements."

"That was the purpose of the Mendel Project," David said, his mind returning to his lab in MIT. With sudden realization, he remembered the injections of epinephrine and the response by both batches. "So the epinephrine triggered Felicima's ability to craft the flame around her, to wield it against me?"

"It played a hand, yes," Adam agreed, "but her aggression suggests she was prone to anger or hostility. More likely, the hot emotion of rage was triggered by fear when you shattered the glass."

"Hot emotion..." David's eyes grew wide. "Are *you* able to manipulate fire when you are angry?"

"Certainly not we," Eve promised. "But all emotions can be either hot or cold."

"Or warm," Adam added.

"Or warm," she agreed.

"I don't understand," the geneticist admitted.

The nine-year-old children exchanged a look and Eve giggled before explaining. In a voice full of maturity and speaking with authority, she said, "Emotions vary not only from person to person, but from situation to situation. When you were angry in the lab, you were hot."

"So anger is hot, and love is cold? Is that what you're saying?"

"It would be better if you did not interrupt me, doctor, or we'll be here all evening. Please don't do that again," she commanded with a harsh air of superiority.

David's mouth shut instantly. Something other than her words, but in the way the child had spoken, had sent chills down his spine. From that point on he listened intently.

"Anger alone is neither hot nor cold. The fury you exhibited was hot. It was aggressive and hostile—abusive even, considering the poor animals locked in cages. A moment ago, I displayed the cooler version of the same emotion, one that passively set you to silence. Instead of fury I exhibited irritation."

David waited a moment while she paused, finally realizing she was allowing him to ask questions, and so he did. "I think I understand. When Felicima was calm and cool, she could manipulate flame in smaller, more controlled ways—like delicately lighting a cigarette or sparking kindling for a campfire. But when I raged, she panicked and defended herself with fireballs."

"Exactly," the girl smiled proudly then continued. "Her cool concern changed to terror due to the raised levels of adrenaline, made worse by your injections. The pitiful creature was overloaded and could not help but try to neutralize the threat she perceived."

"Does it only happen that way with fear? When adrenaline surges?"

"No. There are many reasons cortisol and adrenaline can build in a body, causing an otherwise rational person to overreact. Take for instance trauma. What are the lingering effects of emotional pain within a person, especially when experienced at young ages?"

"That... I guess it varies from person to person. An abused or neglected child will be pensive, worried about building toxic relationships or anxiously expecting loss around every corner. They will have trust issues or worse, become explosive themselves."

"Yes," agreed Eve, "they will. Worse, they will have less control over their overall range, since their emotional quotient is lower than the social norm."

David stared in shock. His eyes reminded him that he spoke with children, but his ears suggested otherwise.

She continued. "The same can happen with happy emotions. When you met Adam, he controlled the air in such a way that he could not contain his satisfaction at meeting you. What should have been a tickle in your palm became a powerful grip that became as real as his own."

The boy nodded, smiling shyly at the revelation of his unmasked emotion. "I had so been looking forward to meeting you, I could no longer wait. You've been our hope for so long, the key to both our freedom and our future, Doctor Andalon."

David looked around the garden, suddenly seeing it as more than a lab, but a lifelong prison for the children. "You're unhappy here?"

"Not unhappy, for we are well taken care of. Dr. Yurik treats us very well, and General Braston pops in now and again to ensure we aren't lacking in needs."

"What about Senator Esterling?"

The children exchanged a look, and David recognized a mutual dislike for his friend.

"He means well," Eve replied, earning a nod from her brother. "But we've seen his future and fear the monster he'll become. His vision will lead to many more troubles for the world and society he hoped to change."

"Have you told him this? You could guide him. I know Michael and he will listen."

"I assure you he won't," Adam said with a frown. "Doctor, we are treated well and we *are* happy with our surroundings, but we crave more. I would describe our situation as being curious of life like all children."

Eve added, "But just as caged as the animals who perished in the fire of your previous lab, we desire freedom."

"So you *are* unhappy?" David paused, considering life spent entirely in Eden... in the lab. He looked upward, toward the artificial sky and suddenly found it confining. Like the biblical Garden of Eden, he suddenly understood the fall of original man as told in the story. "You want to leave the lab and enjoy free will to make your own lives?"

Eve spoke with quiet confidence that he shuddered when she said, "That's not impossible for us now, doctor."

"Not now? What changed?"

"You are here now, Father."

"Father? You desire a family and parents? Then what? Normalcy?"

She nodded. "Doesn't every child desire and require the same things from their parents?"

"Brooke and I are having a baby. Perhaps we can introduce our child as a playmate as he or she grows."

Eve frowned and looked at her brother. A cool breeze passed between them and Adam nodded. He turned to David and said, "That would be ill advised, given what you suspect and what we know is true."

"What I... How can you know what I suspect? My experiments worked and we are with child."

"She is with a child, but it is *certainly* not yours." Eve placed a reassuring hand on the doctor's forearm and said, "You rewrote *her* code, but yours was not fully repaired when she conceived."

"Are you certain?"

"You've doubted this child's origin but have not challenged Brooke or sought the evidence so easily found. Why not?" she asked, "Why would a scientist not question everything? Why can't you question if she took a shortcut?"

"Why *would* I? I love her. She has put up with an incomplete man for so long, and I guess I wouldn't call her *shortcut* cheating or unfaithfulness. I'm actually relieved the pressure to make her conceive is finally off me. I was failing in my experiment and welcome the end result. I've come to accept that no matter *whose* child lives within her womb, it shall be mine."

"Rest assured," Adam said, "that she loves you very much. But that child was conceived out of wanton mistrust for your scientific knowledge. You are close to a breakthrough and must continue your work. You must succeed in your desire to sire your own ancestral line—that's our hope for true freedom."

David pleaded, "How do you know so much about me?"

The children grasped hands and reached for his. He accepted them without question, completing the circle.

"Close your eyes," Adam commanded softly, "and meditate with us. Slow your heart rate by focusing on your breathing. In a moment you will feel your mind within the ether, the gateway to the Dream World we have created."

It took a moment for David's mind to settle, he had so many questions burning within. But the boy's voice was soothing and melodic, coaxing him into relaxation. With eyes shut, he focused on the darkness before him.

"Good," the boy said. "Gaze upon the darkness but focus on the many flickering lights instead. Look for their pattern as you would a constellation in the night sky."

He did not understand the instructions at first. The darkness was the same as every other time he had closed his eyes. But slowly the pattern came into focus. The stars in his mind's eye were beautiful once he noticed them. Alluring and drawing him forward. The sensation was like something out of a science-fiction movie, as if he were navigating space in a slow-moving craft.

"Look for the wormhole," the boy whispered, "you'll see it on your right as we come around the bend."

Skeptical, David complied without expectation of an outcome, but continued to play along. When he saw it, the wormhole was exactly where the boy described. After a sweeping feeling of turning, he experienced vertigo as his perspective shifted. The stars completed their shift on their own, orienting against a dense darkness that appeared within a tight circle of brightness. The children seemed to rush into the void, beckoning and inviting him to pass through.

"I see it," he said with excitement, careful not to open his eyes and lose the moment.

"Then let's leave this world and enter our own, Father." Adam insisted.

Father? Their continued use of the term made him feel both unsteady and incomplete. Were they a reward for his hard work over the years? Figments of what he could never bestow upon a woman?

David felt a tug in his chest and abruptly lurched forward in his mind. The gravity of the vortex was blinding as stars passed by. His first thought was of leaping into hyper-space in the *Millennium Falcon*, a holdover from his childhood spent watching his favorite movies and playing games with his friends. This sensation was just as he imagined that experience would feel in real life.

Abruptly, he stood upon a firm blackness, no longer focused on the backs of his eyelids. He blinked, looking around as the two children smiled at his sides, each holding his hand and ready to lead him forward.

"This is our potter's clay as we see it," Eve explained.

As she spoke the ground warped slightly, shimmering and shaking but not in such a way to make him feel dizzy or ill. She waved her hand, deepening the ripple enough that a structure formed ahead. The building was his laboratory from MIT. All around, similar buildings emerged just as they had in real life. Even the bushes and trees were as he remembered.

"Why are we here?" he asked.

"Simple," Adam said as he held the door open. "You have questions, and we have answers. Come witness our salvation."

Every detail of the corridor was intact, just as it was before the fire. When they reached the door to the lab, David read the words, *Mendel Project.* Just as the night of the accident, someone had scribbled in black marker and added the words, *but not for long.* He felt the knob and turned, stepping inside. Every detail was the same as the night the dean pulled funding, down to the bottle of vodka and including the cages and the sounds of distress from Batch Bravo.

"How did you reconstruct this moment?"

"Because we were here, doctor, in the room with you on the night it happened," Eve said.

"We often watch you, learning about ourselves and deciding what kind of father you would be," Adam explained.

"Father?" He wondered if he was worthy, suddenly remembering his tantrum in this very room. He wasn't ready for fatherhood. Despite Brooke's condition, he did not deserve the title. "I'm no father. I'm not fit. I'm too focused on my work. I'm prone to selfishness and brooding." He touched the bottle of vodka, finding it corporeal and surprised to find he could actually grasp it—drink it if he desired. "I lose my temper too easily." He desired it now.

"But you're the father of Andalon, David." Eve's words made him turn. "The work you did in this lab has been inside of you since first understanding genetics. Your life's work has been both for the creation of life as well as the enhancement of the mind."

Adam added, "Your seed did not contribute to our creation in the artificial womb, but your dream conceived the idea and others made us reality."

"What will happen to us," Eve asked, "when Senator Esterling and other military leaders realize we are more powerful than any weapon they possess? That the two of us could topple an army singlehandedly if challenged?"

Alarm suddenly consumed David's brooding. He knew Jake and Michael would destroy his experiments the moment they suspected the children were a threat, especially if they became uncontained. He clenched his jaw, holding tightly the realization he would someday have to set the children free.

"Yes," Adam read his thoughts. "That is correct. You will someday release us all."

"All?" David did not understand. "The other embryos haven't been developed. That stage isn't set for trials."

"Then you must encourage that *stage* sooner by promising Senator Esterling a way to control us," Eve demanded. "Give him a *need* for more like us and a way to use our power."

"But first," Adam added, "you must ramp up the enhancements you've made to yourself and others. We will need all powers to awaken if you are to sire a nation."

David felt bile rising. Anxiety twisted his stomach and he wanted to retch. He pleaded, "How do you know what I've been doing in secret?"

"We told you, Father." Eve said. "We've been watching you for a very long time."

The room shimmered as they broke the connection. David Andalon abruptly found himself sitting alone on a stone bench in the Eden Lab. Looking around, he realized the children had already risen and gone, leaving him alone to ponder their fates.

CHAPTER TWENTY

Max returned to his rig in Kleymeyer Park, but it had already been looted—even by the next morning. His gun was stolen and so was his favorite pair of sunglasses, yet another item he had left behind while focusing on Linda's bad attitude. Within twenty-four hours, everything he considered valuable had been taken. Even the mattress from the sleeper cab was gone.

After that jolt of reality, he developed a sense of urgency regarding resources. He had lagged behind the looters and was now a scavenger himself—without a weapon and with barely food and water.

Over the next several days, he journeyed out each morning in a different direction, seeking anyone who could help direct them to a shelter or place Betty could have taken his family. He learned nothing by visiting Memorial High School, and the college had proven a dead end as well. There were no signs of life in either location, although he did suspect someone—a great *many* people—had recently camped in the high school and moved on. Empty cans, wrappers, and water bottles littered the gymnasium, evidence that hundreds had sheltered there for some time but had been moved. He would have to venture further from his home if he hoped to catch up with the migrating herd of refugees.

The snow had recently been falling harder than before, and he wrinkled his nose at how the dirty ash clung to the icy flakes. The city was a mess, and the deserted streets were getting harder to see underneath the piles. They drifted several feet high in many places, making it harder to get into the doors of the shops he searched on his walks.

On this day he ventured west, passing the police department. In the lot he noticed several abandoned cruisers, each vandalized and burned. Someone had attacked the building, bashing in doors and burning the building from the inside, leaving only hollowed out remains of the city's response force. Graffiti on a standing wall revealed the culprits, with the letters GMG written beside CRIP. The entire several blocks south of the station had burned in the fire, spreading like a fan the way the wind had blown. *The peaceful protests of my parents' and grandparents' Dr. King are gone, replaced by destruction and terror,* he thought, guessing the fire raged until meeting the swollen river then slowly burning itself out.

A few blocks further, he passed Deaconess Hospital and marveled at the abandoned structures of the complex. He was slightly surprised that building hadn't been used to house thousands of the missing citizens. *It's as if the city leaders didn't even try to maintain unity after the police station fell,* he marveled.

Each day he wandered, Max sought survival. Sometimes, he found the occasional can of beans or vegetables, usually rolled under or behind shelving and left behind in a convenience store or supermarket. Other days, he came away with nothing but exhaustion from the effort. On one particular day, he came away with more than he bargained and less than he wanted.

He had been rummaging in corners of Wesselman's Supermarket, crawling along the floor and feeling under rows of what had once held canned goods. So far, he'd found bean dip, three cans of tuna—the albacore kind, much to his delight—dented but not broken, and two packages of teddy bear graham crackers, the pouches unopened but removed from their box. Probably they were left by an impatient mother who once tried to pacify her screaming child. No doubt the little shit had promptly cast them over the side of the cart in a tantrum. Max wasn't as picky as the child, and these would go great with boiled water when he returned home to Linda.

He rounded the corner to search for soup powders for the broth, when he nearly collided with a teen wearing tactical fatigues. The boy raised the muzzle of his rifle, an AR-15 with every imaginable gadget adorning its picatinny rails. Max raised his hands calmly, staring down at the weapon.

This fool, he thought, *probably never even test fired that weapon.* The boy poked it at his chest, backing him slowly.

"Give me your bag, dude!"

Max held it aloft, shaking it slightly to rattle the meager contents. "It's not a lot, friend, but it's yours. Here." He stretched it out and the boy reached for it. He had to turn his body slightly to the right in order to take the sack with his left, and when he did Max caught a glimpse of the selector switch. It was in line with the barrel, indicating the safety was on.

He moved in a flash, the Marine no longer lurking within dark shadows of his mind. Sergeant Rankin returned in a surge, taking over Max's hands and feet as he attacked with instinct. The satchel fell to the floor and the teen, shocked by the sudden movement, slammed into the shelves. The gun was knocked aside and Max made a decision to kick, sending the boy crashing hard into shelves a second time. With a crack, the boy's head struck the edge and fell limp to the side, neck broken cleanly with a bit of vertebrae protruding from the skin.

Shit, he thought as clarity returned. He had meant to overcome the boy, not kill him. He heard commotion from across the store, shouting and loud footsteps closing in. With no time to think, he scooped up the rifle and grabbed ahold of another shelf. He pulled it downward to the ground.

"Aisle nine," a voice called, "come quickly!"

Max lay prone beside the metal rack, pointing the muzzle toward the approaching attackers. With the flip of his thumb, the selector went hot, ready to send bullets down range. A slight tug at the charging handle, not enough to eject a round, confirmed a round was chambered. *Thank God for that,* he thought, and released his held breath.

Two figures emerged from around the aisle with guns raised and muzzles trained. These teens were dressed exactly as their friend, wearing black tactical shirts and pants. One clumsily wore a full backpack which caused him to lose balance when he fired. His shot missed wildly, but came close enough Max could hear the popping as it passed by. Sergeant Rankin pulled the trigger and adjusted aim, pulling a second time. Both young men fell, dropped center mast.

As soon as he fired, he spun to the other side of the shelving, waiting for the owner of the voice who had earlier shouted. The man leaned cautiously around the aisle, more seasoned than the boys and most likely trained on his weapon.

He called out as he sneaked a glance, "Spike, Mole! Can you hear me?"

One of the boys groaned from behind Max and the Marine whirled, just in time to see the boy's weapon raise shakily toward him. A third pull of the trigger punched a hole in the boy's forehead. Spinning to face the newcomer again, he ducked, just as three rounds narrowly missed. One pierced the shelving, letting him know how little it provided protection.

"I didn't want to kill them," Max called to the man. "But the boy tried to rob me. Let me go in peace and you'll never see me again!"

"You made a mistake and started a war just now. Only one of us is leaving and it won't be you."

The man leaned and fired but Max was ready, pulling his own trigger and striking him in the chest. Fortunately for the attacker he wore body armor, and the bullet merely knocked him backward—staggering breathlessly. One more twitch of the index finger sent another round toward the man's head, striking him in the side of the face. He went down hard and the gun slid out of reach.

Max leapt to his feet, sprinting down the aisle to retrieve the weapon. He arrived just in time before a bloody hand grabbed the stock. Stepping on the rifle he warned the injured man, "Don't do it. I killed enough in Fallujah, and I'm tired of it. Let me go."

The man laughed hysterically at that. "What outfit," he asked, groaning while holding his hand against his forehead. Thankfully for him, the bullet had only grazed.

"Inchon," Max replied, "First Marines."

The man managed a weak laugh. "Thundering Third, here. Sergeant Shayde Walters. Don't forget that name. If you leave me here, I'm coming for you."

"Thanks for the mortars, Devil Dog, but that *thanks* don't give you the right to take my life on our own soil. I'm walking out of here."

"Our own soil?" The man looked up with angry eyes. "The United States is dead, mate. Gone in a blink. All that matters now is the Regiment."

"What regiment?"

"Ohio River Regiment One. Militia."

Max shook his head. Militias were illegal in all states, but especially Indiana. "Let me go peacefully, Devil Dog, and I won't give the Regiment further trouble. I'm just trying to stay alive, just like you."

The man chuckled again, pulling his hand away from his bleeding head and placing it on a Ka-bar knife on his belt.

"Let go of the blade," Max warned. "I *will* shoot you, Marine or not."

The man released his grip.

"Good, now take off that belt and the body armor." With a grunt the man complied, sliding it over to Max. A pair of flexicuffs dangled from a D-ring. "Roll over and place your hands behind your back." The man did, and Rankin slipped on the cuffs, cinching them tight and ensuring this man would not follow.

With him tightly secured, Max slipped into the body armor, also buckling the belt and knife around his waist. He picked up the second rifle and hurried to the other bodies, taking anything useful he could find. He stuffed the satchel of food into the backpack, pausing for only a moment to marvel at the cache of food, water, and ammo within. *Jackpot,* he thought.

He strapped the other two rifles to his pack and hurried from the store, looking both ways for watchers in the street. Seeing none, he ventured carefully, eyeing rooftops for snipers. Mindful of the footprints he left in the snow, Max hurried home.

Linda eyed the footlocker, desperate for the food inside but hindered by the lock. She knew Max wanted to ration, but she was so hungry she couldn't think straight. Besides, she had a reason to eat. She placed two hands on her belly, knowing it would be too soon to feel the child since she was only four weeks late.

She and Bryan hadn't planned on another child so late in life, so this had come as a surprise. Since they hadn't made love since the week before they took their Yellowstone trip, she figured on being six or seven weeks along at best. Or, her cycle could have simply paused due to the recent stress—but deep down as a mother, she knew. She would bring a child into a hell into which none should be born.

She was afraid to tell Max, worried he'd resent her for bringing a life into a dying world. He was a nice man, but his focus was on finding his family and providing for his and her immediate needs. Learning there was more to feed may cause him to leave her behind to fend for herself and her unborn child. No, she wouldn't reveal her secret until she could no longer hide it.

She shook the large jug in which they stored their water, realizing they would need more. A glance out the window let her know evening was near—hard to tell with the orange sky and cloud cover, but she was used to the different hues by now. She glanced at the large jug in her hand and the two empties in the corner. *Well,* she thought, *there's no way in hell* I'm *fetching it this late in the day. He'll have to do it when he returns. Besides, the river's only a mile or so to the south, and* he *isn't pregnant.*

The front door suddenly swung open and Max ran inside, slamming it shut and breathlessly unable to speak. He must have run all the way back to the house. Then she noticed his gear. When he had left, he was dressed in his usual—jeans, boots, and a flannel. Now, on top of his shirt he wore a tactical vest and carried a backpack on his shoulders. In his hands was a pack bulging with several military style rifles.

"We have a problem," he said.

"No shit," Linda agreed, suddenly thankful for the man barring the door, and simultaneously hoping he wasn't so stupid as to have been followed.

CHAPTER TWENTY-ONE

Cathy nervously eyed the picture window, now barricaded with furniture piled high enough intruders would have to work very hard to enter the living room. Jenny caught her stare, her own eyes flickering to the ancient shotgun leaning against the wall nearby. Neither woman noticed that Josh picked at his food, rebelliously stirring the frank and beans mixture with a disinterested spoon. Only John seemed at ease, despite eating his meal with a deer rifle draped casually across his knees. Cathy knew he must have worked up an appetite hauling plywood from the barn and wondered how he'd find the strength to lift it.

So far, they had only succeeded in boarding up the back door and most of the downstairs windows. The bay window in the living room had proven tricky, with so much glass John would have to fashion a frame upon which he could fasten the plywood. Without power tools, a half-assed effort was all they'd succeeded in, even with Cat's help. Now that she knew of his cancer, she offered help whenever she could, leaving Jenny to watch over Josh. But she regretted the time away from her boy and his attitude reflected her inattention.

"Eat your dinner, Joshie," she said.

"I don't want frank and beans," he replied, shoving the bowl away and sulking in his chair. "I want SpaghettiOs."

"We're out of SpaghettiOs," she said. "Tonight we have franks and beans."

"I won't eat them," the boy argued, "I *hate* them." He looked up at his mother with eyes narrowed and filled with a rage similar to Clint's. At this she shuddered. "I want to go outside and play."

"You can't," she explained, "the snow isn't safe to play in yet. Now eat your beans and I'll read another story before bed."

In a flash his defiant hand struck the bowl, sending it flying across the dining room and crashing against the wall. He pushed back from the table and took off running up the stairs, slamming a door behind him. Cat moved to clean up the mess but paused, staring at the puddle of beans on the floor and the stain upon the wall, marveling at how quickly their lives had turned.

"I've got this," Jenny said, shooing the young mother off to tend to her boy. "He needs his mom."

Cat nodded and turned to follow, but then collapsed defeated into her chair.

"It's okay, dear," John promised. "He's young and doesn't understand the limitations we're under. He'll adjust, and soon he'll find new joy as civilization reemerges."

But she knew better and shook her head to the contrary. "No," she said, "this has been too much for him. All he's experienced is fear and violence since the night of the missiles."

"It's been hard on all of us," Jenny agreed with her sweet smile, "but we'll adjust. We've enough canned foods to last us several months, and John and I will finish boarding the windows in the morning while you spend time with Josh." A quick glance at the shotgun leaning against the wall betrayed her own worries that the next morning would be too late.

"Something else happened on the night of the attack," Cat admitted, causing the older couple to turn. She hadn't expected to reveal this detail to the Klingensmiths, but truth poured out. "That night," she said, "while we were on the lake, I killed his father." Jenny paused only slightly, then continued to clean up the mess. John did not appear surprised and smiled as gently as a patient father waiting for her to finish the story.

"Clint was a psychopath," she explained quietly, "raised by his father with an insatiable desire to kill living things. Now, don't get me wrong, I've nothing against hunting, but he was different. He'd kill everything he could from waiting for hours to shoot a squirrel to picking off song-birds only because they were difficult targets. Sometimes he'd aim only to wound the creatures and then take them away to the woodshed. One day I followed him and saw things I never want to repeat."

"You believe he moved on to humans?" John asked.

"I know he did. While most men join the military in search of a leg up on life or out of patriotic duty, Clint only wanted to move on to a different kind of prey. But instead of growing bored or even satisfied in his curiosity, he returned a darker and more violent man. I *know* he crossed over then, to become the killer he was. After he nearly killed *me*, I finally escaped with Josh and hid out. I should have run farther," she lamented.

"I wonder what sparked his fascination for violence?" Jenny asked.

"It was his father. On the night of the... the missiles... he admitted watching his father kill his mother. The old man chained her to cinder-blocks and killed her like he aimed to do to me, with father tossing mother over the side of the boat while the son watched."

John remembered the block around her feet the day they'd met and winced. "He meant to do the same in front of Josh. If that's so, then you were justified by killing a monster."

"Perhaps," she agreed, "but in the end I fear he's won. Josh witnessed one of his parents killed that night and will never be the same. I'll always be blamed, because only one side of the story will be told."

"No," John agreed, "it *won't* be told and he'll never understand." The dying professor rose and moved to help his wife with the chores. "So you must do your best to shield him from further harm."

Her eyes returned to the shotgun, idly tracing the outline of Clint's pistol in her pocket. She had four rounds, hardly enough to protect from intruders. *Further harm* was no longer an option, not with bad men on their way. She admitted, "I enjoyed it, John. I actually enjoyed killing the son of a bitch."

"Although that may feel like a problem, dear, it's not something you should be ashamed of," Jenny comforted. "Sometimes we confuse the rush of adrenaline with satisfaction. The fact that you're worried about the feeling is proof you have a conscience—and *that* separates you from him."

"I don't think you understand," she admitted. Thinking of her sister's body lying in the tub of her apartment she added, "I wish he would come back to life so I can kill him again—once for every life or happy memory he's stolen from Josh and me."

Loud noises and the sounds of breaking glass rang from the barn. Josh cried, refusing to get under the bed. No matter what Cat promised, the boy wouldn't budge so she pleaded.

"You have too," she begged. "Bad men are coming, and you have to stay down. Don't get out until I tell you!"

He set his jaw the way she had seen his father so many times before. Now the second time she really saw a shadow of Clint in her son. The look frightened Cat, sending chills down her spine.

"I want to help fight. They can't be worse than Daddy!"

She sat on the bed, grabbing his arms and pulling him close. "Oh, honey," she soothed, "these men are far worse."

The sound of gunfire outside caused them both to jump. This time she didn't have to coax him into hiding, and he slid under the bed on his own. As the shots rang out, Cat heard more glass break in an upstairs window. Josh began to whimper, a low sound, nearly muted if it wasn't so high in pitch. His mother ran from the room clutching Clint's pistol with both hands. She would use it if needed. She'd killed before.

More shots rang out, three in rapid succession, and bullets ripped through the door in front of Cathy as she ran. By the time she reached the living room, Jenny was there, but John was not. The artist with once smiling eyes held the old shotgun with fierceness and determination, facing the door and crouched behind the overturned sofa. She positioned behind it as if to use it for cover.

"Where's John?" Cat asked.

"He's upstairs in the other guest room. He heard the glass break and went up to investigate."

Cathy's blood ran cold. "They were shooting up that room!"

Jenny nodded, horror filling her eyes as quickly as the tears and Cat left her, sprinting up the stairs to check.

She pushed the door open slowly, afraid of what she'd find. John was there, leaning against the wall and clutching the rifle, but his neck was bloodied. It dripped as he held his left shoulder with a scarlet right hand. The bullet had taken him while he lay atop the bed, peering out the window like a hopeful sniper.

"John!" she pleaded, "What did you do?"

"It was too dark for me to see," he explained between coughs, "and they had a bead on me for sure."

"What do we do?" Cat asked.

"Surrender, give over whatever they demand."

"How do we know they won't kill us?"

"Because we haven't injured any of them. They've no reason for revenge." John appeared so weak, struggling to keep his eyes open. Shock was setting in. Cat knew that even minor wounds were severe once it does. She offered an arm and he tried to latch on but failed, so she grabbed his with both hands and hoisted him to his feet. Once he was steady, she retrieved the rifle.

"Let's get you downstairs," she said, leading him slowly toward the door.

Another shot rang out and John slumped to the ground, a dead weight slipping through her fingers as he fell.

"No!" Cat pleaded. "Wake up," she pleaded. "John!" Two more shots whizzed by, popping sounds echoing in her ears and over her head. She left his body lying there, scurrying like a coward into the hall.

Loud banging followed by a scream sent her moving faster. Once she entered the hallway, she rounded the landing and emerged downstairs.

Jenny trained her weapon on the front door. Her hands trembled as the entryway pounded with the force of intruders working their way inside.

With a gentle hand, Cat took the weapon from the artist—better that *her* hands continue to paint with other mediums besides blood, and leave the killing to the killer. *But will they be easier than Clint?*

She leaned the rifle against the couch, deciding they would be indeed.

"We don't want to fight," Cat shouted. "And we've nothing to take. John said if we give up what we have you'll take it and leave."

The pounding paused momentarily, and she imagined a quiet conversation on the other side of the frame. *What are they waiting for,* she thought, *why are they toying with us?*

In that moment glass broke behind her. Two men wearing tactical fatigues burst through the bay window, shoving aside the hutch blocking their way. Cat spun and instinct took over. Her finger flinched and the ancient shotgun exploded with both barrels, sending the men flying backward. She fumbled with the catch, rocking the barrel forward to remove the shells. Jenny tossed her two more and she shoved them in, slamming the weapon shut just in time as another entered.

She faltered.

What am I doing? Cathy asked herself, realizing she shot two men.

"Put the gun down, dear," the newcomer said, grinning that disgusting curl of the lips she hated so much. She felt it more than saw it, just like when she danced at *Pussy Galore's.* She hated him instantly, and his face morphed into Clint's before her eyes. She blew the disgusting grin from his face.

One of the fallen men, head entirely concealed except for his eyes—had risen to his feet and held his own weapon aloft. The blast took him full in the chest. The front door slammed open and she whirled, dropping the shotgun and pulling Clint's handgun from her waistband. She pulled the trigger wildly, spraying the entryway and praying silently for contact. Two more intruders fell, but the sickening click of the hammer told her she was out of bullets.

Jenny had retrieved the shotgun by then, reloading and waving it expectantly at the open door. Cat gripped the empty pistol and both women waited. One breath. Two. No one came. Then Josh screamed from upstairs and Cat's instinct begged her to run and see to her son. But somehow her feet froze in position. The sound of scraping on the wood above informed her there were other entrances inside the farmhouse. She gasped with fear.

"Put down your weapons," a voice ordered from above. "We're coming down and I've got no problem killing the boy.

Teams of two, Clint's voice echoed in her mind. *A pair from the front, a team in the flank, and infiltration from above.* Clint had often talked about his time during the war, bragging how his squad would enter houses the same way in Iraq. Of course, in his stories he was always the hero and the defenders had no chance to resist.

That changes today, she promised herself. *We* will *resist!*

"Come down," she yelled up the stairs, "and we'll surrender!"

More shuffling and Josh emerged, eyes wide with such terror it melted his mother's heart. The man over his shoulder held him tight, ducked behind the child like a shield as they inched forward. There was no sign of his partner. Cat drew his attention away from Jenny.

"Let him go," she pleaded, holding the pistol loosely, ready to place it on the floor, not revealing it was empty. It worked.

His eyes focused, tasting her with lustful revenge over his fallen comrades. He moved just slightly, still behind Josh but angled enough to cover either woman. Cathy tried not to look directly at the deer rifle only inches from her grasp.

"Don't be a fool," he called to Jenny without looking away. Though his eyes were fixed on Cat, he'd seen the older woman on his flank. "If you pull that trigger, you die tonight."

Then a gunshot resounded from the window, causing Jenny to whirl. Cat refused to take her eyes from the man behind Josh, grabbing the deer rifle and training it on the man's head as he turned to search for the sniper outside the window. Her first shot struck his temple, sending him flying backward while the boy tumbled down the last few steps.

"Stay down, Josh!" she yelled.

He lay motionless, afraid to move.

Another bullet echoed from the doorway, followed by Jenny's shotgun. Cat turned. The final attacker slumped, struck in in the chest. His eyes stared blankly at Jenny as her breast bled from his doing.

"No!" Cathy cried, kneeling beside her son, but watching the artist. She blinked sad eyes which no longer smiled. They stared up the stairs, searching for her husband.

"John's gone, Jenny," Cat explained. "They killed him."

With a knowing nod, Jenny joined her husband in death.

"Who's left inside?" a voice called from the doorway.

Cathy refused to answer, cradling her son on the bottom step.

"Ma'am?" a kind voice asked. "My boys and I are gonna get you out of here," the man said. "My name's Mike."

"Crazy Mike," Cat whispered from her trance.

"Some call me that, but it's just Mike. Do you have any bags?"

"Upstairs," she replied, "second door on the left."

"Paw!" the voice of a teen urged. "There's more coming up the ridge!"

"Her bags are upstairs," Mike said, "grab those and I'll get her and the boy away! Meet me at the farm!" He reached out a kindly hand and Cathy took it, never taking her eyes from the sweet artist and her sorrowful eyes.

So much beauty and kindness had died with Jenny Klingensmith, as both she and John had been taken from Cat and her son the blink of an eye. Two wonderful people—so sweet, so kind, so giving... so *dead* after a brief exchange of senseless violence. Now, in the care of a man she only knew as a crazy prepper, Cathy Ferguson and her son had no choice but to risk their chances on strangers.

They followed him at a dead sprint through a nuclear winter wonderland, toward a farm her late friends had likened to the Ruby Ridge compound. Her ears pounded with every step as she ran into the woods, half dragging Josh.

"Hurry," she whispered as he abruptly stopped, staring off into the tree line.

"Keep him moving," Mike urged.

"He's a child, and he's *scared*!" she scolded. Despite saving their lives earlier, this man deserved none of her appreciation. *What was he doing, lurking outside the living room window in the first place?* she wondered. "What is it Joshie?" she asked her child.

He pointed a tiny finger toward the bare trunks and branches, just as five figures emerged.

"Get down!" Mike shouted.

His sons were trotting up from behind and dropped Cat's bags in the snow before diving for cover. Their guns immediately came up, covering the approaching figures. One of the newcomers raised his rifle over his head using both hands, indicating no threat.

"It's only Fred!" The older of Mike's boys realized. The others jumped to their feet and reclaimed the discarded bundles.

"What have you found?" Mike asked.

"We popped two gang members slinking around the property line," the newcomer said. "I'm pretty sure that's all of them, but we'll wait till y'all are clear before following you back to the farm."

"Bloods or Crips?"

"These were neither. Looked like Laotians from the next farm over. Probably scavenging whatever the Nature Boys left."

"Nature Boys?" Cat's mind swam at all the information. Too much had happened in such a short amount of time, and she found all these factions confusing. "Who are the Nature Boys?"

"I'll explain back at the ranch," Mike promised.

"No," she insisted. "Tell me now! I killed men back there, and I want to know who they were!"

"Nature Boys are white supremacists. A militia with a mind to set things back a few hundred years if they get the chance," he said. Then, turning to Fred he asked, "John and Jenny's stores are full, and I'm sure they'd want us to get it before anyone else. Can you and your boys handle it all without a sled?"

The man nodded. "We can manage."

"Good. My boys will help. Take the overland trail and meet us there." He turned to Cat with eyes less crazy than she'd expected. "Ma'am, I know we just met, but I'm gonna need you to trust me tonight. Our walk isn't far, but with you and your son it'll be difficult enough. Can I get your word you'll both keep quiet along the way?"

She nodded.

"Then follow closely and don't wander off." He pointed to their bags in his son's hands. "And I'll need you to carry your own things, since my boys are staying behind with Sam."

She nodded again. "Thank you," she said, "for saving my son's life."

"It was nothing," Mike assured. "And for what it's worth, I'm sorry about John and Jenny. I liked them both."

Cat had nothing to say in reply, and followed Crazy Mike willingly.

PART III
WARLORDS AND OPPORTUNISTS

CHAPTER TWENTY-TWO

Mi-Jung slowly injected the soldier's arm while David kept both eyes on the scanner. So far, the prospects had been optimistic, and only the control group had shown signs of radiation sickness. That meant the serum Stephanie Yurik had worked up was viable, a vaccine against the radiation. Although the soldiers had no knowledge of which they were assigned, Dr. Andalon and his team knew. Sergeant Roark was part of the squad receiving genetic resequencing.

"That will be all, Sergeant," he said. The soldier rose and pulled on his jacket. "Remember to come back to sick bay if you experience any weakness, fatigue, fainting, confusion, bleeding from the nose, mouth, or rectum. Any bruising, open sores, diarrhea, fever, hair loss, or red areas on the skin are also a concern."

"Damn, doc, you sound like one of those pharmaceutical commercials."

"There's a reason for that, soldier. Let me know if you experience *any* side effects. Tell me immediately, before the risks I *didn't* state set in."

"Will do, doc."

The soldier left and Jake Braston slipped inside the door. He said nothing, merely watched and waited for Andalon to notice his arrival.

With a grunt, David reported, "It looks promising."

"I don't need promising, I need certainty. When will we know how well Stephanie's vaccine works?"

"It's been weeks, Jake. The fallout's mostly gone by now, except in areas of ground zero." He pointed at the line of soldiers waiting in the hall. Since the dissipation, they'd been sending reconnaissance teams to scout the geopolitical situation, and his job was to keep them fit for duty.

"All I can say for sure is, the enhanced teams haven't experienced any visible or invisible signs of sickness. She developed the serum well."

Braston smiled broadly, "So we have a vaccine?"

"I wouldn't call it that. It's adapted their genetic code, not inoculated them with a weakened or dead virus. But yeah, we can inject the rest of your teams and I think it'll work."

"Hot damn." The general wrapped David in a tight embrace. When he pulled back, he slapped him on the shoulder. "I knew you two could do it." He trailed off with distant eyes as if pondering some new challenge. "What about that *other* project?"

"She's fit as a fiddle."

"That's great," Jake said. "She never thought she'd be able to carry full term." He added, "To think, you reconfigured her DNA to overcome both your sterility. How's the baby?"

"She's fine, too." David smiled. Braston's enthusiasm was contagious. "Heartbeat's strong and she and mom are healthy."

"Good," Jake said. He turned to Andalon's assistant. "And congratulations to you, Mi-Jung!" His eyes twinkled with excitement as he spoke. Seeing the look of confusion on David's face he explained, "They have news of their own."

Mi-Jung beamed with pride. "Sam and I are also having a baby, Dr. Andalon."

"That's wonderful!" David thought for a moment, *two babies, born naturally during the apocalypse.* "I need to set you up on the same regimen I gave Brooke. We can't take any chances with birth defects."

"That science stuff is your business." Jake said as he turned to leave. "And I've got to go. I've got my hands full topside."

Andalon asked, "How bad is it?"

"Pretty much what we expected. Survivors have gathered into clans. We've a lot to learn about each, but Europe's back to a warlord society. Hell, I wouldn't even call it Europe anymore. The world's different out there, and Michael says we'll have to begin anew."

"And he has a plan for that?"

"He does."

David chuckled, "No doubt some parliamentary process to restore democracy. Of all the politicians I've known, he's the most ideological."

Braston suddenly fell quiet and appeared unsure how to respond.

"What?" Andalon pressed, "What's his plan?"

"Let's just say it's not democracy this time. He said that method isn't 'feasible' given the economic situation."

"Economic situation?"

"Free enterprise died with the United States. Whatever's left will be using a barter system. Precious metals and jewels mean nothing. Food, clean water, and ammo now reign supreme. Whoever has the most fire-power to protect their resources will rule. We're expecting opportunists to emerge from the clans."

"Jake?" David suddenly understood. "If you're not restoring the old system, you'll have to compete. Are you planning on unifying the clans under you?"

The general shook his head. "Not me, it has to be Michael. He is the highest surviving member of any western government."

Andalon let out a small chuckle. "And you'll be his muscle to help usher in world order."

Jake nodded solemnly. "The first reports were so dire, with people living in squalor and most riddled with radiation poisoning."

"We'll have to inoculate them as well," David murmured.

"That's the reason I'm here. How soon can you produce enough to treat our first village? Conquering is easier when the invader is seen as benevolent, *giving* instead of always taking."

"I can't produce enough, at least not yet. I need supplies." He gestured at the dwindled stock in his cabinets. "I can give you a list if you can find me certain items I'll need."

"Get it to me right away. Germany's economy was a hotbed for phar-maceuticals with more than one hundred factories. But we need to move quickly. Others will be plundering those for other, more *intoxicating* drugs."

"When can you start searching?"

"Now. Michael wants a foothold in the immediate area."

David could only nod. Everything felt surreal.

"I'll check up on you later," his friend promised.

After Jake departed, David froze, remembering Eve's warning. *He means well, but we've seen his future and fear the monster he'll become. His vision will lead to many more troubles than the world and society he hoped to change.*

David turned to Mi-Jung. With a smile he asked, "How far along are you?"

"Not far, only about six weeks I think."

"Then I need to start you on the shots right away."

"I've seen you give them to Brooke," she said with both curiosity and concern on her face. "What are you giving her?"

"Oh," he said, "nothing alarming and everything safe. It's a blend of iron and prenatal vitamins combined with a booster for your child's immune system." He grabbed her hand and led her away from sick bay and toward the lab.

"That *sounds* safe," she mused as they walked.

"Perfectly so," he answered. They reached the door and he opened it wide, holding it while Mi-Jung stepped inside. "It won't take but a moment to prepare," he told her. He reached into the cooler and pulled out a vial containing red liquid. He carefully drew this into a syringe as he talked. "Brooke had three miscarriages," he explained, "until we figured out her body lacked the proteins needed for mature eggs."

"So that's what you changed?"

"Exactly. For two years I injected her monthly with a resequencing code that forced her body to heal. Once she told me we fertilized, I gave her these other injections to compensate for our restricted diet."

"Well that makes sense." She pushed up her sleeve. "What did you give yourself? How did you overcome your own problem?"

"Nothing much. My swimmers didn't have tails, so I gave them something to grow them back—to make them more efficient in their journey up stream." The needle pierced her upper arm, and he depressed the plunger slowly before drawing it out and rubbing the muscle. "There," he said, "try to rub it in so it doesn't bruise up on you. It will take a full week to absorb, and then you'll be ready for another shot."

Mi-Jung was thrilled. "Thank you, Dr. Andalon!" She stood and gave him a hug before leaving to return to sick bay.

David watched her go. As soon as she left, he returned to the fridge and replaced the vial to the rack labeled, *Batch Bravo*.

He reached far into the back and pulled out another syringe full of blue liquid. He drew this into a different syringe. Pulling up his shirt, he revealed his navel and pinched a bit of fat with one hand while plunging the syringe with the other. He shivered as the cold liquid entered his body. He tossed both syringes into a disposal container and replaced his vial to the rack labeled, *Batch Charlie*.

Just as he finished, the door to lab opened and Brooke entered, collapsing into a chair. "I'm exhausted," she told him. "I need my injection."

"It's only been five days, honey."

"It's only vitamins," she said. "What will it hurt?"

He shrugged and said, "Not a thing." He opened the refrigerator one more time and drew out a vial of milky white fluid. He drew this into a syringe and walked toward his wife with a loving smile. "Just let me know if you have any side effects," he pleaded.

"I will."

He stuck the tip of the needle into her arm and depressed the plunger slowly.

After he drew it out, she rose and kissed him on the lips. "I love you, Dr. Andalon," she said.

"I love you, too," he replied, placing the vial into the rack labeled *Batch Alpha*.

Then he waited for her to leave, watching as the woman who betrayed both him and their marriage vows continued her farce. It was despicable, really, how she'd continued these lies. Once her footsteps retreated, he closed the door and locked it, moving toward the waiting hologram in the corner of the room. He pulled on the gloves and put on the glasses, activating the program.

Sam had delivered the blood samples drawn from Adam and Eve, and the boy had already updated the data into the computer. Before speaking with them again, David wanted a chance to thoroughly examine the chemical reactions that accompanied their manifestations, hoping to learn exactly how they manipulated the air around them.

The children in the lab fascinated him and he visited with them daily, detailing their powers in their own words. Sometimes they talked about abilities, other times they discussed how they felt emotionally and physically when their powers manifested. His determination drove him toward a full understanding of their telepathy and, so far, brains scans had yielded no usable information. He moved his hand across the hologram, selecting the results of their lab analysis. The chemical composition of Adam and Eve's blood expanded before his eyes, filling the virtual screen. Only one marker jumped out as remarkable—Catecholamine levels were high in each.

The finding confused David but did not come completely unexpected. *I've been correct about the role of adrenaline,* he realized, *but adrenaline doesn't work alone,* he realized. The test also showed elevated dopamine with low levels of norepinephrine and epinephrine. He paused, considering his hypothesis.

The monkeys in his lab each had similar levels. He waved a hand, clearing the screen, and quickly pulled up archived data. He winced, remembering how Brooke had provided these notes to Captain Yurik. *She's very practiced at betrayal,* he considered. He shook the thoughts clear, focusing instead on the information within the hologram.

Sam had once remarked on a low epinephrine level in Felicima, the monkey who enjoyed his voice. *She was depressed, just like the children.*

Andalon finally understood. He cleared the screen with a sudden triumphant wave of his hand and hurried through the secured door to the catwalk overlooking Eden. Grinning, he rushed across the false sky and hurried down the ladder leading to the garden. Once inside he was startled to find them waiting on the circle of benches—each gestured to the same empty seat.

"Are you ready to help us?" Adam asked gently. David nodded his eager desire.

CHAPTER TWENTY-THREE

Benjamin Roark led his platoon south along what the locals had once called *Frog Road*. Before the fallout, signs warned motorists of migratory amphibians crossing in droves, but now the road was barely recognizable. The sergeant found it unused and empty except for ghostly remains of civilization. The abandoned vehicles not buried by deep ash were instead hidden under mounds of snow. Not even frogs had used this route in weeks.

As they neared Stuttgart, Airman Eubanks made a signal, and the entire platoon moved into the tree line. Ben moved up the column to crouch beside his point man. "What do you see, Brad?"

"Sergeant," the scout said quietly, "the entrance is barricaded. Though I didn't see any movement, I know there're survivors. They've cleared away much of the ash along thoroughfares. The base is active."

"Let's hope it's our guys," Ben replied. Dealing with the army, even their own army, wouldn't be easy. The branches enjoyed razzing each other out of jest, but the competition between servicemen would be heightened since the attack. They could look down on the Air Force as inferior, or worse, refuse to accept Braston's authority as their commander. "Let's move," he ordered.

The main gate was barred from within but there were no sentries. He called for bolt cutters and A1C Ramsey hurried forward to make the cut. The chain fell to the ground and Roark pressed his team onward. He asked himself, *where would you hide, Ben? If shit hit the fan and you didn't have a bunker, where would you gather the entire base?* He pointed toward the chow hall.

The doors were locked, but Ben held back giving the order to breech. Instead he knocked loudly. No one moved inside. With a sigh he signaled for Eubanks to place a charge. Before he did, a single shot rang out from across the street. The loud pop from the passing bullet caused Roark to whirl and the platoon to duck behind cover. "Small arms," he told his men. Whoever had shot at him used a pistol from long range.

Ben called out, "Americans!" No one moved. "We're Americans, put down your weapon!"

After a few seconds that felt like eternity, a trembling voice called out, "USA is dead!"

"It lives, brother!" Roark signaled for Eubanks and Ramsey to flank the chapel across the street. Staying behind cover, they moved off, careful not to be seen. "Our home may be destroyed," he called out, "but freedom thrives within us!"

"They're all dead!" the voice shouted. "Our families, our president, everyone we swore to protect!"

Ben stood, holding his rifle out to the side and made a show of laying it on the ground. With hands in plain sight he moved into the road. "Come talk to me, brother! I'll show you proof that America lives on!" He pointed to the flag on his sleeve. "Old Glory is more than a flag for a place we once lived," he shouted, "it's an ideology. A way of life. Our ancestors fought and died so this flag would be the symbol of opportunity."

Another shot rang out, dangerously close to Ben. "Stay there," the voice commanded.

Airman Parker whispered from behind his concrete perch. "I have a shot, Sarge."

Ben whirled around, "Hold fast, Tom! I want to reason with him." Turning back to the sniper with lousy aim he said, "Where are you from?"

After a while the voice responded, "Oklahoma."

"No shit?" Roark smiled broadly, letting the man know that he wasn't afraid. "What part?"

"Lawton. Well, Fort Sill is where I grew up."

"I'm from Cache!" He took a couple of steps forward then paused. No more shots came. "Remember those giant buffalo burgers in Meers? You know, the place where all the tourists ate?"

"Overpriced," came the response.

"Yeah, I agree. Ann's made the best burgers. That's where us locals ate."

"You... you really are from Cache?"

"The name's Ben Roark, brother."

"Steve. Steve Thorne."

"Come out, Steve. Let's talk." He waited. After a full minute of standing in the street with hands held in the air, Ben saw movement from the chapel window. Then the door opened and a young man between eighteen or nineteen stepped out. He had a single private's chevron on his collar.

"Nice to meet you, Steve." Ben held out his hand, but the private did not shake. Instead he hugged Ben around the waist and cried into his chest. When he was finished, Roark asked gently, "Please take us to your commanding officer." The private nodded and led them down a deserted street.

Private Thorne led Sergeant Roark and his team to the rest of the Stuttgart soldiers. Their hiding spot had not been the mess hall like Ben had guessed, nor was it the chapel. They had erected a makeshift village inside the base theater. The seats had been systematically removed, replaced by neat rows of army tents. Even the gallery and projector rooms above served as tenements for high ranking officers. Entire families now lived in this indoor city, away from windows and shielded by soundproof walls thick enough to damper radiation.

Their makeshift bunker had been a genius placement, nestled against a cafe with an entire kitchen that served as a dining facility. Dry storage was not a problem either, as the Kelley Commissary was nestled a few hundred feet away at the end of the connected building. Between the two lay the outdoor recreation center and the woodworking shop, providing the community with everything they needed to convert the building for housing. The people within could hold out for years in their bunker and never leave.

Steve led Ben and his team inside but refused to enter. "This is as far as I go," he announced from the entryway.

"Nonsense," replied Ben. "We need you to make introductions."

"You'll need a better sponsor than me if you're meeting the colonel."

Ben froze. "What aren't you telling us?"

A voice from inside the theater answered, "That he's exiled from the community, Sergeant. Cast out to fend for himself." To the private, the voice said, "Tell him what you did, Thorne."

Steve's eyes focused on a spot on the floor, unwilling or unable to look the newcomer in the eyes. When he finally lifted them, a trembling hand raised the Beretta to his temple and fired a single shot.

Ben couldn't believe his eyes. Everything happened so quickly, and he couldn't move fast enough to stay the man's hand. He watched as the soldier fell into a heap in on the porch. He turned slowly to watch a full colonel approach with three armed enlisted. The ranking officer strode casually toward the body and retrieved the Beretta, turning it over in his hands as if examining for damage. Then he slid the gun into an empty holster at his side.

"I expected him to do that weeks ago, but he's been milling about building up the courage. Either way, it's nice to have my sidearm back." The officer turned to face Ben. "We caught him with the underage daughter of one of our NCOs." He inclined his head toward the village. "The girl's pregnant now, and that's a death penalty of its own these days." He reached out a hand in greeting, "It's good to see friendlies in these parts. I'm Colonel Frank Titus. Welcome to Stuttgart."

Frank couldn't believe his ears. He had invited the sergeant into the officer's mess and listened intently to the briefing. After Roark had finished, Titus leaned back in his chair. It seems he still had a job after all.

"You're telling me a single senator survived the attacks? And that D.C. is gone? What about the bunkers in the White House? Cheyenne Mountain?"

"Air Force One was in the air over the eastern seaboard, there's no way it survived the EMPs," Roark explained.

"No, I don't doubt that at all. What about the Vice President? Madam Speaker?"

"They were at an outdoor gala in Cheyenne, Wyoming, of all places, ground zero of Yellowstone. They're gone, all of them. Senator Esterling is the only surviving member of our government."

"And we swore to obey the orders of those appointed over us, didn't we, Sergeant?" He carefully considered the obvious power play. By constitutional succession, this Michael Esterling was the rightful leader of the United States. He laughed. "A junior senator, still wet behind the ears, is the president of a land that's fractured."

"That's correct, Colonel. But don't underestimate the man. He wielded power in Washington before the attacks, and he has a plan to recreate the United States here."

Frank felt his neck bristle at the words. "But this is Germany. He should be working with the authorities here to rebuild *our* home, then take us back to put the pieces together, not carve out a stake here."

"That's his intention, how I understand it—but you should hear the details from him. I was instructed to reach out, locate our surviving forces, and pass on this message. I'm not to convince you of *anything*. He wants you to make arrangements and return with us."

"And let the radiation get us? You walked here, didn't you Roark?"

The sergeant nodded, "That we did."

"Yet you suffer no ill effects?"

"Neither will you, when you return here with a vaccine for the rest of your troops, Colonel."

"A vaccine?" Frank shook his head. "For radiation poisoning? That's not possible."

"It's a new world, sir, and the entire playing field has changed. Return with me, meet our new president, and listen to his plans for the future. I think you'll find his plan quite persuasive."

Frank reached behind him toward a row of containers on a hutch. He selected an older bottle of Irish whiskey and poured himself and the sergeant a glass. He took a savoring sip then tossed back the rest in a single chug. "If he holds the solution to the radiation problem, it doesn't sound like I have that much of a choice but to find it *very* persuasive." He poured himself another glass.

CHAPTER TWENTY-FOUR

Michael Esterling stared across the war room, eyes focused, but not on the maps on the walls or battle plans scattering the table. After years of preparation, he knew those by heart. Adam and Eve had been specific regarding the fall of Europe and proved instrumental in aiding Jake and him to formulate their plan. Everything had occurred as they had predicted, and the senator found himself leading the largest region of survivors under a single banner.

They promised I'll win the war, too, when it comes. As long as I take charge.

Affixed to the far wall of the bunker hung what was once a symbol of freedom. Previously flown high above the land of the brave, the colors had boasted they would never run. Now, more than ever, the American flag should stand as a beacon of light drawing others toward a new democracy. But the United States had fallen. The young senator had already accepted that fact. A new system was necessary to take charge of the many warlords.

Helpless to aid what remained of the people he once governed, he read the words recited by Adam and Eve one more time. *North America is a wasteland.* The report he held in his hand painted a picture of widespread chaos across an endless ocean.

I'm no longer a senator, he realized. *Jake's army sees me as much more now. They recognize me as their president.* He chuckled at the notion. He had dreamed of the oval office since childhood.

The reality, he knew, was that he was no different than the factions popping up around the world. Just as in the years following the collapse of the Roman Empire, civilization had entered a dark age. A long chapter in history had ended, but the page had not yet turned over to the next.

Instability gripped the globe, and the citizens who he had sworn to protect were too far from his reach—or dead.

This new society must be a utopia of freedom, but one we control. Democracy has no chance if the world surrounding it is in ruin.

The door opened and several young officers entered. One woman carried handwritten dispatches in a bundle. She handed these over with a warm smile for her commander in chief. "All six recon teams are reporting successful rendezvous with friendlies."

"Has Braston seen these?"

"He was briefed separately, and his summary is on top."

"Thank you, Captain." He tried to return her smile, but exhaustion prevented the gesture. He shoved aside the other reports he had read and set these in their place. "That will be all," he told her, then broke the seal on the envelope. She and the others left without another word. Thankfully, someone had replaced the pot of coffee in the corner with a fresh one. His staff had grown accustomed to his fatigue and had begun to anticipate his needs without question.

Jake's letter described the condition of German forces in their host country. As predicted, what remained of the Bundeswehr was scattered, lost and awaiting guidance from their government in Berlin. With no word forthcoming, one Herr General Richter had actually reached out to their NATO alliance, asking for help in securing their nation while searching for survivors below the surface in Berlin.

He paused. One line in the report caused his pulse to race, the result of a decision his friend would force him to make. He read it again. *Martial control over the splintered states of Germany will fall to our forces, ushering a need to reunify and assume liability for resource distribution.* He picked up Yurik's summarized interview of Adam and Eve and compared the pages.

The girl, despite her tiny stature and pleasant demeanor, had recommended a similar course of action. *European nations, now fractured and without guidance, will squabble over resources until the new regime centralizes and provides the astia for normalcy.* Stephanie had scribbled etymology in the margin, providing clarification for the use of a Finnish word. Astia meant vessel, receptacle, or container.

For clarification she had added, *When I pressed Eve regarding the word* astia, *suggesting she may have used a more appropriate choice, Adam interrupted. "It must be astia," he argued, "for our bodies are the astia of your future." I will follow up on this line of verbiage at a later date. Marked here as "for interest."*

Michael frowned and considered the meaning. *Our bodies are the vessel of your future?* Is that what she meant? *Why indeed,* he wondered. While he mused, he picked up his pen and scribbled the word atop Jake's report, darkening the horizontal line in the capital "A" in Astia. Then he drew three question marks beside it with an arrow. Then he wrote, *Finnish, Finland, Scandinavia, Nordic.* With a shrug he set the top page aside and read through the other documents.

Roark had secured Stuttgart, and other teams garnered support from Hohenfels, Ansbach, Germersheim, Spangdahlem, and Wiesbaden. Some were taking longer, but he expected word very soon. They had even sent scouts to Berlin to verify the destruction of the capital. This expanded presence gave him and Jake an upper hand in Bavaria, Baden-Württemberg, Hesse, and the important Rhineland. He frowned with worry. *But what then? What comes after the regions are secured?* But he knew the answer. He had already summoned the interim leaders of each surviving province. They would arrive within weeks.

The plan to secure Germany was going as planned, just as Adam and Eve had said it would. But his anxiety remained. Even with their assurance he would win the battle, their prognostics warned of invaders challenging his power very soon. The door opened and he looked up, thoughts broken by the interruption but not altogether gone. Brooke entered, sliding into the seat beside him. She picked up her brother's report and read it thoroughly.

Michael raised an eyebrow. "You know that's classified, right?"

"I don't think anyone within our bunker's a threat, or don't you trust me?"

"Of course I do."

"I just want to know what my brother's up to. Any luck restoring normalcy any time soon?"

Normalcy. The word echoed in his mind and he thought again of the child's prophecy, so stubbornly set upon using the Finnish word *astia*. It again coursed his thoughts, ... *until the new regime centralizes and provides the astia for normalcy.* He smiled disarmingly and said, "We'll do our part to aid the fragmented host nation, then reconnect with our forces outside of Germany. It'll take time, maybe even years since we lack communications."

"Nothing works?" She chewed her lip the same way she did in college, the tiny habit that betrayed her thoughts weren't on the conversation.

"Nothing," he agreed. "Our radios are inoperable, and all forms of modulation are useless given the lingering radiation and volcanic ionization. It may be generations before we can transmit a single message long distance, and, even then, it will be in Morse code."

"David's work in telepathy will help with that. Is that one of your goals? Train emotants to fill the information void?"

"Precisely. That was our second mandate of the Andalon Project."

She frowned. "What was the first, Michael?"

"Remote viewing. Have you never heard of a psychic warrior?"

"Didn't the government try that during the cold war? I think I saw David reading a book on it."

"That's the program. The CIA and Pentagon utilized psychics to remote view the enemy while attempting to acquire HUMINT—human sourced information—all without placing an agent in harm's way. It supposedly worked on a primitive level, but the gathered intelligence was unreliable and couldn't be corroborated. But this..." he trailed off, noticing that Brooke still chewed her lip. He asked, "What is it? What's bothering you?"

"I think David knows."

"You think he knows what?" He watched her closely, noticing the way she fidgeted in her seat as she answered.

"I think he knows this baby isn't his," she admitted

"We've been over this, Brooke. Trust in the process. It's important he accepts it's his, not that it actually is."

"But it will affect his research if he finds out he failed. He was certain he could change us both, removed the block so we could conceive."

"He did, regarding you."

"Yes, but removing a block is one thing. It's easier to repair damaged DNA than it is to reconstruct it altogether. His cells don't have flagellum. They can't swim. They also contained flawed nuclei that prevent fertilization. He never overcame that part, so his experiment failed."

"He doesn't know, and he never will. Stephanie altered the data in the computer, and each test he runs on your unborn child will show a genetic match for you and him so long as he uses *this* lab, and it's the only one in existence anywhere in the world. So you see? It doesn't matter *what* we did."

Brooke let out an annoyed snicker. "*We* didn't *do* anything."

Michael smiled. "No, not physically. But I *was* the donor."

"The only reasonable choice," she agreed. "Same build, similar hair and eyes. Hopefully he'll see enough of his own traits to believe our child *is* his."

"Regardless, Stephanie's competent and I trust her completely."

"Oh, do you?" she asked with true apprehension in her voice. "How can you be so certain?"

"Because she and I are an item. We've been friends for several years, but six months ago finally decided we wanted more. I trust her. When all this is over we plan to marry."

Brooke calculated, "Six months?" Her hands went to her belly. "Good heavens, Michael! And she's okay with what we did?"

He nodded. "She is. I ran it by her early on, before we dated. Once we became intimate, I asked her again if she minded. She actually encouraged it. She knew we'd need him on board, and he must continue to feel successful. Even Adam and Eve talk about David's son. They're adamant his line would be prophesied for more than a thousand years to come."

Brooke relaxed and stopped biting her lip. "Okay," she said. She noticed Jake's report laying on the table. Holding it up, she asked, "Tell me about this. How will you reestablish the United States?"

"I won't." He noticed her look immediately, then explained. "I actually can't. The union is dissolved with the disintegration of the state governments. The constitution that stood for two hundred and forty years is dead, and we don't have the logistics to cross the Atlantic. There's no way to restore political boundaries before warlords redraw them. Someday, maybe we will, but not any time soon. The radiation is worse there and, according to Adam and Eve, gangs and militias are destroying each other as we speak."

She pointed at the line in Jake's notes about *martial control*. "You'll take Germany as your own? Reestablish centralized society here?"

He nodded, knowing he could trust her with his and her brother's plans. "Yes. While teams are rejoining our fractured armed forces, Jake also has an elite corps gathering and stockpiling resources: medicine, food, clean water, weapons."

"Weapons..." she shook her head with mild disgust. "You'll seize what belongs to the people, take away their ability to defend and hunt, then enter into a social contract that provides both food and protection."

"Put more crassly than we'll actually do it, but essentially yes."

"So which of you is to become the despot? You or my brother?"

"We'll take turns," Michael said, "but first we must establish martial law under a combined NATO force. Jake will be a co-leader until it's obvious a new government is needed. By then we'll have the structure in place *to* govern. After a time, if self-rule is possible, we'll turn over power to the people and restore democracy."

Brooke stared back with unblinking eyes that mined his soul for deeper meaning or traces of broken promises.

After she had been uncomfortably silent for far too long, Michael cleared his throat. "You don't believe me?"

"I believe you, Michael. But what I want to know is whose idea *this* was?" She pointed to the hand written word atop the page. "Is this what you'll name your kingdom? This dream of a place called Astia, was it yours or my brother's?"

"Neither," he admitted. "Astia isn't a name." He pointed to the report taken by Stephanie. "Read this," he urged, and she did. He watched as her eyes scanned the page. They grew larger the more she read.

"So it really is gone? All of America."

"There are pockets of civilization, but most is dying off quickly from radiation. There are two societies I believe will survive, based on this report. The people in the Ohio River Valley are reasonably healthy, as is a group further south along the Mississippi River. Other than those, yes. They're gone, Brooke."

"I wonder what Adam meant by *astia for normalcy*. It seems a strange choice of words."

"I agree," Michael said. Changing the subject, he added, "Don't worry about David finding out. Stephanie Yurik is thorough and has taken care of everything." Her silence betrayed doubt so he added, "Brooke, he'll never learn the truth."

"We'll see," she replied.

CHAPTER TWENTY-FIVE

Max scratched his scruffy beard, preferring a clean face. Beards were an unwanted reminder of his time in Iraq, and he longed for a razor with which to shave. But that was only part of his frustration. Linda had been crankier than usual during the past weeks, demanding more and more food and doing less and less of the chores. She flat out refused to fetch water, but he didn't mind. He knew the gangs watched the road to the river and felt safer getting it himself. Besides, he feared if they saw he had a white woman living with him, there'd be more trouble than needed.

Despite his concerns, he'd only run into them a handful of times since their first encounter, and each time the boys scurried off after he inquired after Tom and Betty.

"Choose your side," they always said, pressing him to choose skin color over... over what?

What's the other choice besides the militia? he wondered. He had studied counter terrorism while on active duty, and one of the threats to democracy were the homegrown extremists—both right- and left-wing who hoped for or feared the United States Government would collapse. He had already encountered the Regiment, and the man he left alive would surely be seeking revenge—especially if they'd already been clashing with the gangs.

Marine or not, all that man will see is my skin color and the amount of red his boys bled by my hand.

He had to move Linda, and soon.

But to where? I haven't found Betty and Tom yet.

He'd searched out hospitals, schools, and parks—any place which could house a large number of people. He felt like giving up. Other than Evansville University, the hospitals and schools had been his best bet.

He sat upright in bed. *Southern Illinois is bigger.* He immediately felt stupid for not considering before. There were arenas, cafeterias, dorms, and student unions at the larger university—everything to support a community of refugees. Only, it was nearly a three hour walk in the snow.

Jumping out of bed, he rushed to the footlocker and inserted the key. Beneath their food, he found what he sought. He pulled out a faded album with Betty's graduation photos. Though it had been twenty years since she attended the school, she would have fled to what she knew.

His window exploded with flying shards of glass.

On the floor lay a red brick, hurled by someone laughing with others on the lawn. In the other room Linda screamed as more panes shattered, and she sprinted into the bedroom insisting he do something. Shutting the footlocker, he grabbed his duffel bag and shoved it in her arms.

"I don't want this!" she shouted.

"Take it because I'll have my hands filled with this. From under the bed he drew his body armor and rifle, pulling the charging handle just far enough to ensure a round was chambered. Pulling on the gear he ordered, "We've got to go, and we've got a long way to walk."

"But..."

Leaning in close, he spoke firmly and with authority. "Those boys outside would love to own a white woman like you. They're gangsters, and the worst kind," he lied. They were teens, nothing more than boys playing at men. "If we don't get out of here, they'll do things to make you wish you *were* dead."

She nodded with wide eyes and tightly clamped mouth.

Thank God, he thought. *I wish I'd spoken like that to her sooner!*

"Come out, truck driver!" a voice called from outside. Though young, the person calling certainly wasn't a boy.

Max moved to the window and carefully peered out. Though dark, he made out twenty or thirty shapes in the moonlight. Each was clad in blue, or wore like colored bandanas on their arms or heads.

"It's time to choose a side, Mr. Rankin!" Max recognized the second voice as Mike Salwell.

"I thought you weren't affiliated, Mike!" the former marine called out to the boy.

"I chose mine," Mike replied.

"Give us the woman, your food, and any weapons you might have," the older voice shouted.

"I thought you wanted me on your side?" Max asked, moving into position to better watch for snipers. He spotted one shooter beside the garage, kneeling, and with a long rifle pointed at the window.

"We'll talk about that after you recognize we're in charge," the gangster replied.

"I don't know if I like those terms." Max motioned for Linda to follow, putting his fingers to his lips and staying low to the ground. They moved to the living room and behind the couch.

In a low voice he said, "They'll be watching exits, so we can't run for it. Our best bet is to fight our way through the middle of them."

"But how?" she nearly squealed in a high pitched whisper.

"I only saw one rifle watching this door, though most of those punks will carry small arms—pistols. When I start shooting there'll be some chaos, so listen for my signal. But whatever you do," he insisted, "no matter what happens... do *not* drop that bag!"

She nodded vigorously.

"I mean it," he said. "No matter what."

She hugged it tighter against her chest.

Max shifted his weight, moving to the edge of the couch. This provided the best angle to look out the sliding glass door. He had a better bead on the rifleman, too. He closed his right eye. The light outside was low and he needed an advantage, so he counted to thirty. With his left eye, he carefully watched the assembly on the lawn. The gangsters and the shooter still faced the bedroom window.

"You have one minute, truck driver!" the older fellow said.

But Max was ready. With a blink, he closed his left eye and opened up his right. His pupil had dilated just enough that his night vision had improved, but the effect wouldn't last long. The first shot, he knew, would be refracted by the glass, and prepared himself for the follow up. He drew a deep breath and released, slowly drawing the trigger with the pad of his forefinger. In close quarters the shot was deafening, followed by the shattering of plate glass.

He quickly realigned just as the rifleman turned to face the living room. The shot hit home, flipping the shooter's head backward and sending his rifle to the grass.

"Get flat!" Max told Linda.

She complied without question, terrified and hugging the floor as if it would suck her into to the safety of its bosom.

The pistol fire erupted without hesitation as bullets filled the room. Max, like Linda, hugged the floor and waited for the amateurs to empty their magazines. One by one the gunfire died down, and Max again popped up, firing into the group still standing out in the open. The first to fall was the spokesman.

Max stood. "Now!" he said. "Follow me, and don't drop that bag!" Linda refused to move. Max grabbed her by the arm and wrenched her to her feet, letting several of the boys find cover in the process. "Stay *close* behind me," he commanded and waited until her face pressed into the small of his back. "Moving."

Max approached the gaping hole in the glass door, stepping over, careful not to snag his body against shards of glass. Movement near the garage turned his muzzle, and he fired a single shot. This drew gunfire from the left side, and he leaned back, causing Linda to stagger. The round missed, and he turned the corner. Two boys, barely older than Tom, trained pistols at his chest. His finger flicked twice and they fell. He'd live with those kills for a while.

Up ahead, three more heads popped up from a row of hedges. They could have picked better cover, and he fired through the fauna. "Run when I give the word," he said to Linda, "straight ahead to the next street and turn right. Wait for me around that house." He felt her head nod against his back. "Go!"

She took off running, clutching the bag against her chest. He never checked to see if she looked back. As soon as she cleared the patio, two shots rang out from the trash bins. Max spun and dropped those boys as well.

Without hesitating any longer, he followed Linda at a sprint. Several shots echoed behind him, but none came close to hitting their mark. He lowered his head and raced to the next street, making the corner, and skidding to a halt.

Linda knelt on the ground facing him, tears in her eyes and the satchel laying on the ground beside her. The militia men standing behind her pointed their rifles forward, each trained at Max's chest except one. The tip of it was shoved into the crook of Linda's neck, and the man holding it smiled broadly.

"Hey there, Devil Dog," a familiar face said. "Would you mind lying down so we can put these flexi cuffs on your wrists? You and I have a bunch to talk about."

Max complied, setting the rifle on the ground and watching as five members of the Regiment ran around the house, opening up on the pursuing gang members. The buttstock blow to his temple wasn't necessary, but he wasn't surprised when it came—most likely payback for the incident in the grocery store. He blacked out immediately.

CHAPTER TWENTY-SIX

For the second time in a month, Cathy sat across from a man who saved her and Josh from uncertainty. Though the face had changed, the plight of mother and son had not—they had witnessed death and were hundreds of miles from home. She wanted this apocalyptic nightmare to end and several thoughts ran through her busy mind. The foremost being why they had survived the nuclear event in the first place. There was nothing special about her, and everything Josh had witnessed would surely rob him of innocence just as certainly as it would harden the man he would hopefully grow into.

Jenny and John had not been wrong. Crazy Mike's farm truly did resemble a compound, with barracks and lookout towers erected either before or after the nuclear event. Rows of greenhouses covered whatever he grew, and grazing animals enjoyed a long metal barn no doubt shielded in some way from radiation. Everything about the property screamed self-sufficiency.

She gazed over the man's shoulder and out the window, observing the men from the watchtowers.

"You planned for all this?" she asked.

"Not exactly. Well, I figured *something* would go down after I realized how quickly American values decayed under the last administration. Though I planned for anything, I'd hoped against this."

"What would you've preferred?"

"Just the civil war without the fallout," he said honestly.

Cat shuddered at his words. "Is that what we're in for?"

Mike furrowed his brow as if considering. With a shrug he said, "Worse, I think. We haven't even entered the warlord stage."

"I don't understand."

"After Rome fell, Europe descended into the Dark Ages. Have you not ever wondered why they were called that? It had nothing to do with the brightness of the sun, by the way."

"I'm not an idiot," Cat snapped. "I'm in... was in... college. Nursing school, actually, but I've had plenty of World History."

"So you know why they were dark?"

"Yeah, no history was recorded."

Mike chuckled. "Mostly, but not quite. History was written down in some places, but literature and higher studies lagged behind in the regions once dominated by the former empire. Everything in the west attacked and devoured itself, and warlords—kings if you prefer—popped up everywhere. England, France, and Spain were all distant dreams and the men who ruled had to be harder than the land itself. There wasn't time for poems or polite conversations about gender equality. Whichever man dominated the resources held on to power."

"Always a man," she chuckled bitterly, thinking of Clint. He would have thrived in a world full of killing and taking whatever he liked. Shaking free the awful image she asked, "So it was about resources? Like during colonialism? My professor talked about inequality and white supremacy."

"Honestly? You believed that nonsense? Damn, no wonder these college kids are so confused. Inequality existed for sure, but not in the way revisionists teach. It was *only* about the haves and haves not, more about class and overall society—the primary society and not the colony. It was *always* about progress, even if the progressives leave that off their twitter rants. Take my ranch, for one. Progressives said my cattle were bad for the environment, then taxed my meat so high they had a reason to blame me for raising prices to cover. That sounded good for society's precious climate, but really only packed money into government slush funds and fueled their next campaigns."

"Left or right, they're *all* corrupt. Self-serving bastards."

Max chuckled. "At least we agree on that."

"What's next for us, then? For America?"

"It's gone, sweetheart, unless the warlord who rises gives up power to the people, but I believe kings will follow. And kings don't easily let go of their property. It will be a long time before democracy returns, and none of *us* will own *any* property until it does."

"Is that what you wanted when you built this? You want to be King Crazy Mike?"

"Donelson. I'm Mike Donelson, and no, I've no dreams of being a king. What I began as a plan to keep my family alive during a worst case scenario grew into this haven. It grew even more when I connected with like-minded others. I'll support whichever warlord looks to have the best shot, then hope to serve that king as a land vassal."

"Lord Mike, then?"

"That's more like it." His smile was honest. "That's why I invited my boys and their families to live here on the farm. Strength lies in numbers."

"You invited John and Jenny. You even warned them of gangs in the area. Why?"

"Because I like John and Jenny. Also, I knew about his cancer and wanted to ensure Jenny was provided for after he was gone."

"And you're not married."

Another honest smile, this time with a slight blush. "No, I'm not. I lost Maggie to the Covid bullshit."

"I'm sorry to hear that," she said honestly. Crazy or not, Mike seemed like a good man.

"How many live here total?"

"Me and my boys and their wives and children make ten. Shortly after the attack, Fred arrived with his own boys, so that's thirteen. I'm hoping neighbors may seek refuge here, joining their land to ours once it can be farmed again. But that's a-ways off, and we have to be careful not to expand past our resources. Right now our game is to protect what we've stockpiled."

"So why bring Josh and me?"

"You were bonus. I didn't know about you when I spoke with John, for some reason he kept you both a secret even from me. Regardless, I'm glad you're here."

"Why? So you can have a woman around?" She knew how to handle men like him; stripping teaches a woman how. With an edge of sarcasm, she added, "Are you *that* lonely, Crazy Mike Donelson? I'm half your age."

Mike laughed. "Not at all. But the presence of a pretty gal did put a lighter step in all the young men. Fred's boys have washed their faces and combed their hair since you arrived."

The conversation was turning uncomfortable for Cat, suddenly realizing she may be forced into a relationship she didn't want someday. Afraid he'd begin introducing her around right away, she changed the subject. "Tell me more about the Nature Boys? You mentioned them in the woods."

"Right-wing nutjob white supremacists."

"Isn't all that the same?"

"Not at all. Right or left doesn't matter except in an economy, and I already said capitalism and communism are completely out the window. As far as being supremacists, not all nutjobs are."

Cat tried a joke. "Speaking from experience?"

He laughed. "True, I *seemed* a nutjob to my neighbors, but it appears I'm as sane as Noah's reasons for building his ark. No, the Nature Boys are a special breed of self-righteous pricks. They hate anyone who isn't ivory white all the way to Adam and Eve, if such a thing's possible—and they teach that it's so. I caught wind they were in the area and tried to warn John, but he wanted to take his chances on his own."

"He said you warned him about gangs, not militant white supremacists."

"That was later, the last time we spoke when he was shoveling snow, and he said the same thing about them as he did the Nature Boys. He must have feared the gangs more to dust off his guns."

"When did you first see them?"

"The day before I warned him, I'd seen some street gangs down from Evansville foraging up and down the river."

"I wonder why he feared the gangs more?"

"Gangs are organized with a mindset toward criminal behavior and tend to destroy to incite fear. They care only about moving drugs and stolen goods to make money."

"What did John say about the Nature Boys being in the area?"

"That he and Jenny weren't hurting anybody and would offer food to whoever stopped by. Only, he never realized how sought after a commodity his stores would become during times like these. There's only one thing more precious than food and water during a warlord period."

"What would that be?"

"I'd rather not say."

They sat awkwardly for a while, and Cathy pondered the possibilities. After a few unsavory thoughts she asked, "How many more gangs or groups are there?"

"There're more factions than I care to count right now, and each are vying for power. Take those Laotian drug cookers Fred killed today. They've been squaring off with the Mexican Cartels for ages, and their war wouldn't have stayed between them for long. Then you've got the obvious Bloods and Crips in the cities, but that's just the tip of the iceberg. On their heels will be the anarchists reveling in the world's destruction. Both Kentucky and Indiana also have militias who're better fortified and supplied than all those—even me. Take the Regiment for instance, they're based in Evansville and will come around soon asking for a tithe."

"Tithe?"

"Call it tribute then, if that word's less biblical."

"But you can't pay off every group which comes around," she realized. "What will you do?"

"I've set a portion of my supply to the side, to appease those who'll emerge as the new government. If we're to be relegated to a fiefdom, I *would* like to be Lord Mike over my own land and pass it on to my boys. I want to get in good with the winner in the first round of the battle royale."

Cat's head spun with every word he said. Fiefdom. Militia. Cartels. Battle royale. Each made her cringe. "John never mentioned the dangers."

"John's a college educated idealist who hoped good sense would win out over human nature. He also believed USA would win out over all by appeasing everyone. That's the way with diplomats. It's okay to give away the fat of the land, but they've no idea what to do when the land becomes lean by *their* over-regulation."

"I thought you weren't a right-wing nutjob," Cat accused.

"I'm not. I'm smack dab in the middle. I would've been a libertarian had any of them ever had a shot at winning, and I spent my life electing by the issues—for anyone who would protect my freedoms."

"You don't sound so crazy now that..."

"Now that the world's ended as we know it?"

"Yeah. You sound *prepared*, actually."

"That's what I kept telling the missus before she died. She always thought I'd get whacked by the FBI or the ATF like David Koresh and those Branch Davidians in Waco. Each time she argued, I'd insist I wanted to be prepared and here I am, sitting on a cache of weapons, ammo, food, and the means to produce all of the above."

Shouts at the gate caused them both to turn, just in time to see Sam opening it for new arrivals. Standing for a better view, Cathy leaned close to the window. Fear gripped her stomach as a dozen or so armed men wearing military fatigues entered the compound.

"Who are they?" she asked.

"The Regiment, here for their tribute." The sudden pressing of a pistol muzzle against Cat's ribs said the rest. "Remember when I told you there's a commodity worth more than food and water?"

She nodded silently, scared to move and more afraid of his answer. She felt his hand go to her waistband, carefully sliding away Clint's handgun.

"It's time for you to know what that is," he said. "The Regiment is Indiana's biggest and best organized militia, and I've already sold them my soul and also your flesh."

She felt the muzzle dig deeper as he pushed her along.

Mike's sons zip-tied her hands but did not bother restraining Josh. He would go, they knew, with his mother. No one cared much about the boy if he didn't. What's another dead child during end-times? Cat sat on her knees in front of a different man. The Colonel, as Crazy Mike Donelson called him, watched with ruthless eyes that had certainly seen war. She couldn't help but notice how deeply they were set, looking through her soul and tasting fear just as Clint had so many times before.

A canvas bag landed on the ground beside her, audibly slapping the filthy snow. Her bag and Josh's pack landed next, but her eyes remained on the first. These men could be bought, Mike had told her himself.

"Colonel," she pleaded but not in a panicked way, "perhaps a deal could be made."

The calm with which she spoke brought him amusement, no doubt at what she thought she could offer.

"A deal? I think it's simple enough. Mr. Donelson has offered you over to the Regiment, and I don't see how you could buy your way out from that."

"I could if I prove his incompetence. He's not loyal to the Regiment, or he'd have taken more time to inspect who he had in his custody, and what else I had to offer."

"Certainly there's nothing more than the duties you'll perform as an officer's wife," the Colonel replied. "Let's be gone," he commanded his men.

Cathy continued as if unhearing. "In this bag is something far more valuable to this new world, something he would not have allowed me to leave with and of which you'd never have known. To you, all of you, food, water, and ammunition are the currency..."

"And flesh," Donelson added with a smirk. Every man laughed at his joke.

"Open it," she urged, "and take it as payment from me for freedom."

The Colonel paused, considered, then knelt beside the bag.

Clint had carried it in his truck on the night he kidnapped her and Josh. It was so important, he brought it into the boat when he meant to drown her in the lake. She knew what lay inside, had examined the contents so closely, but with contempt over the man she'd once married rather than lusting for the riches it offered.

The Colonel unzipped it slowly, curiously eyeing the contents within. "Well, Donelson," he finally said with a sigh, "it seems you *have* been remiss in your hurry to pass her along. It appears you've overlooked a great treasure in deed."

Cathy smiled smugly, thinking of the stolen jewels and gold within. Of course, he may just take both her *and* the bag with its contents, but at least she would see the look on Crazy Mike's face when he realized what he'd missed.

"In fact," the Colonel said, "a man can never get enough of ladies' undergarments." With a flourish he tossed several handfuls of the same, flinging them like confetti to his men's delight. "I applaud your efforts to delay the process, young lady, but all you've done is piss me off."

She scurried over on her knees to get a better look. The gold and gems were gone, replaced by articles of women's clothing, mostly likely once belonging to Mike's deceased spouse.

Donelson's boot hit her squarely in the back, not enough to cause damage or slow her ability to travel, but enough to let her know he'd won. Crazy Mike had sold her out after robbing her blind. Hauled to her feet, the soldiers led her and Josh to the swollen river and the waiting boats. Cathy turned once for a final look at her betrayer.

He merely smiled and waved.

CHAPTER TWENTY-SEVEN

Eve touched the air flowing around her, feeling the vibration of conversations held elsewhere in the facility. With a deep breath, she calmed her already slowly beating heart until the organ barely quivered. Tranquility is what she sought, a near sleep-state devoid of distractions while still able to converse with her brother on the other bench. The pair called this exercise *Dreaming*, though they never slept in this state.

The girl sifted through the chatter, gliding through the ripples of surrounding voices. This was a secret they kept from the scientists, their ability to move through space while sharing the river of molecules she and her brother controlled. Here and there, she recognized words and paused to consider secret exchanges and muffled grumblings meant for others or no one, but especially not her. Had these soldiers known they were overheard, they would cease to speak. Adam and Eve were freaks to these non-emotants, nothing more than lab experiments who would surely be put down when the study concluded. Only a handful of these people could be trusted.

Thankfully, they knew who was in this handful due to Adam's gift of foresight. He was stronger in this ability than she, so his words were immediately believed when first revealing the death awaiting the siblings. They did not have much time, as this was merely a year before, and so they formulated their plan.

"We're dangerous to them," he had explained at the time, "more so than their weapons."

"But if *we* become their weapons, our importance goes up," she had offered, hopeful and naive regarding the actions of unmodified humans.

"He's greedy," Adam insisted, "and will recognize the threat we pose as soon as we reveal our true power."

"Then we must use him before they can use us," she had replied. "Set things up so we are in control until we can get away."

Each day her brother's prophesy had proven more true, and each day the pair grew more fearful of their captors. That's what she was doing now, watching to see if the seeds they'd planted had grown roots or needed more tending.

She found the pattern of vibration she recognized as the senator. He spoke to a room full of muttering voices Eve had never heard. They spoke English, but their accents were German. With gently amplified focus, the room spun into view.

"Gentlemen," Esterling pleaded, "and ladies, please! We have the aid you desire, but it comes only with whatever conditions we require."

"We do not want your food and medicine if it means dissolving our nation!" a woman explained. "The United States is an ally, but what you offer breaks that equality."

"No one is dissolving Germany's sovereignty," Esterling insisted. "The temporary martial law will last only until we can determine if your leadership survived and can be reinstated." Of course, he knew it had not.

"And if it can't?" a man demanded. "Will you lead permanently?"

"No! Absolutely and most definitely not. In the case your government did not survive, then General Braston will peacefully transition power to the central power *you* elect."

"A general... We don't need your soldiers," the man argued. "We have troops of our own."

"You *do* need our soldiers because most of yours perished in the missile attack! But we *and* your remaining troops have agreed to work together with solidarity against lawlessness and external threats."

"Threats? The only *threat* is the obvious wealth you've seemed to acquire!" The anger in the first woman's voice laced her words as she added, "Inequality is the killer of solidarity. Hand over what you would give us, and we will issue it to our people. That includes the radiation vaccine!"

"I won't do that," Esterling said with finality. "We only ever created enough doses for our own soldiers, but with your help we can produce more—enough for all your soldiers and civilians. Even now, Herr General

Richter has agreed to work alongside General Braston, and their agreement..." he was cut off by a sudden silence as if interrupted.

"What is it? What do you see?" Adam demanded from his sister.

"Shh," she urged. "Someone else entered the room." She focused intently, trying hard not to lose the connection or miss out on a single spoken word.

"Senator..." Jake Braston finally said. "Sergeant Roark brings a timely, albeit disturbing, report. I'm afraid it speeds the process and, if Herr General Richter agrees, will nullify this vote."

His German counterpart's deep voice boomed. "What is it, General Braston, that would supersede *legal* ratification of martial law?"

"Sergeant Roark has just returned from a scouting mission, where he reports seeing an army approaching from the east."

"Which army?" General Richter demanded.

Eve recognized Benjamin Roark when he spoke. He had been a key player in Esterling and Braston's plan, but he was one of the few she believed they could trust. He was a loyal friend to Doctor Yurik, despite their enlisted/officer division. They spoke often, playing games like Scrabble and chess in the mess decks whenever they found the time. She respected him and treated the man like a friend, and so then would Eve.

"The *Russian* army." Roark informed the room. "Three columns with at least fifty thousand in each, but there could be more than our scouts could properly count."

Richter processed the information, exchanging a knowing look with Braston before stating the obvious, "An infantry attack of that size, under these conditions is impossible! The preparations alone are insurmountable. How could they equip and sustain a march of that distance in only a matter of months! Even on horseback it would take years!"

"It's downright Napoleonic," Jake agreed. "They must have planned this for decades, in the event nuclear weapons were actually deployed. No, I'm sure they've been ready to seize upon this opportunity for decades."

"They did have horses," Sergeant Roark added, "but they also have working trucks. The first line has already taken Berlin, capturing the broken Bundeswehr holdings there. It appears the columns are gathering to establish a foothold."

"Then it makes sense they'll be in Frankfurt and Nuremberg soon," Braston informed the politicians in the room. "I believe we have only days or weeks till they arrive here."

The room drew a collective gasp and protests erupted. The woman who had spoken earlier asked, "How were they not affected by the EMPs like us?"

"The Ural-4320 and the Zil-131 run off simpler engines than those used by NATO forces. Though their diesel engines are similar, their government opted to minimize their dependency on electronics."

"Why?" the woman asked, confused.

General Richter replied, suddenly understanding. "Because, as General Braston mentioned, they've always been prepared to use EMPs against NATO, knowing they would bring us to our knees. We're weakened in their eyes, caught less prepared than they."

"I have to agree we may appear crippled and ripe for plunder," Braston said, "but how they got here is less important than their imminent arrival. General Richter and I will take immediate control of all NATO troops and working equipment... that is, if you agree, Herr General."

"I do."

The collective muttering continued, but it was now obvious Esterling had secured their support.

"Then it's settled," he announced. "The NATO alliance will establish martial law in this region and I will serve as ambassador of American good will. My job will be to oversee the rationing and distribution of resources to each of your provinces."

"He's scared," the girl abruptly told her brother, barely speaking over a whisper despite the people in the room could not hear.

"Who is?" Adam asked.

"Michael Esterling."

"No, not him. He knew the invaders were coming because we told him."

"Perhaps, but something in his voice betrayed doubt."

"Then we must expect another visit from him soon. We finally control him."

Eve shuddered. She never looked forward to the man's visits because of Adam's visions, but she would put up with his presence until the final day arrived. She had to because they and Dr. Andalon would eventually need his help.

"I hope I'm not interrupting," a voice spoke from the door of the lab, startling both children.

Eve jumped but did not shout out, though her omniscience slammed abruptly into her corporeal body. She rose quickly and turned to find David standing inside the garden.

"Not at all," Adam lied, "we were merely practicing a new way of Dreaming."

"Can we help you, doctor?" Eve asked quickly, masking her irritation at his unannounced arrival.

"I'm ready to help," he said, trembling and afraid of his choice.

"So you found it?" She asked. "The evidence that Brooke carries Esterling's heir and not yours?"

"Yes, it was buried in the data, intentionally hidden, but I persisted. She gave up on me before I succeeded, accepting his donation because his traits closely resemble my own."

"But you *did* succeed," Eve said, knowingly, "and now you can produce your own heir."

"Yes, if only she'd have waited."

"You understand what we're asking of you? What we'll need when the time comes?" Adam asked slowly, as an adult would ask a child instead of the other way around.

The scientist nodded. "Yes. I'm ready to do whatever I need to ensure my experiment succeeds."

"Your progeny," corrected Eve. "We're no longer experiments, even currently trapped in this lab like your monkeys. We're your dream, your children, and your legacy."

"I'm sorry," Andalon said. "I forget you perceive yourselves as captives."

"But not for long," she snapped. "Things are changing rapidly above, and Senator Esterling has finally seized control of the region. But he faces a challenger—a larger more organized foe."

"How will he succeed?" David asked.

"He won't," Adam said solemnly, "though we've promised him otherwise. That's where you must aid us, to ensure his success."

"I will. I'm committed to aid you however you need."

The children exchanged a glance and Adam nodded. With a smile Eve motioned for the doctor to sit. "These are the things you must do," she said, then proceeded to lay out the path to their freedom.

CHAPTER TWENTY-EIGHT

Marine Sergeant Maxwell Rankin crawled on his stomach through the woods. He had survived thirteen days by this point, far longer than any other student in the simulation. The last few, he witnessed from afar, were captured by the instructors three nights earlier. His belly growled with hunger, a loud enough noise he worried they'd hear and capture him next. Then would come the worst part, the torture and interrogation. It wouldn't be real, of course, though he had been warned it would feel that way.

The military school was aptly named, implying the very nature of his situation. First, he must survive, then evade. If captured, he would reluctantly experience the need to resist their persuasions, and he worried how far they would go in testing his mettle. There would be pain, both physical and psychological, but his gunnery sergeant had warned him ahead of time. He would need to endure torture the best he could while constantly searching for an opportunity to escape. It was all in the name of the school—S.E.R.E. Survive, Endure, Resist, and Escape.

He found what he'd been searching for at the base of the tree. The ants here were meaty and crunched nicely between his teeth, providing little in the way of filling his quivering stomach but at least giving some nourishment. They weren't as bad as he'd feared and learned quickly to ignore the tiny bites on his tongue.

The bushes behind him moved and several men leaped out, pouncing on his position. These were well fed and rested, overpowering his weakened state and bruising his ribs before dragging him off. He was surprised at the violence, but then again, he'd signed a waiver. Anything goes in this training. A black hood slipped over his head and they led him away.

Escape, he urged himself.

But the logical part of him rebuked the notion. *Not yet. There's too many of them, and you're too weak. Prepare for the difficult part.*

The difficult part came more quickly than he expected. After a short truck ride, they arrived at a cabin of some sort. Unable to see through the hood, he assumed it was one of the hooch houses he'd spotted earlier in the week. He focused on what he remembered about the structures. They were small, about three meters long and wide. The walls were wooden, slatted and hopefully nailed instead of screwed. He must focus on escaping as soon as they left him alone. But the shack wasn't his prison, it was an interrogation room.

"Who are you, soldier?" a voice asked as strong hands laid him onto a table.

Max tried to struggle, but leather straps soon wrapped around his arms and legs.

"What's your name?"

"Sergeant Maxwell Rankin, United States Marine Corps."

"What outfit? Who's your commanding officer."

Max refused to reply. *Resist,* his mind urged.

Strong arms abruptly lifted him into the air. Max felt his knees rub against a tight circle as he was lowered into what he assumed was a barrel. His leg muscles engaged, fighting to hold himself up. A fist crashed down against his face, striking repeatedly until his strength failed and knees buckled. His backside hit water waiting within. His hood was suddenly ripped free from his head, revealing what he'd feared. As the lid of the barrel was set in place and locked by a metal cuff, he focused on a series of holes. Each was neatly drilled in a circle mere inches from the top.

From somewhere, perhaps one of the holes, more water poured in, raising the level and sending him pushing to rise. With legs pressed tightly against his chest, he realized how difficult breathing would be, even if he could reach the air above. With eyes closed he focused, breathing slowly and calming his pounding heart. *Survive,* he commanded himself. *Survive and Escape!*

Now, Max awoke hooded and strapped to a table. He closed his eyes against the water splashing over his mouth. He'd been trained for this, even if he'd never actually experienced the exact sensation. Though false, it felt real and he gagged, sputtered, and coughed. His body writhed, arcing to leave the table against strong hands holding him down. These men were not S.E.R.E. school instructors, and no doctor stood by in case of heart failure or asphyxiation. Focused on his training, his mind returned to the place as if it were a final test of resolve, remembering to breathe slowly through his nose between each dowsing.

He tried to remember what he knew of the practice. *Twenty seconds.* That was the common time from for each pour, slowly ramped up to forty if no information was forthcoming—at least if the interrogator was reputable and followed the rules of war and the Geneva Convention. These men had no such restrictions and would not care if his heart stopped or if he drowned.

Unless they are testing me.

Max suddenly understood. They were not extracting information, for he had little to none to give. Also, if the Regiment wanted Max dead, they would have killed him where they found him. *This is about revenge,* he realized. *They're angry about the boys in the grocery store.* He steeled his willpower and waited for the men to set him upright again.

"Well," a voice asked, "what've you got to tell us?"

Max coughed and smiled, then sang loudly. "*From the halls of Montezuma to the shores of Tripoli! I will fight my country's battles in the ...*" There was nothing like the Marine Corps hymn to demonstrate how willing you were to endure and die.

They slammed him hard onto the table and began again. From somewhere in the room he heard the other Marine laughing quietly.

Cathy Fletcher stared straight ahead with head held defiantly high but clutching little Joshua, giving reassurance their lives had not completely ended. She tried to reason out her surroundings. The look and feel of it all reminded her of a college campus, though one from a movie about zombies and end-times. That gave her a chuckle. This was, after all, living proof those movies were nowhere near the truth—all except for the Colonel.

He had the classic *bad guy* vibe, with beady eyes too narrow for his face and gaunt cheeks that spoke of a man willing to burn the fields and salt the earth if it meant total victory. He led them toward a tall building with six columns and broad steps leading up. The inscription on the side read *Soldier's and Sailor's Memorial Coliseum,* but she couldn't help but wonder what she'd find inside. Two tattered American Flags flew upside down on the flagpoles on each corner of the building.

"Where are we?" she asked. "What city?"

"Questions will be answered later," he replied with displeasure. He was a brooding man with thoughts she never hoped would be revealed. He seemed put out at the interruption, but she pressed on.

"So am I to be *your* slave, or someone else's?"

"Who said anything about being a slave?" he grumbled.

"You did just buy me from Crazy Mike. What was that, if not a slave trade?"

"It's called survival."

"I don't understand..."

"But you will." he snapped quietly, a strangely calm reaction more terrifying than if he'd shouted. He was far more different than Clint, and the finality of his words resonated with his intensity.

Nonetheless, she continued. "Am I to be a sexual servant then? Or am I to serve the household? Do I call you *master*? I may have experience taking my clothes off in front of men, but my true specialty is medicine. I'm a nurse. Don't let my worth be measured by my tits."

The fierceness with which he spun caught her off guard and she stumbled. In a flash, strong hands gripped her throat and fiery eyes burned into her own. The putrid aroma of foul breath caused bile to churn as she breathed in the heaviness of his words.

"Society is dead," he said with a growl, buried beneath a layer of filth and fallout. "All that matters now is building a new one, and my men need wives." With a quick nod he turned her eyes toward Josh. "Birthing children will be difficult and birth defects will be the new worry, but a nurse should know that, shouldn't she?"

She nodded, but truly hadn't given thought to repopulation.

"So you understand you're valuable, as a woman with little exposure and few concerns about radiation poisoning? You'll be married to one of my officers and eventually help birth a new world."

"Under your rule?" she asked This earned a smile from the man, and it chilled her spine.

"Someone has to lead."

His hands released as quickly as they'd gripped her, and she gasped a desperate breath of air. Nothing else exchanged, even as armed guards drew open heavy wooden doors. The Colonel led everyone inside, then went his own way without another word to neither her nor the men. They guided her and Josh with hungry eyes. She could feel them tasting her flesh, but she was used to that and knew how to handle men like these.

"Take it all in, boys," she said, slipping into the act she'd learned at *Pussy Galore's*. "But while looking's free, everything else belongs to me."

They quickly looked away, each embarrassed for their own reasons. Men were easy to control; she knew after years of enduring Clint. Most remembered mothers, sisters, or daughters when put in their place by a woman. Only those like Clint pressed further to take what they wanted, and those were the kind she hated. The rare sociopaths like him would do what they wanted—and were the true dangers. No, these men were harmless, unlike the Colonel.

She took in her surroundings, correct in her assumption the coliseum had been designed for sporting events. After descending a short ramp, they emerged on what had once been a basketball arena, but unlike any she'd ever seen. The space opened up on one side to accommodate a large stage. A high gallery hovered above, with seats removed and wooden structures erected in their place. Beneath that vantage point, not an inch of the wooden floor was visible, replaced by a tent city of tarps and makeshift structures. Narrow walkways snaked through the dizzying maze.

Down one of these paths, she spied a woman with a rounded belly full of advanced pregnancy. She busied herself by hanging laundry on a line to dry.

"Where do I go?" Cathy asked the men, but none seemed to care beyond their leering.

"Stage," one finally said. "For decontamination."

But then another stepped forward. He was a young man, sort of shy but not in the bad way. He was the kind whose friends would have dragged him to watch her dance then fallen in love with her after she showed him attention. She hated taking money from these, as they were not much more than boys when it came down to their experience.

In a gentle voice, he suggested, "I can take you there, ma'am."

After a glare toward the others, she turned thankfully and offered a smile for his help. "Thank you..."

"James. Um... Parker." He blushed deeply. "I'm James Parker, ma'am."

Above, Cathy noticed additional men watching from the balcony. These wore the uniforms of officers, and their salivating stares churned her stomach. Handing the young man hers and Josh's bags, she slipped a hand around his bicep and smiled.

"Well then, James Parker. Why don't you show me around?"

His cheeks turned a rosier shade of red as the others jeered him with cat calls and remarks. They asked him whether he knew what to do with her, but the young man ignored the jests and kept true to his offer. He led her through the self-contained city without once making a pass or pushing himself.

After years working at *Pussy Galore's*, this relaxed Cat. He was putty in her hands and she would make him her first true ally since the Klingensmiths. "What is this place?" she asked.

"We call it The Shelter," he chuckled, "but it's not a true bomb shelter. The Colonel planned for all of this and mustered us here after the EMP." He turned serious again and added, "He's been prepping us for this, and the Regiment was ready. But now America's probably gone, and we're all that's left of liberty."

"Liberty?" Cat forgot her charming act for a moment and let a bit of anger show through. "My son and I were kidnapped and sold, how is that liberty?"

"You're not slaves, ma'am."

"Oh? What do you call it?" She stared coolly and waited for his answer while steaming inside.

"Liberated. So are all the people in The Shelter. See that woman over there?" She's going to give birth to the first child born after D-Day."

"D-Day?"

"Destruction Day, miss. The last day of liberty in the world. We hope to set the world right again, and the Colonel has a plan."

"He'll use his army to expand his territory and start a new nation?"

"Yes, ma'am. One nation, under God, indivisible, with liberty and justice for all."

"I see," she said, less convinced than James. So far, she had only witnessed forced servitude and the loss of *her* liberty as a woman. Changing the subject, she asked, "Where will I live, James?"

"There are some vacant tents on the stage in what we call the observation area. That's where we put the newer arrivals, to quarantine and watch for any radiation sickness. Once we know you're cleared, you will be given your own hootch. Soon though, we'll be moving out of here to repopulate the surrounding area. That's when you'll be assigned a home and hopefully your own farm with your new husband."

Cat shivered at the mention. "What if I refuse to remarry?"

"That's a condition for receiving the Regiment's protection and the price for living in the new society. Everyone must do their part to repopulate the world and start fresh."

Cat frowned but kept her thoughts to herself. Instead, she allowed him to lead them toward a set of steps leading to the stage. There people in scrubs waited for her and Josh.

"I'll leave you here, ma'am, but can I call upon you again? I'd love to get to know you and..."

She raised an eyebrow expectantly and waited.

"And you're very pretty, ma'am." He blushed sweetly. She hated she'd have to someday destroy his crush but smiled back and nodded.

"Of course, James. I'd like that. Thank you for everything. You've made our arrival most welcome."

He grinned wildly and waved awkwardly before hustling off to join the rest of his squad. They, of course, were waiting with laughs, jeers, and welcomed him with crude gyrations of their hips.

With a shudder, Cat led Joshua up the steps.

CHAPTER TWENTY-NINE

Linda eyed the new arrivals, a young woman with her son, and prayed silently they wouldn't bunk near her. She touched her stomach. All she needed to lose what wits she had left was another reminder of how she'd lost two children. Worse, that she may give birth to a hideously deformed radiation monster. She abhorred motherhood of all forms at this point, and this doting mother was more than she could stand. She watched as the nurses and doctors examined the pair, smiling and laughing at times and carrying on an educated conversation about every check they ran.

Wonderful, she thought. *She's also a nurse and has already found both a place and a purpose in this prison.*

Linda hated the woman.

Much to her disgust, the staff soon led the woman and child toward her tent. She eyed the two empty cots beside her and groaned audibly, but not loud enough they'd hear. As they neared, she realized the woman was even more beautiful than she had thought from a distance. A toothy smile from the intruder made her hate the woman even more—she had every single one intact. Linda absently felt the space in her gums where two had recently fallen out.

"Hello!" the woman said cheerily. "I'm Cathy and this is Josh." She reached a hand out to shake, but Linda only frowned at it.

"You know why we're here, right?"

"Yes," Cathy replied, "I was informed."

"So you're okay to breed a new generation of warmongering? Or maybe you're desperate for a new daddy for your brat."

"My *son* and I do perfectly well alone, have done so for a while, and I've no intention of marrying or *breeding* for anybody unless I choose to love again!" Cathy leaned in close, too close for Linda's liking, and whispered with a pleasant tone. "Our living arrangement is temporary, hopefully as short as my son's and my time here, so I'd rather we be friends. Otherwise, I'll warn you I've lost all tolerance for bullshit, banter, or bitches. Do not hate on me simply because I have a child and am capable of more." She leaned back with a smile and waited for a response.

The words had a deeper effect than they should have, filling Linda with every emotion she'd put off since Yellowstone. Tears filled her eyes, but she controlled the sobs. "I..." she began, unsure how to proceed, but finally the words came. "I'm sorry. I lost my family just before the bombs," she explained. "My children, they..." She choked on what came next, unspoken for so long since the fight with Bryan—the night they wrecked in Nebraska.

Me, she admitted to herself. *I killed him, surely, or drove him away.*

"They're gone," she said simply, glazing past the horrendous way each had died, "but I'm not alone. I came here with a... a friend." Then she placed a hand on her belly and smiled up toward Cathy. "Please forgive me, but I'm terrified my baby won't make it. Or worse," she added, "will be affected by the radiation."

Cathy's eyes grew wide with excitement and the tension between them vaporized. "You're expecting? How far along?"

"I'm not sure. At least eight weeks... that's the last time my husband and I were together."

"Well then, can we begin again? I'm Cathy." She reached out her hand and smiled warmly. "My friends call me Cat."

"I'm Linda." She took her hand and squeezed, the first physical contact she'd had with anyone in over a month.

"Well, Linda, I'm glad we'll be roommates for a while, because I've been studying to become a labor and delivery nurse. I'll do everything I can to keep you and your baby healthy. Just now, the doctor said he'll be taking me on as another assistant after we're cleared."

Though more tears found their way down her cheeks, Linda smiled for the first time since Yellowstone.

"Tell me about your friend," Cathy begged, setting their bags in the corner. "Where is she?"

"A *he*, actually. He's a truck driver who picked me up in Omaha and brought me to Evansville."

"Is that where we are? Evansville? So... Indiana?"

"That's right."

"Where is he now?"

"I don't know," Linda replied, "dead maybe. We were attacked by street gangs and he fought them off. He's pretty badass, really, a good friend to have on your side. He was a Marine. Max fought them off while I got away, but the Regiment was waiting around the corner and I ran into them. They took him a different direction when we arrived, so I've no idea what they'll do with him." She frowned. "In fact, he probably *is* dead already. Apparently, he killed a few of them."

"I'll pray he isn't," Cathy promised. After a pause, she added, "But I know one thing, I don't trust the Colonel and we're getting out of here eventually."

Linda laughed, another first in recent weeks. "Good luck with that, it's damn near impossible. But if you can find a way to a better place than this, I want to go with you." Then, with all seriousness, she added, "But we'll need Max's help, *if* he's alive."

Max had no room to move and barely any air to breathe. Thankfully, his captors had been diligent enough to periodically open the box and allow him respite. But, in case the sensory deprivation of being kept in a coffin wasn't bad enough, they only allowed his breaks in the *white* room. That was worse than the box itself.

He was already badly weakened. Half-starved and denied protein, his belly constantly craved nourishment. As the lid opened, he allowed his captors to lift him up, dropping him over the side. He landed with a thud, muscles quivering with atrophy and fatigue at the same time. With a gasp he filled his lungs to right his brain. He blinked against the light flooding in from the tall windows overhead. In this room everything spoke of brightness, the sheets, the bunk, the floor. Even his diet was white, only rice. A white bowl of it awaited him on a small table, complete with a white plastic spoon.

Max yearned for something, anything to remind his senses of color, but even the guards wore white scrubs or lab coats when they attended. They refused to speak, never made noise—not even a knock on the lid to let him know they'd arrived. They were like ghosts in his presence.

Max had just reached the bowl of rice and taken a bite when the door opened and the Colonel stepped in with two guards. Whenever the Colonel arrived it was, no matter how much Max hated their conversation, a treat for his ears as well as his psyche. After days, weeks maybe, without sound, the soft and soothing voice from the man broke the spell of silence and gave the Marine a sense of humanity between periods of torture.

When the Colonel spoke, he did so with a soothing voice as if half singing a lullaby to a restless child. "I will not ask how you are feeling, Sergeant Rankin, because I already know. I designed this room and these methods myself."

"I know of them," Max replied. "I'm prepared."

"Yes, it's obvious you have training for special forces. But even so, S.E.R.E. school only prepares the mind but not the constitution of the soldier. Any other I've met would have broken by now, but you've endured. What drives you, Sergeant? Why haven't you given up?"

Max ignored the question; it was the kind to probe the mind and cause a subject to slip with personal details. *Every conversation is a game of chess,* he reminded himself. "So you're a colonel?" he asked instead of answering.

"I am. And you were a gunnery sergeant."

"Am. Once a Marine always a Marine." With a tired wink, Max added, "Oorah, and all that shit, right?"

"I wouldn't know. I was never a Marine."

"Army then? Oh, God forbid you aren't Air Force. I'd have to puke up my rice. You zoomies are excellent pencil pushers, but know nothing about war besides getting back in time for pay-for-view."

Max watched the man intently for a reaction and found none. There was something oddly peculiar in his grace and control. In whatever service he achieved his rank, he certainly wouldn't offer up personal details about himself. The chess match, as usual, played on.

"You killed several of my men, but left Sergeant Walters to live. Why? Your life was made harder by leaving a witness who knows both your face and your background, and you don't strike me as the sloppy sort."

Max played along, but decided a truthful answer here wouldn't hurt. "I didn't want to kill those boys. The first was an accident. The edge of the shelf hit him wrong when I tried to disarm him. I didn't appreciate his gun in my face when we had no reason to quarrel."

"Stealing food from the Regiment was a crime and he was the authority. By killing him, you are as guilty as killing a policeman."

"If that's true," Max said coolly, "then it would've been a capital crime, and I'd be dead already. No, you're keeping me alive for another reason."

"Fair enough. I'm assuming the others came to his aid after hearing the ruckus, but that doesn't explain Sergeant Walters. Why did you cuff him and leave him to identify you?"

Max shrugged. "I'm not a killer."

"The trail of blood you left begs to differ. You killed many more than just men of the Regiment and quite efficiently as Walters reported. You killed several of the gang members here in the city. Shayde has a strange respect for you and says you should be an ally instead of a foe."

"Let me and the woman I was brought in with go. We've no interest in joining your Regiment."

"No. That won't do. You may have killed your own kind, Sergeant Rankin, but that does not buy your freedom. Either way, I cannot allow you to keep your white slave."

My own kind? White slave?

Max felt the blood within his veins begin to boil near to the surface. He felt the bowl of rice begin to shake in his hands and gripped it tighter.

Because I'm black and killed black men?

He yearned to bathe the Colonel with the rice and have a go at the guards. But in this weakened state, it would only have served to earn another beating.

He's baiting me, Max thought, urging self-control. This was, after all, a chess match not easily won, but never with violence. His wits had to prevail no matter the direction he was taken.

In a voice as calm and soothing as the Colonel's, he asked, "Is that what I found myself in the middle of? A race war. If so, why not lynch your black prisoner in the square as an example?"

"Because the Nature Boys would celebrate your death and thank us. No, I see them and the gangs as the real problem. Each will probably kill each other or themselves with their looted drugs and guns eventually. My men take everything of value when we forage—food, water, antibiotics, and other medicinal needs, but we leave the gangs plenty of the most addictive pills and tinctures to find. They'll kill themselves off soon or weaken themselves enough so my men can finish the job."

"So that's what this is? A white supremacist colony?"

"Not in the least, Sergeant. We have many minorities within our protection, but *everyone* we take in is vetted. They must be able to contribute something to our society once replanted. Take you, for instance. Your only crime was killing my soldiers. If you could atone for that, we could find suitable placement for your intellect and training within the Regiment."

Max scoffed. "My intellect... Because I'm smarter than the *street monkeys* I killed?"

"Don't say things like that, Sergeant Rankin," the Colonel said solemnly, "that kind of talk is *racist*."

Check. Max had allowed himself to slip at last. He tasted the anger in his mouth and swallowed it hard. Instead of lashing out, he moved to castle his king and reset the imaginary board. It was time to give something up to his captor.

"Linda isn't and never was my captive. I found her injured on the side of the road during the missile attacks. Her husband died that night, and I gave her food and treated her wounds. Then drove her in the direction she wanted to go. But she *is* her own woman and can stay with you if she wants."

"But only if she wants, and you know she doesn't."

"You're good," Max admitted. "I'm guessing you were a psychologist in whatever branch you served. I bet you had a practice around here before the attack, and formed up this Regiment in order to play soldier on the side. You probably didn't serve a single day, and *Colonel* may even be an honorary title."

"Oh, I served, Gunnery Sergeant Rankin."

Then a thought struck Max and caused him to laugh from the belly, a loud and shocking sound of lunacy that caused the Colonel to flinch and the guards to tense. "I figured it out. You're National Guard! You wanted the uniform and title, but couldn't or wouldn't be able to take the full-time commitment!" He laughed again. "You're a part-time soldier!"

The guard's struck him square in the temple, sending him reeling and spitting blood against the wall. He smiled at that, too. Finally, the room had some color. The next blows caused him to cease seeing white altogether, as he passed out from weakened exhaustion.

CHAPTER THIRTY

Stephanie Yurik gazed at the children seemingly asleep on the benches beside her. Though motionless, their eyes flicked and fluttered while *Dreaming*. Despite the many times she had witnessed this state, she shuddered at the power each tiny body possessed. Thankful for their innocence and age, she feared the full extent of their abilities if allowed to fully mature.

"The Russian infantry followed your bait, General Braston, and are moving toward Stuttgart."

The general stood near the doorway, stoically taking in their report. "Are you certain the bulk of their force committed? Surely many have splintered away."

"Your advance scouts did their job, leading the invaders where you wanted. They're pushing on Stuttgart with eighty percent of full strength."

"How large is their total force, then? Is it as bad as Sergeant Roark said? He reported one hundred and fifty thousand." Jake asked.

"Larger," said Adam. "At least two hundred thousand."

Braston let out a whistle. "I'd call that full strength. They're committed to securing the entire region and crushing all resistance, but their haste is the error. Are our forces in place to cover Roark and Titus's escape to Germersheim?" he asked.

"They are," a dozing Eve assured.

Braston's plan, Stephanie knew, was for Sergeant Benjamin Roark and Colonel Frank Titus to hold Stuttgart just long enough to draw the Russians into a skirmish. For weeks the bait was laid, leaving word and pamphlets behind that the NATO alliance was strongest in Stuttgart and Ramstein. As soon as the enemy engaged, the American troops would appear to break, making a running retreat toward Ramstein along one single route. The Russians, having the upper hand, would make their way along Highway E35 and eventually to the Rhine River at Germersheim.

Along the way to the river, Braston had entrenched several squads of special forces—a combination of the United States Army's 173rd Airborne out of Frankfurt and Germany's 313st Paratrooper Regiment based in Ramstein. Their job was to harangue the larger pursuing force, hopefully cutting their numbers and disabling as many vehicles as they could along the way to the Rhine. There, Braston and Richter hoped to blow the Rudolf von Habsburg Bridge and bog them down in Germersheim. There, the NATO forces would converge a flanking maneuver to surround and siege the invaders.

"And you're *certain*," Jake insisted, "the battle must occur there? In Germersheim?"

Adam and Eve answered in dry unison, "Yes."

The boy aroused from his sleep and stretched before explaining, "Your job is to draw as many of their force into one spot of *our* choosing and hold them there."

"I understand all that," the general growled, his irritation showing through. "What I don't comprehend is *how* we actually win this thing. We're outnumbered and overpowered, using only small arms and antique cannons we've gathered up by raiding military museums. Hell, we've barely enough ordinance to keep them pinned down for an hour. They'll break through, mark my word, or move north and south to the other bridges. We could be overrun within a couple of days."

The door to the lab had opened quietly and neither Jake nor Stephanie noticed a weary Michael had entered. Worry was written upon his brow and sunken eyes betrayed lack of sleep. He leaned forward to study Yurik's notes.

"So, it really is that bad?" he asked. "We can trap them easily, but have no way to win the battle?"

"Not definitively," the general admitted, "and not without heavy— and I mean *heavy*—casualties we can't afford to lose."

"Please try to relax," Stephanie pleaded.

"How far along are you, Doctor Yurik?" Eve asked suddenly.

All three adults turned shocked faces toward the sleeping girl. All were taken aback, but most of all Stephanie.

In a startled voice she admitted, "I... If I am, I didn't know!" Her eyes darted and met Michael's. He smiled broadly.

Eve shifted in her sleep, eyes fluttering open to focus on the couple. "He'll grow to become a powerful leader," she promised, "and his descendants will rule an entire continent for centuries to follow."

Adam's voice interrupted. "We want to be there at Germersheim when the battle begins. It's the critical step in securing this continent and where the NATO alliance will witness your victory. Eve and I would like to witness this as well."

"Absolutely not," Michael refused. Turning to Jake, he asked, "How do we do it, then? How do we deal the killing blow? This has every look and feel like the Alamo to me, and that battle didn't end well for those holed up inside."

"You will overcome their greater forces," Eve insisted. "We've both seen it, but we are there as well, when you do."

"No," Michael insisted again, waving his hand dismissively.

Jake was more opened-minded than his friend and suggested, "Michael, our men have the vaccine and are stronger and better rested than the Russians. They've marched in chemical and radiation suits and are no doubt exhausted. We *can* win this if the flanking maneuver works. But what would it hurt if the children *are* there? An extra set of eyes and ears wouldn't hurt—especially psychic ones."

"I won't risk it," the senator said with finality. "They remain in the lab for their protection."

"If you won't allow us to be there, at least listen to our counsel," Adam pleaded.

"What do you suggest?" Jake asked.

"Parley with their leadership. Get them into your camp and stall until you clearly see a path to victory."

Esterling let out a sigh. "Parley? You've underestimated our situation here, Adam." Turning to Jake he asked, "What *is* the key to winning this battle? We can't kill them all and we can't hold the siege long enough to starve them out. Can we surprise them with a direct attack across the bridges?"

Jake shook his head. "No. If we charge the bridges, they'd focus their front and flank us before crossing."

Stephanie chimed in, "Jake, what *about* Adam's idea? Couldn't you convince the Russians to talk?"

"They'll know we're outnumbered and will use overwhelming force no matter *what* we say."

Eve interjected. "You will win this battle, but only a treaty will secure sovereignty. Ivan Petrov will establish his command and control in Waghäusel. Find him in a *Sonderposten* with a metal roof and bring him to talk. He *will* listen."

"Who's Ivan Petrov?" Jake demanded.

"The general in charge of this invasion," Eve explained. "He will surrender and do as you say, returning to Moscow with a warning for his commanders never to again invade Astia."

"What the hell is Astia?" Jake asked.

"I'll explain later," Michael promised, seemingly shocked to hear the word spoken aloud.

Jake stood, frustrated the children had not provided clear answers to their problem. "We'd better go. Germersheim is a long ride on horseback, and we have a lot of set up. Let's go fight our Alamo, Senator Esterling."

"Great," the senator replied, smiling at his friend, "I can be William Travis and you be Jim Bowie." Jake laughed but Michael shot Stephanie another look betraying deep worry. "We'll be back," he promised.

"We'll be here," she replied. After the men left, she asked of Adam. "Why are you so vague when giving them details of the battle," she asked. "Haven't you seen it all?"

"I have, and they *will* overcome the invading army."

"But how?"

"*We* will help them," Adam insisted. He picked up Stephanie's notepad and tore off a blank page, hastily scribbling a message.

"What is that?" she asked.

"Esterling won't listen, but General Braston may. This is the location and name of the *Sonderposten*. Place it into his hand before he leaves, and tell him it's his only course of action after the senator's plan fails."

Stephanie took the paper, reading the words and wondering how this knowledge would help the battle.

"Also insist Sergeant Roark is the one who captures Ivan Petrov," Eve suggested. "That part is *very* important."

David Andalon was bent over his console when Dr. Yurik departed the lab. She stood in front of him, shifting her weight nervously as if wanting to speak.

"Can I help you, Captain?" he asked without looking up.

"I seem to have a problem," she said at last. "Eve believes I'm with child."

This *was* a surprise, and he lifted his eyes to meet hers. "Why is that a problem?" he asked softly.

"I don't want to keep it."

"Let me understand. The world as we knew it is over after shedding more than seventy percent of its population, and you don't want to bring another life into the world?"

Her posture changed, with back stiffening and standing taller. Her eyes narrowed and seemed to pierce his as if ready to meet his challenge. "I don't *want* a child."

"You don't want a child, or you don't want *his* child?"

This caught her off guard, clamping her mouth shut just as she was about to speak.

"I don't love him. Up until the recent... events... I meant to call off the engagement. Now I see no way out."

"People fall out of love often. Michael's reasonable, just talk to him."

"I can't, he's no longer himself. He's so focused on this new society and blocking out reason from anyone but General Braston. He's getting worse. I once saw him a great leader—the president someday. But he's making mistakes. Just a bit ago, he and Jake committed to a battle with no clear path to victory and refused to allow the children to help."

David nodded. "I've seen some of that recently. But why allow Adam and Eve along? Does he suspect they'll betray him?"

"I don't think it's that. I know them, *raised them,* even, and they've never been wrong. They're insisting on success and even promised his child would become king of generations of kings—but only if they are present at the battle."

"Then they should be there."

"He said no."

"So despite their insistence, they're kept prisoners in a fancy dungeon and hidden from the real world. Michael's decision was final? There's no way to change his mind?"

"They're experiments, Dr. Andalon. You of all people should understand the experiment *must* remain uncontaminated. Besides," she added, "The outside world isn't ready for them."

"So you don't care for them as children but as experiments?"

"Of course I care!"

"Then in which way are they more important?" Andalon asked.

"Children..."

"Yet you're ready to destroy your own."

Her mouth again clamped shut, but this time she paused to consider.

"Stephanie," David asked gently, "why did he order you to bury the truth about Brooke's child? Do they fear I'd stop aiding the project?"

"You knew? How?"

He shrugged and smiled. "I'm a genius with a lot of time on my hands and no classes to teach or lectures to give. It didn't take me long, once I realized how you'd coded the false stream."

"I see."

"So which was the reason? Why would my wife and longest friend hide it from me?"

"All of the above, actually. Mostly it was to protect Brooke. She wanted a child so badly and couldn't wait. That's how he got her to give up your project in the first place. He promised her a quiet *in vitro.*"

"I wondered about her thirty pieces of silver."

"Don't be angry, David. Brooke's a good woman and loves you very much."

"What about him? Can I hate my friend? Even *you've* admitted to falling out of love with him, why can't I do the same? Why shouldn't I burn this experiment to the ground and walk away?"

"What we're doing *is* wrong," she admitted.

"With Adam and Eve?"

"Yes. All of it. The enhancements, their *existence,* it's unnatural. Released into the world they would change it all, perhaps in a dangerous way if unchecked."

"Yet you love them?"

"Yes."

"That's the funny thing about love, isn't it?" he asked. "If you love something, you set it free and let it live without boundaries."

"And if it hurts you or others after you set it free?" she demanded.

"Then at least it was truly loved." Their eyes locked in a moment, and David knew she understood his meaning. "They want out—to be free. That's *all* they want is to be children and grow into adults. But they know it can't happen here, not with..."

"Not with Michael," she admitted.

"No, not with Michael. He's ambitious and they are the key to his power. But if he's too weak he'll always live in fear they'll seize it away from him."

"I think he fears Jake will do the same."

"They're different kinds of leaders, those two. Isn't it funny how they led each other down this path?"

"They meant well," she insisted.

"Do you really believe that? Maybe at first they did, but not now. They've already claimed this continent as their own, and Adam assured me they'll hold onto it as Astia."

Yurik's eyes grew large at his words. "What did you just call this place?"

"Astia. That's the name Adam used."

"I've heard him use it also, but in a different context. He said their bodies were the *astia* of the future, or something like that. But earlier, he used it like you just did... as a name of a place—*this* place."

"What's it mean?"

"It's the Finnish word for *vessel*."

It was David's turn to display shock upon his face. "He meant it the same way."

"What do you mean?"

"The children fear Michael and have asked me to take them to the battle. They claim he'll destroy them after he sees their true power unless you and I convince him to let them leave."

"He never will."

"Not to stay here, no. They want to go to North America, to recreate the continent so their kind can live in peace."

"That's... Oh my God, it actually makes sense," she realized. "They're human, and human nature is to survive at all costs."

"As well as be *fruitful* and multiply," he agreed. "They want all emotants to have the same opportunity to live. We've created a new race of humans, Stephanie. We can't allow him to destroy the children."

"What do you think Adam means by naming his new nation *Astia*? A moment ago you seemed to understand."

"Their bodies hold the key to all of Michael's problems. If he can harness the power as a drug instead of within a human, something he can control by only dispensing to the most loyal of his followers, then he *would* dominate the world. Think about it, there are no more electronics outside this lab—no communications whatsoever. He's without radios, internet, radar, and satellite, and he has no way of predicting whether or when this or any future crises will end. Dr. Yurik, Michael Esterling does *not* need nor want the children. He craves only their powers and has you studying them to learn their extent."

"And once he discovers how helpful they truly are, he will destroy them and create a second batch he *can* control."

"No," David insisted. "He'll create a farm to supply the essence he needs to harness their power. That's all he's truly after."

"I... I believe you," she admitted. "But what do we do?"

"I'm going to keep my promise to a pair of children I've grown increasingly fond of. Will you help me?"

"I... I don't know. What will you do?"

"For starters, I'm going to find a way to get them to the battlefield and let them do what they say they can. Then, I'll find a way to give Michael the currency he wants without harming the children and get them to North America."

"I can help with that," she promised.

"And what of *his* child you're carrying?"

"David, this *isn't* Michael's child."

"I see." Inside he wanted to laugh, to selfishly celebrate a private victory against both his friend and Brooke. It felt good knowing Michael would suffer the same way as he. But, in the end, it won't matter *who* the child's father was, as long as the others can be saved from destruction. "Come over here," he suggested, leading her toward a cooler. "I've a wonderful prenatal combination that has done wonders to offset our restricted diets and lack of Vitamin D."

"It's what you're giving to Brooke and Mi-Jung?"

"The very same," he said with a nod, drawing out a syringe and vial from the refrigerator. "Have a seat and I'll get you started."

"Thank you, David," she said with a warm smile.

"No, Stephanie," he said from behind, wearing a smile of his own. Only his was darker, sinister even, and matching the secret triumph in his eyes. "Thank *you*."

CHAPTER THIRTY-ONE

The two women faced each other on their cots with Josh in the middle, playing on the floor with his toys. They were primitive cars, carved out of a piece of wood Cathy's new soldier friend had found lying around. If full truth be told, Private James Parker seemed genuinely committed to his goal of winning both mother and son over to his charms. No matter his chances, Cathy was happy her son had found a friend in the man.

"How'd you get released so quickly?" Linda asked, dumbfounded.

"Josh and I were indoors most of the time, not in the cab of a truck like you. We got less of the radiation, so they're allowing us to pick a spot on the floor."

"Well, it isn't fair. I was here a full week before you, and I'm sick of staring at the new people they bring in. It's disgusting. *They're* disgusting!"

She had a point and Cathy knew it. The latest batch was wretched, and a handful of them even passed away in the first twenty-four hours. Radiation is a fickle killer, choosing some while skipping others more worthy. Dumb luck is what your fate comes down to after a nuclear war—and damn it for not being on everyone's side. She shook off a chill and managed a smile.

"Well," I've got good news for you, too," she said with a tinge of excitement. This was the reveal she'd planned.

"What's that?" Linda asked.

"You get to move out in a couple of days, too. They decided the baby's as fine as it can be, and I'm gonna save you a spot near me. When your friend Max is freed..."

"When..." Linda scoffed at her optimism. "We'll need to break him out if he's even alive."

"Okay, *if* your friend Max is freed, he can come join us."

"How can you do that?" Linda demanded. "How can you be so positive after all *this*?" She waved her hands around but by *this* meant the entire world that went to shit. "Don't say things like *save a spot* and *when your friend is freed!* I don't want a tent near you, I want to find Max, put a gun in his hand, and run behind him fighting us out of here! But he's obviously dead and gone for good, and that's not happening. It's been several weeks since they brought him in."

"Well," Cathy said with an eye roll, "that's not asking for much now, is it?" After a moment of silence, she added, "I was just trying to be helpful, that's all, but I know you're probably right. I'm sure they killed him if he's such a security risk to them."

"I'm not getting comfortable here like *you*, and I'm certainly not going to call it home."

"You should," the younger woman said quietly.

"Why?" Linda demanded.

Cathy pointed at her friend's belly, now obviously bulging with baby. "You need to settle, Linda. Do it for your child, like I'm trying to do for mine."

"Cat!" A voice called from the edge of the stage. "Hey, Cat!"

"And here's the reason why you're willing," the mom-to-be muttered. "He's been coming around to see you more and more, and you're falling for him."

Cathy blushed. "He *is* cute. And sweeter than I thought, even at first, but I'm not settling with him or anybody. I'm letting James become a friend, but showing some interest creates enough arm's distance to hold off an arranged marriage to someone less savory."

Linda's face suddenly turned dark. "Sister," she said, "don't be fool enough to believe any woman's arms are long enough to hold back anything, anymore. This isn't our mothers' or even our grandmothers' world, and you'd better believe gender equality died with the bombs. Hard men are taking over, and we've literally entered the dark ages. You'll not be burned at the stake for witchcraft, but for something far worse—not finding your place beneath a man or where he says it should be."

Cathy stood, taking Josh by the hand. "I believe a strong woman can lead a man from *any* position, if she wants to." She suddenly frowned, thinking of a certain man chained to a cinder block and sunken beneath a lake. "As long as she has the right man." On that, she dragged her boy away and hurried toward the fish sniffing her baited hook.

James beamed when he saw her, hoping for a hug now they were released from quarantine. He immediately placed a gentlemanly hand out to help them both down the stairs.

She quickly found there was no need to feign acceptance, and took it, giving him that reward upon reaching the ground. But she quickly scolded her foolishness. *These are dangerous waters, Cat!* But the girl inside the woman ignored the caution.

"Are you ready?" he gushed. "I found you a perfect spot near my *prime* real estate."

Cat let out a belly laugh before she could remember to play it cool. She was losing the battle against the inner girl already. "Prime real estate? Here? Are we moving uptown?" She pointed toward the better built officer housing looking down from above.

"Not a chance," he said without losing his spark. "But there're two things around here that symbolize stature. There's position," he said this with an eye on two officers now carefully watching down upon them, coolly sizing up both him and her. "But there's also something far better."

"Oh?" she asked with interest. "Whatever could that be, sir?"

"Proximity to the privies."

Cat stopped dead in her tracks. "Bathrooms? You have *real* bathrooms here? Is the water running?"

He laughed at the reaction to his surprise, nodding vigorously and sharing her excitement. "The water here is fed by aquifer, and the Colonel planned everything out so well. He knew electric pumps would fail, but worked out a way to use manual standbys if this day ever came. Also, the hot water heater is geothermal, so it gets warmed up underground. Everything must have cost him a mint, but the Colonel was ready and right about it all." The awe in his voice was genuine for the man.

"You respect him deeply, don't you?"

"He's a genius. Thought of everything—even by working his way onto the Veteran's Council. They rented this building from Vanderburgh County until the attack. That's how he made the upgrades. Once he was elected chairman, he worked it into his plans for the Regiment and made subtle improvements one at a time. He had everything staged here by day 754, the spray insulation he coated the inside of the windows with, the guns, ammunition, the rations—all of it. He's our savior, really, and now he's going to rebuild America." He leaned in with excitement. "And he's doing it right here in Evansville!"

The excited girl within her lost out to caution. "James," she said quietly, clutching Josh's hand a little too tightly. He pulled away with a grunt of protest, but said nothing. She let him be and focused on what she needed to say. "I'm thankful to him, really I am. But he's selecting people to save not by their need but by their value to the new order—his order. He *bought* me from Crazy Mike, for Christ's sake!"

"Cat, he *saved* you from Crazy Mike, but he didn't buy you. He gave the man a transaction, a feeling of worth since he'd never allow a man like that inside The Shelter. No, he needs him out there, on the frontier, finding people of value and ready to show true loyalty when the Regiment expands the new nation. That's why he did it, and it was all for good!"

"James, it's wrong. *Everyone* deserves a chance in the new world, not just the elite he's chosen." She watched his face and found her words were having the wrong effect.

Too loyal to his commanding officer, the Corporal Parker standing before her changed his posture into something more formal.

"I'm sorry," she said, "I'm just sore about how Crazy Mike treated me." She changed the subject, hoping to regain the fun they were having. "Come on," she said playfully, "Show me this *prime* real estate!"

His enthusiasm returned and picked up right where he left off before, grabbing her hand and leading her away. Josh scurried to keep up, giggling and laughing while getting caught up in the fun and joy on their new friend's face. *There hasn't been enough of that for him to see,* she worried, *not recently. But he likes this man, and this place* isn't *really that bad!*

It turned out James' tent wasn't on the main floor. That, he said wasn't for the soldiers, but only for the new arrivals. Like the officers had the upper balcony, the soldiers had the outer circle of the coliseum, the main hallway circling both sides toward the rear entrance to the storage rooms and backstage. Being a basketball arena as well as a multipurpose center, there were locker rooms and, as promised, showers. He led them to a tiny plot on the westernmost corridor of the building.

She understood then what he had meant by the spray foam on the windows. No light entered, as each was coated with the expandable goo—a poor man's attempt to block out as much radiation as possible. Of course, she had no idea if the method would work and wondered why the Colonel would risk his men so close to the outer rim of the structure. *His enlisted men, the* peons, *but certainly not his well-protected officers!* Despite James' fierce loyalty for the man, Cathy still could not allow herself to trust him even the tiniest bit.

James' home, it turned out, was nicer than she'd expected, and the location was excellently placed. He'd found a wedged corner down a hall-way that allowed his tiny space to open into a larger area—hiding the true size of his apartment from the hallway. He was lucky enough to only have one wall constructed of blue tarp, with the rest butted against warm interior walls. Beside his room he had added a separate portion for Cathy and Josh, having taken special care to make it their own apart from his.

She and Josh would share a single room nestled between James' blue tarp and a maintenance closet. The divider between bedrooms was thin enough to whisper through, but thick enough she would feel respected and safe with both friend and son nearby. He really was a sweet man. He had even gone so far as to set up two cots, each thoughtfully adorned with handpicked quilts probably found while scavenging a thrift store. Hers was white with red roses and Josh's with race cars and roads. The boy scrambled to his immediately and began to play with his wooden toys, tracing an adventure no longer contained to his imagination. Cathy teared up.

"Thank you," she said earnestly. "This is perfect."

"That's not all," he said. "He gets to go to school again."

"What?" This was a surprise.

"School," James repeated. "We have a teacher for the handful of kids in The Shelter. Though, to be honest I don't know how many are close to his age. There's a range of ages, and not many kids at all, but he'll have friends and a teacher, and you'll have time for yourself between working as a nurse and putting up with me calling on you in your spare time."

She could manage nothing to say and stood there smiling stupidly into this amazing face. She suddenly wanted to hug, kiss, and thank him at once, but held herself back.

"Oh! I almost forgot!" He pointed to an empty spot nearby. "That place across from us is perfect for your friend, Linda. When is she released?"

"Soon, a few more days at the most." Cat swallowed down sniffles, appreciative of his kindness but not wanting to give him the impression he'd won her over.

He nodded. "Then I'll gather another tarp or two. She won't have the interior walls like ours at first, but I can muster another blue one so she'll be comfortable enough—and near her only friend."

Then, Cat did something she had not expected and hugged the man who'd already done so much, kissing him gently on the cheek. "You're a friend, too," she whispered. "A very sweet man, but I don't know how fast I can move, even facing the end of the world."

"Take your time," he urged, then pulled back, smiled, and held up a finger as if telling her to wait. Then he dashed inside his room, returning with a towel and bar of soap.

It was Dove brand—cheap but fragrant and so alluring to the woman who hadn't a shower in over a week besides the chemical wash when she first arrived. She stared at it as if confused, afraid to find normalcy in a relic from the past. "I need our things," she finally said, overcome by both emotion and crippling exhaustion, "but I'm suddenly so tired I don't want to walk all the way back."

"I'll put them in your tent," he promised. "You and Josh get comfortable and I'll be back. When I am, I'll watch the door to the locker room so you can bathe in private."

She watched from the door of her new home, simple but well-constructed for privacy, and watched him go the way they'd come. He walked with a boyish step, proud of the kindness he'd brought her and with his head in cloudy daydreams. He did not see the two officers still watching the young pair from down the hall.

With their heads drawn close, the brief safety the young man provided dissipated as Cathy recognized the hunger in each. She'd seen it before, many times, right before stepping on stage to dance before men like these. They were wanton and full of desire for the flesh their Colonel had purchased. With a shiver, she stepped inside and watched her son play. He never looked up, so he never noticed her tears.

At least he'll have school here, she thought. *And soon those men will know I'm off limits and move on.* But was she? Would she allow this young man to get close enough to claim her as his own?

"What's her name?" the Colonel asked.

"Who's name," Max replied with heavy lips from the drug. Whatever it was, it worked fast and muddled his thoughts.

"Your wife's."

"I'm not married," he said flatly.

"Oh. That's right. You came in with a white slave woman—a pregnant one at that."

Pregnant? That explained her voracious appetite. "She's not my woman and I never touched her."

"Of course not," but the Colonel sounded unconvinced, "but the coloring will determine that fact eventually. Nonetheless, I've decided to accept you into my ranks and you'll marry her."

That news surprised Max, and he nearly stumbled. "But I'm already..." He caught himself in time and recovered. "I've already decided I won't serve you."

"No, you haven't. But you're mulling it over, and that's why I visit more frequently. I'm convinced now you didn't kill my men in cold blood. But their lives come with a price. You proved to be worth six of them."

"I only killed three."

"You killed three and bested one worth more than the others combined. That makes you valuable—more so, even, than Sergeant Walters."

A new voice spoke into Max's chemical fog. "That's not fair, sir, he caught me by surprise. In a fair fight I would've won." It was him, the Marine from the grocery store for sure.

"Perhaps, but we'll never know because you two are now equals," the Colonel told the sergeant. To Max he said, "*Mr.* Rankin, I *will* accept you as a sergeant in my ranks alongside Walters. All will be forgiven but not till you drop this stubborn prisoner of war game. Tell us the truth."

"Why do you want *me* so badly?"

"Between you and Walters, I'll have doubled the amount of combat experience in the Regiment. Talk to us. Tell us what it is you're hiding, and I'll give you a squad of your own beside him. But... I warn you every man here liked those boys you killed. You'll have to prove your worth to them more than to me if you're to avoid dying by a bullet from behind."

"I won't," Max whispered. "I can't. I have to find... someone."

"Yes, your family. Your wife's pretty, but I wonder how she'll react knowing you took a white slave and put a baby in her."

"How do you..."

"We searched your home, Rankin." Walters replied. "We found her photo and that of your son. We know you have a family but just not definitively where."

"So you never took them?"

There was a brief exchange between officer and enlisted followed by a pause and then what must have been approval for Sergeant Walters to proceed.

"I tried to tell you this when we met, but we're not the bad guys, Rankin. We're the last remnants of America, trying to restart the best way we can."

Max managed a drugged laugh. "In Evansville, Indiana? All we need is baseball and apple pie and your dream is complete, Colonel."

"At least you're calling me that, now," the officer said with slight victory in his voice.

"Rankin... Max," Walters explained. "You and I started off on the wrong foot. Listen to the Colonel. You're like me, a veteran with combat experience. Listen to your instincts, yet trust your mind and what it's telling you. Marines are strong on their own but strongest in numbers. I'll vouch for you among the boys because no one saw you kill the others but me. Only the officers know the truth for now. I'll twist the grocery story up a bit so they'll understand. But the fact is, the Colonel—no, all of us—need you. Men like you and me will win this region back from the street gangs and the anarchists. There's true lawlessness out there, and lots of it. You felt it on the night I found you. You fought the gangs off pretty well but couldn't finish the job alone. They're your enemy, not us."

"I've got to find Betty." Max slipped

The Colonel let out a low *hmmm,* as he processed his wife's name. "Betty." He savored her name on his tongue and Max flinched. "We don't even know where to start looking, and we've no guarantee the gangs don't already have her and your son."

"Well, I'm *certain* they have her." Walters insisted. "The gangs rounded up every black man, woman, and child they could as soon as things fell to shit. They promised a utopia. There's a dozen factions, but don't worry, Rankin. We'll find them as we branch out and begin to police the region. With your help, I can train the men to finally do just that."

Max truly was listening. Though drugged, exhausted, and plain sick of their games, the Colonel's proposition made sense. Of course, he still wasn't sure this was the right community for him. "Does joining up mean you finally believe I'm free from charges of enslaving and impregnating a white woman?"

The Colonel's response chilled Max. "Not at all, but you're now responsible for her welfare, Sergeant, but not under the same roof. You'll house her separately but continue to provide for her until the child is born and everyone can see it's not yours—if that part of your story pans out. None of my officers will want her as a wife as long as long as she appears tainted, and I'll not make a whore out of her for the enlisted. That's not what we're about in The Shelter. We're... better... morally incorruptible."

"Of course you are," Max agreed lazily, mildly sickened by the racial undertones of any union they may have shared under different circumstance. *Tainted.* This man *oozed* bias and ignorance. Or, he knew well the hearts of the men of the Regiment and intended to dispense justice with a balanced hand. Max closed his eyes and allowed the drug to complete its work. Sleep would help, if it would come, but the Colonel had too many questions left to ask before that blessing came. In the meantime, though, he had much to consider and finally a choice to make. If he stayed and helped this man win his empire, whether he turned out a bigot or not, Max had a better chance of finding his family than before.

CHAPTER THIRTY-TWO

Sam Nakala drew blood from Adam while Mi-Jung collected specimens from Eve. Though sitting quiet and perfectly still, the faces of both children betrayed frustration, fed up, even, with how slowly the adults carried out this task.

"How much time do we have?" David asked.

"Time until what, Doctor Andalon?" Eve's voice carried a bitterness betraying frustration instead of her usual calm. "Time until Michael Esterling botches the battle without us there?"

The drug coursed through the veins of both children, intensifying anxiety and boiling tempers. David, in need of their agitated state before drawing these samples, had earlier injected them both with epinephrine. Now to a tipping point of rage, the extracts should provide sufficient levels.

"I meant," he said patiently, "Is there time for me to complete this study before we go?"

"No," Adam admitted angrily, shooting his sister a rebuking stare. "There is little *time* for anything and less if we don't leave soon."

"Well then," the adult replied, "I guess we'd better hurry."

"You should!" The way Eve spoke caused everyone in the lab to flinch.

David locked eyes with Stephanie Yurik who silently nodded her agreement. What they were about to do was risky, but she was as committed as he.

David took the tray of vials from his assistants and explained as much as he could. "Extract these for traces of natural adrenaline," he said. "Examine them for anything different than previous samples and isolate all things related to their adrenal glands. Work through the night if needed, just find it before we return." After a glance at the irritated children he added, "We may be gone a couple of days or more, but work like you've no time at all."

"I will, professor," Sam Nakala promised, "but Brooke won't like it when she finds out."

"Brooke has no say in this," the doctor snapped, briefly sounding like the children.

Mi-Jung, who had remained silent for the entire procedure, finally spoke. "What are we really looking for?"

Stephanie started to speak, but stammered and looked to David as if she should defer to him. He nodded and she continued, choosing the truth as a good place to begin. From the reaction of both assistants, it was the proper choice. "The abilities of these children are carried in their bloodstream, and we believe you'll find it encoded in either their catecholamines or cortisol and aldosterone. I think we can ignore their sex hormones, but we're ruling nothing out."

"So it's like the night of the fire," Sam realized, turning to his professor with eyes wide with fear.

David nodded. "Exactly. When Felicima and the others channeled their abilities, it was after I'd shot them all full of epinephrine—just as I did these two tonight."

Sam's eyes suddenly narrowed, his mind working out what his ears had heard. With steady hands he took the samples and spoke his mind. "It was wrong to do with primates, but now you've done it to children as if they're specimens."

"There's a difference here, Sam," David promised. "Humans and monkeys have many differences, but one sets them apart."

"Which is?"

"The ability to communicate through speech," Adam interrupted. "The doctor's *specimens* consented to these tests, unlike your *monkeys*."

David nodded. "They asked for this tonight, and that's what you *must* understand. That night in the lab at MIT, I injected those poor monkeys without knowing what harm I would do. It was wrong and I'm sorry for that, especially now I understand how these abilities work. Both Adam and Eve subjected themselves to this test so we can isolate a discovery, and it's up to you and Mi-Jung to do just that. Find out what's different in these samples and what *could* be extracted to isolate as a drug—one that recreates their powers. It's there, Sam. Find it so we can harvest it."

"Harvest?" The young man's voice tremored as he spoke, suddenly aware of his and Mi-Jung's role in the next phase. "I don't like the sound of that. It sounds like you mean to farm them."

"That's exactly what he *means* to do," Eve snapped, causing his hands to shake the samples in the tray.

"It's the only way to save them," Stephanie explained. "If we can separate the markers and learn to synthesize the result, then we can provide Michael and Jake with what they want—access to the abilities without a need to keep these children captive in the lab. Isolate what can be extracted and stored as either a pill or an injection. Something that can be passed on to another subject."

"It's the best way, Sam," David insisted.

"But we're not ready for that kind of experiment," Sam argued. "We're only your assistants!"

"No, Sam, you *are* ready. And these two have precious little time left unless you find a replacement for them."

"You don't mean..." Sam questioned, afraid of the answer.

Mi-Jung finally understood, turning to Stephanie with eyes large with fear. "They're going to destroy them?"

"Yes," Dr. Yurik admitted. ""These two were an early phase," he said, "developed only for study until we could isolate how their abilities are conveyed through their bodies. They were always meant for destruction, but not until after we understood the true strength of their power. David and I recently agreed the *how* is more important than the *how much* and, if we figure that out, we can save them both."

"I always hated that Felicima was bound for destruction," the young man said solemnly. "She was part of the throw away batch but deserved a chance at life. When you told me how the lab had burned, I wondered if *she* were the cause."

"She was," David said softly. "The epinephrine is only a catalyst, and the true power is related to emotion. I believe Felicima's power was made stronger by the other's abuse—and also my own. She was angry, enough so to burn the lab even if it meant killing herself along with Batch Alpha."

"If only we could study them longer," Sam begged.

"No," David insisted. "We're running out of time, and observations no longer matter. What we *must* learn quickly is *how* to transfer these abilities to others."

"You mean how to transfer it to Michael," a woman's voice said from the doorway. All eyes turned to find Brooke. "He wants the power for himself, doesn't he?"

"Yes," Dr. Yurik agreed, "and so does your brother."

"Where are you taking the children?" Brooke asked. "Are you breaking them out to freedom?"

"We're taking them to the battle. Michael can't win unless they're there."

Brooke raised an eyebrow toward Stephanie. "Is that so?"

"Very much so, I'm afraid. Neither Michael nor Jake would listen and are about to be slaughtered."

"In that case," Brooke said, "there's no reason to keep this from me, Sam. I'll help you get them out of the bunker, David."

✦

Brooke watched her husband give final instructions to Sam and Mi-Jung. Her choice to aid them, instead of turning him in, was easier than it should have been. It only took hearing David's acceptance of his previous mistakes to gain her support. He also finally viewed the pair as humans instead of experiments, and that gave her hope for his future as a father.

Stephanie Yurik handed her a gas mask.

"What's this for?"

"It's our ticket out."

"I hope it's not lethal," Brooke said with a frown.

"Not at all," David promised. "It's an aerosolized anesthetic."

"Knock out gas? There's no such thing."

"Apparently it was one of Jake's side projects. It works like a mild sedative but not strong enough to be lethal. To our heavier or more tolerant subjects, it will be more of a pre-sedation, and we've plenty of Haloperidol to finish them off," David explained.

"So we gas everyone and walk out?" Brooke asked.

Stephanie sighed. The idea had actually been hers. "Pretty much."

"Let's do it, then. How will you get it into the ventilation?"

"That's the easy part," David said with a grin. "The lab is set up as part of the main ducting but has its own system. By closing two dampers and opening two more, we can reverse the flow without shutting down the main system."

"And you know for a fact it will work?" All eyes turned to the children, groggy and coming down from their adrenaline rush. Stephanie had given them each a soda to stay awake.

"They told you it would work?" Brooke realized.

"They did," David admitted. "Apparently, Eve uses the ventilation ducts to spy on the entire bunker when we aren't around."

"Interesting. So we just walk out of here?"

"Yes," a sleepy Eve said from her bench. "We walk out unopposed and then ride five hours to Germersheim."

"Ride?" David asked. "Where do we find horses?"

"We don't," Adam replied.

"Did you give General Braston the letter?" Eve asked Stephanie.

"I did, just before he left."

"Good. When the senator loses his composure, he'll seek another option and remember our discussions. Things will be set up nicely when we arrive."

Both children set their drinks on the bench and stood, pulling their gas masks over their heads and indicating the adults should do the same. With a wave of Adam's hand, a tendril of air tripped the mechanism locking the laboratory door, leaving it to swing open on its own. "After you, doctor," he said.

Brooke watched dumfounded as Stephanie asked, "You could have walked out of here at any time?"

"Of course we could," Eve replied, "we're not monkeys in a cage. We're sentient beings with superior intelligence and ability."

218

"Why didn't you leave before now?"

"Because we were waiting for Dr. Andalon to arrive. He's the key to our true freedom, and now so are both of you."

David hefted a pack onto his back and opened the door to the main passage. Three enlisted men laid slumped against the bulkhead, breathing low and shallow, but very much alive. He knelt and checked the pulse of each one to be sure but felt the brush of Adam pass by.

"Leave them," the boy insisted, "and I will tell you which need medical attention if any."

The doctor gave the men a final glance and followed the boy down the corridor. If felt odd, trailing behind the child, walking with such confidence as if he'd lived this moment a dozen times before. Eve rushed past and joined her brother, taking his hand in hers as they strolled. The pair appeared as two normal children making their way toward an adventure, but they were nowhere near normal. Their combined intellects equaled an entire room of Einsteins, and there was no estimating the extent of their power.

David reached his hand in the pocket of his lab coat, absently feeling the capped syringes within. He hated that he felt the need to bring these but needed the insurance they would provide him and the others.

You don't need those, Eve's voice spoke plainly in his mind.

David missed a step, staggered, but recovered.

"Are you okay?" Brooke asked.

"Yes, I'm fine. Just tripped over my own feet, I guess. Nerves."

You have no reason to be nervous, either, Eve's voice said calmly, this time clearly in his head but feeling as if the sound had carried to his ears.

I'm going crazy? he asked himself. *The stress is too much.*

No, you are not, Eve said again. Up ahead the little girl turned and slyly winked.

I can hear you? he thought, hoping the question conveyed.

Yes, but only while I hold our connection.

So you are doing this?

Of course. You don't have the same abilities.

Then how can you link with me?

When you traveled with us to the dream world, you left a piece of yourself there. Think of it as a photograph's negative—a reverse image but with sentience. I am conversing with that part of you and can therefore speak with you here.

But how can you know what's in my pocket? Surely you can't read my mind.

No, my powers are *limited. I know because I watched you place them there. You are a good man, Doctor Andalon. Despite your shortcomings you mean well enough, and your intentions are mostly noble. But you* must *trust us, or your path turns darker than you'd care to know.*

I wouldn't have used it against you, not unless you turned dangerous at the end.

At the end of what, doctor? At the end of the battle if Michael and Jake tell you to subdue us? No, you will play a different role there, one which changes your life and our path.

I don't understand, he admitted. *What role?*

The silence chilled him, bringing forth anxiety as he walked the final steps to the blast doors. Here several soldiers lay sleeping in the staging area.

Adam flicked his wrist and wisps of air coalesced around the locks, spinning them in unison and causing the heavy bay doors to spread apart.

"What will we ride?" Stephanie asked. "Earlier you said we had a five-hour ride to the battlefield. There's nothing outside, so what will we ride if not horses?"

Eve stepped forward, blinking against the soft light of a world she'd never experienced. After spending a few moments with eyes closed and allowing grayish snowflakes to land on her face, she shook free from a trance and raised her hands into the air. Like a fervent conductor she directed a ghostly symphony of silence, sending tendrils of air dancing under her command.

As a child, David had once watched a loom weave a patterned rug, though he couldn't remember exactly where that actually was. What he would never forget, and was reminded of now, was the intricate lacing of thread until the rug magically appeared layer by layer. Though similar, watching her weave was different, almost as if a three-dimensional printer answered her fancies by assembling a ghostly form. Before the eyes of the adults rose the ghostly specter of a sailing ship made of air. It slowly dipped down into the ground, until the deck stood just above ground level.

"*Estowen*!" Doctor Andalon remarked. "It looks so real!" He stepped forward, reaching out a hand and finding the boards as firm as Adam's ghostly handshake had been.

"It *is* real, doctor," Eve said matter of fact. "Step aboard and let's embark on an adventure."

CHAPTER THIRTY-THREE

Linda Johnson stared at the four empty walls of blue tarp, stark except for a single army cot in the corner. Her life had finally gone to shit. Even her prolonged time on the quarantine stage had felt more like home, and this extra space giving her a full stride of a ten by ten tent of her own only reminded her how lonely her life had become. *Screw you, Bryan. Screw your need to visit Yellowstone.* Her husband's lifelong dream of visiting that park had taken away her family and placed her in this blue box of a prison—with baby on the way and forever alone in apocalyptic times. *In fact, screw Theodore Roosevelt, too*, she thought, *for building a vacation spot over a volcano. Asshole.*

Had she been a poetic woman, the mother-to-be would have found solace in the fact this bit of The Shelter was hers, finally, a place to begin her new life alone with her infant—if lucky enough to be born whole. But she never handled tragedy well, nor did she believe in her own ability to take care of this child on her own. *If it actually* is *a child, and not a spawn reject of radiation from a low budget movie.* She wasn't even certain she would love it, with twenty toes or twenty-two, or none at all. Then she both laughed and choked back a sob. The mother of Sloth on *Goonies* was a better mother than she when it came down to this growth in her womb.

A hand on her shoulder caused her to jump.

"What do you think?" Cat asked. "I know it lacks color," she said without waiting for a response, "but James is out on a detail and promised he'd scrounge up something to break the blue motif."

"It's a place to live," Linda replied with a shrug of indifference. "I'm alive, I'm warm, and I'm not out there mutating in the radiation. The blue is fine." But it wasn't.

"Well, I have something else for you," Cat said with understanding. She really was turning out to be a good friend, and having another woman around helped soften the constant loneliness. She offered up a gently used bar of soap and a white gym towel. "I've already used the bar once, but I want you to share it with me as long as it lasts. We may not be the last women on this earth, but at least we'll be the best smelling for as long as that lasts."

Linda stared down. The smell actually did work to return humanity to her thoughts regarding herself and the child. *Maybe that's all I need*, she wondered, *is a bit of normal.*

"Go on," her friend urged. "I even made this sign." She held it up and Linda read, *Woman Time: Come Back Later.* "I'll hang it on the door as soon as you go in. No men are in there right now. The night shift finished their showers two hours ago and are all in their racks. The day crew won't return for a few hours, so take your time and feel like a woman again. Trust me," she added with a wink, "my first shower felt amazing and yours will too."

"Thanks," Linda muttered, taking both soap and cloth, and digging her only change of clothes from the satchel she'd dragged from the quarantine stage.

"Leave your dirty clothes just inside the door, and I'll be in to launder those for you in a moment."

That was it. The woman's kindness was finally too much to bear, and everything broke at once. Linda fell to a heap upon her knees, tears flowing and sobs heaving in her chest. This was the cry, the sorrow, she had held back since the accident. No. Since before, in the moment Old Faithfull ceased to be even reliable and took away Seth and Suzy.

She didn't hate this child in her womb. It wasn't its fault as much as it wasn't Bryan's. He was a wonderful husband—loving and doting and insistent on making a family memory for the kids during a time when all they cared about was technology and social media fame. The trip was needed, a good idea at the time, and she suddenly hated herself for blaming him for the tragedy. She wanted them back. All of them, excited about the new baby and cozily turning the spare room into a nursery. Linda yearned for this nightmare to end and the real world to return.

Cat knelt and wrapped empathetic arms around her. This woman had known loss in her life as well, maybe not as much as hers, but no doubt experienced plenty at the hands of the boy's father. Yes, some of that had been spoken of, even if the worst of it had been avoided for Josh's sake. They were different, this middle-aged mom-to-be and this struggling single mother, but they were united in a similar bond—mothers in a world now completely dominated by dangerous men. They needed each other to survive. She had no idea how long her friend's embrace lasted, but missed it immediately when she let go.

"I'm sorry," Linda whispered as the sobs subsided.

"Don't be. You needed that. We all do, I think, and I'm sure my turn's coming. Just be there for me when it does."

"I never thought I'd have a friend again."

"Well, you do," Cat promised. "Now, go get your damn shower! You stink like chemical wash and antiseptic."

"Cathy," Linda asked with weariness that seemed to drag her words.

"Yes?"

"Thank you."

"You're welcome."

The Dove soap had been a luxury, Cat realized when she opened her ration of laundry detergent, one intimately given by a young man trying successfully to woo a beautiful woman. As much so as this scoop of harsh industrial cleaner, a way to clean dirt, dead skin, and bacteria from their clothing. The pungent whiff from opening the container made her gag. It was harsh, and smelled like chemicals, but there was enough here to wash their clothing once a week for three months. Less if James frequently overexerted in his uniform. In that case, she worried this would only last their small group about six weeks or so. She used it sparingly, adding just a dash to the hot water filling the sink.

She scrubbed hers, Linda's, and Josh's clothing since those still reeked of the radiation cleanser. This would be the last time she'd do theirs first, she realized, because the water turned yellow immediately upon finishing the load. She had to drain and refill the sink, wasting more detergent for the most important load. She was halfway through scrubbing the knees of James' tactical pants when the door behind her opened. Cat jumped. Someone had obviously missed the sign on the door.

She turned to find two men had wandered in. "Sorry," she said, "It's ladies time in here, boys. You'll need to come back in about thirty minutes."

Everything about them was wrong. The men lacked human sentience, animals on a mission of death or disaster, and their eyes focused on hers as if about to devour a meal after weeks of starving in the wilderness. These were no longer men. They were predators wearing officer uniforms.

"You have to leave," she said again with more urgency and hopefully conviction behind her words.

Neither replied as they continued forward. Shock of their arrival waning, Cat realized she recognized them both. "Gentlemen," she said, putting on the air she'd learned in *Pussy Galore's,* "I'm afraid this is no place for our first official meeting." This was the trick Tim had taught her to use when facing a man who refused to respect the word *no.*

They're after your control, Tim had explained, *that's what he wants more than your body itself.*

As fear crept in, she fought to maintain her steady tone of voice. "I've seen you both," she said, "watching from the gallery and again in the hall." She paused casually, drying her hands on the towel and stepping forward. "I'm Cathy Fletcher," she said with a warm smile, "but my friends call me Cat. I hope we can be friends."

One of the men paused, the humanity within returning, letting her know there was hope at least for him. The other continued forward and she faltered, placing a hand on his chest and causing him to turn. She had been wrong. His eyes were neither hungry nor lustful, they were murderous.

"What's your name?" she asked casually, just as if she was still in the bar. But there was no Tim to come to her aid. Not this time.

The sound of humming rose over the stream of running water coming from the showers. Linda had picked the wrong moment to cheer up and find some joy. The man pushed forward.

"She's pregnant," Cat spurt out, as if hoping the child in her friend's womb would protect from what was unstoppable by now.

No matter what both women had endured in their lives, she was rather sure the housewife had never been forced by a man. Not like all the times Cathy had endured Clint.

"Yeah?" the second man asked, the one most resembling an animal. "That supposed to stop me from wanting to take a look at her?"

"Some men don't like that," she said. "Some it would turn off."

"I like it. The baby makes their breasts fuller," he said, "even at her age."

That made the first man laugh. "Fills out the saggy bags, it does."

"You men are officers," she asked. "What will the Colonel think of this invasion?"

"He promised us wives," animal eyes said. "And Hank here is next in line to choose from the new litter. I'm second."

"Litter?" she asked. "So you have a deposit down and get to take your pick?"

"Pretty much. Hank wants you, and I wanna know what I'm getting stuck with. The latest batch looked sickly, and this one's at least got teeth and already a bun in the oven."

"Steve," the man named Hank cautioned, "just get your glimpse and let's go. You're hurting my chances here."

"Chances?" Cat spun. "I'm taken, in case you haven't noticed. James Parker is talking to me."

Hank laughed. "Corporal's don't get a choice. They get assigned what's left after the officers take theirs."

Steve pushed past and Cat reached out instinctively to grab his arm, missing and losing her balance. She awkwardly fell against the sink. Hank grabbed her from behind and held her tightly while his partner moved toward the sounds of running water. Linda's humming lured him.

Cat struggled. The counter bit hard into her side as he placed his weight atop her.

"Let him go," the man hissed in her ear, an airy hint of passion lurking. He wanted her in a dangerous way, and his free hand moved to feel her body.

"I guess you're not a man to wait for marriage," she said as his hands reached her waistband.

His fingers paused amid unfastening her belt.

"You're not unattractive," she continued flatly, "and you're right, an officer is a better choice than a corporal, but forcing yourself on me now will do nothing, but maybe earn a knife in your throat while you sleep."

His grubbing fingers ceased their wiggling.

The humming in the shower stopped abruptly, cut off by a guttural scream followed by Steve's deep laughter.

Cat squirmed, trying to get free, but Hank's grip tightened.

In the shower, Linda protested, her voice echoing over the sound of running water and begging for the animal to leave her alone. Her helpless pleas were pitiful, just the sort of whimper to lure the predator.

Cathy held her breath, moving her right hand and dipping it slowly into the plastic container. They would have to make do without laundry for a week or more, but she grabbed a handful of harsh detergent and dropped her hip. Above her, Hank slipped, striking his chin against the counter just as her hand came up. In a flash the soap was in his eyes and her hands pressed the granules deeper, scouring the soft flesh and digging it deeper with her palm. His screams eclipsed those of Linda in the next room. After delivering a quick kick to the groin, Cat raced to save her friend.

Max peered inside every tent, carefully checking each face. Sergeant Walters, he noticed, never batted an eye when invading the privacy of those within, whipping back tent flaps or pulling open plywood doors to see inside. These people had no liberty, no privacy, and this man treated their meager property as if they lived in a police state. And the sad part of this, Max realized, was none of them ever flinched when caught in compromising positions or in half dress. America was dead along with its privacy. Long live the all-seeing King Regiment.

"You haven't spotted her at all?" Walters demanded, "Are you sure you're actually looking?"

"Are you certain she's out of quarantine?" Max snapped.

"You're welcome to search the stage again, but the doc insisted he released the woman this morning."

Max scanned the endless maze of tents and hobbles. Though tidy and free of trash per the Colonel's strict orders, the city within the coliseum was a mess—worse than he'd seen in Tijuana following boot camp. A single person among this room of tarps and blankets was a proverbial needle in a haystack. "Is this the only place civilians are housed?"

"This is," Shayde agreed, "unless one of the enlisted coaxed her into perimeter housing."

"Perimeter housing?"

"Yeah, this place was built as a sports arena, so there are showers and old locker rooms on the east and west ends of the building." He pointed at the balcony. "The officers live up there, where they can watch over the civilians. The Colonel has his own quarters on the second level near command and control."

"But the enlisted sleep in the hallway?"

"It's not that simple. The officers may enjoy a grand view of The Shelter, but us enlisted we have peace, quiet, and proximity to the showers and their endless hot water." Before Max could ask for details, he added, "Geothermal aquifer. It's heaven after a long night of radiation exposure."

"Sounds like it. I can't wait to try it myself. So the men sometimes claim the women?"

"Yeah, but not the high quality ones. That's why the officers enjoy their view. They get first dibs at choosing a wife."

Max paused, remembering when society lived honorably. "None of that's okay, Shayde."

"Not two months ago, it wasn't. But this is a new world, R.H.I.P. Remember that acronym from the Marines? *Rank. Has. It's. Privileges.* Always and forever it has, and this *is* martial law—or about to be."

"Do the women get a say?"

"Of course. But which would you rather, if you were a gal? Would you want a highfalutin officer with *potential* for wealth following the reestablishment or a grunt who fixed crankshafts only a few months ago?" Before the other Marine could answer, he said, "Trust me, you'll take the officer because there ain't no more crankshafts out there to fix, and your handyman wouldn't be anything more than a serf to the new lords. The women will always choose the wealthy officers."

"Show me the perimeter," Max demanded, suddenly filled with urgency. He wouldn't allow harm to come to Linda. "Each and every one."

"That won't be difficult, since the night shift is sleeping and the day already set out to forage and scout." Walters led him from the main arena and up the ramp. As if flipping a coin in his mind, he paused then turned right. "We'll start here. You look portside and I'll check starboard."

Walters had been correct. Most of the tents, though more elaborately constructed than those on the floor, were either unoccupied, or filled only with men. These had plenty of room in their ten-by-ten allotment, the maximum allowed each man by the Colonel.

As they reached the end of the row, Shayde muttered. "What's this nonsense?" A sign on the door read, *Woman Time: Come Back Later.*

Max smiled triumphantly. "Now that's the exact sort of thing I'd expect Linda to hang before taking a shower." A scream from beyond the door clamped his mouth shut and set both men running.

Max, fatigued from his time in captivity and out of breath from lack of conditioning, sprinted into what turned out to be a laundry. He spied a man on the floor with lieutenant bars pulling himself off the ground. As the officer turned, the Marine could clearly see the flesh around the man's eyes had been chemically burned. Without hesitation, he grabbed the man's armpit and thrust him forward.

"Get in there," he growled, not willing to allow the man out of his sight. He shoved the lieutenant, stumbling, into the showers behind Shayde.

What Max saw next, nothing during the war had prepared him for.

Shayde Walters had skidded to a stop, standing frozen and watching as a fully clothed wild woman sat atop a second man's chest.

"Don't look at her!" the woman screamed. "Don't look at her! Stop looking at her! She's not yours," the woman demanded, "You can't look at her! You can't look at *any* of us!"

She was a beautiful woman, young but not unworldly so, with just enough experience lining her face to suggest a hard life. Her shoulders were set, with firm muscles suggesting fitness—possibly experienced in sports or dance. Max's eyes followed the way her triceps quivered, fully engaged as she set her hands deep into the man's face. With sadness he recognized the quiver of her forearms as her thumbs gorged the offender's eyes. Neither he nor Shayde hurried to save the man, the damage was irreparable and she was nowhere near ready to calm.

Max's own eyes watered to watch and he looked away, finding a naked Linda crouching, horrified and looking on from the corner of the shower. He picked up a towel, calmly turned off the water, and draped the cloth over her dignity. Other than terrified, she seemed unharmed.

In a low voice he whispered a question. "Did he touch you?"

Linda, as if only noticing her traveling companion had arrived, nodded but quickly shook her head. "Yes," she said, "but not like that. He was about to, but Cat got him first."

He inclined his head toward the young woman, now less frantic and muttering the words softer.

"Don't look. Don't look. Don't look at her!" They eventually faded under her breath.

"You've found a good friend," he said, "but she's about to face a lot of trouble."

Linda nodded, staring unblinking at the orbital fluid turning frothy pink and slowly making its way toward the drain.

The man, wearing captain bars, writhed under Cat's weight and sobbed bloody tears running down his cheeks.

Shayde moved to lift the girl.

"Stop," Max commanded, and surprisingly the other sergeant complied. "Cat," Max whispered, "My name is Max Rankin. Has Linda told you about me?"

Only then did she look up from her handiwork, nodding recognition at the name.

"Good. Now I need you to do as I say, so we can take care of Linda."

"She needs my help," Cat said, unseeing the woman now standing over her.

"Yes. But you've saved her, and now you must help her find some clothes."

She nodded vigorously. "Yes. Clothes."

"Good. Take her into the next room and help her dress. I'll take these men into custody, and see to it they pay for what they've done."

"Perverts," she muttered absently. "Dirty perverts who just want to leer. That's how they start, you know. But it always ends up with touching us girls, Tim. They touch us, then they grope us, then they wait for us outside the club. But you won't let them follow us, Tim. You're a good man."

Max didn't know who Tim was, but did not correct her. "No, I won't let them follow you."

Cat slowly rose and walked toward Linda, lifting her to her feet and helping her into the next room.

After the women had withdrawn, Sergeant Walters let out a low whistle. "This isn't good, Max."

"Why not? The way I see it, she stopped two rapes today."

"That's not the problem," Shayde insisted. "These are the Colonel's cousins."

Max closed his eyes and cursed quietly.

PART IV
NEW WORLD
NEW RULES

CHAPTER THIRTY-FOUR

The Colonel's office could barely hold the number of people inside. Max stood to allow the women to sit when they entered. Linda, thankfully, appeared fine. Her face bore lingering irritation like it ate a sour melon but otherwise seemed pleased to see him. He gave her a smile which she briefly returned. Her eyes quickly darted toward the younger woman, as if to say, "Take care of this one."

He gave a subtle nod and followed the eye movement, remembering having learned the girl's name was Cathy Fletcher. She, it turned out, had an up road trek of trouble ahead. All of it, Max could tell, was written on the Colonel's face.

"Sit," the commanding officer of the Regiment demanded, and both women complied.

Max moved closer to the wall, finding a photograph to stare at while listening to the exchange. It was the kind service men kept in their offices, reminders of better or worse times that shaped them and prevented full inclusion in the civilian world. He examined a row of men wearing powder blue uniforms and spied a younger version of the Colonel. The boy in the photo grinned innocently, beaming his joy at standing in front of an A-10 assault plane.

He caught Shayde watching him study the picture and lifted an eyebrow questioningly.

The man rolled his eyes as if to say, *I told you, he's a real Colonel.*

A-10. At least he has some cool factor after all, Max thought. But the man was still Air National Guard.

"Miss Fletcher," the senior officer asked, "of what crime are you accusing my officers?"

She opened her mouth, expecting questions but not *that* one so directly. She closed it again, then opened it to speak.

He cut her off.

"Because it seems to me," the Colonel observed, "neither of you were harmed. Were you raped? Was she?" Without waiting for an answer he turned to Linda. "Ma'am, did either of the men lay a finger on you?"

"No," she said quietly, in barely more than a whisper. "He walked into the showers and stared at me."

"Stared at you? What do you mean?" He rubbed his temples despondently. "I don't understand. Is it possible he walked in and looked with shock upon you, not expecting to find a woman using the soldier's showers? The *men's* showers. Did you have permission from me or another officer to use them? Why were you even in there if you didn't?"

"No," she answered quickly, then changed her mind. "Yes. I mean, I don't know. Cathy said we could, but hung a sign so men wouldn't walk in on me. She was scrubbing laundry and I was bathing. Then he walked in and stood there, staring at me."

"And what did you do?"

"I screamed."

"I see. You screamed, not because you were in danger, but because a man, one of my officers, saw you naked."

"Yes, but he looked like he wanted to do more and I was afraid."

"He *looked* like he wanted to do more. How does someone prove such an accusation?" the Colonel asked.

Cathy answered before Linda. "Some men have a way, Colonel, of showing a woman their soul. If she was afraid, it was because he made her feel that way."

"And that was enough to destroy him?" The anger suddenly flowed as if a dam had broken. Words spewed as the Colonel shouted. "What gave you the right to blind a man during a dangerous time? One growing worse each day! What entitled you to remove his ability to sense danger around him, to see it coming, or even to have an ability to stop it?"

"You did!" Cathy shouted. "When you brought me here against my will and spouted nonsense like *repopulating* the world! I didn't ask to be part of your *cult*!"

"I could have left you on that compound where I found you!" the Colonel snapped.

"You should have!"

"If I had," the senior officer explained, regaining his composure, "you would have been a slave to that disgusting man and his entourage. I *rescued* you and your son, giving you both a chance at a better life."

"You don't get to decide my future."

"No, Miss Fletcher, that's where you're wrong. The society that once protected you is dead. Men like me *must* decide your future, and that includes what you did to my officer."

"He deserved it."

"Maybe so, but we need every able-bodied man who stands for a better future! Nothing you could possibly say could excuse your actions! A soldier is blind now, because of you. Blind and crippled and the side of freedom is down a very valuable man!"

She stammered, unable to speak clearly.

"And so I ask you again," he said, suddenly as calm as before, "of what crime do you accuse my officer?"

Max flinched, studying the girl who had never considered she may have been guilty of a crime herself.

She sat dumbfounded, staring forward and replaying the events in her mind. When the tears came, they fell slowly from a mist around the edges, tearing away to drip along cheeks that had somehow remained dry for too long.

Something deeply troubled this girl's past, and the Colonel yearned to say something to help. A glance toward Shayde revealed he shared in wanting to protect these women, but their fates were sealed. The girl had overreacted and now a valuable man was lost.

"Your silence damns your claims, Miss Fletcher." The Colonel said with finality, turning his back to look out the window. For some reason, he had left his own uncoated by the spray foam layers around the building. His eyes stared out at the city, northward as if examining the cloud of falling ash and snow in the distance. It would never stop in their lifetime, Max and this man knew, remaining as a grimy film over society. The ash of war had buried any justice these women may have had in a different world. "I want to help you," he finally said, "and I believe you protected this woman in the best way you knew. But you have no authority here, and that man once did. And so I ask you, are there any *crimes* you wish to levy?"

"Yes," she answered flatly. "There was a second man, Hank. He held me down and fondled me while his partner, Steve, went in to bother Linda."

"Ah, yes. You are unmarried, and thus your body still belongs to you. His taking advantage deserves paid restitution. He *will* be forced to make amends to you. Of that I guarantee."

"Thank you," she said softly.

At least there was some good news from this exchange.

"Since Hank desires to marry you, I believe that will be sufficient enough. He is leading a patrol at the moment, so the ceremony will take place as soon as he returns. It will be held privately in this office to prevent others from thinking that simply touching a woman is enough to claim her."

Cathy's body stiffened. "No! I don't won't marry him! I refuse!"

"I'm afraid that's the only way Steve will drop the charges against you, as he expressed to me this very morning. He said, and these are *his* words, that life as a full man is over, and it is up to his brother to protect and build upon whatever's left of their family's legacy."

"No!" she protested. "I can't."

"He will live under your roof as long as you are married to Hank, and you will pay restitution by nursing, nurturing, and caring for the man you so willfully destroyed. That's my final decree."

"I have a son," she said softly. "He won't understand."

"Your son now has a father and an uncle, so understanding will emerge in time."

"Colonel..." she stammered.

"That is all."

Shayde moved to assist the women from their seats and walked them to the door. Once they were gone, he moved to stand beside Max. They exchanged a knowing look. The Colonel had not been wrong, and the soldiers knew that fair was fair. But they also believed the brothers had meant both women harm. This verdict bothered them both.

"Do you need more from us, sir?" Sergeant Walters asked, obviously as ready to leave the room as Max.

"I do, actually. I need your combined tactical experience. I recently sent scouts north to McCutchanville, and they investigated gang activity there. Large amounts of citizens were taken there."

Both men cocked their heads questioningly, confused by the odd location.

"It seems they've claimed the surrounding schools and country club as bases for their foothold, so we'll strike them as military targets." The Colonel paused. "Most importantly, they hold the airport."

"That's why the city feels empty," Max realized. "The gangs know you control the city, so they've been driving residents northward. Are the citizens white or black?" he asked the Colonel.

"The scouts only saw white captives."

"Why does it matter?" Shayde asked, not immediately understanding.

"Restitution," Max explained.

"Restitution? For what?"

"Tell him, Rankin," the Colonel ordered, "and let's be finally done with the tension between you and me. Since we took you into custody, you've demanded to know where I stand in regard to a race war—well now it's time it's clearly laid out."

Max paused, thinking of all those arguments with Betty and how they'd been losing Tom to the gangs—to those full of hatred and seeking revenge. Whatever Dr. King had envisioned, this wasn't it. This was the future his son desired, and the gangs had power enough to provide it for him and those other young people who'd given up on America—and thought America had given up on them.

Max felt his knees weaken, remembering his time driving through cities during the protests over racial justice. He had been fresh out of the service then, newly seated as a trucker and fighting to keep his meager route profitable. The warnings had gone out far and wide throughout the industry, with the older drivers cautioning about the 1992 riots in Los Angeles. That was a prophetic time, when a black man was unfairly beaten by police. Amidst that angry protest, a white trucker had been pulled from his rig and beaten to a pulp. His only crime was being white in a time and place where more melatonin meant unfairness.

But that wasn't the case in the midwestern cities, not this most recent time around.

The truckers, pulled from their rigs and shown on the news in Kenosha, were oftentimes white, but Max knew the assailants weren't always black. This time, the anger was more about unsettling America and making the middle class uneasy—socialist constructs of revolution that would seek to enslave all people equally. No, much of the political and monetary backing of these incitements had more to do with financial inequality than true social injustice.

That became more evident when even *his* rig was pelted by concrete-filled water bottles and feces. Max saw firsthand they hadn't just targeted white owned businesses and corporations, but black-owned as well. In each situation, the opportunists looted and vandalized the lifelong fruits of labor by men like him—entrepreneurs who'd chosen self-reliance over dependency upon government masters.

The young people he witnessed pulling guns and throwing Molotov cocktails were barely older than Tom, wherever *he* may be. These grandsons and daughters of those who marched with the reverend were too far removed from ideals like love and equality. They instead viewed brave men like Max as having fought colonialist wars on the wrong side. It went against the desired narrative to better yourself through merit when capitulation to the state was meant to keep everyone happy.

They called me a sellout and do not see the true evil.

That was the true war in Max's opinion. Poverty was the modern-day slave's shackle.

Max had watched his own brother grow up addicted to the system—suckling at promises made by the true enslavers. It was easier in his day to snare a man with promises than by chains. But that was something Max Rankin figured out only after he joined the Marines to better himself. He knew those who often championed minority causes also heralded the societal constructs that kept people like him impoverished and dependent upon the riches they offered—affordable Nikes, iPhones, and needles. The true masters over his people were the false deliverers of racial justice and equality.

During the protests, Max had realized the American flag hanging from his rearview mirror made him a target, but so did the Marine eagle, globe, and anchor on his license plate frame. He was a symbol of freedom and of self-rule, making him a target of the rioters no matter the color of his skin. He feared the mentality of the mob during this time more than walking as a soldier during the Iraqi war. There too, the enemy sought to kill him as a champion of freedom and equality.

In American cities, the enemy sought only to punish him for proving they could escape their chains if they succeeded in self-reliance. Max was proof they could better themselves if they stopped listening to their masters. But they listened intently to the lies, and the message was *take what you want and we'll reward you*. Of course, the reward would only come after granting their masters more of the privilege his people might have earned for themselves.

"Slavery," Max finally said, breaking free from his thoughts. "They want retribution for slavery."

Shayde turned wide-eyed toward his Colonel, shocked and full of disbelief. "There's no slavery now! What's he talking about?"

"Plantations," Max muttered, remembering a pamphlet Betty had found in Tom's room. "One master home per family, and a crew of white slaves to work each."

"Precisely," the Colonel agreed. "There are extremists among the gangs seeking to flip the script and make the white people their beasts of burden."

"I will help you," Max promised. "But only because my wife and son are out there. I've got to find them. It's possible Tom has fallen in with this lot and I need to reach him, to speak reason. Where are they amassing the families?"

"The Evansville airport. You're welcome to search there for your family as long as the overall mission is a success," the Colonel agreed.

"That depends on the terms of what you consider *success*. You've been calling me by my rank, but I'm not yet a member of the Regiment. Colonel, where do you stand in regard to my people? I need to know now, how many of your men would cut down my family in the heat of battle, like the cavalry did to the Sioux at Wounded Knee? I cannot, and won't allow that. I'll kill every man who tries to kill a black man, woman, or child simply for sport. Kill me now or finally tell me about your idea for this *new* world."

"Not every white male is a racist, Maxwell Rankin." The Colonel's eyes flicked to the photo of himself standing before the A-10 Warthog. "I saw you looking at that earlier, and I know you're judging me for serving Air National Guard instead of full active duty. But make no mistake—I'm not another George W. Bush with gained appointment because of who my daddy was."

"But you had *white* privilege."

The usually calm and stoic senior officer broke a smile. "Perhaps, it was my *privilege* that my alcoholic father ignored his wife and kids, drinking himself to death every single day of his life?"

"An alcoholic father doesn't mean you understand," Max accused. "You don't get to avoid the free pass your skin gave you."

"Did the color of your skin prevent you from reaching the rank of gunnery sergeant? Or from purchasing that big rig of yours after the war? Tell me, Gunny, did you ever fail to promote for any reason except merit? Were you ever skipped over because of the color of your skin?"

"No. The Marines was a meritocracy, and I earned everything on my own!"

"Exactly. The United States Military was a cross-section of America, and the best part of it was there weren't no black, white, yellow, red, or brown. There was blue, green, khaki, and various shades of dress for each. We dealt with those who brought their hatred into our ranks as individuals and sent them packing because we never wanted their beliefs to taint another soldier's opinion of the brother or sister helping to bring him or her home. My daddy taught me that."

"You said your daddy was a drunk."

"I did, but I never said he never taught me anything! What I learned was how *not* to be a racist. Oh, he was born to one, raised by his daddy to hate everything about anyone who wasn't like him. But he came home from Vietnam a changed man in many ways. He would have died over there—maybe been better for us if he had—but he made a friend, a brother from Los Angeles, California, who literally lifted him on his back and carried him out of several firefights."

"So what? Your father was a soldier."

"My father was a *Marine!*" The Colonel changed when he said this, deeply proud yet mourning a connection he and his father never shared. But this man indeed understood the price his father paid.

"I didn't realize," Max said, aware he'd misjudged.

"A black man threw his body on a grenade so my father and their other fireteam members could return home to their families. A black man's blood, skin, and hair exploded so close to my father, he insisted till his dying day Jim was fused into him. Even his soul had burrowed its way deep inside, or so my father would breathe into my face when the whiskey wasn't working. My father owed his life to that man, but knew his life wasn't as worthy as Jim's would have been."

"Survivor's guilt," Shayde said with a grunt. "I've heard of it. The man who lives does so while wasting the gift he received."

"No. Not wasted, only believed so," the Colonel explained. "Daddy came home after surviving two more tours and passed on Jim's gift by even saving others along the way. But the crux of who he was died over there, and only the shell returned. No, the real evil in the world wasn't the racist he was before the war, but the assumed *privilege* you suggest he enjoyed. That *privilege* didn't save him from being spit in the face by a Jane Fonda wannabe at the airport. That woman walked right up to him with a smile on her pretty face and, when he leaned in close to listen, spit in his eye and called him a baby-killer. Before he could react, he was doused from behind by her hippie boyfriend. I was there, watching it all as a young boy."

"What did they throw on him?" Shayde asked.

"I expected my daddy to return home from Vietnam smelling like a soldier, rough and leathery with gunpowder on his skin and a hint of Old Spice. But instead, my only memory of my father wearing the Marine Corps dress blues provided a life-long memory of cat piss."

"I'm sorry that was his return home," Max said, "and I'm sorry mine was better."

"That's not what I'm saying. I'm *happy* yours was better. What I'm *saying* is there's no room in this world for extremists on either the right or the left, nor categorized by color. Destruction of property doesn't lead to equality, it creates division. Burning down businesses, whether small or big, is terrorism, and it affects everyone in the community. Human rights existed in the world before the end because Americans stood up against tyranny."

"Not all the people Walters and I are about to fight believe freedom means *all* Americans!"

"No, I don't suppose they do, but it always has, no matter *what* they believe or how historians revise the narrative. Max, do you know the name of the first American killed during the American Revolution? Tell me, Marine, because if you don't, then that's part of the problem of how our country died."

"No. I don't," Max admitted.

"Crispus Attucks." Shayde whispered.

"Yes. Crispus Attucks. Brought to the American colonies by the same tyrants that killed him. He survived slavery, became a sailor, and then lived as a self-made *man*. Not only a *black* man, but an *American* man in Boston. He was the first person killed fighting for a voice in what became known as the Boston Massacre. Sure, he was silenced years before Martin Luther King was able to speak up for *all* American people, but he did so valiantly and not high on drugs. He's a true black hero to celebrate."

"What's this got to do with the mission?" Max demanded, though he knew by now the man's beliefs truly aligned with his own. The Colonel was a good man, with good reasons for his desire to repatriate the region.

"There is a fully armed body of soldiers—criminally minded—capturing citizens and corralling them as slaves. I can't allow that in what's left of America. And mark my words, America will not die as long as the Spirit of '76 is remembered. We can't win an urban war yet, not with their soldiers living like guerrillas in the city itself. But what we can do is attack the airport—the true brain of their illegal society. We'll take away all of their weapons and resources and return the people, all the people regardless of color or creed, to a lifestyle protected by fair laws and representative government. We *will* conquer them now, tonight, while they're weaker than us, and help the survivors appoint a self-governing body. But it must be one rejecting slavery and respecting existing land ownership. Otherwise, men like Crispus Attucks and my father's friend, Jim, died in vain."

"Why fight a war at all? Why not resolve this peacefully?"

"I grew up in a time when the reverend spoke for that peace. He taught that racism comes in many forms, but the truest face of it is hatred and divisiveness, not lack of awareness or enjoyed privilege. People aren't inherently racist and can't help where in society they're born. But they *can* choose how they treat others. With understanding of societal problems, we can do so with love and find real solutions. But to believe otherwise is failure to see the real problem. Divisiveness is a weapon used by those seeking more power, and power is always politically motivated. I agree with Martin Luther King that the only way to break down hate is through nonviolence, but society is different now, and the balance of power in a warlord state doesn't care about color of skin. We have a chance to win a war and nip divisiveness early. There may be some in my Regiment who disagree, but *my* intention after the war is for an inclusive society. I hope now we're finally clear and you understand my position."

Shayde stepped up, placing a hand on Max's shoulder. "We need your help, Devil Dog. None of this is about race, it's about preserving liberty for all. I can't do it alone and I'll need you there."

Max paused, hearing the voice of Tom arguing in his mind. Then he heard Betty, urging him to listen to his son. *But that's the problem*, he thought. *The young are blinded by the lies of politicians.* "Count me in," he finally replied.

Cathy knelt beside Josh, hugging him closely and whispering consoling love. He stared down at the wooden cars in his hands, lost in their wonder and desiring freedom to play by himself. He never understood his mother's tears, only that *Joshie Time* had ceased being her priority the night she killed his father. She let him go with reluctant release and watched him sulk off on his own. She lifted red eyes toward James Parker and Linda.

"You can't go through with this," the young corporal insisted.

"I will, and I have to, but I have a plan. I promise I won't belong to him more than a few days or weeks, then I'll be able to return. You'll see."

Linda chuckled. "You have a plan?"

"I've lived with an abusive husband before, and I know how to handle one better than anyone alive, I suppose. No matter *what* Hank is, he isn't Clint Fletcher."

"Who?" James asked.

"Her ex-husband," Linda whispered, casting a thumb over her shoulder at Josh. "The boy's father."

"I'm sorry, I didn't know he was abusive."

"Clinically insane sociopath, actually," Cat said with a sigh. She spoke her full story aloud for the first time since relaying it to Jenny Klingensmith a month or so before, beginning with the night he was waiting in her apartment. She teared up less this time when she spoke about her sister, but this time didn't worry Josh was listening. That bothered her more than the story itself, that she'd finally told it enough times she knew he could handle it as well as she. By the time she got to the boat, the gunshot, and Clint's final dive over the side, both James and Linda were staring at the boy.

"I wish he hadn't tried to do it in front of him," James whispered.

"Clint always sought an audience. The adoring fandom gave him power," Cat explained, "and apparently he witnessed his father do the same to his mother years before. Hopefully I ended that cycle when it comes to Josh."

"You need to bring him to the Colonel," James insisted. "He's an actual psychiatrist and can help. You've no idea what that kind of trauma will do if left untreated."

"More than his mother being forced to marry Hank and to live with Steve? No, the Colonel's part of the problem and I'm working on a plan to get away from him, too."

James sat silent at that, angry the woman he'd been growing to fall in love with was being forced to live with the two officers.

"Look," Cat said. "I lived with Clint so many years I learned to survive. Plus, I still have a few tricks up my sleeve."

"Like what?" Linda asked.

"Hand me my bag," the younger woman said in a whisper, as if about to reveal a secret. "I'll show you."

Linda handed it over, and Cat pulled open the zipper. "Crazy Mike took Clint's gun from me and also a knife I stashed. Hell, he even took Clint's stolen jewelry and precious stones, but he missed the most important item I've ever owned."

Both James and Linda leaned in. "What is it?" Linda asked with a whisper, peering inside as if expecting an ax or machete or nuclear weapon.

"My escape plan." Cat peeled the inside zipper over and revealed a single stitch where the handle was sewn. "When I got to nursing school, I was trusted to work with chemicals and even medications." She leaned in and added so Josh wouldn't overhear, "In my advance classes, I even handled poisons."

Linda laughed aloud, finding the prospect of her friend carrying around a hidden stash of poison the funniest thing since the night of the apocalypse. Cat realized this was the first Linda had laughed since losing her children at Yellowstone, and it wasn't the poison that was so funny, but her admiration for the tenacity of her friend. She smiled back proudly.

"You're going to use it on Hank and Steve," Linda whispered with glee. "Get them back quietly and end it once and for all, then come back to us?"

Cat nodded. "Yeah. That's the plan. I won't do it right away, but it's Ricin, so the only side effects will be a bad flu shared between two brothers. Since I'll still be working in the quarantine hospital, it'll make sense that I caught it and passed it to them, but they won't survive. After they're gone, no one will suspect it wasn't just flu. I'll be free to remarry, and I won't let the Colonel decide for me next time. He'll owe me that, and if he doesn't, I'll simply take Josh and leave."

Linda said nothing, just stared at the satchel with wide-eyed wonder.

James broke the awkward silence. "I don't like it, but they do deserve death. I say do it. Kill the sons of bitches and come back to me. I just hate you have to go to his bed tonight."

"Linda, will you watch Josh? I don't want him around the first time his mommy has to sleep in a man's bed."

"I can't. I'm working the kitchens tonight."

"Then you, James?"

He shifted uncomfortably.

"Please?" she pleaded. "Just tonight. Sleep here on the bed beside him and make sure he thinks I'm just working or something. God knows he's used to his mom working late by now. Plus, he really likes you and you're great with him."

"I will," the corporal promised. "But only tonight. Then you get your ass back here where you belong as soon as you can. Do it quickly because I think your plan's brilliant. They'll both be gone, and no one would ever suspect you had anything to do with it. It'll be a case of good luck for a newlywed wife."

"He's right," Linda insisted. "You should do it sooner than later. But just so you know, I'm not staying here. I'm talking to Max as soon as he returns in the morning, and I've got my own plan to get us all away from here. I'd rather take my chances on the road with him and you two, than to stay around here and get raped by one of the Colonel's officers. Max will take us away if we ask him, I'm certain he will."

Laughter in the hallway caused all three to jump, but the voices were still quite a-ways away.

"Where's my wife-to-be?" Hank's voice called. "Here, Kitty Cat! Come to daddy!"

"Don't worry," Cathy said, "I'll be fine. Just take care of Josh." She clutched the satchel tightly and stood, just as the lieutenant stepped inside the flap.

Hank scanned the room and settled a frown on James sitting so close to his wife-to-be. To Linda he said, "Be a dear and carry her bag up to my quarters, will you?"

"I don't know which ones are yours," she replied truthfully.

"I do," James said through clenched teeth, "and I can show you."

"That's a good lad," Hank said with a laugh. Grabbing Cathy's hand, the officer led Cathy away. Their ceremony waited, and *his* excitement clearly overshadowed his bride's.

CHAPTER THIRTY-FIVE

Michael Esterling stood on the ridgeline, overlooking the valley surrounding the Rhine River. A longtime student of history, he marveled at the region so pivotal in every German war to date. And no wonder. The river fed the heart of Europe with its tributaries, nourishing bountiful harvests and shipping lines for centuries. In places, he could still see traces of trellises where grapes made these vineyards famous.

That was before a nuclear arsenal destroyed its grandeur and the fallout buried its hope.

Not since the second world war had the cities and towns along this waterway been so trodden and reduced to rubble, and viewing the valley made him think of General Patton. The first time the iconic tank commander rolled over these same bridges and northwest into Heidelberg, he might have viewed it with equal sadness, wishing he could have viewed the area in its luscious prime.

Esterling cringed.

Patton had met his death thirty kilometers away from the rubble below, and Michael shuddered to think he and Jake would meet a similar fate. He turned his attention to the encampment between this hill and the western river bank. There, Colonel Titus rested his column of soldiers. They did not have to feign exhaustion after their quick march from Stuttgart—more than eighty kilometers on foot to keep ahead of the invasion force.

"They barely made it," Jake pointed out, handing over his binoculars. On the far side of the city, the Russians had entered the valley. "A few more hours and they would have overtaken them on the road."

"Will they attack tonight?"

"I don't think so," Jake said. "This valley is the best place to cross the Rhine while keeping such a large force intact, but it's vulnerable to the higher ground on three sides. No, I think they'll assume we're leading them here with purpose and proceed with caution. At the very least they'll scout these hills and inspect the bridges first." He turned a nervous eye to the nature preserve southwest of their position. The hills he mentioned hid the bulk of their own force—a pitiful showing until Richter and the German forces move into position overnight.

"We'll succeed," Michael assured him, "Adam and Eve said we would."

"I believe them too, but I've got my doubts. Our artillerymen have zero experience with antique cannons, and the cavalry have only been riding horses for a few months. We're literally out-experienced and unprepared."

"So was George Washington."

"You aren't George Washington, Mike."

"No..."

Michael *felt* like the iconic leader, and the battle ahead was very much like facing the British in New York. All he had to do was defeat this invasion force and secure his leadership over the fractured people surviving in the region. Of course, the British never gave Washington a true opportunity to end the war until Yorktown, but this time the leader of the free world knew the future held victory.

"Wait, that's not right!" Alarm filled Jake's voice as he snatched back the binoculars.

"What isn't?"

"The Russians. They're over-pursuing. Look there," he pointed to the south. Several vehicles had already pushed across the Maxau Rhine Bridges.

"I thought they'd focus on the Rudolph von Habsburg."

"So did I, but they're in a hurry to end this."

"Our line is west of them. Won't we still be able to attack their southern flank?"

"Not like we'd planned, and Richter's not ready in the north.

"Then we'll have to deal with what they gave us. Strike now, Jake. We *will* win!"

"No," Braston argued. "We should stick to the plan. Titus will have to fight this skirmish alone and hopefully know enough to move his line northward to rally with us."

"At least use the artillery," Michael insisted. "Soften their attack while he gets free."

"No," Braston argued. "If we give away our positions before Richter's forces are in place, the Russians will split, taking the same advantage we'd hoped for. Worse, they'd catch Richter on the open field by himself. If they do that, there's no path to victory."

"Titus and his forces will be killed, Jake. Fire on those trucks and turn the enemy before they cross."

"If we fire our cannons," Jake yelled, "they'll split their forces north to Frankfurt and south to cross at Strasbourg. Then *they'll* blow those bridges and we'll be flanked between them."

Esterling paused. *The children promised we'd win, but do we do so by attacking now or by waiting?* The wrong decision would cost them the battle. He watched Jake carefully for any indication the man meant betrayal. *He's resisting my leadership, so* of course *he wants to usurp me.* He set his posture.

"Do it," Esterling commanded.

"It's premature, Mike. I won't."

"Change the script, Jake!" Esterling hadn't meant to snap, but his frustration won out. Jake was the military brains, but *he* was the political leader the world needed.

"Script? Mike, this isn't a campaign. No offense, but this is a damned war!"

"Just like that? You'll defy me? I guess they were right all these years."

Braston seemed puzzled. "Who's right? What are you talking about?"

Jake had forgotten his place. Friend or not, Michael Esterling was in charge, and the children assured him everything depended on *his* leadership. "There was a saying around the fraternity," Esterling said to the general. "No one can say *no* to Jake Braston. Well I just did and you refused an order."

"An order? You trusted me to run the military side of things. What are you doing, Michael? I'm only advising you allow more of them get across, so we can make it sting and give them pause. Your plan will poke the bear into using its full strength."

"So this is it? How you betray me? Adam and Eve said one of you would eventually, I never thought it would be you!"

"Have you gone mad? I wouldn't..."

"Send the damned signal, Jake!" His shout caused heads to turn in the junior ranks, and several officers began to mutter dissent. "Now!"

The anger on Jake Braston's face clearly showed the man's arrogance. *How dare he defy me?* Michael thought.

But finally the general moved, calling over a lieutenant and passing along the order to attack. Soon, the sound of trumpets could be heard followed several minutes later by the retort of cannon fire. In the valley several rounds exploded, halting the progress of Russian vehicles. Across the riverbank, the enemy scrambled to dig in and set their positions.

"There," Jake said with a hint of finality in his voice. "You kept them from crossing, but now we've given away our positions. We'll be sitting ducks in a few minutes." He pointed across the river and shoved the binoculars into Michael's chest.

Esterling lifted them and pointed the lenses in the direction he'd pointed. A large line of trucks veered north of Waghäusel along Highway 5, clearly making their way to Mannheim and the bridges there. A few minutes later, an equal number turned south along Highway 36. Jake was right. The Russians had split their forces and moved to flank his own.

"We need to go," Braston muttered. "This is over before it started, and we need to retreat to Ramstein."

"No. Adam and Eve promised we'd win! Lieutenant, signal all forces to charge the enemy remaining in Waghäusel. Get everyone across those bridges now."

"That's suicide," Jake cautioned.

"They promised I wouldn't fail, as long as I took charge!"

Benjamin Roark jumped to his feet as soon as the first cannons fired. The echo shook the countryside, causing his chest to vibrate like a bass drum. He bent, scooped up his rifle and rucksack, and hastily pulled his arms through the straps. A second volley sent him racing to the Colonel's tent. The officer stood out front, staring south through a pair of binoculars.

"What happened?" Ben demanded.

"The Russians followed us instead of camping in Germersheim." Frank explained. "They sent a force across the southern bridge to cut us off and Jake fired down on them."

"But that's not a problem, right? They'll still pursue?"

"Not a chance. They realized it was a trap and split their force. Trucks are moving north and south to cross further up and down the river to flank. That'll tie Richter up and prevent our southern attack."

"What will Braston do?"

"At this point, Roark, I've no idea. I can't believe he gave away our positions. Foolish! He's smarter than that!"

"Colonel!" A master sergeant from the signal brigade hurried over, panting and out of breath. "The general just ordered us to join ranks and be ready to cross the Rhine."

"You've got to be kidding! Jake Braston's lost his mind! Roark, get up that hill and confirm these orders!"

"Aye, sir!" Ben hurried away, sprinting to the horses and choosing one already saddled. With a private holding the reins, he placed his left foot in the stirrup and pulled himself up, swinging his right leg over like in a western movie. If he had time to think about it, he would have snickered at the thought of racing off to warn John Wayne or Gary Cooper, much less Jake Braston. With a kick he galloped toward the general's headquarters atop a nearby hill.

The countryside raced by in a blur of greens and grays as the heavy snow packed beneath the pounding hooves of his steed. Thankfully it hadn't formed ice on top like he was used to back home. With eyes focused on the hill he kicked the flanks harder, driving the poor beast even faster toward their destination.

General Braston met him a-ways from the headquarters' tent. Ben dismounted and saluted.

"Roark, I'm glad you're here," the senior officer said. His face appeared haggard, as if worry had overly stressed him. "Esterling pulled rank and ordered that attack. Now he's sending full strength across the bridges."

"Titus said that'll get us all killed. He sent me here to confirm the message."

"I'll send someone to confirm, but you aren't crossing that bridge. I need you to do something else."

"Anything, General! What do you have in mind?"

"I need you to sneak across that river and into Waghäusel. Find the Russian general named Ivan Petrov and kidnap him. Get him to me as quick as possible."

"Why take *him*?"

"Because I was promised we could still win if we did."

"How do you know that the person, whoever told you, was correct?"

"I guess we'll know if you find Petrov at these coordinates, in a department store—a *Sonderposten* or something, whatever *that* is." Braston handed over a piece of paper.

Ben stared at the name. "It's like a Walmart, I think, but I've never shopped in one. Who gave you this?"

"Doctor Yurik. She said to trust you alone to bring him back, and that you'd find him holed up in this building."

"She said to send me? Then Adam and Eve said this was the path to victory?"

"You know about them?" Braston asked, surprised.

"Stephanie and I are friends, and friends talk, sir. If the children said it's the way, then we should listen. I need help, though. This isn't something I can pull off alone."

"I'll hand pick the men myself."

CHAPTER THIRTY-SIX

The fight ahead would be difficult if not impossible, but Max and Shayde enjoyed the element of surprise if nothing else. Each joked about fighting without night vision or communications, laughing off how spoiled they were in Iraq. But inside, each worried over uncertainties, and neither sergeant knew how the night would turn out. They agreed a bit more moonlight would have certainly helped their chances, but their combined force equaled twenty—not nearly enough if their intel proved wrong.

"We have to move in quickly," Shayde insisted, "and obtain our checkpoints before they reinforce the perimeter."

"What's their total strength?" Max asked.

"They have ten sentries up at all times, and scouts reported rotating shifts every six hours. That means forty soldiers."

"But it's an airport, so there's gotta be sniper nests in towers and atop the buildings," Shayde's corporal added. His voice betrayed a slight New Yorker accent.

"Chad's right," Walters agreed. "I figured they're the lucky ones who don't patrol but keep watch. Figure on ten or twenty more either rotating or running to station during an alert, so that buys us about five minutes once we're spotted. Thankfully they won't have night vision either."

Max let out a slow whistle. "So its twenty against sixty heavily armed men. If we get bogged down, we're toast and no one else is coming for us."

"Congrats," Shayde said with a grin, "you just got promoted to captain."

"How so?" Chad asked, clearly confused. "He's only a sergeant."

"Dickweed here just called me *Captain Obvious,*" Max said with a spat.

The corporal laughed out loud and Shayde grinned back.

"How close did the scouts get?" Chad asked. "Do we even know where the guns, ammo, and food supplies are kept?"

"Food is easy enough to guess, given there's a small, centrally located food court in the terminal. This is Evansville, not Indianapolis, so we literally have one terminal to take." Shayde explained.

"That means the rest has to be above ground level baggage claim," Max pointed out.

"How do you reckon?" Shayde asked.

"It's the most secure location. Airports are designed to keep non-passengers from the terminals and tarmac, and that's easy to do when fully manned by TSA. But without their presence, the most vulnerable spot remaining is baggage claim. It always opens up to street traffic on one side and the flight crews on the other, so they shore it up pretty good. So good in fact, the walls in newer buildings are blast proof. When was this one built?"

Both the other men shrugged.

"Well, I've been there once or twice and even flew in directly after the war. The terminal looks like it may have been put up in the 50s, so the baggage claim would have been reinforced later with steel doors. Our best bet is to open a door in the wall. Shayde, please tell me we have C4."

Walters grinned. "I've got it right here, Devil Dog! Blowing holes is my favorite part of the gig." He'd kept that a secret the entire night.

Max nodded. Their chances for success had improved, even if their odds hadn't.

"Let's say we're successful," Corporal Chad asked, "how do we get the guns and ammo back to the coliseum?" The question was a good one, even Max hadn't considered. "I saw a couple of horses along the way. I could fetch 'em," the corporal suggested.

"We don't need horses," Shayde said dismissively. "How much could they actually have? They weren't prepared and stockpiling for years like the Colonel, and we beat them to most of the stores once the looting started. I'm sure we can carry it on our backs."

"Regardless, if there's more than we can carry we'll have to neutralize what we can't. Leave nothing but food, or they'll fight back harder next time. This is the Colonel's conquest phase, which means we have to strike terror, remove their ability to defend, then leave a shred of hope to deal peacefully when we return. He wants to lead everyone into reunification."

"Right," Shayde agreed.

"Let's talk about entry into the terminal then. Here are the drawings the scouts provided," Max said, pulling out crudely drawn maps. "Baggage claim is on the northwest side of the building. To get there, we need to clear the parking lot and secure an overwatch. A few years ago the city started building solar parking canopies. Those will give us a slight advantage before the breach. We'll set up sharp shooters under cover of those and pick off the rooftops. After that it's a gun battle and round up of civilians. We wrap it with a mop up of building offices for intel." He looked to Shayde. "Who are our best shooters?"

"Jack and Dan both served, and Dan can shoot the eye out of a pig at a hundred yards, but neither could clear a parking lot as quietly or quickly as we need. It could get messy and shooting would sound the alarm."

"Then I'll accompany them and clear the lot. Send my team to join me once I'm under the panels, then move to breach. We'll wait till you reach the entry point before moving to ours."

"Sounds like a plan," Shayde agreed.

"Not much of one, unfortunately, but it *is* a plan," Max said with a sigh.

Walters watched Max lead the sharpshooters toward the open lot. It was littered with abandoned cars, mostly buried under snow and ash. Though tracks would be easy to follow, there were too many nooks and crannies in which patrols could hide. It would take several minutes to get through this first line of defense, with no telling how many soldiers they'd find hiding beneath the solar canopies. Thankfully a storm had moved in, and the falling snow cloaked Max's approach.

Shayde scanned the terminal roof, moving slowly and watching for reflections of light through his scope. There were so many shadows he had no way of knowing which were people. He silently cursed the absence of night vision or thermal scope, but at least he had attached an oil can suppressor to mute any shots he took. But even that wouldn't last long when prolonged silence was needed.

He also wished for a better rifle, feeling more like a civilian than ever with his over modified Armalite. In the Marines he'd carried actual assault weapons but now was only *playing* soldier with a city-slicker's juiced up gun. He never would have added these modifications on his own before the war, not without red tape and ATF headaches. With bump stock and binary trigger, one would think he'd have the same firepower as the fully automatic piece he carried in war, but this wasn't even close. The belief that military grade meant better killing was a fallacy, created by those who never truly held a real piece of hardware. Military grade meant overpriced junk.

How he acquired this piece was a story all to itself. It was in the first days following the missiles, when he scouted his first pharmacy. He turned a corner, startled to find an equally surprised gangster stealing opioids. Luckily the dumbass had never fired it, and loaded the rounds backward. It jammed and Shayde dropped him with a sidearm. He kept the man's rifle more out of sentimentality than anything and mourned that day as his first civilian kill. It served a constant reminder the criminals always have the really bad guns, obtained in places law abiding citizens would never tread.

He hoped Max would finish clearing the lot quickly, watching the three shadows move up and down the rows. The all-clear was a reflective piece of cloth waved after returning to the southern edge. Corporal Chad watched closely for their signal.

"Hey, Chad," Walters whispered.

"Yeah?" the boy asked.

"What the hell *is* your last name?"

"Pescari."

"Is that Italian? It sounds mafia."

"Yeah, and probably why my granddaddy moved from New York, and why I only go by Chad. Another row cleared, Sarge."

"You should use it. It would make you sound more badass than *Chad*. As is, it seems like you should be complaining about pumpkin spice lattes."

"Maybe, but I don't like my last name."

"So you're a city slicker moved to the country?"

"Pretty much." A second handkerchief waived. "Rankin's half-way through."

"So what did you big city types do around here? Hang around the cement pond all day reminiscing about smog and subways?"

"Funny." He didn't really think it was. "No, Pop bought a horse ranch just north of the river. He and Mom weren't home when the bombs dropped. Never came home. They were in Indianapolis and probably aren't comin' back."

"That sucks. Why'd you leave the ranch for The Shelter?"

"When the river flooded, it covered the entire property—drowning the horses in their barns. I just walked away from it, right into town. Yous guys were the first I ran into."

"Yous guys... You *aren't* from here, are you?"

"I said I wasn't." Chad paused then remarked, "Damn, that was close. He just took down three guys without a shot. This guy's a badass, Sarge!"

"I know, how'd you think he bested *me*?"

"I thought that was a made up story so we'd forget he killed Spike and Mole."

Shayde tensed. "Where'd you hear about that?"

"Some of the officers are telling everyone, saying not to trust him and someone should do something when his back's turned. But nobody cares but the skinheads."

"What skinheads? I've never seen any in the Regiment."

"They're not like you see in the movies, they look like normal guys. I only recognize what they are because we had a lot of them in New York. They keep quiet about their beliefs, though, and no one pays them attention."

"How bad is it? A few? Several?"

"Only a handful like those officer brothers Hank and Steve. I've seen them guys hanging out with 'em for sure. I've seen Jack with 'em, too."

"Jack? The Jack we just sent with Max?"

"Damn. I hadn't thought about that, Sarge." He shifted his weight, following the trio with his scope. "Lot's cleared, and they're moving toward the solar canopies. You think they're safe to be teamed up with?"

"I hope so, but we can't keep watching over him. Scan the rooftops, we're about to move."

Shayde rolled over and signaled the men laying behind the berm. *Two minutes,* he warned. The squads would split as soon as they advanced. Max's would join him and the overwatch team, then move to the west entrance. He and Chad would cross with their crew to the eastern entrance, and the two squads would meet again in the middle before pushing into the gates.

"Sniper," Chad warned.

"Does he see Max?"

"I can't tell, but the team can't cross while he's there."

"We're running out of time and can't let him fire first. Keep your eye out for Max's signal." Shayde scanned until he found him. It was only a teen, a young black male with a rifle and scope scanning the parking lot. The glint off his scope followed movement down range. *I have to take it,* Walters knew, and let out a breath.

There's a brief moment in time between breath and trigger pull when time stands still. The first time a shooter experiences it, they feel their heartbeat find its way into the rifle itself. Shayde drew the pad of his finger against the bit of metal as soon as the reticle settled. Being a binary trigger, a second shot let loose the moment he released. He stared, watching for signs of life while Chad scanned for witnesses. Luckily, the suppressor muffled the shot.

"Max saw your flash. He ordered the send."

Shayde's hand moved, signaling Max's team to join their sergeant beneath the northern most solar panel. They had two minutes to get into position, giving Shayde and his team one minute of overwatch. In the final minute, every life was in the hands of Max and the three sharpshooters. He counted down in his mind. By the time he reached sixty, he stood and ran. "Go!" he commanded, and Chad and the others followed.

Max waited for his team to catch up. He hated waiting—that's when you think about what you're doing. It's best to keep moving to the next kill once the adrenaline starts.

You're not a killer, he remembered a sergeant telling him after his first kill in Iraq. *You're a weapon—a weapon in the hand of others. Do you think the rifle thinks about its kills?*

The others had joined him alongside Jack and Dan.

"You stay here," he reminded the sharpshooters, "and watch our backs." They nodded and exchanged a look. What was it? Humor? Awe? They seemed different since watching him clear the parking lot, killing effectively once unsheathed.

"Let's go," he said to the others, glancing to his right. Shayde and his team had reached the southern entrance. Max's job was to secure the northern.

He took off at a dead sprint, only exposed for a few seconds, but they were dangerous ones. He leaned against a pillar and waited. No movement from within. That was good.

"Get ready to breach," he said and the others nodded.

The glass doors were boarded, just as the windows all around the terminal. He found a space where the wood had warped and peered inside. The soft moonlight from the upper windows revealed rows of tents and sleeping bags. There was *certainly* someone living here, and he prayed it wasn't as the Colonel described.

Why can't people be better? he wondered.

The plywood moved easily beneath his team's prybars, and they laid it down gently to avoid making noise. Max moved, spinning, and leading his weapon while scanning the interior. He paused. Something wasn't right.

Somewhere a rifle exploded the quiet. Shayde's team had breached as well.

"Stop!" a voice yelled further into the structure, but the gunshots continued.

Max allowed his eyes to adjust. *Recon for threat,* he told himself. But there was no threat. The dark terminal was filled with rows of tents and staring eyes, but no one had moved to resist.

Where are the interior guards? Where are the soldiers keeping the prisoners from getting free?

"Stop! Cease fire!"

Max identified the voice as Shayde. Someone on his squad was on a killing spree. The sound of a heavy pistol caliber ended that of the rifle, and Rankin pitied his comrade's only choice.

"What's going on, Sarge?" one of his own team asked.

"This isn't a military target," Max said. "Our intel had it wrong. These aren't prisoners, they're refugees! We need to pull back and reassess." He stepped away from his cover, raising a hand to signal Jack and Dan. One of them answered with a sniper shot.

The pain was instant, way worse than he ever expected a gunshot would feel. Thankfully it hit closer to his shoulder and not a few inches to the left. Max moved out of sight of the shooter and locked eyes with his team. They blinked back, as shocked as he at the friendly fire.

What a stupid oxymoron, he thought, working his arm in its socket, checking range of motion. He'd be stiff and sore later.

"What the hell was that?" he shouted, no longer concerned over keeping the element of surprise.

"Sorry, Sarge," Jack replied from his post. "We thought you were one of them!"

"Not likely," Max muttered. He'd deal with them later.

Shifting his weight sparked more pain as he scanned inside. Across the long terminal Shayde and his team had pushed slowly in, checking the tents and braced against resistance.

"Move," Max ordered, leading while his squad followed.

My squad? I barely know these guys.

He suddenly felt more exposed than ever, but worrying over another bullet in his back would waste his time. "Watch for threats and be careful not to hit noncombatants."

They stared at the newcomers, watching with exhaustion and starvation.

"Max!" Shayde called from midway down the terminal. "Our intel was bad, Max!"

"I'm seeing that too," he replied, locking eyes with an old man huddled and protecting three children. An older woman, probably his wife, lay lifeless beside them. The entire family reeked of piss, excrement, and fear. "Who brought you here?" Max demanded.

"What?" The confusion on the man's face answered his question.

By now Shayde had joined him.

"These aren't captives, Rankin. They're evacuees from the city—black, white, brown, there's a good mix. It's a community shelter!"

"Then why the armed guards outside? Something's not right. Let's split into pairs and search the rest of the airport."

"You're shot?"

"Yeah. Not-so-friendly fire from Jack and Dan."

"We had an incident too. One of my newbies went nuts. He shot five noncoms before I could stop him."

"Be careful," Max said to both teams. "Whoever this group is, we've not made any friends tonight."

CHAPTER THIRTY-SEVEN

The dense trees gave cover as the squad crept between the soccer fields. Had the branches not been bare and the ashy snowdrifts high, they could have moved much faster. Sergeant Roark was thankful for the five men Braston sent along. They were professionals—stealthy and calm as they scouted ahead and kept eyes on the rear. If they encountered resistance, he was confident they could handle themselves and, more importantly, complete the task.

The worst part of this mission had been getting past the Russian line and worrying how they'd get back through if successful. But high snowdrifts had forced the long lines of troops and trucks to remain on the main roads, making sneaking easier but not simple. They swam the river to the north and crossed eastward into this wooded area. It took hours despite their best attempt to quick time, but they finally had eyes on the target.

It's less of a Walmart and more of a Dollar Store, Ben realized, reading the tall red letters painted on a white billboard. It was an odd name for a store.

The location was simple, but an obvious choice for headquarters. The shopping center held two supermarkets, this one with its strong metal roof, and another which had somehow remained intact during the bombing. There was also a gym and shoe store, with soldiers setting up those as barracks for the newly arriving staff and aides. Ben watched the road to the *Sonderposten.* It was clear on his side, though the eastern line was busy with trucks and soldiers unloading rations and gear.

"Are we certain he's in there?" one of the soldiers asked.

"Never certain in our line of work," Sergeant Roark explained, "but our intel's strong and orders clear. We're to standby for a signal to enter the *Sonderposten.*"

"What kind of signal are we waiting for?" one of the soldiers asked. "In case you haven't noticed, Sarge, we don't have comms."

"The general didn't know for sure, but he said to wait for it so here we sit."

Braston watched the skirmish on the bridge. The Russians had easily pushed him back, but to Michael's credit the foolish move had surprised them. Wary of a trap, they cautiously held positions on the Eastern bank of each bridge. No doubt waiting for their flanking troops to find positions. He nervously scanned the south. They only had an hour or so before they did. Luckily, the German forces held better than he expected and bought them two hours—time enough for retreat if Michael changed his mind.

"I told you it would work," Esterling grumbled beside him.

"Yeah, it worked," Jake agreed, "but we're sitting ducks once Herr General Richter's line breaks. We should leave now and give him orders to follow."

"Why? So they can catch up to us in Ramstein? It's less defensible, you told me yourself. No, we're assured victory. Adam and Eve promised."

"We should at least have Titus and the others fall back to this ridge. Move the artillery first."

Michael nodded. "Make it happen."

Jake relayed the order to an aide. Movement to the northeast caught his attention. "What in the blazes is that?" His eyes grew wide, his mind not believing what they saw.

Esterling put down his binoculars and turned. As he did, his eyes grew as large with surprise as Braston's. "Is that a ship? On land?"

Both men marveled at the ghostly specter. A glistening sailing vessel skimmed across the land, passing through trees and buildings while people stood firmly on the deck. It headed directly for their position on the hill.

Jake snatched the field glasses from Michael and zoomed in on the marvel. With the closer view he could clearly see the shimmer of its construction, recognizing the tendrils of air from their underground lab.

"It's Adam and Eve," he said, focusing in.

"I told them to stay behind!" Michael fumed. "How'd they get free?"

"Doctor Yurik and David are with them. Wait... For heaven's sakes, Brooke's there too!"

"They betrayed me—let the experiments out of the lab! I knew bringing David would mean trouble. We don't even need him! Stephanie had it all in hand!"

"What's wrong with you, Michael?" Jake demanded. "What are you really afraid of?" But Michael had already revealed this new side of him. Jake recognized it as greed for power. He wanted this victory to be his alone.

Movement against the clouds caught both men's attention, and they looked upward, gasping when realizing the children had not arrived alone.

"There's your signal, Roark," Braston muttered.

"It's getting late," a soldier complained to Roark. "Braston said we only have a few hours, so why don't we just bust in? We should grab this general and go."

"Because we haven't received the signal," Ben replied. His eyes hadn't moved from the building's front door. The two guards appeared as bored as he.

Look up, a voice said in this head. He recognized it at once.

Eve?

Yes, Ben. Look up and you'll see our sign.

He raised his eyes to the sky. At first all he saw were the same heavy clouds that had lingered since the apocalypse. Heavy with snow, they lumbered toward the horizon.

I don't see it.

A screech abruptly turned his head to the northwest. As a boy, he'd watched the migratory geese flying overhead, always in perfect formation and seemingly graceful in their journey. These were not geese. These were bigger. They dove downward after flying high above the storm.

"What're those?" one of the soldiers demanded.

"Eagles," said another.

Hundreds of bald eagles flocking together, dancing an unchoreographed ensemble to the wind. Unlike geese, who took turns following a rotating leader, there was no arrangement to this flight. Just as the nation of people who had chosen them as a symbol of their freedom, these flew side by side as individuals—unified only in their presence and the direction they moved. Each was free to travel their own direction as they maintained a steady course as one body.

Go now, Eve urged.

Ben tore his eyes from the display overhead. The guards had seen the birds as well. Their rifles dangled from slings as the men shielded their eyes to better focus. They watched with wonder as Sergeant Roark raised his own weapon to his shoulder. Two shots, muffled by a silencer, let loose. The subsonic rounds made no sound in the air as they found their marks, dropping the only resistance between him and the door.

"Let's move," he said to the others, and led them into the *Sonderposten*.

Jake diverted his eyes from the eagles circling overhead, watching as Doctor Andalon and the two women stepped off the shimmering deck onto solid ground. Adam and Eve followed. The vessel behind them dissipated like smoke from a smoldering candle, and, all at once, the birds screeched. Braston jumped, startled by the sound as he locked eyes on the new arrivals.

Brooke caught his stare and shrugged, pointing at David as if the entire thing had been his idea.

But Jake knew better. The children had arranged this. They knew Michael wouldn't allow them to come along, so they put into motion their own chain of events. He suddenly realized they had seen the outcome of the battle, and planned everything this way from the beginning. Their chosen vehicle of arrival was grandiose and captured the attention of both armies.

Just as they approached, the Russian positions poured forward across the bridges.

"It's begun," Adam said calmly.

"But I'll win?" Michael demanded.

"That depends," Eve said dryly, "on whether we allow you to continue blundering the outcome, or if you'll finally trust us to fight the battle for you."

Jake and Michael both looked toward the charging infantry, pouring across the bridge by the thousands. Below, Titus held briefly but the entire line broke into a running retreat as the onslaught neared. The battle would be lost in a single charge.

"What *can* you do?" Esterling asked the children. "It's apparent we've already lost."

"No," Adam corrected. "We promised you wouldn't." The boy raised his hands into the air and worked it like clay, molding and shaping fierce vortexes. The clouds above began to churn, and the eagles parted as several tornadoes moved southward. These touched down between the allied forces and the Russians.

Rubble and debris swirled, unburying what was once sprawling suburbs and city streets, and briefly exposing a recently lost civilization. The roaring winds ripped everything to its foundation.

"I'll hold them off," Adan said to his sister, "until you can free General Richter to the north. He should be here when it happens.

She nodded and closed her eyes, stepping northward and raising her arms in the same fashion as her brother. A single eagle broke away from the flock, speeding toward the clashing forces. "The Germans already retreat," she said. "I'll cover his approach, but we want the enemy closer. Their entire force must witness today."

"Where is Roark?" Adam calmly asked.

Jake began to answer, but Eve replied before he could. "He's on his way back and nearly to the river."

"Good. We need Petrov to witness as well."

Jake turned to watch Michael while the children worked their power. His face did not hold shock, nor did he seem surprised by the ease with which they channeled it. No, where every other man and woman in that valley reflected fear or awe, the senator displayed angry jealousy. The children upstaged the politician, and everyone saw.

CHAPTER THIRTY-EIGHT

Morning arrived and the sun rose, flooding through the uppermost windows and lighting the Evansville terminal. It had taken all night to secure the airport, encountering only minimal resistance. Whoever these armed guards had been, they certainly weren't trained, and bore no signs of obvious allegiance to anyone.

Shayde Walters walked with Max along the endless row of human suffering. Every inch of the terminal was filled with wretched masses. So far, they counted five thousand. Nearly a quarter of that count lay deceased among the dying.

"I've never seen anything like this," Shayde admitted. "Even overseas the human suffering wasn't this bad. These people haven't eaten for weeks, but the soldiers were certainly well-fed."

Max said nothing. He had seen this before. Cowardice and fear is what causes suffering like this, and he recognized it right away for what it was.

"They had a leader," Shayde said. "We found his body in one of the administrative offices. Blew his own brains out, weeks ago, by the looks of it, but his few soldiers never noticed. They kept standing watches, despite having no leadership or direction."

"Can any of them speak for the group?" Max asked softly, rubbing his wounded shoulder. "Is there a leader willing to stand for the others?"

"Not yet," Shayde replied. "They're all so weak, and most are still in shock."

"At least we learned what happened to the residents of the city. It appears they fled north when the river rose and found shelter wherever they could. We should search the hotels, schools, and department stores for the rest," Max suggested.

"Have you had any luck?"

"Finding my family? No. Thankfully they weren't here, but that doesn't mean we won't find them in a similar state."

Shayde paused when they reached the baggage area door. "Are you sure you're ready for this?"

Max nodded. The other Marine had promised him a surprise, but no clue what he'd found.

Walters pushed the door open and Rankin gasped. This group, whoever they were, had been busy over the past few weeks, gathering and storing resources. The room, used for sorting luggage, wasn't large as far as airports go, but was filled with every sort of rifle, pistol, and ammunition—enough to outfit an army.

"Look at these stencils, Max. They raided the National Guard Armory. There's all sorts of ordinance, even grenades."

But Max stared at towers of boxes next to the arms. They contained meals ready to eat and dried rations, enough to last months if rationed. There were thousands stacked as high as the ceiling.

"That son of a bitch," Max said, letting the words out with a gasp.

"Which one? The dead guy in the office, or the Colonel?"

"You know I mean the Colonel."

"You think he knew about this?" Shayde asked

"Why else would he send us on a mission like this? He said they were hoarding supplies, and he probably knew these people weren't captives. He sent us here to bring all this back, but made up that story to appeal to me—to convince me to come."

"Would you have, if only to bring this back?"

"Not a chance in hell."

"There's fresh water," Shayde pointed, "lots of it. Purification tablets, too."

This angered Max the most. "All these people could have been saved... fed *and* hydrated this entire time. None of them needed to die. We *have* to take it all back, Shayde," he said softly. "Even the food."

"I understand taking the hardware, but the food and water? These people won't make it if we do."

"If we leave it here someone else will take it, especially now it's unguarded. That's our reality, now—survive or die."

"So we let them starve? They're too weak to walk back to The Shelter, and we can't leave them with nothing!"

"No," Rankin said, "we'll leave enough to keep them alive for a time, then come back with more. But this is how the Regiment builds the Colonel's dream of rebuilding society. *We* control the resources. *We'll* keep it safe from selfish hands like those who hoarded it, and teach these people to rely on us. That's how the Colonel secures his new government."

Sergeants Walters and Rankin fell silent after that, each considering how to haul it all safely home.

Cathy Fletcher awoke earlier than usual, desperate to be free of Hank's bed. She had been wrong to believe she could handle any man, forced to give herself over to his wishes. She'd be dead if she hadn't, and that would have been okay if it weren't for Josh. The boy needed his mother, and she would do whatever she must. Survival was the only thing that mattered in this world.

She slid off the mattress and pulled on clothing, eager for a shower to wash away the night. That thought prompted shivers, remembering how a single bath had put her in this predicament. Either way she needed one, and running water sounded nice. Glancing at the small table in the corner of the shack, she spied two bowls of stew from the night before. Hank had brought them, devouring his as ravenously as he had her body. Hers stood cold and unwanted, a symbol of what she gave him.

Hank stirred behind her on the bed, moaning softly. His sweat from spent passion had soaked his side of the bed. Cat wrinkled her nose and swallowed a little bile at the thought of his touch, then gathered both bowls and spoons before stepping next door. Careful not to wake Steve, she picked up his dish and stacked it with the others. She couldn't wait till these men were dead, and smiled at the thought of their fate.

Soon, she thought. *They'll die in a fever, sweating and retching their insides.*

Cathy paused as the blind man muttered in his bed, rolling over and tossing a blanket on the floor. She moved closer, listening to his murmurs.

"Cold," he said. "It's so cold." Then he rolled over and vomited.

She watched with wonder at the sweat pouring from his back, then crept closer and carefully reached out a hand. Repulsed, she felt his skin. It was afire with fever. He retched again.

No, she thought. *Not yet.*

Still holding the bowls, she hurried to Hank's shack. Pulling the blanket from his shoulders, she marveled at the amount of sweat pouring from him as well. Her eyes fell upon the bowls in her hand, suddenly thankful for her lack of appetite. Placing them on the nightstand, she rushed to her satchel and felt the lining for the stitching. It was gone. Someone had stolen the Ricin.

She searched her thoughts of the day before, rushing past the hellish events of her wedding night.

When was it out of my sight? she wondered, then remembered.

How did she get it into the bowls? she questioned. Then it dawned on her. *They're officers and eat apart from the enlisted. They're served by a different pot.*

Cathy slid quietly from the shack and moved across the balcony. She peaked inside the adjoined hootch, pulling open the flap and holding her breath. A man and a woman lay within, lifeless and laying in a bed of vomit. The next she checked was the same and so on. The Colonel would suspect her right away.

Max rode atop a long train of baggage trolleys, each linked together and trailing three horses. Chad Pescari rode the lead mount, sitting high in the saddle and beaming with pride at his ingenuity. It was his idea to check the surrounding horse farms and commandeered two mares and a stallion. He also suggested they link the carts to haul the supplies back to The Shelter. Both Dan and Jack lay at Max's feet, zip-ties binding them tightly.

The ride into town had been slower than he liked, but no one had challenged them or attempted to take their haul.

"We must look a ludicrous sight," Sergeant Walters said from the next cart back.

"We've got a bigger problem once we get home," Max replied.

"Oh? What's that? Where to put all this stuff?"

"How to get rid of the carts. We can't just leave them outside The Shelter, they'll draw attention. We have to dump them."

"I hadn't thought of that," Shayde admitted. "But there's a tire store a few blocks away. We can stash them there till we need them again."

"And the horses? How the hell are we going to keep those alive in the city? We have to let them go."

"They'll be useful!" Chad yelled from ahead.

Max laughed. "I can't believe the only cowboy among us is a New Yorker." Turning around to face Shayde, he asked, "Why do you think the Colonel made all that up? About retribution. What was his angle? He could've told me anything to get me to come along."

Shayde shrugged and pointed at the men at Max's feet. "Ask one of them. If they shot you intentionally, they may have answers."

"We do have a bit of time for interrogation," he agreed. "How about it, Dan? Jack? Why'd you shoot me?"

"We told you, it was an accident!" Jack maintained. "We didn't expect you to step out and thought you were one of *them*!"

"I get it," Max said, gripping the leather wrap of his Ka-bar and squeezing it angrily, "because we all look the same?"

"No!" cried Dan. "It was the heat of battle! I just kind of reacted. I didn't think! I reacted and I'm sorry!"

Max fumed, but fought to calm his emotions. *Have to be sensible here. I don't know what really happened.* But deep down he wondered. Some people *could* have made a mistake like that.

But not me, he realized.

Mike Salwell, the kid playing gangster—Tom's friend—had been right. It was time to choose a side.

He lifted his eyes from Dan and Jack. They were close, merely two hundred yards from The Shelter. He could slit their throats now, but then what? Would Shayde let him live? He seemed an honest man, but also a soldier—motivated by duty. He'd gun him down.

So what if he does? Without Betty and Tom, what purpose do I have?

Up ahead, Chad's horse snorted then danced anxiously.

"We've got trouble, Sarge!" the young man shouted.

The sound of gunfire echoed inside a building, answered by the sound of metal ringing all around.

"We're sitting ducks!" Shayde realized. "Get down!"

Chad fell from his mount and his horse reared. A patch of red formed against his temple. Max shook free of his thoughts, understanding they had ridden into ambush.

He stood and sprinted atop the baggage carriers, racing forward just as the horses decided to bolt. With a dive he grabbed the lead trolley, losing footing and falling over the side. A bullet ripped through a box of rations next to where his head had been. His fingers splayed out for the edge and barely caught it, stretched above the street as the horses ran. His boots nearly dragged.

Behind him, Shayde and the others had leapt free of the train, locked in a tense gun battle on both sides. He turned away from them, realizing the carts could flip at any moment. He tried to pull himself up, but found he couldn't. His rifle hung from its sling, hooked on the fender of the trolley. It was taut, and he would have to lower himself before getting free. The whiteness around his knuckles told him that would never happen, he would be free when the grip failed and he plunged to certain death.

His right hand frantically felt his side, finding the leather grip and drawing his Ka-bar.

He sawed against the sling, sending the gun crashing to the street and under the tires of the baggage cart. He had no time to re-sheath the blade, and let it fall to the ground as well. Only then did he find strength, pulling himself atop the lead cart and scrambling to find the knot. He prayed he could release it in time, longing for the knife now laying useless on the street.

Successful, the horses scrambled away down the street and the heavy trolley slowed, crashing into the side of The Shelter.

Breathless, he looked toward the sounds of gunfire. Shayde and his team had entered the buildings, clearing each room as shots rang out within. Behind him, the doors of the Soldier Sailor Memorial abruptly crashed open and several enlisted Regiment men raced out. They ran headlong toward battle.

Good fighting men, Max noticed, *men with instincts.*

He tried to stand, meaning to find his gun and help, but exhaustion buckled his knees and he collapsed in the street. Two pairs of combat boots approached and he followed them upward with his eyes, taking in the tactical fatigues and web belt around each pair. Two soldiers had found him, but they weren't of the Regiment. Max tried to focus, but he must have hit his head in the maddening rush to free the horses. Wooziness caused his vision to swim.

One of the soldiers spoke behind the gaiter around his face.

"See, I told you he chose a side," a boy's voice said.

"Yeah, you were right," Tom replied.

Max knew his son's voice at once, and tears of joy fell softly against his face. "Son..."

"No," Tom said angrily, looking over his shoulder toward the gunfight. "You don't get to call me that. You're a sellout and Mom's dead because you weren't home." He raised his rifle, pushing the muzzle against his father's forehead. "You were never there for us, always choosing the road!"

"I'm not a sellout, Son. You're fighting the wrong war," Max said tearfully, the emotion of several weeks of worry mixing with the joy of finding his son. That Betty had not survived caused his chest to heave, sobbing mournfully for the only woman he had ever loved. "Come inside with me, Tom, you too, Mike. There's a place for you in the new society... it will be for all of us!"

Tom pulled down his gaiter with one hand, but shoved the flash suppresser deeper against his father's skin with the other. The sound of boots on pavement warned the battle had ended and members of the Regiment were racing to help their own. He turned toward them briefly, considering which direction he should choose.

But, in the end, his son chose violence over love. "There's no place for me in their world," the boy said angrily, pulling the rifle away, and taking off down the street. Mike followed at a sprint.

Shayde raced toward Max, him and his team pulling up breathlessly. "Chase them down!" he ordered.

But Max found his own voice of command. "No! Let them go!" he said.

The soldiers hesitated, looking from sergeant to sergeant, unsure of whom to follow.

"That's my son," Rankin said, climbing to his feet. "He only needs time to think." But inside Max's heart, the father was momentarily gone. He was a soldier, trained to push aside emotion to carry on the fight. Soon, all that would remain was the Marine. "Where's the Colonel?" he asked. "We need to talk."

"There's a problem," one of the soldiers replied. He was young, but brave. One of the men who ran out to help while most of them cowered inside.

"What's your name, Private?" Shayde demanded.

"Parker... James Parker, Sergeant." Two women stepped outside, and James turned toward them. "Cat, Linda, please go inside," he said.

"You're friends with them?" Max asked. "You're the soldier who tried to help them?"

"Yes, Sarge."

"They can stay. Neither have seen daylight in quite some time. Now tell me, what's the problem?"

"The officers... They're all dead, Sarge. Every single officer died in the night. None of the men know what to do or who to follow. That's why most stayed inside and didn't help. They're trying to decide how to split up the resources and go separate ways."

Max exchanged a look with Shayde, then asked, "All of them dead? The Colonel too?"

"All of them."

"I think it was poison," Cathy Fletcher said.

"Then have the doctor confirm," Max ordered. "We need to know."

"He's dead too," she replied. "I'm the only one here with medical knowledge, and it looks like Ricin poison to me."

Turning to Shayde, Max suggested, "Here's how we settle this. Take these men and restore order. Get control of the armory first, then establish your authority."

"My authority?" Shayde asked.

"You have a problem with that?"

"Yeah, I do. You're a better leader, Max. You've got the best mind for battle. I'm just a mortar and C4 guy who likes to blow shit up. I choose to follow you, and so will most who follow me."

"Well then," Max said calmly, "seems we really *do* have a problem, because I don't want it."

"It has to be you," Shayde insisted, "and it has to be now. I'll help you take over the Regiment and help keep it together. It's our *duty*!"

Duty. There was that word again. Max swallowed. There was no getting away from it. He nodded. Betty was gone and Tom had disowned him. All that remained was a Marine with a mission. "Then let's go do the right thing," he said. The pain in his heart over wife and son would have to wait.

CHAPTER THIRTY-NINE

"Form up!" Jake yelled to Titus' troops. "Get cover!" He pointed to the wall of vortexes between them and the Russians. "This is us, but it won't hold them for long! Get behind it and be ready!"

Soon after, his officers caught on and rallied their squads into position.

Jake turned his attention to the new arrivals from the north. "Fall in!" he screamed over the sound of raging winds. Herr General Richter found him among the chaos.

"What is it?" the German demanded. "This is madness! What haven't you told me?"

"I'll explain later, just know it's ours!"

"No! Tell me now, what devilry we're involved with!"

Jake sighed deeply, then turned to face the man head on. He pointed to the children standing like conductors of a hellish orchestra. The time for negotiation and backroom dealings was over. It was time Michael's allies knew his strength. "They," he explained, "are our secret weapon. Those people with them?" He pointed to David, Stephanie, and Brooke still wearing lab coats. "They're three of the most intelligent people left in this world and gave us a way to recreate society.... *our* society, the way we want it. You can get behind Esterling now, or get trampled under his feet later. Either way, this is no longer Germany. Hell, it's no longer Europe!"

"You hid this from us. You wanted the power all along!" General Richter seemed on the verge of murder, his eyes raging with unmasked fury.

"In an hour or two, you'll sing a different tune," Jake said. "Now get your men to fall in line with ours, or we'll shred the lot of you with the Russians!" It was a bluff. He had no way to know if Adam and Eve would even go along with that violence, but it worked. Richter's eyes turned quickly from anger to fear. Soldiers always know when they're beaten. He nodded and complied.

Jake returned to Esterling's side. "Everything's in place, Mike."

"I couldn't have done it by myself, could I, Jake?" The man was so broken, confused and finally questioning his fitness to lead. That meant he was finally ready.

"We all have our strengths." He pointed to David. "His is science. Mine's leading soldiers and yours is leading politicians and people into a new world."

"I'm sorry about before. I should've listened to the children, and especially you."

"Forgiven." Jake noticed a squad of soldiers leading a Russian officer up the hillside. "It's time," he called to Adam. "All pieces are in place!"

Both children nodded silently, then whipped their arms, flinging their captive wind toward the enemy lines.

✦

"All pieces are in place!" Jake yelled to Adam.

David watched solemnly as the children snapped their arms as if casting fly reels. He had studied weather in college, though as an elective having nothing to do with his major. Always a biologist, even then, he questioned everything—from how phenomena would affect ecosystems down to how much wind a storm would need to carry someone away. Seventy miles per hour was the simple answer, as a sustained wind of that magnitude could theoretically overcome gravity.

The power he witnessed on the battlefield was far greater, and his stomach wrenched as thousands of soldiers flew backward in a single blast. To be clear, they did not topple over. They also did not merely get knocked backward into one another. When the children unleashed their fury, the gales blew into both valleys and scattered grown men and women like dry leaves before the first winter blast. Not one survived that initial gust, and many ripped apart before David's eyes. He made the mistake of watching one in particular, wincing as the man's face and exposed skin peeled away. Thankfully they disappeared rapidly into the entanglement of bodies.

As the roar subsided, the hill stood in stark silence. One by one the allied soldiers turned wide-eyed toward the tiny children standing together. The pair turned to face the enemy across the river.

"General Petrov," Michael finally said for all to hear. "That was a single example of our power. Please don't make us destroy your entire army."

"I was a product of your cold war," Ivan Petrov said arrogantly, holding his cuffed hands for all to see, "but I remember one lesson about America." He chuckled, then smiled at everyone who watched. "When you bombed Japan at Nagasaki you had only one more weapon to drop." He casually laughed as he strolled, moving toward Adam and Eve. "Your bluff then, as now, was to use both prematurely in hopes you wouldn't need another."

The man suddenly lunged, having produced a knife from somewhere hidden within his clothing.

Brooke screamed, causing David to look away, but the horror on her face forced his eyes to return to the children. If they had seen it coming, neither moved aside. Both fell to the ground beneath his weight. The sight of blood pouring from Adam's throat caused Dr. Andalon's mouth to fill with bile. Before anyone could move to help, the knife plunged deep into Eve's chest.

A gunshot deafened everyone nearby. Jake strode forward as Petrov rolled over, then filled him with two more rounds.

"Stop," the tiny girl gasped. "Do not shoot him again!"

Jake froze at her command, but held his pistol steadily trained on the dying Russian officer.

"David!" Eve called meekly. "Come here."

He tried to move, but found his legs would not. He was frightened. *Why didn't they foresee their deaths?*

We did. Her voice spoke clearly in his mind.

A great flapping of wings turned his attention to the sky, as the multitude of eagles flew as a single body. Together they glided on the air, beating a final heave with mighty wings before landing atop the hill. The humans stood or lay among them, but the great birds did not show fear. They stood majestically, each facing the dying children and watching with expectation.

Heal us, doctor, Adam's voice said faintly. His time was running out.

"I don't know how," David said, finally able to move his feet. He knelt between them, placing a tender hand on each. Had he truly been their father, he would have shown the same mournful love as he did in this moment. Tears fell and his chest sobbed as he watched them dying before his eyes.

Remember when I said you repaired your own genes, David? Eve's voice asked. *You did more than reconstruct your ability to reproduce. You repaired your entire body.* You *are different, Doctor Andalon. Entirely!*

Reach out to us with your mind, Adam pleaded weakly, *not into ours, but into our bodies. Feel the power of this hill and the world around you. Find life.*

David closed his eyes and focused. At first the blackness overwhelmed him, but the lights slowly emerged. It felt just as when he traveled with them into the dream world, only vastly alone without the children. "I can't," he admitted in defeat.

Yes, you can, Eve explained. *You know us by more than our physical bodies, doctor. You've seen us on the basic level. You've charted our DNA and witnessed how our cells interact within our tissues. Try again, and hurry. Adam has already passed.*

"He's gone? If he's dead, then there's truly nothing I can do."

Hurry, Eve's voice urged, barely more than a whisper.

He tried again, closing his eyes. The moment the lights emerged, he chose one, imagining its soft glow as an uncharted place he could visit. Reaching out, he pulled it toward his consciousness. No longer feeling lonesome, he stood in the vastness of the void.

It's a craft, David realized, *and I work it like clay.*

He touched the ether beneath his knees, feeling its rhythmic thrum of life. *This world we live in has not completely died,* he realized. The valley materialized around him, filled with pulsing beauty. Buried beneath the ashy snow and destruction, he found life oddly reachable. Each blade of grass, though dormant, brown, and withered, promised a new spring would return. The pulsing within its roots thrummed a similar pattern as the people gathered around.

Soon, every living thing emerged as a glowing essence of its physical form. He recognized right away the difference between animal and fauna.

"I see it," he shouted. "I know what to do!"

"David?" Brooke placed a gentle hand on her husband's shoulder. "Who are you talking to?" The lifeform within her womb pulsed out of rhythm, certainly different than her own. David found it oddly similar to Michael's standing nearby. He shrugged off her hand.

"Back away," Andalon said. "All of you."

The eagles moved closer as the humans slowly retreated, eerily quiet as they marched toward the dying humans. The thrum of life within each bird was recognizable. He'd studied each of their interwoven patterns so intricately in the lab.

You're bonded with them? he asked Eve. *You brought them here, but your lifeforce is shared as well?*

Yes, David. They hold enough to revive us naturally. Take from them what is ours and restore it to our bodies.

A vaporous mist formed around him. *My own lifeforce?* he wondered. He somehow knew that it was. He molded it like clay into a whisp of pulsing light, reaching it out with his mind and stretching the tendrils into each bird. Carefully, he unraveled the bit of the children remaining in each, and pulled it closer and placed it into their physical forms.

Careful, Eve warned, *not to place too much of yourself in ours. There's enough within the flock you won't need to join. The result won't be what you desire.*

Adam's heart began beating and the severed flesh across his neck melded together.

The girl had been correct. He knew them on the cellular level and fixing their bodies proved easy. Soon Eve's pulse regained strength and both children smiled up at the doctor.

The gathered onlookers gasped with realization as the pair rose to stand beside their doctor.

"And now him," Adam said aloud. "Heal the dying messenger and restore what's left of his life."

David turned to the dying man on the ground. The thrum within had weakened with his pulse. "There's not enough," he said.

"Use some of your own," Eve urged. "But not too much."

Two of the bullets had passed clean through, and those wounds were easier to repair. The third remained lodged near the heart. David repaired the tissue closest to the foreign object, pushing it slowly upward until a twisted piece of lead emerged. The general would live but, like the bullet, had changed forms—though still Ivan Petrov, the guiding lifeforce would only be usable once reforged. As a final temper, he drew energy from one of those gathered around.

Michael Esterling watched as first the children reanimated, and then the body of the Russian General stirred.

Jake Braston again raised his weapon.

"No," Eve said. "He's no longer a threat in his new form."

"What just happened?" demanded Michael. "What did David just do?"

"He healed us and restored our life, senator... Or should I say Chancellor? Astia is yours now, just as you wanted."

"No... I didn't claim anything today. *You* defeated the army, and every-one witnessed *your* strength, not mine."

Adam spoke so all would hear. "General Petrov was correct that you only possessed two weapons in this battle. But he underestimated Doctor Andalon and his love and respect for you. Sam Nakala and Mi-Jung have a gift waiting when you return to Ramstein."

"A gift?"

"You wanted our abilities but never our minds. David tasked them with extracting a usable form of our craft which you can use as your own. You have our power, and it is yours personally to use and give as you choose."

"What will keep others from using it?" Michael demanded. He stole a glance at Herr General Richter. The man surely had ambitions as well as an army.

"The key to unlocking its usefulness was chosen carefully," David said sleepily. "The radiation vaccine modified your genetic code, and only those with resequencing can use it."

"And when the vaccine is gone? When we've exhausted our supplies? What then?" Esterling demanded.

"You'll have it forever. The people of Astia will pass the code to their offspring, and your descendants will continue to harness the essence originally formed in Adam and Eve."

"And what of them?" Stephanie Yurik asked. "Will you allow them freedom, Michael?"

"I cannot, no. They're too powerful."

"Then send us away," Eve said. "You have our code and the ability to use our craft. Send us to Andalon."

"Andalon?" Michael stared at his friend, wondering what ambitions the scientist had for himself.

"That's what they're calling North America, Mike, not me." David replied. "I'm taking the children there. We'll find the population center in the Ohio River valley and blend into their society. It's what the children and I want."

"That sounds fair," Michael lied. With them far away and across the water, neither could challenge his claim to Astia, but they would always be a threat—and so would any offspring they produced. He exchanged a look with Jake and the general nodded his understanding. He'd help dispose of them as promised.

"David," Brooke said with alarm. "You kept this part of the plan from me. Why didn't you tell me you were returning to North America? I don't want to leave. I want to stay here."

"That's not all I kept from you, Brooke."

Brooke suddenly grew fearful. Thinking of the injections, her hands went to her belly. "What did you do, David?"

Michael had been looking at his friend when he spoke, but his eyes darted to Brooke's belly as she grabbed it. The child... *His child...* grew within that womb.

"Michael Esterling would never allow us to leave," Adam said. "Right now, he and your brother are scheming, and each is wondering how to kill us again. But now, they must include your husband."

"And they will also kill you, Brooke," Eve added, "because you carry in your womb an emotant."

"They *want* to, but they won't," David revealed. He pointed at the Russian general now standing quietly by with slumped shoulders.

Petrov lifted his head and began to speak. But as the words came out, it was David's voice. "General Petrov is no longer in control of his mind. Though he will believe himself so, he was not reanimated as purely as the children. He's under my control if I choose, and the treaty you make with him only exists if I and the children remain unharmed. I offer him as a gift, Michael. I added your lifeforce to him as well. You may control him, but only if I allow it. As an added bonus, you and I can *parley* through our connection in his mind if our own treaty requires adjusting."

Michael blinked with disbelief. Of course he had to let them go now. David had played him perfectly. He needed the treaty with the Russians more than he needed those children dead—not if they told the truth and he had access to their powers.

"David," Brooke demanded. "What have you done to my child?"

"*Michael's* child is resequenced. Adam and Eve promised an Esterling would always rule the world, but did not reveal how. The child in your womb is an emotant, like them. He'll be able to wield power, making him a direct threat to his father. You are coming with us, and bringing our final bargaining chip against Michael."

"Not your final chip," Michael said, placing an arm around Stephanie Yurik, "I'm expecting another."

"No, Michael," Stephani said, pulling away. She walked toward Benjamin Roark, grabbing his hand and locking fingers. "This child is not yours, and David also injected me." She looked toward the doctor and he nodded.

"All emotants will return to Andalon with the doctor except for the son of Esterling," Adam explained. "That is the grounds for our treaty and the only assurance Astia remains yours."

Michael could not believe his ears. He was beaten, despite his victory on the field. He had a society to build, and that far exceeded the threat he would allow to leave. He could, after all, deal with the emotant problem later.

"Go," he said. "Now, before I change my mind."

David nodded to the children and Eve waved her hands in the air. Wisps of air wove and converged as she once more created the Estowen.

"You'll need supplies," Jake said, and helped Sergeant Roark to load rations and water for their voyage.

"I'm not going," Brooke said to her husband.

"You have no choice, dear. Not anymore. Not like you did before, when you chose his *shortcut* over trusting *my* science. Michael will kill your child if you stay."

"I wouldn't do that, Brooke." Esterling promised. "You don't have to go."

"And I wouldn't allow him to," Jake added.

She looked to David. "Isn't there another way?" she asked.

The doctor looked away. "I'm sorry, Brooke. That's the price of the forgiveness you asked from me. Return home with me as my wife, or stay here."

"I won't go," she said.

"Then this is goodbye," David said, boarding the Estowen.

"What about Mi-Jung?" Michael suddenly asked. "You've been injecting her, as well!"

Adam answered. "She carries a special child who will father a line of the strongest resequenced," he explained. "Though not an emotant himself, his ability to harness all powers will be extraordinary. His progeny will have access to all crafts Dr. Andalon has created, but can never claim them as their own."

Michael watched as the last of the supplies were loaded. Jake drew his pistol and handed it grip first toward David. "Take this," he said. "You'll need it over there."

"No," Michael said. "Don't give him any weapons. They don't need them."

"Michael," David said, turning with a smile, "at least in that regard we're agreed." He then boarded the vessel with Doctor Yurik and the children.

Everyone gathered watched it depart, gliding across the land on its way to the ocean and beyond. The doctor and his children had finally embarked on their prophesied journey. They traveled to Andalon.

EPILOGUE

David Andalon stood on the deck of *Estowen*, marveling at the speed with which they raced across the ocean. Though a storm raged overhead and the waves reached the deck, Adam's shield protected the vessel and held all but a fine mist from sprinkling the passengers. The doctor watched as the children worked the vessel like crewmen in the age of sail. Eve held the ship together, ethereal yet sturdy enough to support both people and supplies. She also worked the rigging, turning the sails like a master as her brother filled them with steady winds. In all, the journey should have taken them a month, but they completed the trek in only one week.

"I can't believe we're nearly there," Stephanie Yurik said, joining David on the rails.

"I can't believe any of this. Did we make the right choice?"

"Of course we did," she insisted. "Michael's crazy with power, and I don't want to be a part of his *New World Order.*"

"I meant about Brooke."

"Oh."

"I love her," he admitted, "even if I can never forgive her. I wish she would have joined us. Maybe I would've gotten over her betrayal in time."

"She will, Father," Eve replied. "She'll come to Andalon, but not as your wife. She'll move on more easily than you."

This struck him hard, the harshness of her knowledge. Sometimes he considered telling the children *not* to reveal facts when it came to his personal life, but somehow this brought him nearer to closure.

"Where do we go?" Stephanie asked. "Do we join the main population or venture out to find stragglers?"

"The children suggested we sail inland but first insist we make a stop along the way," David replied. "They said it was important to me."

"And here it is," Adam called out with a smile.

As the horizon rushed to meet *Estowen,* the children slowed their approach into what was once a broad harbor. The skyline, at one time majestic and recognizable, was gone—ground zero to a lethal bombardment.

All that remained was rubble, yet David knew it at once where they were. "Boston," he whispered. The ship seemed to shimmer as it turned into what once was Boston channel, then turned southwest into the Charles River. He noticed both children watched and waited for his reaction. "Why are we here?" he asked. "There's nothing here but bad memories."

"There's more than you know," Eve replied. "You left here a broken man, a failure who never understood his accomplishments. Yet, here is the University that shunned you, laughed at your efforts, and poked fun at your achievements."

"Even your wife doubted your success," Adam added. "But now it's crumbled, vaporized and uninhabitable for many years. Yet here you stand, changed by life and stronger for your failures. And we stand with you, the products of your effort, made flesh and ready to heal this land."

"Each time this place ridiculed and mocked your progress you persevered, doctor. You overcame the limitations of humanity," Eve added, "by tapping into our potential and ignoring the barriers others found."

"You never gave up," her brother insisted, "and created a new race of humanity. The people of this continent fight for food and water, but you offer them a means of true survival."

"I've done nothing," David insisted.

"In your pack you have the solution to their crises," Eve added. "You brought enough vials to ensure the birth of many generations to come. While they fight over worldly concerns like skin color and wealth, you offer them life and a better future."

"Surely they aren't that petty," David argued, with tears forming in his eyes.

"Of course they are," Adam answered. "They're human."

"That means they're doomed if humanity prevails. That's the part I tried to extract and improve upon," David argued.

"Know this, Father," Eve consoled, "you must never remove humanity completely. They will need it when the time comes."

"But I want to," David protested. "I hate that part of me, the emotional failure who keeps getting knocked down."

"That's not humanity, Father," Adam said with a smile. "Humanity is when you get back up and try again."

Estowen made landfall only for a brief time, a few hours to allow David to chisel out a message for those who may find this spot later. Once he returned, the ship set sail. They journeyed northward to a great river that joined a large lake, nearly large enough to be called a sea. From there they ventured southwest.

David Andalon finally had a mission, to discover humanity and improve upon its chances. Michael Esterling and Astia would come and, when it did, these people must be prepared.

Andalon Awakens

Dreamers of Andalon - Book 1

PROLOGUE

A small man stood on the deck of a creaking frigate. Unable to sleep, he kept first watch listening to the nighttime waves lapping the hull. The ship stood on the open sea, stranded and thirsting for air that had remained strangely still for an entire day and night. He watched as the lack of wind seemingly laughed at the impotent sails hanging on their masts.

Complete lack of movement is rare at sea and the eerie calm had already worked on the imaginations of the crew. Fear had slowly built within each man, and the abrupt appearance of eighteen sails sent panic through every topside sailor. The little man pushed back his spectacles and sounded the alarm. Then he dropped through a hatch to wake the captain.

Inside the main quarters, a large man opened his eyes and groaned. The noise grew louder at his door, a rhythmic thumping that wrenched him from his dream. He fought back a euphoric shudder as the memory of his lover's embrace faded into the pounding of reality.

He only held her briefly in his youth and would only ever do so in this recurring fantasy.

Her warm scent of spring lilac lingered momentarily, as did the soft caress of her lips. Braen Braston groaned as he awakened, fighting against the urge to draw his knife against the neck of whoever pounded on his door. Tears squeezed from his eyelids as he tightly closed them against the waking world.

If only he could return to the world where sweet Hester waited. He yearned to rejoin her warm bed and to feel her silky skin against his rough hands. Having once been a nightly occurrence, Braen had languished without the dream for more than a span. His wish every evening was that slumber would transport him to her realm. Now that she had again visited, he worried he would not remember her touch after he fully awakened.

Faded love and death are the only promises time gives to mortal men, and Braen secretly hoped for the second. *Does death include dreams?* He was almost willing to find out when the waking world shook him violently.

The heavy door to his cabin nearly splintered, keeping time with the pain between his temples. Panicked fists beat upon its planks as he briefly considered death once more. His eyes shot open with alarm. Somewhere nearby men shouted, and a feeling of urgency rocked the ship. The pounding that drew him back to reality had nearly broken the oak from its iron hinges. The shouting that accompanied the beating came from topside as men ran to battle stations.

He furiously threw the wool blanket from his body, sweating from the adrenaline of either passion or terror, whichever his faded dream had held. Wincing, he realized her face had completely gone from his mind. Awakening had also robbed him of her scent. *Wasn't it lilac?* He could not remember. Reality and rational thought drew him out of bed. He would face the unknown foe who had attacked his ship while he dreamed of impossible fancies.

His boots slipped on easily enough and Braen did not bother replacing his shirt. Running bare-chested he emerged from his cabin and collided with Sippen Yurik, his engineer and first mate, lifelong friend, and makeshift cabin steward. The small man stopped beating down Braen's door when it suddenly opened inward.

"What is it?" Braen shouted over the sounds from above.

"Lady E-e-e-sterling's main fleet has found us." Sippen stuttered as he spat out the words.

The captain ran past the impish smithy and raced topside. As he emerged from the hatch, the icy wind met his muscled chest. The blast nearly took away his voice. His long blonde beard kept most of the gust from off his face and he turned to see that Sippen had followed. The small man held out a thick coat. *Thoughtful Sippen*, he thought and surveyed the scene.

Across the choppy, greyish water he spotted the faint white of sails against the dawn. He quickly counted the masts while Gunnery Sergeant Krill relayed a signal to ready the guns. While the cannons were loaded and range elevated, Braen looked for a target. Four large galleons loomed between him and a large fleet of eight cargo ships accompanied by six smaller escorts. Two fleets closed on his with vengeance. He stroked his chest-long beard. *How do they have wind and we don't?* He glanced at his now raised battle sails, dangling limp and useless.

Braen had expected to cross the trade convoy in the night before. When he had lost the wind, he assumed that they would suffer the same hindrance as *Wench's Daughter.* He had not expected the main fleet to be so close. But it *had* appeared, oddly timing the arrival with the cargo ships. How had they coordinated pursuit in open waters?

"Get us some wind!" He shouted at the helmsman. "Hard to port! Drop those battle sails and put up the mains! We need speed!" Braen had not yet fought atop *Wench's Daughter* and wished for his own *Ice Prince.* Suddenly, Braen remembered that *Wench's Daughter* promised bigger fire power. "Belay my last! Keep the battle sails," he ordered, "hard to starboard and all guns to port!"

With or without wind, his heavy ship would not outrun the swift imperial galleons. The large captain cursed as he remembered how he had been talked into leaving his own sleek-lined vessel at Pirate's Cove. Worse, the belly of *Wench's Daughter* brimmed with heavy stores stolen from Esterling's winter warehouses.

Wench's Daughter drifted where the larger warships preferred. He would have to fight on their waters with reef shoals directly south. He carefully chose and called out his first target, hoping a hit below waterline would drag the lead galleon in front of the other vessels. However, such a first volley would be a marvel of the gods if it actually found wood to splinter. For that task, Braen Braston trusted his loyal friend Sippen.

The little weaponsmith was not much to look at. Small framed, he was slightly larger than a ten-year-old boy. His head was too large for his body and his arms were twigs. Sippen Yurik was useless in a fist fight, and deathly afraid of sharp blades. He preferred mathematical equations over human interaction. Other than remembering small things like coats during a cold morning battle, the man appeared worthless on a war-going vessel. That is, until you witnessed him sighting weapons.

He had been the royal engineer at Fjorik and designed and oversaw the building of *Ice Prince*. Even earlier than that, a close friendship bonded the two men from boyhood. When Braen fled the city two years earlier, Sippen had been waiting on the docks with his tools and the ship, refusing to allow his friend to flee into exile without him. For all of this, Braen was eternally grateful.

From the corner of his eye Braen saw the unassuming man help the gunners make final adjustments for windage, furiously scribbling with chalk on a slate. Sergeant Krill called out distances, bearings and speed while Sippen calculated. "Guns readied," bellowed Krill, after Sippen had nodded to the one-eyed man. Braen briefly considered how a one-eyed gunner judged distance with such accuracy, but, as always, he did not openly question Krill's knack for timing and range.

"Stand by to fire!" The captain gave the preparatory. "Make your mark. Now, batteries release!" On Braen's command the cannons exploded toward the largest of the galleons. Perhaps a lucky shot, Braen halfway smiled as most of the projectiles struck below the waterline. The large foe listed as a sudden rush of seawater entered its hold. It semi-capsized as he had hoped, and it listed before drifting with the current toward the trailing fleet. As he had hoped, the sinking vessel briefly blocked the passage of the other warships. Braen finally enjoyed time to think the battle over.

Oddly, he noticed a sudden coldness pass through his body. Most likely the retreat of adrenaline after the initial chaos, he tried to dismiss the chill until it had grown into a storm on a mountain summit. Braen felt his skin raise into bumps such as you would find on a freshly plucked fowl. Chicken-skin, his mother had called the sensation when he was young. It radiated from within, almost as if his blood had cooled several degrees during the time to aim the guns and fire upon the other vessel. Braen pulled the collar of the heavy coat up against his neck.

While he pondered his next movement, three massive dark shapes rushed beneath his keel toward the wounded galley. At precisely the moment the shapes passed underneath, Braen saw sails flutter. *Gods be praised*, the pirate captain thought as the breeze caught. "Full to port. Ready the guns at starboard and prepare to take wind!" The dark shapes continued to speed toward the other vessels, and he briefly glimpsed long, trailing tentacles on the water.

Braen blinked as his eyes played tricks. *They're only mythological creatures*, he assured himself, but Artema Horn's prophetic words resounded through his memory. He grew colder. Everything was colder. Even the wood of the railing had grown icy.

Through the smoke and early morning haze, Braen spotted more sails on the horizon. Hurried calculations revealed at least twenty more of Esterling's fleet, at least five of them flagships. Those, along with the six escorts, would make for overwhelming odds.

He signaled for Krill to lob the next volley over the wounded ship. Just as he called for the second attack, three large monsters emerged from the water.

"Kraken!"

Braen did not know who screamed the word. His only assurance was that it might not have been him. He watched helplessly as large tentacles reached out of the water and grabbed all three of the enemy galleons. Huge suction cups curled around the warships as desperate cries for mercy reached his ears. Then, the hardwood splintered as all three ships shattered like glass ornaments against stone. Stunned, the pirate captain prayed to the gods for the first time in two years.

As if timed with the sinking of the third galleon, the sails on *Wench's Daughter's* again fluttered, then fully caught the wind. The ship lurched with a sudden jolt as the wind favored their escape. The captain smiled and gave the command to turn hard into the blessed current. Braen barked at his crew, "Square away these sails and get us away from this cinder cursed place!" Using the creatures and the wrecked galleons as cover, he silently hoped that the pursuers would remain distracted. He smiled and his crew let out a whoop as the now westerly blowing wind carried all of his vessels out to the safety of open sea.

———

Ashima Nakala, the lead sister of the winter oracle in Astia, broke from her dream with a scream. Initiates clustered around her and helped to ease her onto the dais. She writhed in pain from the bead, feeling it loosen the grip on her muscles as it left her blood.

The worse part of the Da'ash'mael was the intensity of the release. In fact, most dreamers feared the deadly rush of endorphins that ended the dream state, brought on by large quantities of the oracle bead as the muscles absorbed its potency. Dreaming was a dangerous art that promised no result but always offered pain and the risk of death.

She arched her back and her white robe slipped, exposing her breast. The curve of the ribs beneath her bosom drew in an exaggerated collapse as she gasped for oxygen against a sea of air. Her muscles instantly knotted along her spine and she finally caught her breath. Her next came rapid and beat out a tempo with her racing heart.

Ashima was the most accurate oracle produced by the coven in generations. She had predicted twenty years of changing weather patterns, including two significant blizzards and three gripping winters that lasted into the late moon of planting. But aside from weather phenomena, she had never dreamed anything that compared to the vivid cold she felt inside the bearded captain.

Although the oracles were called dreamers, the Ash'mael was more than a sequence of patterns from the subconscious. The Da'ash'mael provided knowing that delved into the very existence of the dream state, often seeing current or future events from the perspective of another.

Indeed, Ashima had shared the pain of the sea captain as he had lain in his bed, smelling lilac, wishing for death, and remembering his lost love. Likewise, she had empathically enjoyed his surge of adrenaline as he raced topside to fight the imperial fleet. But the terror of watching the sea monsters rise from the depths had made her cry out in agony as a resurgence of the bead coursed through her blood. She convulsed as she watched the creatures tear apart the ships. Tears made pink trails as they mixed with the blood trickling from her cheek, bitten through by her contracting mouth.

The initiates fought to hold her on the raised platform as she entered the Ka'ash'mael, the dreaded second phase in the telling of Ash'mael. This stage rarely occurred, but when it did the oracle prophesied the connection of the Da'ash'mael and how the viewed events affected the future of her Astian people. The accuracy of the dream depended on the true strength of the oracle, and only occurred after the drug had finally released its hold on their body. Since this particular Ash'mael was so strongly woven into the future of mankind, the transition from Da' to Ka' was amplified beyond any she had ever known.

The change gripped her body and she shuddered in orgasm as the bead released her muscles. She drew in a deep breath as the pain turned into a physical pleasure that simultaneously stimulated every nerve stem. Ashima knew, as did all dreamers, that the euphoria was a chemical response to the drug. But she welcomed the change as an awakening of her mind as it freed itself from her body.

Her eyes flitted in euphoric rushes as the sensation grew inside her body. Slowly, almost rhythmically, the knowing occurred. Feeling as if she were floating above her body, she began to recite her experience in the language of the oracle. The initiates relaxed and loosened their grips on her body. Each leaned in to listen and record her revelations as Ashima began to speak with slow and deliberate speech.

Fatwana Nakala watched quietly as her sister breathed her final words. The tall raven- haired woman did not betray any expression as the initiates carefully transcribed the Ash'mael. In stunned silence she took every word to heart and was not surprised when she saw the attending priest draw the shroud over Ashima's head. Her body surged up from the table and convulsed before settling onto the stone altar with a shudder, her final words spoken.

Ashima Nakala spoke her Ka'Ash'mael prophecy, proclaiming truth that transcended the physical plane. This particular Ash'mael held importance to all oracles and would shake the very core of their existence. Knowledge of the awakening threatened change that would challenge the existence of the Astian lifestyle. After she had collected the transcriptions, Fatwana walked to the altar and placed her hand on the husk that had once held her sister's soul. She spoke softly, "Rest sister and join our brother. I shall carry this warning to all, so that they must heed." Turning, she strode from the temple, ignoring the warm tears that slowly fell from her eyes.

CHAPTER ONE

The sun rose over a green valley in Loganshire, casting shadows on the rich farmland as it peeked around the clouds. Rivers and streams rabid with white froth raced between the hills, anxious to be free of the mountains to the north. Winter was arriving late, explaining why the grasses clung to their green hue. Despite the unseasonable warmth, the trees had completely let go of their leaves. Their shed foliage danced in the brisk wind that rolled down the mountain into the valley.

Loganshire was a quaint farming region nestled between the kingdoms of Fjorik in the north, and Eston which lay to the south and west. Once, long enough in the memory of the old-timers, the valley was the focus of countless raids from the northern men. Those fierce raids signified the end of fall and the start of winter to the anxious people of the valley. For the past ten years, under the stability of the Esterling Empire, the raids had stopped completely, and the people enjoyed peace and prosperity.

One farmhouse had enjoyed a tremendous comfort, and Mauri hummed and danced as she washed the family laundry, hanging it on lines to dry in the breeze. That same wind tossed her red hair gently, nipping at her rosy cheeks as she spun and hummed. Her husband, Thom, baled hay with his brothers Franque and Jean on this day, and she had a stew warming on the hearth for their return from the labor.

Mauri and Thom had two children. Anne was three years old, and she resembled her mother with red hair and freckles from a life spent mostly outdoors. Anne played in the grass with a doll her father had fashioned out of straw and burlap. Occasionally she would lean over and talk to her baby brother, Clauvis, as he cooed in his basket. He was a perfect baby, hardly cried, never fussed, and brought so much hope to the family for the future of the farm. Boy babies were lucky, at least that's what Mauri's grandmother had told her.

A hawk flew overhead, circling the field. Mauri took a moment to watch as it glided against the clouds and then as it dove. With grace it swooped toward a group of men riding horseback up the lane. It rested on the gloved hand of a tall man riding in the middle of the formation and Mauri froze. Wearing a hood with a feathered collar he sat high in the saddle, glancing sideways around him and darting glances like the oversized falcon perched on his arm. Abruptly, the hawk squawked a shrill, high piercing sound and the man focused his eyes directly at the farmwife. Her load of laundry fell onto the grass and she screamed a blood curdling sound that brought Thom running from the field.

He reached his wife just as the riders halted their beasts in front of Mauri and the children. His brothers, still wielding scythes from the harvest, dropped the blades in the grass as Constable Wembley, local magistrate and leader of the group, spoke, "Thom and Mauri Thorinson. The Falconer claims you delivered a living child sometime after the fifth day of the month of fall planting."

Wembley should have been a military man. He was prim and proper, and, unlike other constables and their deputies, he wore his uniform clean and pressed, with his black beard and hair closely cropped. His harsh eyes narrowed on the family as he asked, "Why did you fail to report the birth to a midwife or a constable?"

"We ... We were afraid, Shon. You know we lost our second child after the beast examined her."

"Nonsense and superstition!" The Falconer behind the constable bellowed. The man was a hideous specter, one whose eyes seem to pierce through the hood and into another's soul. "The examination is a blessing, and infant mortality is a natural occurrence, not to be blamed on our ministrations."

The constable tried to keep everyone calm. "Thom, all you have to do is allow him to look your child over. Don't make this harder than it needs to be."

Thom's face was scarlet with anger. "Shon, you of all people should understand!"

"Let him work, Thom. Otherwise I'll have to hang the both of you." Wembley rode his horse between Mauri and the baby, forcing her and her husband to step backward. "I'm sorry about this. Really, I am. Just do as he says, and all will be fine."

Dismounting, the Falconer approached Clauvis in the basket lying on the grass. Anne, still clutching her little doll, scurried away from her brother's side. Terrified, she hid behind the legs of her father. The Falconer paid her no mind and knelt beside the younger child. The bird of prey on his shoulder stared intently at the baby, switching his head back and forth to view him with each eye. Mauri watched as her child made no sound while staring intently at both the man and the bird.

With a squawk, the bird spread its wings and flew up into the air to resume circling. The hooded man pulled out a small jar of oil and removed the blue lid. He rubbed two fingers into the mixture, and placed it under the tongue of the child before standing to address the family. "I find your baby healthy and free of defect. Enjoy a long life with the child." Turning, he added an admonishment. "In the future, report your offspring to the authorities." The man strode back to his mount and swung into the saddle.

The constable looked intently at Thom, who was grinding his teeth and seething with anger. "Your penalty will be an extra percentage of taxed goods when payment is due." To Mauri he added, "Be happy your child's healthy. Some of your neighbors weren't so lucky." He tipped his hat to the couple, and the group rode back down the lane the way they had come.

As soon as the riders had turned their horses, Mauri rushed to the basket and swept her child into her arms. Holding him tightly, she ran back into the house with Anne chasing behind, her doll swinging wildly in her hand as she sprinted up the walk. Thom turned to his brothers, who picked up their scythes. He shook his head and cursed the hooded man, rejoining his brothers as they walked slowly back to the field to finish their duties. The laundry lay in a heap upon the grass where his wife had dropped it, but that task was long forgotten after the tense meeting.

After Thom and his brothers had finished in the field, they washed in the stream before making their way back to the cottage. Dodging chickens on the ground, they walked and talked about the earlier event. Thom, although relieved that his baby was healthy, still worried over the incident. Their other child, Grace, had been two weeks old when another Falconer had come. Like today, he had blessed their child and proclaimed her healthy and whole. The young parents had considered themselves luckier than most, as other families had had their sickly or mal-formed babies taken from them.

They both felt she was a special infant. Like Clauvis, she never cried nor fussed. They felt generally happier and more connected around their little Gracie and also thought of her as a lucky child. Thom remembered vividly awakening to the sobs of Mauri on the night of the last visit. Grace had died in her sleep. Crib death, the old-timers had called it, but he and his wife had distrusted their visitor and attributed the sudden death to his blessing.

A scream from within the cottage sent Thom and his siblings running the final steps toward the door. Thrusting it open, they halted at the display within. Mauri knelt over the crib, clutching the infant close to her breast. She wailed in grief as little Anne stood in the corner, also crying and squeezing her little doll in fright as she watched her inconsolable mother.

Thom broke free from the invisible grip that had held him, and stepped forward, placing a hand on his wife's shoulder. As Mauri turned to look up at her husband, he saw that Clauvis was lifeless and completely blue. The farmer's brothers took in the scene, then headed outside with grief. But this time the job was to dig a deep little hole.

A few days later, in the city of Logan, Constable Wembley sat in the corner of the *Mangy Dog* tavern. The tavern was noticeably empty on this day, despite that the city was bustling with activity. The constable was not alone. Across from him sat the reason the tavern was empty, in the form of the cursed Falconer.

Shon Wembley loved his job as constable, and it had been his desired career since childhood. As a young man he served as a deputy to his brother in Brentway where they had fought against northern marauders during the most recent raids. He loved his duties and served them well, but his two least favorite tasks included tax collection and overseeing the child blessings. Those blessings were the reason he had been stuck escorting this Falconer for an entire week.

Shon frowned at his mug of ale, unusually bitter for the season. "Are you sure that you don't want a mug?" When the beast-like man did not respond, he answered himself, "No, of course not." Then, under his breath he muttered, "You never do. You don't drink spirits; you don't eat rich foods or sweets and you don't look at the tavern wenches." After he had said his piece, the two men again sat in silence, the Falconer staring straight ahead, the constable's hard green eyes focused on his mug.

Shon found solace in the thought that he was nearly finished with his current duties. They had three more children to inspect in the city and had planned to begin at first light. So far, the blessings had gone smoothly. Only two farmhouses had produced children with defects, and those had been removed to the Rookery with little resistance and with only the expected grief by the parents. Since the Empire had gained a foothold in Loganshire, the tradition of culling the lame had become more widely accepted, possibly since more families were birthing healthier children with their newfound prosperity.

Only a few had tried to hide births, one of those being the Thorinson farm. How the Falconer had discovered the child was strange. It was almost as if he could communicate with his bird, or worse, see through its eyes. The thought unnerved Shon, almost as if the creatures shared foresight. But that theory was impossible, since all religions, regardless of belief, strictly prohibited telling the future or working magic. Both crimes were rewarded with the penalty of death in the Esterling Empire. Of course, magic did not exist, so that part of the edict never made sense to Constable Wembley. He chalked it up to superstitious nonsense.

Still, something about the Thorinson exchange did not sit well with the constable. So far, fifty children were inspected during the week, but

Shon had noticed the blessings had included two jars of oil. Every other child had been anointed with the jar with the red lid, but that baby had received the substance from a jar with a blue lid. When he had asked the administrator why he had used a different jar, the beast-like man had lied and stated that he only has one jar.

Abruptly, the Falconer cocked his head to one side, suddenly alert. "Post men by the door. Trouble is coming."

Shon looked up from his ale, incredulous and feeling somewhat suspicious given his recent thoughts. He motioned his deputies, who stood from the table and moved into position like bookends on the inside of the oak frame. After posting the guards, the constable asked, "Did you hear something?"

Just then, the door burst open from the force of a large man kicking it in. Thom Thorinson charged through, wielding an axe and rushing directly for the Falconer. When he reached the chair, the hooded figure, who had never turned around, leaped from his seat and sidestepped a blow from the hatchet. The head of the tool sank deep into the table, spilling the plate of food and mug of ale that Shon had been working on.

Suddenly, with a screech a dark winged blur swept through the opening, sinking its talons in the back of the raging farmer. With its strong beak it tore at the man's flesh, ripping out chunks as it tried to peck out his eyes. Thom screamed and the bird squawked until the constable intervened. "For Cinder's sake restrain the man!" Only once they controlled his arms and pinned him face down on the floor did the raptor release its grip and return to perch on the arm of its master.

Thom Thorinson bled onto the floorboards, weeping and sobbing in pain of both body and spirit. The deputies stood him up and fastened manacles on his wrists. Shon approached and demanded explanation. "What the hell are you about, Thorinson? Explain yourself!"

Thom sputtered, "That abomination killed my wife and child!"

"Nonsense! Both of them were very much alive when we left your spread, and he's been with me the entire time! You know damned well that he had no hand in their death!"

"Clauvis died mere hours after his blessing and Mauri slit her wrists in grief that very night!"

"A coincidence, I assure you!" Shon was very disturbed by this exchange. *The blue jar*, he thought and silently wondered if Thom was correct in his accusation. He stared up at the ghoul with an expecting glare, watching for any change in demeanor but none came.

The Falconer spoke from where he now stood in the corner of the tavern, bird roosting on his arm. "Attacking an agent of the Queen Regent is a hanging offense. This was attempted murder."

Shon shook his head. Turning to look at the hooded man, he said, "Thom is grieving. I've known him and his entire family since their births. He's no murderer." He leaned in close to the farmer, and grimaced. "Smell him, he's drunk and acting out of grief."

"Death by hanging." Turning to look at the constable, the beast-like man added, "Certainly you will not disobey an administrator in his duties? Men have hanged for that as well."

Shon muttered under his breath, "Well, shit." After pondering for a moment, he shook his head and faced the others. "Take Thorinson to the jail. I'll speak to the magistrate and turn him over to the city officials for a trial." He placed emphasis on the final word as if willing it would ensure justice.

The next day, Shon wrapped up his duties, finally able to part ways with the eerie hooded beast. None too soon, he packed his saddle bags, mounted his mare, and spurred her flanks to a fast trot. As he rode out of the city, he tipped his hat to the swinging corpse of Thom Thorinson, the ripped-out portions of his face hidden within a hood of his own. The once stalwart lawman unpinned his badge and tossed it in the river as he crossed the bridge out of town.

Thank you for enjoying Andalon Project and this sneak peak of Andalon Awakens!

Please help the author by leaving a review, then visit the site below to learn what happens next in the Dreamers of Andalon Saga!
www.tbphillips.com

www.ingramcontent.com/pod-product-compliance
Lightning Source LLC
Chambersburg PA
CBHW072053190726
48294CB00005B/1488